FIX THEM UP

Reader Reviews for *Fix Them Up*

'A binge worthy small-town romance!'

'I can't remember the last romance novel that made
me this warm and giddy'

'This book is a beautiful blend of love, loss, and self-discovery'

'If you're looking for a feel-good read with some heat,
small-town charm, and authentic ADHD representation,
this book is perfect!'

'I cannot believe this is a debut novel, Maggie Grant has
produced something wonderful here'

'I absolutely adored the setting of Everly Heath, it's like
someone's picked up Stars Hollow and dropped it in
Northern England'

'From the first page I was completely hooked and it had
everything I love in a romance novel from the grumpy x
sunshine trope to the small town with the nosey but
caring community!'

'This story didn't lack for anything, with healthy amounts
of banter, spice, and plot. What a brilliant debut!'

'This book had me screaming and kicking my feet
throughout the whole thing'

'Just wow! This book was a roller-coaster of pure emotion and the best book I've read that shows ADHD and dyslexia and how hard it can be living with those on such a raw relatable level'

'I have gone through all of the emotions reading this story. It had me captivated. It's definitely a page turning, one more chapter kind of book!'

FIX
THEM
UP

MAGGIE GRANT

Bedford Square

Publishers

Originally self-published in the UK in 2024

First published in the UK in 2025 by Bedford Square Publishers Ltd,
London, UK

bedfordsquarepublishers.co.uk
@bedsqpublishers

ISBN
978–1–83501–410–3 (Paperback)
978–1–83501–411–0 (eBook)

2 4 6 8 10 9 7 5 3 1

The manufacturer's authorised representative in the EU for
product safety is Easy Access System Europe, Mustamäe tee 50,
10621 Tallinn, Estonia
gpsr.requests@easproject.com

Typeset in Bembo Std by Palimpsest Book Production Limited,
Falkirk, Stirlingshire

Printed in Great Britain by CPI Group (UK) Ltd, Croydon CR0 4YY

To the girls with brains wired differently –
Even when the world feels suffocating, remember this:
you are intelligent, brilliant, and bloody mesmerising.
And to eight-year-old me –
it took a while, but the words found you eventually.

As someone with dyslexia and ADHD, I *might* have been forgiven for being late to my dad's funeral had I not fucked up the eulogy. The morning had pointed towards success. I only snoozed my alarm twice. I tamed my frizzy hair into a respectable bun. I applied my eyeliner accurately and didn't spill coffee on my black dress. I even ate breakfast. Usually, I'd forget to eat until the afternoon and then almost pass out.

Ordered.

Calm.

Absolutely no chaos.

I was as positive as I could be on the morning of my dad's funeral. And then, my mum texted.

10 am sharp in the foyer.

Another text a few moments later.

Don't be late.

I tried not to flinch as my mum sighed when I joined her and my stepdad, Graham, in the bright white foyer of the hotel. I wondered how often Mum had checked her watch. Graham gave me a sympathetic smile, his towering frame hunched over like he wished he had been made smaller. The foyer smelt of floral bleach, and the bright lighting made our funeral black look stark. Graham looked like Slender Man. The colour dwarfed my mum, making her look more sparrow-like than usual. And me – well, I was

1

ginger, so the black made me look paler, if that was even possible. On a good day, I resembled the transparent fish I once saw at the aquarium in Brighton.

Stood together, the three of us looked like lame, sad Goths. The tinny speaker at the front desk played Carly Rae Jepsen's 'Call Me Maybe', making me want to giggle hysterically.

'All okay?' Mum asked. There was only one answer she wanted to hear.

I nodded. 'All good.'

Graham touched my shoulder. 'You look lovely.'

I smiled tightly. 'Thanks, Graham.'

I wanted to say something sarcastic, like *Thanks, Graham, it's dead dad chic!* or *Wednesday Addams is my style icon*, but it would garner a dark look from Mum. She rarely understood any humour other than *Mrs Brown's Boys* reruns.

We climbed into Mum's sensible Volvo, Graham at the wheel, and drove to Everly Heath Church. It had been my dad's local church, although he hadn't been religious. But tradition prevailed, and he was baptised and married my mum before Everly Heath's congregation. As we drove through the town, it was greener and leafier than I remembered. Not that I had visited very often. Everly Heath – the little town outside Manchester – felt very distant to me. But I couldn't deny it was pretty.

Red brick Victorian houses flitted by. Huge oak trees that must have taken root over a hundred years ago. Families pushed prams. Kids ran ahead, their parents shouting for them to slow down. An elderly man walked a scruffy little dog. It was peaceful. It reminded me of some of the expensive neighbourhoods in London, around Hampstead Heath.

Everyone in Everly Heath was going about their day, oblivious that today was supposed to be a sad day.

The day I was going to deliver my dad's eulogy.

'Fuck!'

Graham almost veered into the other lane, and my mum whipped her head around. 'What?' she demanded, and Graham looked at me in the rearview mirror.

A familiar dread and shame filled my system.

I'm such a fuck up.

I repeated the sentence in my head like Hail Marys. I couldn't even deliver a fifteen-minute speech at a funeral without cocking it up. Now I had to face my mum's disappointed expression, familiar to me through failed tests and tense parents' evenings of the past.

'I forgot my speech notes. They're in the hotel room. I need to go back.'

I checked my watch. We were half an hour early, so I might make it.

'Don't you have notes on your phone?' Mum said snarkily.

Irritation flared, and so did my nostrils. 'You know I can't read on my phone. I printed it on my paper. I need the paper.'

The pale yellow paper and large font meant the words were less likely to do a silly little dance, which would result in a skipped line or two.

'Katherine –'

'It's okay. I'll drive Kat back, and we'll be there in time for the beginning,' Graham said.

Uncertainty flickered across my mother's face. She was about to step into a church full of her ex-husband's family, most of whom she hadn't seen in fifteen years. She was biting her lip. She was nervous, even if she would never admit it.

'No. I'll drive Mum's car. I'm still on the insurance. I'll drive there, grab the notes, and then come back. You guys can do the welcoming and stuff.'

Graham frowned. 'Are you sure?'

'Yes,' I bit out, instantly feeling guilty for snapping at Graham.

My tall, gangly stepdad walked into my life when I hadn't wanted a replacement dad. I was still harbouring hope that my actual dad wanted to be in my life. But Graham never held my teenage surliness against me. He slotted in neatly, often running interference between Mum and me.

From the back seat, I leaned forward and whispered, 'Sorry.'

Graham answered me with a pat on my hand.

Mum and Graham climbed out of the Volvo, and I jumped into the front seat, stress and sweat forming on my brow.

'See you in a bit.' I started the engine and pulled out of the church car park.

Twenty-five minutes later, I returned with a sense of déjà vu.

The car park was full.

I should have seen this coming; it was a small car park, and basically every person in Everly Heath had been invited, thanks to my uncle Brian and auntie Sandra being the most popular residents in the town.

I checked my watch.

Three minutes to go.

A black BMW had its reversing lights on, and I let out a breath. I flashed my full beam, and they reversed. As I shifted into gear, a white transit van hurtled past me at speed, nabbing the spot last minute.

My mouth fell open. I blinked furiously, hoping I'd imagined it. I watched as a tall dark-haired man appeared out of the van, his phone in the crook of his neck, completely oblivious. Fury filled my stomach, and my face burned.

I beeped my horn loudly and the man turned around, confusion on his face. He returned to his call, so I beeped again. Finally, he put the phone down and approached the car, a bored expression on his features that only fuelled my fury.

4

'Are you fucking kidding me?' I exclaimed out of the window, gesturing wildly.

'Can I help?' he asked innocently, a Mancunian lilt to his deep voice.

The man stopped outside my open window, and some little goblin part of my mind registered he was undeniably attractive. He had deep, soulful brown eyes, a scruffy beard and hair just long enough to tuck behind his ears. I shook my head, ignoring how my heart raced as his eyes flickered across my face like I was a fascinating specimen.

'That was my spot. You came in at breakneck speed and stole it.'

An understanding registered in his eyes, and his face turned from curious to unreadable.

He shrugged. 'You were taking too long.'

He pulled his phone back out of his pocket, swiping it open. He squinted as his thumb shifted through what I could see were the green messages on WhatsApp.

'Excuse me,' I said, waving a hand in front of his face, 'I was waiting for the woman to reverse out of her spot. You overtook me and stole the spot. It was my spot. I'd appreciate it if you moved.'

'She was already gone, and you hadn't even indicated yet.'

I took a deep breath.

It's fine. Don't fly off the handle, Kat. Use your words.

'I really need that spot. Today is –' A little voice told me if I mentioned it was my dad's funeral, that I would start welling up. And I was not wasting tears on this dickhead. 'Today is a big day for me. A significant day. And I know you'll do the gentlemanly thing' – the man glanced up from his phone, his eyes glimmered with humour – 'and park at the rectory car park over there.' I gestured to the auxiliary car park down the road from the church.

He huffed a laugh, and then his phone blared a loud ringtone, making me jump.

'No can do, I'm afraid.' He picked up the phone, answering it softly. 'Hey, sweetie.'

I could feel my face heat with fury. This guy was speaking to his girlfriend while I was negotiating a parking space for my dad's fucking funeral. He didn't give a shit about the panic on my face or the plea in my voice.

'Hey, dickhead.' Fuck negotiation. I was never destined for the UN. 'Can you move your fucking van?'

The man cocked an eyebrow. His eyes did that scanning thing again, and the side of his lips lifted. Was he… was he finding this funny? No way.

How was he so calm when I could barely contain my rage?

It made me want to say something *really* outrageous.

He returned to the phone. 'Sweetie, can I call you back? Okay. Love you.'

I made a vomiting noise as he put the phone down, and then he changed. He went bolt upright, and he was… tall. He had to be over six feet.

He placed his hands on my window, leaning in. 'No can do, Red. You'll have to park at the rectory yourself.'

'I am *not* called Red. Why on earth −' The penny dropped. 'Right. Ginger. Red. Very creative.'

The man's lips twitched. 'Actually, it was more a comment on the colour of your cheeks right now.'

'You're a prick.' I don't think I'd ever called anyone a prick. Or at least not to their face. I started the car, preparing to roll the tyre over his foot. 'Can you get your hand off my fucking car?'

He leaned forward. 'What's your name?'

'If I tell you, will you give me the parking space?'

'Probably not. You're not from around here, are you?'

Fury boiled, and I made a very unladylike noise between a grunt and a scream. I followed it up with a 'fuck you' and shifted the car into gear, leaving him standing there. I watched as his face broke into a smile and he shook his head, and then walked off into whatever pit of hell he'd appeared from. I mounted Mum's car on the grass verge of the church graveyard and figured the vicar could shout at me later.

My dress got caught in the door as I climbed out of the car, and I made that frustrated noise again.

'For fuck's sake.'

I ran into the little room at the front of the church where Mum and Graham were waiting for me, relief crossing their faces.

'All okay?' Mum asked.

You can't say she doesn't have a strong brand.

'All good. I got them.'

'Then chop, chop.' Her face was drawn and tense. 'Your uncle saved us a spot at the front of the church. We held off as long as possible, but the vicar has to start soon. Really, Katherine. Of all days to be forgetful.'

I squeezed my eyes shut as self-hatred flooded my system. My mother hated nothing more than being late or being perceived as a nuisance. Funnily enough, I was often both.

I pushed open the arched door, and my mouth fell open. The church was full. And it wasn't a small church. Every single pew was full of people, most I didn't recognise. I halted, but Mum bumped into me, pushing me forward. As I shuffled towards the front of the church, my gaze snagged to the front row, locking eyes with my cousin, Lydia, who wore a form-fitting black dress and smart black trainers. Even for formal events, you couldn't get Lydia out of trainers. I wouldn't be surprised if she had been born with them bonded to her feet.

'Hey,' I said, relieved to see my cousin's smiling face. We didn't see each other often, but you didn't need much time to like Lydia. She has this infectious positivity that hangs around her like a halo. I lowered myself into the pew next to her.

'You okay, Cuz?' Lydia smiled, giving my hand a quick squeeze. That was all I needed for the tears to well. Christ, we were so repressed in this country.

I replied with a watery smile. 'Yep.'

'You'll do amazing,' She whispered, squeezing my hand again.

The priest started, and I was handed an order of service with a picture of my dad on the front.

Jim Williams
13 February 1958 – 12 June 2022

Holding it was surreal. It was confirmation that he was really gone. In the picture, he had the same curly red hair and the same heart-shaped face as me, but it had gone round as he'd put on a bit of weight in his older age.

The echoey silence of the church made my heart beat faster. The sound of the priest's shoes hitting the stone floors filled my ears, much too loud. My head spun as the priest took his space at the pulpit and, in a deep booming voice, gave an overview of Dad's life and upbringing, touching on his ties up north in Everly Heath before he moved south to Reading to live with Mum and me. The priest artfully navigated my parent's divorce.

'... And despite Jim and Paula parting ways, they always remained friends and continued co-parenting their daughter Kat.'

I gave out an uncontrollable bark of laughter that echoed through the church. My mum shifted forward, her eyes wide. Fuck, that had been loud.

'Sorry,' I whispered to no one in particular but everyone in the church at the same time.

'Don't worry about it,' Lydia whispered back, covering her palm over mine and giving me a reassuring squeeze.

'... And I'd like to ask Kat up here to say a few words about her father.'

My head whipped around to see the priest looking expectantly at me.

Fuck. With all the stress of the speech notes and the dickhead parking spot thief, I hadn't had time to mentally prepare myself for this.

I stood up, shaking slightly and approached the pulpit. I looked out at the sea of black and felt the church spin. I exhaled, realising I was holding my breath, and began.

'My dad – where do I start?' I forced a laugh, glancing at my family sitting in the first pew.

My uncle and auntie looked up at me, smiling. My uncle Brian, a doppelgänger for my dad, gave me a small, encouraging nod. I couldn't find any source of embarrassment in their features. This was their town, after all. They knew most of the guests invited, unlike me.

I cleared my throat, shifting my gaze away.

Focus on something else.

'We, ah – we weren't close before he passed. I think I'm allowed to say that.' I frowned. 'But I have fond memories of him growing up. Taking me to the park on my bike. I had stabilisers until I was like twelve. But he never made me feel bad about that. Sorry, I'm rambling.'

I took a deep breath.

'I have fond memories of my dad growing up. Every summer, he used to take Mum and me camping in Devon. Even though Mum and I hated it, he was the best at camping.'

The crowd chuckled.

'Because we hated it so much, he'd let us bring anything we liked to keep us comfortable and happy. One year, he packed an entire box of my Polly Pockets. And I had the house, the car, everything. He didn't even blink an eye; he just picked the box up and put it in the boot.'

My heart was beating in my ears.

'When I was about eight, my hamster, Gerald, died. Mum was out, and I was distraught, crying… really quite hysterical. Dad, being Dad, panicked and had no idea what to do or how to make it better. So naturally, he built a Viking-style funeral pyre for the hamster in the back garden.'

Louder laughs erupted.

'We stood side by side. Solemn. I said a few words, and so did he.' I burst into deep, hearty laughter that shocked me. 'When he went to light the fire, it wouldn't light. So he got some brandy from the drinks trolley… and poured it on the pyre… then it lit up so much that it almost singed Dad's eyebrows. Mum came home to the smell of burning, only to find us laughing in front of a hamster funeral pyre like we'd lost the plot.'

I smiled. 'He was a great dad in those moments. Supportive. Even at school, when I struggled, he never pushed me. He told me to do my best. "All you can do is your best, Kat," he used to say. I just wish –' My knuckles went white on my speech notes.

All my long-suppressed resentments came surging forward. I couldn't help but think about how these nice, warm memories were mixed in with missed recitals and birthdays.

I scrunched my eyes closed, thinking of all those milestones he'd missed…

'How do you grieve someone who was a great dad until I was ten years old, then invisible for the other seventeen?' I whispered, glancing down at my notes.

FIX THEM UP

A drop of liquid had landed on the page, smudging some of the black ink. I wanted to glance up to see what was leaking until I realised it was coming from my eyes. I touched my wet cheek.

The church was silent, eerily silent.

'Sorry, that was an inside thought,' I tried to joke, but my voice broke.

I looked down at the front pew. Uncle Brian and Auntie Sandra had their hands clasped and brows furrowed. My cousin's mouth was in a thin, straight line, uncharacteristically grave. My mum and Graham were trying to communicate with me through their eyes, their expressions saying wildly different things. I tried again to make words come out, but my chest was painful and my breath shallow.

One other recognisable face was a few rows back. Dark hair, eyes to match. The man from the car park, his quiet amusement replaced with pity. His eyebrows pinched together, his mouth downturned. He had a deeply pained expression like he was looking at a gravely injured animal without being able to save it.

And that was it.

The last straw.

'I'm sorry. I–I can't do this,' I blurted out, stepping off the pulpit, walk-slash-running to the back room of the church, locking it behind me and sliding down the door. I gasped deep breaths, like I'd been underwater for centuries, and tears rolled down my cheeks.

The same phrase was repeating in my head:

I'm such a fuck up.
I'm such a fuck up.
I'm such a fuck up.

Chapter One

Kat's To-Do List

- Milk
- Bread
- Cheese
- Lunch? <u>NO MORE PRET</u>
- <u>Stop</u> thinking about funeral
- <u>Stop</u> thinking about Dad's stupid house
- Client rebrand prep
- Therapist???

'Kat!' Willa's melodic shout bounced off the stark white office walls, giving my co-workers Clara and Kieran – a.k.a. the twins from *The Shining* – a rare opportunity to look up from their laptops.

As graphic designers, staring at screens was what we did best but Clara and Kieran were robots. They hadn't looked up from their screens since nine this morning. Meanwhile, I'd got up three times to make myself a coffee. Twice, I was distracted by a notification on my phone and then I wound up reorganising the stationery cupboard. I'd finally made the coffee, for it to go cold beside me anyway.

Willa, my boss and best friend, came hurtling around the corner to where I hid in my little booth. Willa was wearing a nude structured dress, blonde hair styled in immaculate waves. Willa stepped into my booth I'd picked four years ago. I figured if I was having a bad ADHD day, I could hide my hyperfixation in my little booth. Last month, it was the Russian royal family and the conspiracy theory that one of them survived their downfall. My cubbyhole meant the office could be spared from my Wikipedia rabbit holes.

I was praying Willa hadn't cottoned onto my most recent hyperfixation.

Willa threatened to freeze me with her icy-blue eyes. The two of us met at university when we were studying graphic design. Willa had always planned to start her own agency. She'd even told me that first semester that it was the plan, making me feel sufficiently inadequate, given I didn't know what I was having for dinner. But that was Willa – a force of nature. We were the same age, but I always looked up to her like she was my big sister, something that an only child like me could only dream of having.

'Willa, I can explain –' But I stopped myself.

Last week, I forgot to send a client brief. The week before that, I'd called in sick because I'd felt so heavy and tearful that I couldn't get out of bed without bursting into tears. Then, of course, there was a general state of tardiness that followed me around like a bad fart.

I am such a fuck up.

Since the funeral, I had been a liability across every single aspect of my life, and I wanted to fix it. I desperately wanted to fix it but couldn't pull myself out of the ditch.

'Did you hand our biggest client a business card with your used gum on it?'

Clara and Kieran exchanged looks.

I winced, 'Ah – yes.' A strangled noise came from Willa. 'But Alan seemed to find it pretty funny.'

Alan had been perplexed when I'd wiped off the piece of gum and handed the card back to him. I would have handed him a new one, but I'd forgotten to order more. What else was I supposed to do? Dinosaurs like Alan didn't know how to AirDrop. I wasn't even sure if Alan had a phone.

'They just called me.'

'Oh.'

'They want you off the account.'

My mouth fell open. 'No. Alan was fine! He laughed. I'm sure he laughed.'

Willa groaned. 'Kat, that was your last chance to impress them. They have itchy feet! They're one foot out of the door. Especially after you went on that call with a penis straw!'

'They were left over from Sam's hen do!' I exclaimed. Sam was our mutual friend from University. 'What was I supposed to do? Throw them away?'

'That would have been better than using them on a call with a load of strait-laced white blokes, Kat, yes.'

I winced. 'I'm sorry.'

Willa sighed. 'I know.'

Willa deserved better than this. Before Dad died, I hadn't been a perfect employee, but I got the job done. I thought once the grief had subsided, things would go back to normal. But it had been eight months since his funeral, and nothing had changed. Autumn, my favourite season, came and went. So did the red and gold lights of Christmas and New Year. I walked through them, numb and disinterested.

It was February and I was still going through the motions each day. Every night, I lay wide awake, staring at the ceiling, unable to sleep.

Willa should have someone focused on client work, someone present, someone who coaxed clients back, not gave them the ick. After all, Willa had her own problems. Clients were fleeing Horizon Creative by the day and Willa was more and more desperate by the day. She even asked me to write client pitches, which was *not* my forte. My spelling was atrocious.

Willa ran a hand down her face, paused and then turned to Kieran. 'Kier. You're on the QRS account.'

Kieran flinched but nodded – the ever-loyal robot lapdog.

'Kat, let's talk,' Willa angled her head towards her office.

I walked past Clara and Kieran, looking down at their laptops like nothing had happened.

Freaks.

I followed Willa to her office; my eyes couldn't help but be drawn to her round bum. I was no better than a man.

'Your arse looks insane in that dress, Wills.' This was not appropriate for work, but given we were old uni friends, I figured we were well past the usual employee-employer relationship.

'No sweet talking,' Willa added over her shoulder, 'but thank you.'

Willa was in her 'slay your enemies' look today, which had been getting more action than usual recently. I wondered if it had something to do with Aidan, the sales director of *Dunamis*. Willa insisted there was nothing but hatred between her and Aidan, the son of her dad's best friend, but I wasn't convinced. There was always a weird energy about them. Sometimes, I spotted them marching out of the lifts, bickering, only to part in a huff to their separate offices.

Then, I would see Aidan staring at Willa as the two of us trotted through the foyer for after-work drinks, not a hint of hatred on his bespectacled face – instead, a sad sort of longing. I asked Willa about their strange energy because I liked my head on my shoulders.

'Right,' Willa announced, settling into her pink velvet office chair.

Was she going to fire me? Oh my god. Was I about to be fired by my best friend? Because that would be a new low.

I blew a curly strand of hair from my face. 'Willa. Please. I swear I'll put together some extra client pitches. I'll do sales pitches for you in person if you want. I *will* pull myself together.'

'Relax, Kat. It's nothing bad. Sit down a sec.'

I lowered myself into one of the two chairs opposite her huge desk, which was organised with pastel highlighters and Post-its – the complete opposite of mine, which was littered with wrappers and bits of paper with gum squished in. Willa's office was painted a muted plaster pink. It was subtly girly – the kind of pink that wouldn't put off her dad, who might question if she would be taken seriously with Barbie-pink office walls.

Willa flicked her wrist. 'Okay. Explain.'

'Explain?'

'The house listing. Every time I look at you, you're staring at it. In the office. When we go get lunch. Even when we're at Elias's, and I know you usually like to stare at Elias.'

'I think you mean you like looking at Elias.'

'Don't change the subject.'

Elias's was the Italian bar and restaurant opposite the office. Willa and I went every Friday for after-work drinks, sat at the bar and ordered Campari sodas. It helped that Elias, the owner, looked like a tanned Greek god. Unfortunately, he was very gay but declared that he adored us anyway. And the feeling was mutual.

I took a deep breath. 'My dad left me this house. It's his childhood home. It meant a lot to him. At least, I think it did. You know we weren't… close. For years.'

'Right.'

'Well, he has left it to me. It took a while for probate to go through, but the solicitor called me last week and confirmed it. It's mine. And I had no idea he'd even bought it. I think it was going to be his next project. I was going to sell it and try to buy a flat here. But I could only afford somewhere between here and Reading nearer Mum and Graham.'

'Womp womp.'

'Well, exactly. I'd prefer somewhere a bit closer to work…'

Willa's nose wrinkled. 'And somewhere *fun*.'

'Hey! Reading isn't so bad.' Willa raised an eyebrow. 'But, yeah. I'd prefer somewhere in London, but it's so fucking expensive, Wills. And I spoke to the estate agent in Everly Heath, and they said if I do some work on the house, it will go for loads more.' I waved a hand. 'Something about it being great for new families. Especially with the size of the garden.' My voice picked up speed. 'So I thought I could renovate it. I've always loved the idea of a fixer-upper and this is probably my only opportunity.'

I left out that I woke up with a sick feeling in my stomach. I left out that sometimes I wondered if I'd ever get over it – get over Dad's death and the mess I'd made at the funeral. I left out that I thought it might give me some closure, some peace.

'Okay.' Willa looked away, nodding. 'I'm giving you extended compassionate leave. I can't afford to pay you for it, but your job will be here when you get back.'

'What?' The blood drained from my face. 'No, no, it's fine. I don't need it. It's a stupid idea. I can't just uproot my life.'

Willa rose and sat in the chair next to me. She grabbed my hands – a rare moment of physical touch from Willa.

'You know I love you.'

I tried to pull my hands back. 'Stop being mushy. It's freaking me out.'

'Shut up.' She squeezed my hands. 'You need to hear this. Since the funeral, you've been crap. I know that sounds harsh, but you have. I wanted to give you time to process and grieve, but it's been months, and you aren't yourself. And I know grief doesn't go away, not completely. But it does get better. Slowly. But in the last few weeks…' Willa paused. 'You're coming into work more and more pale. You look drained. You aren't the usual you.'

I opened my mouth to object, but nothing came out.

'I wouldn't expect you to be fine. But I also wouldn't expect you to be getting worse. I can see you ignoring it and trying to push on. You need time off. Especially after what happened at the funeral –'

Embarrassment flashed hot, 'I'm fine. I'll pull myself together. I know you need all hands on deck –'

'Renovate the bloody house, will you?' Willa snapped, pointed at me. 'I've seen your Pinterest boards. They aren't listed as private, you know. I know what you're like when you have an itch to scratch, especially when it's something creative. That's why we need you here. Clients love it. So *do* the bloody thing and come back. I'll give you two months. Then I need you back and focused. We're planning to pitch to some big clients, and I need everyone with their heads in the game, okay?'

Willa patted my hand and panic pressed down in my chest. I stood up, as Willa sat back down into her office chair.

'This is unnecessary. I don't even want to go. It rains *constantly*. It's not like I've any friends up there. I barely know my family. It's ridiculous. And Mum would spit feathers –'

'I'll say this as gently as possible because it's what you need to hear. And because we have no HR. *Stop* listening to your mum. You are strong and capable, but the more you listen to your mum –' Willa exhaled. 'Look, I like Paula. Mainly because she likes me.'

Mum approved of Willa almost immediately when she saw how accomplished she was. *A business owner and so young!* Mum had gushed.

Willa pointed a manicured finger. 'You don't take risks when you listen to her. You get scared. Go and do the damn thing.'

Willa made it sound so simple, but she was right about one thing. I didn't take risks like this. Mum hadn't needed my diagnosis to train my impulsivity out of me. If I were a boy, my ADHD would probably have been endearing. I would have run around. I would have fidgeted a lot. I would have been disruptive in class, maybe – an endearing nuisance.

But as a girl, it wasn't so cute.

As a girl, it was repetitive thinking, daydreaming and anxiety. It was all in my head. It was constantly forgetting things and letting people down, especially as I was diagnosed late and had been forced to mask my symptoms.

'It's not that simple,' I said uselessly.

'It is now. 'Cos you're fired.' Willa smiled like she was giving me a gift. 'I've seen your plans. You have an eye for this stuff, Kat. Trust yourself.'

Chapter Two

Our breaths were visible in front of us at each exhale. Mum and I were halfway through the four-mile trek across the Chilterns. We were wrapped up from head to toe, the cold February air making my nose cold. The Area of Outstanding Natural Beauty had a handful of familiar walks we'd taken as a family. With my dad as a kid and later with Graham when I was a surly teenager. But as men came and went, Mum and I walked these routes on Saturday mornings.

It was a special place for us.

Or at least Mum's favourite place. She loved the rolling green hills, the otters she'd manage to spot in the rivers, and bird-watching with Graham at the weekend.

I hated the outdoors but never had the heart to break it to her. I didn't want to lose this rare connection. And I didn't want to be lectured about my health and London's pollution.

I chose the Chilterns, with their beautiful surroundings and unin-terrupted countryside views, to break the news to my mother. On the train over, I'd repeated the story to myself. I was moving up north to renovate Dad's house, whether I liked it or not. After our chat last week, Willa had given me the rest of the week to get my shit in order. Hand over to Clara and Kieran. By now, Willa would have revoked my access to the office. I had no choice but to go forward with the plan. She would have made it that way on purpose.

Her warning rang in my ears.

Don't let your mum convince you out of it.

I knew I should *tell* Mum. Be bold. Brave. But I really wanted her blessing. And I didn't want to have to beg for it.

I heaved a breath, a combination of my unfitness and my anxiety.

'Mum –'

'How is work?' she asked, her tone swift and demonstrative. My confidence plummeted.

'Good.'

'You think you'll stick this one out?' she mused.

I took a sharp inhale of breath; the noise of our boots crunching on the hard ground grew loud.

'I've been there four years, Mum,' I said gently.

'I know, but I know you can get… restless. You've always been restless, even as a baby.'

'Well, I think Dr Harris explained that one.'

I'd gone for my diagnosis with Dr Harris at university after a lecturer had suggested I might have ADHD. I came out of the examination room, Dr Harris having announced I was having twins! She diagnosed me with dyslexia and ADHD. I remembered looking at the psychology report like a flash of lightning had struck me. It all made sense. It all slotted into place. There was a reason for the struggles: the missed appointments, constantly running late, the feeling of being bored and unmotivated. The euphoric highs when that strike of motivation hit. The lows, when I couldn't move, no matter how much I wanted to – my feet stuck in sinking sand.

It all made sense, and I had a community of people who felt the same way.

Despite that, inadequacy lingered.

Mum scoffed. 'I'm still not sure she was a real doctor. They say that some of these places aren't proper clinics. They sign whatever paper you want them to.'

I closed my eyes.

'You know, they didn't have these labels when I was a kid. Now everyone has some problem –'

'Mum,' I warned, 'let's not get into it.'

I'd had this argument with her a million times and I was so tired. Tired of justifying my diagnosis.

'Katherine,' she continued, ignoring my pleas, 'you were a bright child. Sure, you had some… organisational challenges. But you were bright, clever. You just didn't apply yourself.'

Anxiety rose like bile in my throat. My eyes and nose stung with tears.

'Mum, can we please change the subject?' I asked as calmly as I could.

She relented, and we walked in silence for a few moments. We passed a couple hiking back down the hill. Mum and I gave them a courteous nod. I looked up at the clear blue sky, trying to calm my nervous system, which had gone into overdrive.

'Have you called the estate agent?' Mum asked. She probably thought it was a less controversial topic, which made me want to laugh. Or cry. 'We can do it remotely, I checked. We can send them some keys. Then, they can value it. I can't imagine it would get more than what your father bought it for before –' Mum gave a constipated look. 'You know.'

Before he died was what she meant, but she couldn't say it. 'You know' was the extent of the conversation we'd had about Dad's death since the funeral. While I empathised that some people felt icky about death, it wasn't enough for me. I wanted to talk about him. I needed to. I craved to say how I was feeling. I wanted to claw at my skin and scream into the sky. But Mum shut down every attempt I'd made to talk about him, and she was one of

23

the few people who knew Dad. Graham rarely met him. My friends had never met him.

Mum was the only person who could relate to how I felt, but she was content to shove it all under the carpet.

'I haven't yet, no —'

'Oh, come on, Katherine. You need to move quicker than this. It could take forever to sell that house. Not all housing markets are like the one in London. I imagine it's a lot slower in the Northwest.'

'Actually, from my research, they are having a bit of a boom at the moment.'

She raised an eyebrow. 'You have time to research the housing market in Manchester but no time to call an estate agent?'

'Well —' I took a breath, wondering if she'd interrupt me again. But she didn't. 'The reason I did some research was because I did call the estate agent.'

My mum's eyes lit up. 'Oh, fabulous. Why didn't you say that?'

'Well, I had an interesting conversation with a chap called John. And he said that because of the market right now, that I could get a lot more for it, if I did it up a bit. You know, a lick of paint. A new bathroom and kitchen, perhaps.' I added the last sentence with such airy grace that I was worried I would fly away.

Mum's face contorted into confusion. Then repulsion.

'How would you renovate a house two hundred miles away? It would be hell. It's the kind of thing you need to be there for, making sure everything runs smoothly.'

'Yes. Exactly. I was thinking that perhaps, maybe, I could move up temporarily to oversee the renovation.' I winced, waiting for the onslaught.

Mum gave a peel of laughter, like it was the most ridiculous thing she'd ever heard. She glanced over at me, and her face dropped.

'You can't be serious.' She sighed like she was tired, and not because of the gradual incline of the slope we were walking up. 'Katherine, don't be ridiculous. Renovate the house, for what? A few more thousand pounds? I can't imagine you'd get much more back –'

'Well, John said it could be up to seventy thousand pounds more.' My words came fast now, desperate to escape. 'And that would get me a flat in a more central location. A bit more central. Not somewhere on the outskirts of Reading –'

'And what is wrong with Reading? There are plenty of houses you could buy here, I'm sure.'

My mum was oblivious. She seemed to think that houses were growing on trees. We were living through a very real housing crisis. And I'd looked at houses in Reading; they were as expensive and competitive to buy as in London. Regardless of whether I picked a small flat in London or a little house in Reading, I needed as much cash as possible to buy.

'It would take me two months –'

'Two months?' she squeaked. 'And leave your *job*?' She said it like my job was the be-all and end-all of my life. Like it was my reason for living. And it really wasn't. I was grateful to have a job that allowed me to hang out with Willa every day and rent a room in London, but I'd always felt I was missing something.

Some greater calling.

'Ah, I see,' Mum said knowingly. 'This is another one of your schemes. What was the last one? Calligraphy for weddings, wasn't it?'

A lump in my throat formed. A shroud of shame hovered over me.

'And the one before that – scented candle making. I think you sold a few of those.'

I'd sold ten before I lost interest and shut down my Etsy storefront.

25

'And then, you were convinced childcare was your calling. And you wanted to become a nanny.' Mum smiled like none of this was hurtful. Like she hadn't pinpointed the biggest insecurity I had about myself – I had no follow-through. I was flighty. I'd never amount to anything.

'But, Katherine,' she continued, 'this is a lot more than a hobby or what do young people call it – a side quest?'

'A side hustle,' I added quietly.

'This would be spending thousands of pounds on a house. A house that might not make it back. It's too big a gamble to take. Would you pay for all the work or do it yourself? Because if it's the latter' – she huffed – 'well, I dread to think what could happen. You could hammer through a wall and fuse the whole house, for Christ's sake, and then pay for a whole rewire. Would you have a job to return to?'

I didn't mention that Willa had given me the time off. Unpaid. She would probably throw herself down the hill we were currently climbing. I stared at my boots with every stride, lost for words. Mum, however, was not lost for words.

'You would hate Everly Heath. I doubt they have any of that Deliverloo you love so much. You would be bored, Katherine. Let me tell you, people are cliquey around there. They keep to themselves and look after their own. I wouldn't count on your aunt and uncle helping out. You have to think, Katherine…'

The lecture continued for another two miles as my mum made her case against renovating Dad's house. I didn't mention any of my emotional attachment to the place. It was pointless. She wouldn't understand. She would say the man had never played a significant role in my life.

Mum didn't notice a few tears escaping down my cheeks as we finished the walk and climbed into her car to drive home.

I didn't tell her I had already packed my suitcases. I didn't tell her I was catching the train to Manchester in the morning. And I didn't tell her that I was clinging to hold myself together long enough so I could be put back together again.

Chapter Three

I stepped across the threshold, and a distinctive old-lady smell hit my senses — damp with a hint of lavender. The smell provoked memories of visits to my granny: chocolate biscuits dunked in tea and little tuna sandwiches for lunch. I scanned the hallway of the 1930s semi-detached house. *My* house. I pressed a shaking hand to the ache in my chest. Thinking of this house as mine and not Dad's was still jarring.

For the past eight months, I had become accustomed to pushing emotions down like pressing a buoyant beach ball below salty waves.

So far, it had only hurtled above the water once.

Don't think about the funeral.

As if that tactic had got me anywhere.

As I looked at the hallway, the beach ball threatened to come up. I pressed my head against the door frame. What have I got myself into? What was I thinking? Would renovating this house even give me closure?

I took another deep breath and tried not to spiral at the sight of a broken door latch hanging precariously from a rusty nail. I'd need to sort that out today if I wanted to sleep safely tonight. I mentally added it to my ever-growing list, but I knew I'd forget it quickly unless I wrote it down. *Your head is like a sieve*, my mum used to say, *straight in, straight out.* I tried not to take it personally.

Anaglypta wallpaper adorned the walls, cemented on in the 1970s, seemingly never to be removed again. Popcorn ceilings and thick swirling green carpet led up the narrow staircase from the hallway. Some of it looked… wet and sticky. Like there had been a leak at some point. I shuddered. A suspicious brown stain marred the ceiling; I didn't want to know the source. The damp intensified through the hallway.

This wasn't as I remembered it. Sure, it had been dated when I'd visited as a kid. But it had been warm and homely and looked after.

Some original features, like picture rails and skirting boards, remained. But someone had ripped out the original stairs and replaced them with horizontal bannisters to 'modernise' the look of the hallway. But the teak was chipped and flaking off now.

Various mismatching but equally loud shag carpets were on display as I moved through the house. The living room boasted a bold geometric orange carpet, and the dining room showcased a green swirly one. The small kitchen at the back of the house had avocado green units and old-school appliances. I tentatively opened the oven door to see it completely black on the inside.

'No home-cooked meals for me,' I muttered.

Upstairs was a matching green bathroom suite, equally grimy and dirty. The house was silent apart from the ticking of the ancient boiler (the villain behind the E energy rating) and the loudness of my brain screaming a never-ending to-do list. Even though it was only a modest three-bedroom semi-detached house, it hadn't been touched in years.

Hire a skip. Remove the carpets. Steam the wallpaper off. Ditch the electric fireplace and tiled surround. My mind rattled off more and more demands.

Okay, I thought, *let's get started.*

★

Time blurred, and I wasn't sure how much had passed when I heard a loud 'Hello!' call from the open front door.

I glanced around, coming back into my body. My tongue stuck to the roof of my mouth and a bead of sweat formed at my neck. I could almost hear my hair curling and growing, like some disturbing cartoon version of myself. I glanced down. I was holding a bleach spray, cleaning the bathroom sink upstairs. I put the bleach down and made my way downstairs, seeing the chaos I had created in the last few hours – so many half-finished jobs. The hallway was littered with partially ripped-off wallpaper; in the bedroom sat a suitcase that had been opened and rummaged through alongside a deflated inflatable mattress. I'd gone to fetch the pump but had got distracted setting up the kitchen, and I knew I'd left the cupboards open downstairs.

'Fuck.' My head fell into my palm.

I'm such a fuck up.

I felt like an eleven-year-old child again. It brought back the smell of Mum's deputy headteacher's office. Her disappointed expression when I told her I'd forgotten my maths homework, PE kit and food tech basket on the same day. *You need to be more organised than this, Katherine. I can't always be there to hold your hand.* My mother shook her head. Post-diagnosis, my mum's remarks didn't change much. It shifted from *You just need to apply yourself* to *It doesn't mean you have an excuse, Kat.* She didn't understand that my lack of focus wasn't laziness or for want of trying.

'Kat?' The loud voice called from the open front door again, pulling me from my thoughts.

I ran down the stairs to find my cousin Lydia standing in the hallway. She was brandishing two bottles of prosecco like they were awards, and she'd swept the board.

She raised the bottle above her head. 'Surprise, bitch!' She accosted me into a bone-crushing hug, her long blonde hair making its way into my mouth. Our height difference (me, five foot five and a half, Lydia, five foot eight) was even more apparent when we hugged, which was rarely. We were 'weddings and funerals' cousins, mainly due to the distance. Lydia was a born and bred Mancunian, like all the paternal side of my family, while I was raised in Reading.

'How's it going?' Lydia asked, her faint Mancunian accent coming through, the first I'd heard since arriving. Sometimes, it hurt to hear it; that lilt evoked memories of late-night phone calls from my dad after missed milestones – apologies for absences at dance performances, school award ceremonies, and first days at school.

I shrugged. 'Not too bad.'

Lydia looked around the place, probably seeing the destruction in our wake, but didn't comment directly. My familiar friend, self-doubt, was waving like Forrest Gump in my head. There was so much to do, and I couldn't even complete one task without a breakdown.

How did I plan to renovate a whole house if I couldn't clean one?

Lydia looked around the hallway, picking at the plaster. 'So, Uncle Jim left this place to you? You had no idea?'

'I got a call from a solicitor.'

The subtext was obvious.

He hadn't told me because we didn't speak.

Lydia's blue eyes, the Williams family eyes we shared, met mine and softened.

'I'm so sorry, Kat.'

I tensed.

'It's fine. Anyway. I'm going to renovate it myself.' I pulled my curly hair up into the bobble on my wrist.

'You're going to renovate it?' she squeaked, eyes going wide.

31

Great. Even *Miss Motivation* herself doubted me.

'It was Dad's childhood home, and your dad's too.' I nodded towards Lydia. My uncle looked so much like my dad, with darker red curls and crinkly eyes, that I'd struggled to say more than a few words to him at the funeral last year. Looking at Brian felt like looking at the sun.

'I know... but I know you and your dad... were strained. Everyone would understand if you wanted to sell. Let someone else renovate it.'

Were they talking behind my back? This is because of the funeral. They saw how I messed up and thought I would choke at this, too.

I shrugged, attempting nonchalance. 'It feels right to bring it back to life. Let someone else build memories here.' My nose began to burn. 'Plus, it makes more business sense. I met with the estate agent, and he reckons if I spend money on a few basics, it will sell for a lot more. Then I can use that money to buy a place in London.'

'Does that mean I get to see my cousin more than a few hours this year?' Lydia smiled and threw her toned arm around my shoulders.

'Yep, you have me for two months.'

Lydia's lips pulled back in mock disgust. 'Alright. Don't overstay your welcome, cuz. This town isn't big enough for two Williams girls.'

I chuckled. 'I'm sure it will survive.'

'We'll have to warn the town crier.'

Lydia's town. Dad's town. My paternal family had set down deep roots in Everly Heath. But I'd always felt like an outsider on the few occasions I'd visited, even before my parents' divorce. I'd been a pre-teen, an infamously awkward age, and while everyone had been friendly and welcoming, I'd always felt anxious and awkward compared to the relaxed way everyone talked to each other. There was a rhythm, but I didn't have the hymn sheet.

Lydia ruffled my sweaty hair. 'Where shall we start, then?' She eyed the hallway and kitchen.

'You don't have to help, Lydia. I'll manage.'

'Nope, nope, nope. Not having this, you're just like your dad. Never accepting any help. I will be here either way, so tell me what to do or else.'

We agreed that Lydia would work upstairs, and I would tackle downstairs. Three hours of arduous work later, we'd done a deep clean of the whole house while listening to a true crime podcast. I'd heard Lydia exclaim the occasional 'Bastard!' and '*It's the brother!*' and snorted. Satisfied, we collapsed on the living room floor with plastic cups and a bottle of prosecco.

Warmth spread through my chest. It was addictive, that high. It spurred me on. When Lydia left, I would smash out that to-do list and kick arse. But in the meantime, I was quite happy to enjoy the company.

'How's work?' I asked while topping up her glass of prosecco.

'Busy. Really busy. But I have no clients tomorrow, so I can be naughty,' she replied haughtily and took a swig.

I raised an eyebrow. 'Aren't personal trainers supposed to be, like, super healthy?'

Lydia shrugged. 'All about balance. Plus, if I can't celebrate my cousin moving home—'

'—temporarily,' I reminded her.

Lydia rolled her eyes. 'Yes, temporarily, but still. What's the point of all this' – she gestured to herself – 'if I can't enjoy life?'

To say Lydia was in good shape was an understatement. She was tall and lean, features she got from her mother's side of the family because the Williamses were all short, stocky, and usually ginger. Lydia always wore bright sports gear, today favouring yellow and orange, and her long blonde hair was perpetually tied up into pigtails or space buns. She had the energy of the Duracell bunny and the spirit of a children's TV presenter. I stared at her toned arms. *How the hell did they even look like that?*

'I work hard, but it is my full-time job,' Lydia added, as if answering my mental question. 'Most people don't have time to work out because they have actual lives. And families. Or see exercise as a means to an end, which I get. But I love it. I live for it.'

I nodded, wishing I understood that mentality. I liked graphic design, sure, but I didn't live for it. Some days, I wondered if I even liked it all that much.

'Speaking of work. How did you swindle the time off?' A curious tone entered Lydia's voice.

'Extended compassionate leave. Unpaid, but still. My boss, Willa, was understanding. She also lost her mum last year. Plus, I think two months of not paying my salary was appealing. They aren't having the best time, financially.'

'Well, I suppose that's a silver lining. The extended leave, I mean.'

'Yep. Thank god for dead dads, huh?'

'I didn't mean it like that.'

'I'm joking, Lyd. You're right. It's a relief to be able to focus on this: new carpets, a lick of paint. The only big job will be opening the kitchen into the dining room to create an open-plan kitchen-diner. I looked it up, and I don't need planning permission if I'm not extending. Even if it would be much better if we could…'

Lydia jumped up, and I trailed after her. We looked at the wall separating the dining room and the galley kitchen.

'Yeah.' Lydia nodded. 'But if you knocked this wall down, it would be huge.'

I nodded. 'I could even create a little snug here. I think there is enough room for a TV and sofa.'

'I can see that.'

'And over here,' I gestured to the centre of the room, 'once the wall is gone, there is enough room for an island, with barstools for three at least.'

I began designing the space in my head. My mind flooded with Pinterest-like images of arched bookcases and gorgeous parquet flooring. Soft plaster-pink walls contrasted with deep navy cabinets – a cosy breakfast nook by the window. I was itching to pick out the perfect tile for the backsplash. My mum and Graham's Edwardian terrace house resembled an eccentric library. Annotated novels and travel books doubled as coffee tables, cups of tea balancing precariously on top. I loved it but always longed to put my own stamp on a house. I hadn't expected it to be my dead dad's childhood home.

'What did your mum say about you moving up here?' Lydia asked wryly.

My mum had never made her dislike of the North unknown. When my parents got married, my dad agreed to a wedding with all his friends and family at Everly Heath Church in exchange for moving down south to Reading, where my mum was working at a school. It seemed like an even exchange in my head, but now that I thought about it, ultimatums probably didn't set a good tone to start a marriage.

'She...' *Should I lie again?* I lied to get out of trouble all the time. At this point, I was worried it was pathological. But something about Lydia's earnest face and helpful spirit made me want to be honest.

'She doesn't know,' I admitted and waited for the gasp. My mother was scary as fuck. Even Lydia knew that.

I didn't hear any reaction, so I looked up to find Lydia staring at me, a fearful expression on her features.

'What?'

Lydia whistled. 'You grew some balls.'

'What do you mean?' I protested. 'It's fine. It's two months, and we're not in each other's pockets, so I'll be back in London soon.'

Lydia's eyes widened, 'This is what it feels like to be in the rebel alliance.' I ignored Lydia's comment.

I groaned and threw my head against my cousin's muscly shoulder. 'Please help me.'

'Hang on. You talked me through it. You have it all planned out.'

'I don't. I will get overwhelmed and stressed and get carried away and spend too much. Everything I want to do will cost a million pounds. And maybe I could justify half of it if I was staying, but I'm selling,' I said so fast that I ran out of steam towards the end.

'Okay, okay. Let's break it down,' Lydia patted me on the shoulder. 'What first?'

'Builder quotes.'

'Oh!' A light bulb appeared over Lydia's head, illuminating her dirty-blonde hair. She grabbed my arm. 'Some family friends of ours, the Hunters, could help. They're builders. I'll give you Kevin's number,' Lydia added, searching for her phone.

'Do you think they'd be available?'

'Oh yeah. They always do favours around here, especially for locals. I bet if I twisted his arm—'

'I'm not local.'

'No, but your dad is. Was.' She flinched, then recovered. 'And I am. I'll call in a favour, don't worry.'

She grinned, infectious; it made me smile back.

'That would be great. Thanks, Lyd.' I looked around the dusty dining room. 'God, there's so much to do. I don't know where to start.'

'Why don't we make a list together, now?'

A list would be helpful. It would be even more helpful to get the words out. To speak it all out loud. I forced down the instinct to say no. To insist I could do this alone. She'd already offered the Hunters. I couldn't take up more of her time. I couldn't be more of a burden.

'That would be great. Shall we start upstairs and work our way down?'

Lydia grinned. 'I'm opening the next bottle of prosecco.'

Chapter Four

Kat's To-Do List

- ~~Find builder!!!~~ Call Kevin Hunter – 07000 900463
- Call locksmith
- ~~Deep clean house~~
- Call Mum back (plan what to say!!!)
- New light fittings
- Cast iron radiators
- ~~Arched bookcases in alcoves~~ Shelves in alcoves
- Fitted dining nook? Research prices
- Bifolds? Research prices
- Sockets that don't spark (electrocution is not a vibe)

A loud bang echoed from downstairs, and my crusty eyelids flew open. My mouth was bone dry, and my head pounded. I craned my neck, listening. Had I imagined the noise? I lifted my body. I'd slept face down on the half-deflated mattress. I glanced down to see my boob hanging out of my pyjama top. I wiped my mouth where spit had dried on my cheek and rose to my feet. My head was pounding, full of blurry memories of Lydia and me drinking prosecco from plastic cups, burning scented candles and dancing to Taylor Swift.

A soft mutter of 'Ow, fuck' floated upstairs, making my head whip around to listen. My palms began to sweat out last night's prosecco.

Who the fuck was in my house?

My heart jumped as another shuffle sounded from downstairs. Someone had broken into my dad's house. My house.

My head sloshed around as I unplugged the little lamp I'd brought and brandished it before me. I tiptoed down the stairs, pausing to assess the sound of whoever was in the living room.

An obnoxiously loud ringtone went off, and I heard a man's voice.

'Ey up,' a deep voice said. I could hear the tinny replies on the other end as I pressed myself against the wall in the hallway so I couldn't be seen.

Who the fuck breaks into an empty house? There was nothing to steal. Did he check through the window, see the sight of half-empty boxes of cleaning solutions and think, *Oh yeah, I need some more bleach for the downstairs loo?*

'Alright.' His voice echoed, bouncing off the bare walls. 'There's nowt we can do about it now anyway, Jack. I know. We'll order some more and take the hit. I know you are. It's fine.

'Alright. Talk to you later.' The man hung up, and I could hear his footsteps approaching.

Any second, he would come around the corner and see me. What if he was armed? What if he was going to kidnap me and submit me to human trafficking? My thoughts spiraled. All the murders and kidnappings from my true crime podcasts eddied around in my brain.

It was fight or flight, and I chose both.

I let out a battle cry and held the lamp above my head, jumping out into the doorway.

'Fucking 'ell!'

39

A notepad fell to the floor as the criminal caught the lamp I'd half-thrown in his direction with ease. He held it up, his eyes wide like it could explode any minute. In my hungover strategising, I'd thought I'd throw the lamp and run like some sort of grenade.

I saw the face in front of me – a familiar face.

'You,' I seethed.

Car park man. The man from the church car park was standing in my living room. The man who had callously stolen my space and then had the gall to attend my dad's funeral.

'What—I—' the man sputtered. Confusion and shock crossed his features, one after the other in a comical display, like a cartoon character.

'Come to steal something else?' My hands went to my hips. 'What do you need now? My kidney?'

His gaze travelled all over me, his face flickering through emotions I couldn't read. Dark eyes caught on my bare legs, and I couldn't help but notice the way they dragged up my body. I shifted my stance, crossing my arms, suddenly conscious I wasn't wearing a bra.

'Well? Cat got your tongue?' Since when did I say old-timey shit like that? This house was clearly rubbing off on me.

His cheeks flushed at my question, and I felt a morsel of glee.

He held his hands up like he feared another lamp being thrown in his direction. 'I – I didn't know you were Jim's daughter. I wouldn't have—'

'Wouldn't have stolen a car parking space from his daughter at his funeral?'

The funeral. Cue full-body cringe. He'd seen me break down. He'd seen me flee the church. White-hot embarrassment flooded my body.

'I didn't know.' He took a step closer. 'I wouldn't have – I would have given you the space.'

'Mm-hmm.' I nodded sarcastically.

As we stood closer, the juxtaposition of our clothes was even more apparent. My silky floral pyjamas, exposed legs, and probably questionable morning breath, while he wore a long-sleeved fitted black tee, utility trousers, and steel-capped boots. He ran his hands through his dark brown hair that curled at his temples. The scruff around his face was more like a beard than it was that day at the funeral. He had deep brown eyes that I couldn't deny were inherently attractive.

He was totally out of his comfort zone.

It almost made me laugh.

I stepped back, tucking my hair behind my shoulder, attempting to make it look less dishevelled.

'Next question. Do you want to explain why you're committing domestic burglary?' I said haughtily, a bit high from making a man about six foot three blush.

He frowned. 'You called me.'

I huffed a laugh. 'I certainly did not.'

He spoke slowly. 'Yes, you did.' He pointed to the front door. 'Your door is broken. It was half open. I figured no daft sod is going to sleep in a house without a door that can at least shut closed.'

It was my turn to blush. I'd forgotten about the broken lock, and after the second bottle of prosecco, I hadn't cared. After Lydia got an Uber home, I stomped upstairs, collapsed on my makeshift bed and went to sleep.

'I –' I opened my mouth, attempting to reclaim some ground, but came up with nothing.

The man raised a single dark eyebrow. 'I got a voicemail from an unknown number at one thirty in the morning. Two women, sounding pissed as farts, asked if I'd come around and look at the house. As soon as possible. It sounded like an emergency –'

41

'No –' I opened my mouth to challenge, but then – *oh god*.

A memory hit me. Lydia and I still sat on the living room floor, calling up her family friend on my phone and leaving a voicemail. It was a messy, drunk voicemail that probably made no sense.

'Now I'm realising it was you and Lydia. The cousin. Brian and Sandra's niece.'

'How do you know my auntie and uncle?'

He crossed his arms. 'We're family friends. My parents and Lydia's parents were close.' He flinched and corrected. 'Are close.'

My eyes narrowed. 'She said it was Kevin who was coming to take a look.'

My eyes trailed over him. His arms were crossed over a wide, defined chest. This was not a Kevin. No one with arms like his was called Kevin.

'Kevin is my dad. He's out of action at the moment. Knee op.'

I groaned. 'Lydia.' She could have warned me that it was her annoyingly handsome friend we were drunk dialling at one thirty in the morning.

The man chuckled, shifting his weight in a way that was a bit too casual for me.

'She's a bit of a menace.' His gaze shifted to the two empty prosecco bottles in the corner of the lounge, then back to me. Judgemental much?

'She never mentioned a cousin.'

'We don't see each other much.' I lifted my chin. 'So we were catching up.'

'Lydia's good at "catching up". She does that every Friday.' I thought he was joking, but his face didn't change or soften. He was so… stoic. It appeared he'd recovered from his obvious discomfort about seeing me again after the funeral and had resumed whatever this persona was. Big grumpy builder, I was guessing.

'I'm Liam.' He slipped his hands into his back pocket and produced a business card.

Did builders usually have business cards? The card was black and simply designed, if a bit too masculine for my taste. But then, he probably ordered it on some boring website without a thought. It read Liam Hunter, Partner, Hunter Building and Construction. The logo was abbreviated to HBC.

'This could be a bit more exciting, you know.' I lifted the card, the criticism tumbling out.

Liam's eyebrows drew together. 'Excuse me?'

'This design — it's boring. You could design something that represents…' I gestured towards him. 'You. Or your brand.'

'It's just a business card. Not a dating profile.'

I laughed humourlessly. 'If you don't care, how do you expect anyone else to? Design is important. It's how we want to be seen in the world. It's how we represent ourselves.'

I don't know what possessed me to pull out my first-year design modules for a bloody builder.

'I — I'll leave you to it.' He took a step away.

After he broke into my house, I offered him free design advice, but he looked at *me* like I was the weirdo. Incredible.

Liam took another step back. 'I can come by again when you're expecting me.'

His eyes glanced down so briefly to my bare legs that I almost missed it. God, I'd run down the stairs half-dressed, screaming like a hungover banshee, and ranted about the design of his business cards, only to find out he was here because I'd called him. Not to mention, his first impression of me was calling him a prick and then having a breakdown on a church pulpit.

I needed to get this man out of my vicinity immediately.

There was no way I could hire him. He knew too much.

He was halfway out of the house when I called back. 'You know what? I think I'll be fine.'

He twisted his shoulders to look at me. 'Fine?'

'I've changed my mind. I don't need a Kevin, a Liam, or whatever your name is.'

He turned back, that eyebrow cocked again. 'You've changed your mind?'

I crossed my arms. 'I mean, I need to look into options anyway. I can't hire the first builder who walks into my house unannounced –'

Frustration flickered in Liam's eyes. '*You* called *me*.'

'Yes, I know. But either way, I don't want to hire the first builder. I need to compare quotes.'

I had no clue what I was saying, but I knew I didn't want to work with this man who had seen me at my worst. He'd seen me angry. He'd seen me cry. He'd seen me hungover. If I were a mafia boss, I'd call in a hit on Liam.

Liam sighed. 'Look – Lydia asked me to look into it, so I'm going to. She is family, which annoyingly means you are too.'

I bristled at his words. 'It's my house.'

'And you need it renovating.' He glanced around the hallway like it was a pit of despair. Rude, again.

'I'll tell Lydia that I'm not interested. You're set free of your… obligation.'

'Let me guess. This is because of the car parking space, isn't it?'

'No.'

Those brown eyes flickered with heat. 'Yes, it is. Admit it.'

'Well, could you blame me? It was my dad's funeral.'

'*You* were the one late for your own dad's funeral, not me.'

I reared back, reeling. 'Are you kidding me?'

Liam winced. 'I didn't –'

'Well, you did,' I snapped back.

Oh, he'd done it now.

I stepped forward, trying to look as intimidating as possible, which was challenging when I hadn't brushed my hair yet.

'You know what? I don't need some entitled, rude builder with an attitude problem. I need someone who will help me, and you are decidedly *unhelpful*. I don't need this.' I shooed him towards the door. 'There isn't the right synergy here.' I gestured between myself and Liam like Willa does when she explains why clients leave our roster.

'Synergy.' Liam gave a bitter laugh that didn't meet his eyes. 'Fucking Southerners,' he muttered loud enough for me to hear as he retreated to his van.

'Nice to meet you, Kat,' Liam shouted sarcastically over his shoulder.

'Ditto,' I shouted back.

I tried to throw the door shut in a dramatic statement, but it bounced back softly, not matching my vibe. I gave an irritated huff-slash-scream and stomped upstairs to wash the hangover shame off my body.

Then, I would hire the best damn builder in Greater Manchester.

Chapter Five

'Six months?' My shrill voice cut through the overgrown garden to the point I was sure the neighbours four doors down probably heard.

'Yeah, I'm afraid so.' Mac's tinkling laughter came down my phone. 'We've got a load of jobs on the go as it is. Six months is a best-case scenario. It could be longer; we can't always predict problems. I'm sorry.'

Mackenzie's Construction was the third company I'd rung up, and it seemed the safest bet. Mac was an experienced builder, with generations of builders in her family. Unlike the first builder I'd called, she came with a load of recommendations; she'd quoted for the work without seeing the house and wanted the total paid upfront before she'd even started. Sure, I didn't know what I was doing for the most part, but I could spot a cowboy builder when I saw one.

Renovation TV shows were always my go-to when I was home sick from school: *Grand Designs*, *DIY SOS*, *Location, Location, Location*. I used to revel at the moment the materials arrived late; they were over budget by a hundred grand, or the project got rained off. Who didn't love some Schadenfreude on a rainy Wednesday afternoon when you couldn't breathe out of your left nostril? I'd always loved the idea of managing a renovation project; obviously, I could do it so much better than the people on TV.

But I was stumbling at the first fucking hurdle – finding a builder.

'Is there any chance of… speeding things up? I can pay a premium.' I cringed at the desperation in my voice. And at the idea of spending more money than needed. Dad had left some money to renovate in his will, but it wasn't unlimited. I needed all the cash I could get if I wanted to buy somewhere in London.

Mac's reply was instant. 'Nothin' I can do, I'm afraid. A lot of the projects have contracts and have paid deposits. You'd struggle to find any builder ready to start as soon as possible. I certainly wouldn't trust anyone who could, if I'm honest. Things have really picked up in the last year. Unless you can find someone whose arm you can twist, or you could try blackmail.' Mac chuckled.

Broad shoulders and deep brown eyes came to mind. The only person I could have leveraged or strong-armed into helping me, I had now threatened with a light fitting, pissed off, and sent packing. I paced back and forth in the garden, creating a pathway through the overgrown grass. Panic tightened my throat. I needed to refurb the house and sell it in two months.

Two months.

As if sensing my self-doubt, my phone rang, and the caller ID read Mum.

'Hi, Mum,' I squeaked.

I'm twenty-seven years old. I'm an adult. I make my own choices.

'What's wrong?' My mum's voice was laced with concern. Fuck. How did she know already? It was my voice. Or maybe being a headteacher for the last fifteen years had engrained some 'shit's about to hit the fan' sixth sense into my mother.

'Nothing, nothing. I'm fine.' I kept my voice as even as possible.

All fine, apart from the fact I'm lying to you. I've moved two hundred miles to renovate a house with no builder, and I've managed to royally piss off the only one who might do me a favour. Other than that, I'm fine.

Totally fine.

'Hm.' I hadn't convinced her. 'What are you up to at the weekend? Graham and I were thinking we might come into London –'

'Oh,' I said, shock in my voice. They never visited London, so of course, now was the weekend they wanted to visit. 'I'm busy, I'm afraid, Mum.'

'Oh.'

'Yes, sorry.'

'You can't reschedule? What are you up to?' The tone had panic rising in my chest. Had she caught me?

'I'm – ah. I'm with Willa.'

'Oh, that's no problem. Just bring her along. On Saturday? Because we could come in on Sunday –'

'Sunday, I'm helping her with some work. All weekend, we are working. Some client pitches that she's panicking about. She's having some problems, you know, with clients leaving.'

If I threw Mum a bone and gave her something to worry about in my life that wasn't this house, she'd focus on that. Divert.

'Okay.'

'Actually, we'll be doing that for quite a few weekends.' I bit my lip. God, I hated lying. 'See, Willa is doing a lot of away days. And the weekends work best for all of us.'

If I said I was busy on the weekends, Mum had no choice but to accept I was busy for the next few months. She was a teacher, so she couldn't arrange to see me in the week.

'Well, I do hope everything is okay, Katherine. If your job is at risk –'

'It's not. Really, it's fine. You know Willa's dad would never let anything happen.'

Mum gave a satisfied hum down the phone.

'So, the house,' my mum said, and I jumped like she'd appeared beside me. 'Where are we up to with the estate agent? Do you need me to help look at some documents?'

I absentmindedly kicked over a ceramic hedgehog in the grass.

As much as I resented how my mum approached my disability, I did appreciate having her look over dense documents for me. My dyslexia meant I missed a lot of detail, and my ADHD meant I hated boring tasks. Thanks to my eReader's large print, I could read a book in a whole evening, but if you asked me to read over a client contract, I'd rather throw myself out of the office window, thirteen floors up.

'It's all under control,' I said firmly.

'Are you sure? I can call them.'

'Mum. Come on. It's fine. I can sort it.'

'Okay.' She sounded unconvinced.

'I know you're there if I need you.'

That was a bit too emotional for Mum, so all I got was a stiff, 'Good.'

'Katerina!' Graham's voice boomed down the phone. He was usually soft-spoken, but he was being silly, probably to defuse the tension between me and my mum.

'Hi, Graham.' I smiled.

'It's lovely to hear your voice, but your mother and I are leaving. We're going foraging in Greenmoor Wood. I'm wrestling the phone from her as we speak.'

I laughed. 'That's fine! Thanks for checking in.'

'Okay, darling. We will speak to you soon. Your mum sends kisses.'

My mum never sends kisses. Not even on texts. But I respected Graham's attempt to soften her phone call. When I first met Graham at fourteen, I was resistant. In my defence, fourteen-year-olds don't like anyone. But he won me over eventually, with his warm eyes set behind round spectacles like a benevolent library teacher that might help you save the world.

49

Unlike my dad, he was academic. He worked as a curator of the Egyptian collection at the Ashmolean Museum at the University of Oxford, so he and Mum understood working in education and the bureaucracy that came with it. They shared the same passions and eccentric hobbies – foraging for Mum and bouldering for Graham. They planned to retire in a few years, downsize and use the money to travel for the year – Egypt, Peru and South America. It was the absolute opposite of my idea of a holiday, but I was so excited for them. Mum had never visited anywhere.

I said my goodbyes to Mum and Graham and stood in the garden, twisting my watch from side to side. I needed a new plan – one that might include persuading a pissed-off builder to help me. I bit my lip. I needed to persuade Liam to reconsider.

I would happily exchange my pride for the ability to say 'I told you so' to my mum.

Before I could begin hatching my new charm offensive, a chubby little fawn pug entered the garden through the open gate. Its buggy eyes looked at me as if it was surprised to see me there, gave me a look that seemed to say, 'Oh well', and it brought its front and back paws together to take a dump on my lawn. My mouth was agape.

'Noodle!' A panicked voice came from the front drive. Around the corner came a woman who must have been in her early sixties. She had light grey hair styled in cornrows and stylish cat-eye frames adorning her face. She wore blue jeans, a bright orange jumper, and walking boots. A dog lead was hanging around her shoulders.

'Noodle!' She gasped as she took in her pug, now squatting around my garden, looking slightly constipated.

'Oh, I'm so sorry. He's never done this before. He doesn't usually run off, especially into a neighbour's garden. This is *so* embarrassing. Wait until I tell our Steve. He's going to be so mortified. He prides himself on Noodle's good behaviour. When we took him to puppy training, he was the best in the class.' She rushed over to Noodle, pulling green dog poo bags out of her back pocket. 'I am sorry.'

She spoke all this at *Gilmore Girls*-level speed, and it took me a while to process what was happening.

I smiled – because what else could I do – and said, 'Don't worry about it. The garden's a mess anyway. What's a bit of dog poo?'

The woman laughed, glancing around at the overgrown garden. 'Don't you worry. You'll get it sorted in no time. Rose struggled to keep on top of it towards the end.' She smiled sadly. 'And then we never heard from the new owner when it sold. Sometimes, we saw a gardener come in and do a cull – but that hasn't been for months.' She extended her hand. 'My name is Pat. Patricia. I'm number twenty-four. I live with my husband, Steve.' As Pat hadn't picked up the dog poo yet, I didn't hesitate to shake her hand. Her hands were warm and soft.

I smiled. 'I'm Kat. And it was my dad who owned the house. He passed away last summer. I think he was probably the one who arranged the gardener now and then.'

Pat's face almost caved in on itself in sadness and pity.

Panic rose in my chest.

She held onto my hand, pulling it closer to her. 'Oh, I'm so sorry. How awful. And me blabbering on about the garden. Please ignore me.'

I shifted my weight. 'There's nothing to apologise for. We weren't that close.'

Pat's piercing brown eyes seemed to be scanning me, peeking through closed curtains, so I changed the subject quickly.

'Noodle is very cute.' I leaned down and petted him on the head. He rubbed his flat face into my jeans.

'Thank you.' She beamed down at the rotund dog. 'We adopted him – he has a lot of health problems, like most pugs. We would never buy, especially this breed. I disagree with it.'

I nodded, and Noodle got bored of me and trotted around the garden, snorting away.

'Have you got a hus – partner moving in with you?' Pat stuttered through the question. Those eyes were curious, if not a little nosy. In fact, she was definitely nosy.

'Ah, no. No husband,' I said, giving Pat the answer to her silent question – I was straight. 'I've come up to renovate the property, sell it, then I'm moving back down south. Hopefully, I'll buy somewhere in London. It was my dad's house when he was growing up, so I feel like I should –' I didn't know how to finish that sentence, so I left it hanging.

'Oh, that's lovely.' Pat threw a palm to her chest. 'Well, if you need any help, you know where to find us. Our Steve has a shed load of tools, and we know quite a few tradesmen. Have you found a builder?'

I gave a tight smile. 'Almost sorted.' There was no chance I would mention Liam, in case Pat knew him. She had the air of someone who knew everyone.

Pat smiled brightly, and I couldn't shake the feeling that I had become *something* in her mind. A project, maybe? It made me a bit uneasy, but she was warm and friendly, and I couldn't afford to turn away friends who might help me.

So, I gave her a morsel more.

'I think it's going to be a bit stressful, the renovation. But I'm hopeful I'll get it all sorted in time.'

'Of course you will.' She glanced at her watch. 'But the working day is over.' She took on a motherly tone, which jarred against the memory of my own mother's harsh words. 'Why don't you explore the high street? It's small, but you should have a mooch.

You must visit the social club. It's the committee meeting today, so everyone will be there.' Pat clapped her hands together. 'Oh yes, we'll get you sorted in no time. I'll message our Sandy. She works behind the bar and can get you in as our guest.'

'Guest?'

'Yes, guest.'

'Is it like a golf club? I'm not dressed—'

Pat burst out laughing. Then heaved a breath and kept laughing.

'No, no,' she said between laughs. 'Golf club.' She wiped her eyes. 'It's nothing like that. It's a social club – like a working men's club?'

'Oh. Like *Phoenix Nights*?'

I'd never watched it, but I knew the premise vaguely – a working men's club full of balding white blokes nursing their warm pints of ale.

Pat barked a laugh. 'I supposed it used to be a bit like that. Until we had a' – she pinched her thumb and forefinger together – 'little coup and kicked out the old guard. Now, it's more… representative of the area. It's a pub but also a community centre, I suppose.' Pat touched my shoulder. 'Trust me, you'll have a riot and find someone to help you with this.' She gestured to the house with its broken roof tiles and thick, overgrown bushes that obscured the windows.

God, it looked like a mess.

I didn't want to admit it, but Pat was right – I could do with all the help I could get.

'Which way is the high street?'

Chapter Six

As I walked up Everly Heath High Street, I wrapped my trench coat closer around me. The pavement was icy beneath my feet, and I made a note to buy some better shoes if I headed into Manchester at the weekend. Another gust of wind whipped around me. I squeezed my eyes shut. I was freezing even in a coat, gloves, thick tights, and a woolly dress. This would have kept me warm in London. They clearly weren't kidding about it being colder up here.

I approached a building resembling a miniature town hall with its columns and red bricks. A sign above the door read EVERLY HEATH SOCIAL CLUB. The soft light coming from the windows made the social club look cosy – a little port in the storm. Opposite the social club was an arcade of charming little shops with a Victorian lead canopy, housing an independent coffee shop, a delicatessen, a bakery, a wine shop, cheesemonger's, and an old-school hardware shop. It was nothing like I remembered as a kid.

It was something out of a fucking Hallmark film.

All I remembered from my childhood visits were the rapid noise of windscreen wipers, relatives that pinched my cheeks, and cold sausage rolls. Suffice to say, I hadn't been all that impressed.

But I had to admit that Everly Heath was kind of... cute.

Tentatively, I stepped into the social club's arched porch and through the double doors. The room was split into two *very* different events. In the left-hand room, a man with a grey pony-tail in a silver waistcoat was crooning a Dean Martin tune while a single disco ball spun, with an audience of about eight clapping women, all in their sixties.

On the right-hand side, a football match playing on a big projector garnered a much bigger crowd of men and women wearing red football shirts and silent disco headphones. The head-phones flashed bright neon colours, a comical contrast to their grave expressions as their eyes tracked the ball.

The door banged closed behind me, and *every* head in the room swivelled towards me.

About forty people stared at me curiously. I gave a weak smile as I shuffled to the bar, desperate to find Sandy and justify my existence. I walked up to the bar, my foot tapping repeatedly. I was beginning to get desperate when a blonde head appeared from a room behind the bar.

My stomach dropped. Oh god.

'Hiya, love.' My auntie Sandra hadn't looked up yet, busying herself putting away pint glasses. 'Have you got your membership card?'

Her voice sparked a memory – the church – the musty smell, incense, and candle wax. Panic rose in my throat, and my cheeks were red with shame. Before I had a chance to flee, Sandra turned around and faced me. Her dark green eyes went wide, her mouth a perfect 'O'. Sandra always had the perfectly quaffed blonde bob, and today was no exception.

'Kat? What –' She rushed around the bar.

'Hi, Sandra,' I said meekly. She pulled me into her chest, and the dark sludge of shame filled me.

Sandra pulled back, her hand coming up to my cheek as she inspected my face. 'What are you doing here? Are you okay? Do you need money?'

I laughed despite myself. 'No, no. I'm fine. I'm sorry. I thought Lydia would have mentioned it. Dad left me the house on Evanshore Road.'

'Evanshore Road? Where our Brian grew up?'

'Yeah. He bought it a year ago and didn't tell anyone.'

Sandra frowned. 'Why don't I get you a drink, and you can tell me all about it?'

Ten minutes later, I had explained the whole plan to Sandra, but I hadn't touched the pint of Guinness in front of me. I stared at it like it was my worst enemy. Sandra had been supportive, offering help if I needed it and promised to tell Brian, too.

'We'll get that house sorted out in no time, love.' Sandra patted me on the arm. 'I'll add it to the agenda for tonight.'

'The agenda?' I frowned.

'The quarterly members meeting is happening in –' Her eyes widened as she checked her watch. 'About fifteen minutes. Shit.'

'Oh – don't worry about putting it on the agenda. Please,' I insisted, as Sandra's attention moved away.

'Ray!' she shouted to the man crooning in the silver waistcoat. 'Ray! Five minutes, then we need to set up.'

Ray halted mid-way through 'Fly Me to the Moon', his face turning chartreuse. He stomped his foot. 'Sandra, I am mid-set.'

'Ray, I told you –'

Ray threw down his cravat. 'They would have never done this to Ol' Blue Eyes. I'll tell you that for free! Every week, Sandra. I never get my slot –'

He continued to argue with Sandra, who cocked her hip and argued back. Ray had moved on to complaining about football taking precedence over 'culturally significant performances' when the door swung open, and a burst of colour walked in in the shape of my cousin. Lydia scanned the room, finding me perched on a table between the two events, not wanting to side with either.

'Mum texted me that you were here. Oh my god.' Lydia gasped as she stared at my Guinness. 'How on earth are you drinking that?'

'Well, I usually like a Guinness, but after last night, when *you* led me astray…' I cocked an eyebrow.

'It wasn't my fault!'

'You Uber Eats'd that last bottle of prosecco!' I exclaimed.

Lydia winced. 'I thought we needed one more.'

'Everyone knows you never need one more.'

Lydia grinned. 'It's so weird seeing you here at the club. It's like seeing a teacher outside of school. Did you get a nosebleed on the M6 coming this far up north?'

'You know I don't have a car. Never needed one.'

Lydia shook her head. 'Londoners.'

I rolled my eyes. 'Go get a drink. It's my round.' I handed her my card.

'Thanks, cuz. I'll get the next one.' Lydia bounced off to the bar, chatting animatedly with her mum.

I nipped to the loo and on my return saw a familiar dark-haired man beside my cousin.

Liam.

A shorter man with dirty-blonde hair and dimples stood next to him. The blonde man and Lydia stood with pints and amused expressions while Liam stared straight ahead. He hadn't spotted me yet, thank god. The football match had finished, chairs and tables being lifted and moved as Sandra conducted the room like an orchestra. I was frozen, unsure if I wanted to go and stand near Liam. Was I going to have to grovel? Did I want to grovel? Fuck. I should have spoken to Lydia about this earlier to get her onside.

'Kat.' Lydia waved. Broad shoulders tensed as I slowly walked towards them.

'Hi,' I said to no one in particular.

Liam's eyes finally met mine and began an unreadable scan of my face. Those eyes flickered down, taking in my body too. The perusal was lingering, and judgemental and my stupid face went red. Which was really inconvenient when I remembered what Liam had called me at the funeral.

I raised my head to meet Liam's gaze, but his expression was vacant. It revealed nothing. The lights were on, but no one was home.

Lydia smiled brightly. 'Kat, this is Liam. He's the builder I mentioned last night.'

'We've met.' Liam's deep voice sounded resigned. Grumpy.

'We have,' I added uselessly. Lydia handed me my pint, and I stared at it.

'I'm Jack.' The dark-blonde man grinned and extended a hand. 'I work with Liam.'

I gave a sickly smile. 'My condolences.' Jack gave a strangled laugh like he hadn't expected my joke.

'When did you meet?' Lydia frowned, eyes flitting between Liam and me, finally sensing the tension in the room.

'Ah —' I began.

'I went around this morning like you asked, Lydia. At eight.'

Lydia's head swung to me, eyes wide. 'Eight. As in this morning.' She probably recalled stumbling into the taxi at three o'clock in the morning. I'd had a measly five hours' sleep before Liam turned up, seemingly unannounced.

'Yup,' I added.

'Your cousin wasn't in the best mood,' Liam said, sarcasm dripping from his words. He turned to Lydia. 'Before you mither me, she's gone with someone else.'

'About that.' I bit my lip. 'See, I made some calls today. And it seems like everyone else is booked up.' I breathed. 'I'm going to struggle to find someone in time.'

I glanced up at Liam, trying to assess his reaction. He watched people filing in for the members' meeting.

I cleared my throat. 'Liam.' His eyes flickered to me, then quickly away. 'I was wondering if you might be able to look into it.'

He took a sip of his drink. 'Look into what?'

The bastard was going to make me ask. Or beg, maybe. His expression was neutral and utterly infuriating. Lydia's eyes were wide, bouncing between us like it was the final at Wimbledon.

'If you could look into helping with the house,' I said through gritted teeth. 'Please.'

The last word was hard to get out.

Liam's eyes were indecipherable. Clearly, he didn't like me, but I waited patiently for his reply anyway.

Come on, give me something. Anything. Just don't say no.

Liam and I locked into a staring contest. In my periphery, I watched his chest expand with each breath. His hands were clenched at his side. His face gave nothing away. It wasn't until he took a deep breath that I knew what was coming.

He exhaled, delivering the final blow.

'No.'

Chapter Seven

'Liam!' Lydia smacked him on the shoulder, 'Come on!'

My eyes stung, and my head lowered, hanging off my shoulders in defeat. Why was I even doing this? Why didn't I sell as my mum had suggested? Did I care all that much about my dad's legacy anyway? He'd been AWOL for most of my life, for fuck's sake.

It's because of the funeral.

I felt so much shame and anger at myself for fucking up at my dad's funeral that renovating the house felt like a path to some sort of redemption.

Lydia continued with her campaign to convince Liam, but I ignored it. I needed to come up with a new plan. I could sell it. Yeah, it wasn't that big of a deal. I'd sell and move on. If I went home tomorrow, Mum wouldn't need to know I'd been gone. I'll get the train back and forget any of this happened.

This could all be some strange, vivid dream.

'What renovation?' Jack asked, pulling me from my mind.

'It's Kat's house,' Lydia explained. 'She was… left it recently and wants to renovate it.'

I was grateful she left out the dead dad details.

Lydia continued, 'It's a 1930s semi. It's a fixer-upper, but it has tons of potential. But Kat has a tight turnaround to renovate it before she moves back to London. She wants to buy there.'

I coughed, my voice croaky. 'The market is a nightmare, so I need as much cash as possible.'

'How tight a turnaround?' Jack scratched his jaw.

'Two months.' I shrugged. 'That's how long I've been given off work. I might be able to stretch it a bit, but not much more.'

Liam huffed a laugh. 'Two months.'

Lydia frowned now. 'Is that not possible? There isn't any major structural work to do.'

'I've seen her house. It needs gutting.'

'I know. This is my last resort.' A scowl overtook my features. 'You are my last resort.'

'Charming.' Liam looked at me, then frowned, like my foul mood disappointed him. 'There isn't anything I can do. It should have been booked months ago. In fact, if you could ask all of your lot to schedule in your gentrifying in good time, that would be great.'

He stared straight ahead and took a large gulp of his drink.

'Well, unfortunately, I couldn't conveniently schedule my dad dying,' I smiled sardonically. 'And who exactly is "my lot"?'

Lydia rolled her eyes. 'He means Londoners. Southerners. He's bitter because we've had a load buy up here recently.'

'They've priced themselves out of London, so they've decided to price us out of houses here instead,' Liam rumbled.

'I don't know what's up your bum,' Lydia said. 'They all want building work.'

'And they want a personal trainer and their green juices,' Liam said pointedly.

'I know. Unlike some, I'm not complaining. We doubled members at the gym this month.' Lydia shoved Liam, causing him to almost spill his drink. 'Stop being such a downer. I know Kevin manages to squeeze people in all the time.'

Liam's eyes flared. 'Yes, and now his knees are fucked; he doesn't know the meaning of "retirement", and he hasn't had a holiday in about fifty years.'

'Kevin is fine,' Lydia insisted.

According to Liam's tense expression, this was a sensitive topic, and I was struck that my cousin and Liam must be very close if she could comment on Liam's family like that.

'Kevin is fine because I pick up the slack. I'm sorry, but no.' He turned to me, his eyes glimmering with intensity, 'Even if we had the right "synergy", we don't have any time.'

Jack cleared his throat. 'We're finishing early on the Joneses' extension, Liam. I can take over from you, and you could take on this project,' Jack suggested in a light tone as if he was used to pitching ideas carefully around Liam.

'Absolutely not. The Joneses have sticks up their arses. I need to manage it.'

'Manage the stick up their arse?' Jack asked in mock confusion, making both Lydia and me laugh. Liam delivered Jack a droll look.

'Liam, come on,' Lydia protested. 'Mum, Dad and I will help too. We can all chip in.'

'*That* sounds like fucking chaos.' Liam crossed his arms, all corded muscle and veins.

Gym bros were a turnoff for me, but Liam didn't look like he hit the gym. I knew without seeing... all of him... that Liam didn't have one of those perfectly sculpted bodies. His arms were a byproduct of his job, freckled, tanned, and defined from lifting heavy materials.

'Take a picture, Red. It will last longer,' a male voice whispered.

I lifted my gaze to find Liam's eyes sparkling, his lips struggling to stay straight. I flushed and opened my mouth to protest, but a mic made a horrible squeak, making everyone wince.

Lydia's hands came to her ears, and Jack and Liam grimaced.

'Excuse me!' Sandra's voice pierced the room. 'The club committee meeting starts now. If you are attending, please take your seats. If not, the back room is free, and Beverly will be there to pull pints.'

'I only like you pulling my pints, Sandra!' a rather portly man with a receding hairline shouted, making everyone, including Sandra, laugh. Even Liam huffed beside me. It made me wonder what his actual laugh sounded like, if he ever made the noise in his miserable life.

'Oi!' Brian shouted. 'That's my wife.'

My uncle can't have noticed me when he came in, sitting front row to his wife's performance. The man who flirted with my auntie held his hands up in defence, and more laughs pealed through the room.

'God, Mum and Dad make this a bleeding pantomime. Come on.' Lydia shifted us to find seats. 'They fill up fast. This is like a stand-up special, with juicy court proceedings and a dash of a *Corrie* Christmas special all in one. You do *not* want to miss it.'

Lydia leaned down to pull out a bag of Wine Gums, silently handing them to someone above us. I looked up to find Liam looming above me. Silently, he took the sweets from my cousin.

'You're sat in his seat,' Lydia whispered with hushed humour. 'I've never seen him so stressed.'

'I'm not stressed,' Liam grumbled, ripping open the Wine Gums and throwing three in his mouth. Our chairs were so close that our arms were brushing, sending a cold shiver up my arm. Liam flinched like I'd burnt him, so I shifted in my seat further away from him.

God, why did I ever think I could persuade him to help?

'Right,' Sandra announced. 'Let's get started. Chair, would you like to come here and give us an overview?'

A tall woman with braids approached the stage, and it wasn't until she turned around to address the crowd of about seventy people that I recognised her.

'She's my neighbour,' I whispered to Lydia.

'Oh, yeah. I forget Pat lives on Evanshore, too.'

Pat adjusted the mic. 'Good evening, everyone. It's lovely to see all your shining faces. Yes, even yours, Peter.' She gave Peter a sickly smile. 'We'll move onto your –' she picked up several pieces of paper like they were Noodle's dog poo – 'several proposals after I've given an overview of the club's achievements for the last few months.'

Pat presented the club's financial successes and called for volunteers for the dementia-friendly afternoon tea and announced a whole roster of events: kid's crafts, yoga, vinyl nights, and the makers market, which I made a mental note to put in the diary because the barbecue sounded amazing.

'Jesus, it never stops here.'

'Since Mum and Pat orchestrated their coup, things got busier around here.'

'Now these meetings take forever,' Liam grumbled. 'The best kind of committee is a committee of two when one doesn't turn up.'

I snorted and Liam looked at me curiously.

I shrugged. 'What? It was funny.'

'Right, let's move on to member proposals. A reminder that if you want to make a proposal, you should submit it a week before the meeting, but we're not as strict as we used to be, so if it's late, we'll do our best to include it,' Pat said, causing some grumbles to break out amidst the grey and balding of the meeting.

'Peter,' Pat barked, 'as you're like a *dog* with a bone about these proposals, why don't you come up here and have your say?'

A man dressed in browns and greens stood bolt upright from his seat and approached the stage. His flat cap hid his face until he turned around. I never liked to judge someone by their looks, but with Peter, it was inevitable. He resembled Ebenezer Scrooge, with a surly expression and a face lined by frowns and scowls. He stood by the side of the stage, bickering with Pat about something or other, and nattering broke out across the crowd.

'He doesn't look happy.'

Liam huffed. Did that count as a laugh?

Lydia chirped up, 'Peter is bitter because he used to be chairman, but Mum, Pat and some of the other ladies managed to swindle him.'

'How?'

Lydia grinned. 'They managed to sneak a vote past the committee, which meant a public vote for the chairman. Before, it had been decided by a select few deemed "proper members". It was very cliquey. An old man's club. Women weren't allowed in until 2010, let alone be on the committee.'

Liam grunted. 'And I bet they wish they'd kept it that way when Pat won by a landslide.'

'Have you got something against women?' I levelled at him.

'No, I haven't got anything against women, Red.'

'Liam is grumpy because now everything is a lot –'

'Louder.'

Lydia leaned forward and whisper-shouted at him, 'And that's because women like to communicate, unlike you, you caveman.' She glanced at me. 'Mum oversees the subcommittees.'

'There are subcommittees?' I asked, incredulous. I had no idea so much… administration went into running a social club.

Liam piped up again. 'They've got subcommittees about the subcommittees.'

Liam was chattier when he had something to complain about.

'There is a grounds committee to keep the beer garden nice and tidy, a wine and beer committee, and a membership committee.

Those are the boring ones. Pat and Mum gave those to the old guard to keep them happy. Then, there is the Christmas committee. I head up that one,' Lydia said proudly.

'Lydia the Elf.' Liam shoved another three Wine Gums into his mouth.

I turned to him. 'Are you overseeing the snacks? I hope not, or there wouldn't be any left.' Liam followed my eyeline to the half-finished packet of Wine Gums, his expression souring.

'I haven't eaten all day.'

'Nutritious. You're a regular Joe Wicks.'

My traitorous brain couldn't help but flicker down his large hands clasped around the bag of sweets. Liam tracked the motion, and I could see the penny drop. Liam's lips curved, but my head whipped to the front to stare at Peter stepping onto the stage.

Peter cleared his throat and tapped the mic, making a screeching noise erupt over the speakers.

'Is this working?' His voice was sooty, like he smoked fifty a day. 'I propose that dogs be banned from the social club. It is no place for smelly, snorting creatures who piss on the carpets. All those who agree, raise their hands.'

About a third of the room raised their hands.

Lydia hummed. 'That's more than last time.'

'He's proposed this before?'

Lydia rolled her eyes. 'He does it every meeting. And he gets closer every time. He does it to spite Pat because she brings in Noodle. But he's good as gold.'

'Next,' Peter announced, 'I propose we ban the insolent makers market that we have used club money to fund –'

'We aren't funding it, Peter. We bought a new marquee. The old one had holes in it,' I heard a woman shout across the room. Peter's face went bright red.

'I am speaking, Eman.'

'Eman is the treasurer,' Lydia explained.

'The markets are a public nuisance. Closing the high street on a Saturday? What if there is an emergency, and the police can't get through?'

'This is a waste of our time,' Liam muttered under his breath.

Peter continued, 'And that doesn't even mention that we are letting non-members into the club. Now, in my time, this was fine on the odd occasion. But every month? Absurd. We are a members' club.' Peter pounded his fist like he was at the pulpit.

I jumped when Liam piped up beside me, 'People pay thirty quid a year to drink discounted pints of warm ale, Peter. This isn't Soho House.'

I raised my eyebrows, surprised that Liam had even heard of Soho House.

'Liam, I would have expected you to understand –' Peter said, indignant.

Liam stood up. 'Well, I don't. Would you get a move on? Some of us want to get home for tea.'

A small, unexpected glimmer of respect grew in my chest. Liam sank back down into his seat, and I'm sure my eyes were bugging out of my head.

'Those in favour,' Peter grumbled, and a few hands, maybe three, were thrown up.

Lydia raised her hand. 'I don't get his problem. The markets are fun! They only allow independent businesses to rent a stall. I know for a fact his daughter has a jewellery business. He'd rather short-change his own daughter over letting Pat win.' Lydia shook her head. 'Unbelievable.'

I grinned. 'This is kind of fun.'

'Right?' Lydia grinned, throwing more popcorn into her mouth. Pat returned to the mic, and a hush fell over the crowd.

'Next, we have AOBs and general notices. We have one from Sandra Williams.' Sandra made her way up onto the stage.

'What is she going to speak about?' I leaned towards Lydia, curious.

'I have a quick one. We need some help.' Sandra scanned the room. Who was she looking for? Her face lit up when she spotted where I was sitting.

My stomach swooped.

No, she wasn't – no.

'Or I should say, my niece, Kat, needs some help.' Sandra pointed, and my palms began to sweat as every single head swivelled towards me.

Chapter Eight

My face burned like a bushfire. Sandra announced my arrival at Everly Heath like I was the fucking queen on a tour of the UK. 'My niece, Kat, has moved up here from London. She is renovating a house on Evanshore Road.'

'Rose's old place?' someone shouted out.

'Yes,' Sandra said.

'Didn't Brian and Jim live there when they were little?' another voice piped up.

'Yes, they did,' Sandra explained. 'The house has sentimental value to the family, so Kat would like to renovate it. Then, it will be put on the market.'

'She's going to do it up and then sell it?' a woman in her fifties asked.

'Typical,' someone mumbled.

All of those eyes shifted back to me, judgemental. Whispers broke out amongst the crowd.

Thank you, Auntie Sandra.

Now I was the gentrifying southerner, here to make a quick buck. Liam chuckled beside me. 'Try and win them back now.'

'It's her choice. It was her late father's home,' Sandra insisted, and some of the murmurs stopped. 'She would like to bring the house back to life so that another family can build memories of their own.'

I spotted some nods and shrugs amongst the members. I didn't love that Sandra mentioned Dad, but I supposed in a town this gossipy, it was only a matter of time before people put two and two together and realised I was Jim Williams's daughter.

'So, I would like to ask anyone – tradesmen or women for help. She's looking for a builder. And before you lot start' – Sandra glanced at Liam – 'the Hunters are busy with their lot. They can't spare any work.'

So, Sandra must have had a word with Liam. How had she done that so quickly? God, between Pat and Sandra, I wouldn't want to mess with the women of Everly Heath. They worked quickly.

Sandra continued, 'I thought I'd bring it to the club and see if anyone knew of any trustworthy tradesmen –'

'I might be able to spare some time,' a ginger man piped up. He glanced behind, greeting me with a warm smile, and hope bloomed in my chest. 'I can come over tomorrow –'

I felt a movement and then a tall shadow loomed over me.

'I'll do it,' Liam's voice called out, resolute.

Sandra's mouth fell open. 'Oh. Are you sure, Liam? I thought –'

'I said I'll do it.'

I stood up, looking at Liam. 'What are you doing?' I said through gritted teeth.

'I'm solving your problem, Red.'

'I didn't ask you to.'

'Hm, that's funny. Because about half an hour ago, you were begging me –'

'I didn't beg.'

Or I hadn't got around to it.

'– and asking if I'd come and take another look.'

'Yes, but –' I faltered. Why was I disagreeing? Wasn't this what I wanted?

70

'There might be someone more suitable here.' I gestured to the crowd watching our interaction with wide-eyed fascination.

Liam crossed his arms, and his biceps rippled – actually rippled like something from a cartoon. It was ridiculous.

'There isn't. Trust me. It's better that I say yes than you being bartered in front of every idiot with a hammer. It could take us all night.' Liam shifted his attention back to Sandra. 'I'll sort it. I'd end up having to fix whatever these lot cock-up anyway.'

'You know some of us are professionals, Hunter,' said the ginger man who had offered to come around tomorrow.

'Jason, I wouldn't wish your tiling on my worst enemy.'

Jason shot up in his seat, going beet red as laughter trickled out amongst the crowd.

'Jason.' Sandra's sharp tone had Jason sitting back down. She turned to Liam. 'Lovely, Liam, thank you.'

'Oh, you've done it now, Hunter,' Lydia muttered under her breath.

'It's fine. I can handle it.'

'If you say so,' Lydia said in a sing-song voice.

Liam sat down, his face forward, and all I could do was stare at him, dumbfounded.

'Close your mouth. You look like a goldfish.' He turned and looked at me, a glimmer of something in his eyes. A challenge? Entertainment, perhaps? I wasn't sure.

'Why –' I sputtered. 'You clearly hate me –'

Liam's eyes closed briefly. 'I don't hate you.'

'Okay, you dislike me. Semantics. Why would you help –'

In a hushed tone, Liam said, 'You might not know your family very well, but they are good people. The best people. Your aunt is like a mum to me. I owe her. So I will help you out.'

Liam sat back, watching the next item on the agenda in the

meeting. I wanted to ask more, but here wasn't the place. Not when so many members seemed to be eyeing us up curiously.

It was when Sandra called the meeting to a close that the onslaught began – it was like every single member of the Everly Heath community lined up in front of Liam. Liam sighed and got up to talk to the first lady, a woman in her mid-sixties. She had a wide, feline smile on her face.

I turned to Lydia. 'What is going on?'

'Liam just opened the floodgates. He's been putting in major boundaries since he took over from his dad. Kevin used to do a lot of favours for people – he was the first to bend over backwards for people. Liam put a stop to it. Well –' She glanced down at me. 'Until you, apparently.'

My cheeks burned, and unanswered questions rang through my head. What had changed his mind?

I sat and waited for Liam to finish speaking to people. I wanted to speak to him. I wanted to know where I stood when it came to the house and the next steps. Liam was speaking to the fifth person – a young lad who couldn't be eighteen – when I decided to get a pint while I waited for him. When I came back, he was gone.

'He managed to escape,' Lydia explained when I looked confused, holding my pint of Guinness and a Coke Zero for Liam – his usual order, according to Sandra. I tried to hide the way I deflated.

Later, I piled into an Uber. After another drink or two with Lydia and Jack, things were too hazy, and I was too lazy to walk. Plus, I used the excuse of the persistent drizzle that had sprinkled down all evening, glossing the roads and the trees like the Lancôme juicy tubes I had coveted as a kid.

I spotted something new attached to my door when I got to the house. A new shiny silver lock was neatly screwed into the wood. While the door was knackered, the new lock shone in the porch light.

A key was Sellotaped to the frame, with a note which read:

No more strange men "committing domestic burglary".
   I'll be in touch.
   -L

Chapter Nine

Kat's To-Do List

- Find the old to-do list
- Thank-you card for Liam? Is that weird?
- ~~Call Liam~~ Wait for Liam to text

I hated waiting. I'd always hated waiting. As a kid, it was the queue at the ice-cream van. As a teenager, it had been waiting for the DVD release of my favourite films so I could rewatch them again and again. As an adult, it was waiting for the latest season of *Grey's Anatomy* to come onto Prime Video, even when I promised myself not to watch yet *another* season. Impatience should be my middle name instead of Jane.

So, it wasn't surprising that I spent the days after the social club with shaking legs, praying for Liam's text to come through. But he took his sweet time, and I was sure he was doing it on purpose to torture me. It was only Liam being evasive. After Sandra's social club announcement, I'd had numerous visits from locals.

The day after the social club, Davide and John knocked. They were a gay couple with matching bright white teeth. They brought over homemade pastel de natal and asked about the renovation progress. I showed them around the house, and they ummed and ahhed over my plans.

Davide patted my arm maternally. 'We were doing up our Victorian house last year. I had to do all the design myself. It was a nightmare. I'd never had so much — what did you call it, darling?'

'Decision paralysis,' John chirped up.

'Yes. Decision paralysis. An interior designer is like gold dust around here; we don't have anyone local.' He leaned in. 'And some of the Cheshire ones are a bit *Real Housewives*, if you catch my drift,' he added with a wink.

'I don't think that will be a problem,' John said, the more strait-laced of the two. 'Pat said Kat is a designer.'

'Oh,' Davide said, his palms coming to his cheeks. 'I'm so sorry —'

'No, no.' I laughed. 'I'm a graphic designer, not an interior designer.'

Davide waved his hand. 'You will have a natural eye for these things.'

On the second day, I was mid-shower when the doorbell rang again. Rita and Jamal were an older couple. Jamal was shorter with a receding hairline and Rita had perfectly quaffed greying hair and a cashmere jumper.

Coastal grandma jumped to mind.

'We're number twenty-six. Next door to Pat and Steve.' Rita smiled. 'Pat suggested you might need some food, with the state of the kitchen, so we brought you this —' She handed me a foil-covered dish. 'It's cottage pie. It's still warm if you want to eat it now —'

'Or we have a microwave if you ever need to use it,' Jamal said with a crooked smile.

'Thank you so much,' I said, genuinely overwhelmed by the

gesture. 'Wow – I don't know what to say. Thank you. I really appreciate it.'

'It's no problem.' Rita smiled, patting my arm. 'It's what neighbours do.'

On the third day, my phone finally buzzed with a random number, and my heart lurched. Liam. It had to be Liam, *finally*.

'Hello?' I answered tentatively.

'Oh, Kat. Thank god.' Auntie Sandra sounded out of breath, and I felt sufficiently guilty about my disappointment. 'Lydia gave me your number; I hope you don't mind. I wondered if I could ask for a favour. We're hosting an event at the club this afternoon. Afternoon tea for some elderly folks from the community. We asked for volunteers, but no one signed up. We paid it no mind 'cos Pat and I can cope ourselves, but she's got a cold' – my auntie inhaled to continue – 'and given everyone is a bit older, she doesn't want to spread it. Do you think you might be able to help? I wouldn't usually ask, but—'

'Of course.'

'Oh, you're a lifesaver.' Sandra sighed. 'Thank you.'

'I'll be there in twenty,' I agreed, and we hung up, feeling warm and fuzzy that I'd been able to help.

As I walked through the club door twenty minutes later, the club had been transformed into a function room. Sandra was throwing ivory tablecloths onto six large round tables. Several bouquets of flowers sat in ornate vases. The usual heavy wooden chairs were replaced with elegant limewash Chiavari chairs.

'Thank you for coming in so last minute.' Sandra squeezed me into a hug. She wore a dress with vibrant pink and orange peonies. Meanwhile, I wore jeans and a stripy T-shirt paired with beat-up trainers.

I ran my hand through my hair, unruly as ever. 'Was there a dress code?'

'No, no. Don't be silly,' Sandra said. 'Pat and I like to make an effort because the old dears do. It's not compulsory. I need you back of the house anyway.'

'Auntie! You shove me in the back because I didn't come dressed in my Sunday best?'

Sandra rolled her eyes indulgently. 'I see Lydia is rubbing off on you already.'

I helped Sandra set up the tables, copying her formation. After the first table, we got into a steady rhythm, and by the end, the tables looked beautiful. The ivory tablecloths complemented the pink, yellow, and green of the bouquets in the centre of the tables.

'The flowers are beautiful,' I remarked.

Sandra nodded. 'Rebecca, the local florist. She donates them every month. Lovely girl.'

'She is talented.'

'She is indeed.' Sandra turned to me. 'Kat, do you think you could get some extra napkins from the back, please?'

'Of course.' I'd not been in the back yet, but I guessed it was the room behind the bar that Sandra dipped in and out of. I headed around the bar and through the doors and stopped in my tracks.

I almost did a double-take when I saw Liam dressed in chef whites. He was cramped in the small kitchen, his focus on the tiny cucumber sandwiches he was placing on tiered ceramic stands. He glanced up as I walked in, and his eyes flickered across me. Lingering in places, he lingered all over me – my legs, my breasts, up to my neck, and finally, my face. For a moment, I wondered if he was checking me out, but his resting bitch face slotted into place quickly, ridding me of the absurd thought.

'Kat.' Liam nodded.

'Liam,' I repeated in the same tone.

Liam returned to assembling sandwiches. 'Sandra roped you in, did she?'

'What are you doing?' I blurted out.

'I'm skydiving. What does it look like I'm doing? I'm making sandwiches. They get here in half an hour, and I'm behind.'

'I presumed they'd just buy them in. From a caterer or something.'

'No.' Liam wrinkled his nose like someone else making sandwiches was out of the question.

'You come in every month and prepare tiny sandwiches for elderly people. By hand. In this tiny kitchen.'

'They are just sandwiches.'

'Why?'

Liam's dark eyes lifted from the sandwiches, and he gave me a look. I wasn't sure what the look was trying to convey, but it sent a weird feeling up my spine.

'I have a heart, Red.' Liam sighed. 'They might not remember today, but they'll have had a good time. We play some music, and they sing along. They never forget the words, even now. And the care home appreciates it. There isn't loads for people with dementia to do, to get out and about. Funding cuts.'

I opened my mouth and closed it again. Liam looked up again at the expression I couldn't keep off my face.

'If you're going to stand there, gawping, you can help. Chop this.' Liam held out a cucumber, and I could feel a blush creep up my skin. There was something about the way his hand was gripped – nope. Not going there. Abort, abort.

I cleared my throat. 'Sandra said something about napkins.'

'She can wait.'

'Oh,' I said. 'Okay.'

I washed my hands and stood beside him. Our hips accidentally brushed, and I pulled back like lightning struck me.

'No, not lengthways.'

Liam's body came around me. I felt the heat of it first, then the warmth of his hand coming over mine.

'Thin, round slices like this.' He guided my hand, his hand dwarfing mine. Liam was gentle, and I stared as the knife cut through in smooth, measured slices. Liam's breath was at my neck, and I suppressed a shiver.

'There you go,' Liam murmured, his voice low. He stood back, going back to his station, and we stood side by side again. I was annoyed with myself that I had liked his body near mine – stupid, stupid body.

'Thanks,' I said hoarsely.

Then, I realised I'd let a man show me how to cut a fucking cucumber like I wasn't capable of doing it myself. I'd been hypnotised by his body and the warmth rolling off it.

'About the house –' I blurted out.

Liam cocked an eyebrow, waiting for me to finish my sentence.

'Are you still going to help? I didn't hear from you.'

'Have you been waiting by the phone, Red?'

I could feel my face burn. 'No.'

Liam's lips twitched. 'I'm moving some stuff around. Give me some time.'

'It's time-sensitive –'

'I'll get it sorted on your schedule. Don't worry about it.'

'I –' I took a deep breath, trying to calm myself. 'How can you be so casual? We need to set a timeline. Some parameters –'

'I do this every day, remember. It's no stress.'

We chopped in silence as my mind whirled. I'd been taught that everything needed a plan, even if I screwed it up. Liam seemed way too cavalier about this.

'Where do you live in London?' Liam's voice made me jump out of my busy thoughts.

'Oh. I share a flat with some people near Camden. But I gave my notice when I moved up here. I miss the location, but living with six people was getting old.'

Liam's eyes bugged. 'Six people?'

I shrugged. 'Not that surprising in London.'

'I think I'd end up killing someone.'

I chuckled. 'I've been close. Especially when one housemate kept eating my leftovers.'

Liam whistled. 'Cheeky.'

'I know, right? Leftover pizza is sacred.'

'It's breakfast.'

I grinned. 'Exactly.'

Liam and I smiled, and then I glanced away, refocusing on the task at hand.

'I'm moving back. I'll end up buying somewhere further out. I will miss Camden.'

'Overrated,' Liam grumbled.

I raised my eyebrows. 'London is overrated?'

Liam grunted, and it made me laugh.

'What's your beef with London?'

'Everyone's miserable.'

I snorted. Oh, the irony.

Liam continued, 'And rude. It's overpopulated and overpriced. Too many Prets and not enough good pubs.' He arched an eyebrow at me. 'I'm sure you noticed the Guinness is shite.'

'Well, yes,' I said. I'd had plenty of foamy, expensive pints of Guinness in packed pubs, standing next to finance bros in their quarter zips. 'But it's a great city. Sure, there are downsides, but there's always something exciting to do. Somewhere amazing to eat. Great theatres and art galleries.' I sighed. 'I love the galleries.'

'We have all of that here, too,' Liam said, a stubborn edge to his jaw.

I snorted. 'I'll believe it when I see it.'

Liam turned to me. 'Is that a challenge, Red?'

'Maybe.'

'Okay.' Liam dusted off his hands. 'Let's make it interesting. I bet you that you end up falling in love with this place. I bet you that you never go back.'

I gave a melodic laugh. 'Are you kidding me?'

'I'm serious,' Liam said, lifting his palm.

'You're on. Easiest bet I've ever made.' I lifted my hand. Then, I paused, lifting my pinkie finger. It would be so much funnier this way. There was something funny about making a grown man pinkie swear.

'Let's pinkie swear on it.'

'Deal.'

Liam wrapped his finger around mine, and I tried to ignore the hum of awareness that buzzed up my skin. Liam's eyes were on me again, a faint smile on his face. Truce – was this some sort of truce?

He cleared his throat and returned to assembling sandwiches, and I pretended not to be disappointed about his focus moving elsewhere.

'It's nice that you do this, you know. You, Pat, and Sandra. I didn't say it before because I was shocked to see you in chef whites.'

'New kink unlocked, huh?' He gave me a side-long glance. My face heated. When I went red, I went *red*. Tomato. The curse of the gingers.

Liam grinned. 'We raise the money to cover the food and drink costs. Just because they are a bit poorly doesn't mean they shouldn't have a pint. Or a glass of prosecco for the *ladies*.'

'You know, that's a dated view that women aren't supposed to drink –'

'I'm winding you up.' Liam bumped his elbow against mine. 'I don't have a problem with you sinking Guinness.' His tone was light, even if it didn't reflect in his face.

'I don't sink Guinness.'

'Sure, Red,' he said, laced with sarcasm.

'Can you stop calling me that? It's a bit immature, don't you think?'

'Definitely immature,' Liam said, 'but unfortunately for you, I find it entertaining.'

I rolled my eyes, and Liam's lips twitched. It was the most relaxed I'd seen him, jovial even. It was… nice. I felt like maybe we had thawed some of the ice between us.

We arranged the sandwiches next to cakes and scones on the tiered stands.

'How many people are coming?' I asked Liam as he arranged another five stands. He kept bringing more from his car. I was standing uselessly, watching his large hands doing delicate work. It was such a juxtaposition that it threw me off.

'Do you always ask this many questions?'

'Answer them and I'll stop.'

'About fifty in total. I store the stands at my house because there's no space here.'

'That's… nice of you.'

'Yes, you've mentioned how nice it is. Several times.'

I narrowed my eyes. 'It's an impressive operation.'

'It was all Pat's and Sandra's idea. It's their baby.'

Sandra's voice behind us made me jump. 'You're being too modest, Liam.' Sandra collected the stands, arching an eyebrow at Liam. 'We couldn't do this without you, and you know it.' Sandra touched my shoulders. 'Love, would you help us work the room out there? We like to have a chat with everyone while they are here.'

'Sure,' I glanced at Liam, 'unless –'

'As helpful as you've been, I can manage on my own.'

I nodded, disappointed to leave the small kitchen, where I had the excuse to watch Liam working. I walked back into the main room and was welcomed to the sound of Glenn Miller playing over the speakers. Every table was full, with some guests chatting happily while others were quieter and withdrawn.

Sandra touched my shoulder. 'Some have more severe symptoms than others. It can show itself in very different ways, too. My dad, God bless him, struggled with fits of anger. He was so frustrated with himself. But others are more easygoing and relaxed. Why don't you start on Dot's table?' Sandra pointed to the lady dressed in a black-and-white polka-dot blouse with immaculate black trousers.

Dot was inspecting her manicured hands like they didn't meet her standards. She had perfectly coiffed white hair, which came down to her shoulders. Impressive, considering she must have been in her late eighties. She had bright red kitten heels with a matching red gloss handbag. She was glamourous. She was terrifying.

But I took a deep breath and approached her table anyway.

Chapter Ten

'Hi.' I smiled brightly. 'I'm Kat. I love your top.'

Dot shifted in her seat and looked at me, perusing me from the top of my head to the bottom. My grin remained plastered on my face while she assessed me.

'Moisturiser.'

'Moisturiser?'

'You have dry skin. You'll regret it at my age if you don't moisturise. Just like I regret not using sun cream.' She rubbed her forearms absentmindedly. 'We didn't know, of course. I used cooking oil when I honeymooned in Cornwall with my husband. I covered myself with olive oil. Extra virgin, of course.'

I laughed. 'Of course.'

'My husband wasn't by the end, though.' She winked, and I snorted.

She played with the ring on her left hand.

'Do you mind if I sit?' I asked, pointing to the chair.

'It's a free country, doll.' She shrugged, and I realised that was all the enthusiasm I would get.

'How long were you married?' I asked.

'Sixty-seven years this year. I don't like to stop counting, even though my Archie passed' – she frowned – 'it must be ten years now since he was gone.'

Large hands came down on Dot's shoulders, and her hands came up to cover his.

'Thirteen years, now, Dot,' Liam said gently. His chef whites were gone, replaced with a light blue jumper that brought out the light brown in his hair. His relaxed blue jeans fit his muscular legs and had an irresistible worn-in look. They made me picture him pulling those jeans back on in the morning after…

No.

Nope.

I was not completing that particular dirty daydream.

Dot patted his hands. 'Yes, you're right, love. That's it. Thirteen now.' She smiled sadly but then seemed to remember that Liam was here, and her face transformed.

'You. Sit with me. I never see you anymore. Always up a ladder, working.'

Liam put his hands up. 'Okay, okay. Gimme a sec.' He dragged a chair between me and Dot.

Dot gasped and grabbed his hands. 'Oh. Are you getting more handsome? If I was twenty years younger.'

'Cougar.'

Dot glanced at me. 'Liam, have you met…'

'Kat,' I repeated.

'Yes, Kat. Sorry, love.' Dot smiled.

'No problem.'

Liam's eyes trailed over me. 'Yes, we've met. Kat called me a prick the first time we met.'

I choked.

'What did you do?' Dot asked Liam, her eyebrows drawn.

'I stole her parking space.'

'Liam,' Dot said, her lips pursed. 'Really.'

'At my dad's funeral.'

Dot's eyes went comically wide, and Liam gave me a dirty look as if to say, *You didn't have to add that particular detail.*

'I deserved it,' Liam said, his eyes not leaving mine. I could feel my cheeks burning, but I wasn't sure why.

Dot clicked her teeth. 'Your mum brought you up better than that, Liam.'

'I know.' He glanced at me. 'But in all fairness, I couldn't help but want to get under her skin.' Liam's lips lifted. 'She made it too easy.'

'You sound like your brother,' Dot said, shaking her head. 'How is that troublesome brother of yours?'

The light left Liam's eyes as he smiled tightly. 'Last I heard, he was in Peru hiking Machu Picchu.'

'He needs to be careful. That's dangerous business.'

'Ren will get it out of his system soon enough.'

'I used to teach them both piano,' Dot explained for my benefit. 'Liam always practised his scales. You were competent enough.'

'"Competent enough", what a compliment,' Liam said, and I held back a smile at his tone.

'But Ren, well, sometimes he wouldn't turn up. His mum would be so livid with him, and he'd bring me presents to apologise. Sweets or some flowers he'd picked. He was so much trouble but always loveable. Cheeky.'

'Yep, that's Ren,' Liam said, an edge to his voice.

'How's your mum?' Dot asked.

Liam took a sharp intake of breath. 'She's good. Still gardening.'

'Oh, good. I haven't seen her in a long while.' Dot looked into the distance. 'After I stopped teaching the two boys, we became friends, Lily and I,' Dot explained. 'We were thick as thieves. I'll have to drop by and see her soon.'

'She'd like that.' Liam squeezed Dot's hands.

'Right, can I get you ladies a drink?'

'Oh, I couldn't.' Dot changed her mind quickly. 'Maybe a small glass of port.'

'Port.' Liam looked at me. 'Guinness?'

'I'll have a prosecco.' I glanced up at him. 'Someone told me that it's more "ladylike".'

Liam held my gaze, and then his eyes flicked down me, lighting little fires along my skin.

'You're ladylike enough. Guinness?'

'Thank you.'

As he walked away, I was tempted to fan myself. Had he... had he been flirting with me? It was so hard to tell. He kept his voice so even and his face so schooled. I watched the muscles in his back flex as he reached up for the port on the top shelf behind the bar and poured Dot a generous measure.

I blinked.

Was I attracted to Liam?

'I give it a year,' Dot said, shifting my gaze away from Liam.

'A year?'

'Until you're married.'

I frowned. 'Married? Oh, I'm not in a relationship—'

'Our Liam.'

'Oh. We're not – We're not together.'

Dot ignored me. 'You remind me of Archie and me. We used to bicker too, but we'd always make up eventually.' Dot waggled her eyebrows. 'Making up was the best bit.'

I laughed awkwardly. 'We're not—'

The music grew louder, and I realised a little dancefloor had formed in the middle of the social club, just in front of the bar. Liam brought our drinks back, offering his hand to Dot and leading her onto the dancefloor, like they'd done this a hundred times. Other couples joined them, swaying to 'String of Pearls' by

Glenn Miller. My heart gave a horrible swoop as Liam gave Dot a twirl, and her smile widened.

As the song faded and 'Moonlight Serenade' started, Dot leaned in and furiously whispered something in Liam's ear, causing his forehead to crease. He shook his head, but Dot persisted, speaking more animatedly. Eventually, he nodded, then scanned the room. His eyes locked onto mine, that unreadable expression returning. With a determined, unwavering stride, he made his way over to me. He held my gaze as he stopped before me, and I felt the heat rising in my cheeks.

'I've been told to ask you to dance.'

'You've been told?'

'Yes.'

'Well, that's not a nice way to ask, is it?'

Liam's jaw tensed. 'What do you mean?'

'I mean, you could have asked me. You didn't have to specify that an eighty-eight-year-old lady had strong-armed you to ask me. Besides, you don't seem the type to cower to a demand like that. You seem all' − I gestured to his face − 'unmovable.'

'Will you dance with me or not?' Liam said, his voice low.

I laughed. 'Not with that face. Seriously, I'm fine.'

'Red. Please, will you dance with me?' His eyes bore into mine.

'You want to dance with me?'

'Yes.' The word came out strong from his chest, his eyes widened like it surprised him. He glanced away and added, 'It will make a very kind, very sweet lady happy.'

I glanced behind him to see Sandra and Dot whispering, small smiles on their faces. 'We're being set up.'

'Bingo. She gets it.'

'Stop being a dickhead.'

'Look. She looks frail, but I did all my piano homework for a reason. She can be bloody terrifying when she wants to be. We'll dance. Make her happy and forget all about it.'

Liam offered me his hand. It was the first time I'd actually looked at it properly. It was huge, tanned, and pale, white scars all over. How would they feel in mine? Warm, maybe.

I glanced behind him again to see the anticipation on the faces behind Liam.

'Don't step on my feet,' I said as we clasped hands.

His hands were warm and rough, as I expected. I suddenly lost the ability to move. I was stuck, sinking into the ground. The realisation of my poor coordination flickered across Liam's face. Resigned, he drifted his palms across my waist to my lower back.

I glanced up at him and found he was staring down at me. From this angle, I realised how much bigger Liam was. I was not a small woman. At five foot five, I was bang on average. But I had always been mid-size since I was a teenager. I resented my wide hips and full arms when Kate Moss graced the front of *Cosmo*. I'd never felt small, even when I wanted to. But Liam towered over me, the heat of his body radiating through my clothes.

Liam's lips were in the shell of my ear, his voice low. I could feel it vibrate through his chest, which was so, so close to being pressed against mine.

'One minute, thirty seconds more, and we're done,' Liam murmured.

'I bet you've said that before.'

A throaty laugh sounded from Liam, and surprise rolled through me.

'I can't imagine you playing the piano,' I said out of nowhere.

I felt Liam tense.

'Too common for piano, huh?'

'No, I didn't mean it like that. I meant I could see you more on drums.'

'Our mum wanted us to learn. She never got the chance, so I think she wanted to make sure we did. She grew up on a council estate, so once my dad started earning some money, I think she thought piano lessons were what the middle-class kids did.'

I nodded. 'That makes sense. I wish I could have done creative stuff. But my mum signed me up for extra maths and English.'

'Did you struggle at school?'

'Understatement.'

'That bad?'

The curious tone in Liam's voice opened me up, so I was honest. 'I hated school. I hated the exams and the pressure. I was always at the bottom of the class, and my mum –' I stopped, unable to process the disappointment I'd brought to my mother. My shoulders tensed, and then, as if sensing my unease, Liam stroked his thumb across my back. It was simultaneously comforting and maddening.

Now it was my mouth that couldn't move.

'Distracted?' Liam murmured, that voice smooth like honey. I glanced up to find Liam much closer than I'd expected. His eyes bore into mine, intense and fiery.

'I'm fine,' I squeaked.

Liam hummed. 'You were talking about your mum.' His thumb was still there, moving back and forth, driving me to distraction.

'My mum was a teacher,' I managed to get out, 'so she was disappointed when I did badly at school. So I worked twice as hard.'

'Sounds like you.'

'You don't know me.'

'I think I am getting to. You're bloody stubborn.'

I raised my chin, meeting his eyes. 'I prefer determined.'

'Determined,' he repeated, humour lacing his voice. 'What does your mum think about you being up here?'

I huffed. 'She… ah. She doesn't know.'

'She doesn't approve?'

'No. She doesn't… she didn't think I could do it. She knows about all my quirks.'

I could hear Liam's frown. 'Your quirks.'

'I'm a scatterbrain. Unorganised. Flighty. I get bored easily. I try to keep it together; I use coping mechanisms to keep organised and on top of things, but it's exhausting keeping the plates spinning. They call it masking. I realised when I got my diagnosis that I'd been doing it all my life. I looked at how everyone else behaved and copied it.'

'Masking,' Liam repeated like it was a new word.

'Yeah, people with autism do it too. The world isn't built for us, so we mould ourselves to fit.' I huffed. 'Sometimes, I think I've masked so much that I don't know my real personality. Is this one I came up with to hide?' I shrugged. The silence made me feel like I'd overshared, so I laughed and added, 'Who knows.'

'It sounds exhausting. Does your mum not understand that?'

I nodded, smiling sadly. 'It can be. And no, she doesn't.'

The music stopped. Liam and I stepped apart, but our eyes were still locked on each other.

'My disability…' I paused. It still felt weird to call it that. 'It was partly why I was late to the funeral,' I said, my defences rising. I wanted to explain myself. 'Not that it's an excuse. But I forgot my speech notes, and they'd been printed on this specific paper to help me read. It stops the words wiggling around, and I know that sounds ridiculous. I rushed back to get them, and I was running late –'

'And then I stole your car parking space,' Liam said, his voice low.

'Well, yeah. But it was my own fault. I should have been more organised.'

'I was late too.'

'Oh.' I hadn't thought about that. 'Yeah, I suppose you were.'

'I'm sorry,' he said, his lips in a flat line. 'I was in a rush. Jack had gone into A & E again, I was stressed, and I acted like a dick.' Liam glanced down. 'If it helps, I wanted the ground to swallow me up when I saw you stand up there and I realised who you were. I'm not religious, but I was convinced I would burn up and go straight to hell.'

My lips twitched. 'There's still time.'

Liam glanced up, spotted my expression, and his lips turned upwards, too.

'So, I'm sorry if I threw you off. The speech –'

Oh no. We were *not* going there; it was way too deep.

'I'd rather not talk about it if that's okay,' I said, and Liam searched my face. For a moment, I thought he would push on and ask more of me, but he nodded.

'Sorry, I didn't mean to overstep,' he said, running his hands through his hair. 'I've – got some cleaning up to do.'

He was awkwardly looking for an out of the conversation.

I nodded. 'Thanks for the dance.'

Liam's eyes scanned me again. He nodded and went to turn away.

'I never said thank you for the lock, by the way,' I blurted out.

Liam turned back. 'It was nothing.'

'Well, it means I can lock my door, so I appreciate it.'

Liam looked me in the eye, sincere and unguarded.

'It's important you feel safe here,' Liam murmured, the words making butterflies explode in my stomach. A kaleidoscope of new images of Liam flitted across my mind. Liam fitting a new lock. Liam standing up and agreeing to help me. Liam dancing with Dot and preparing tiny sandwiches.

'I'll come around tomorrow,' he said over his shoulder. 'I'll be there around ten. Make sure you're decent this time.'

A choked laugh bubbled out of me.

Chapter Eleven

'You're going to have to move out,' Liam said casually, a pencil hanging from his ear.

We stood staring at the walls in the box room for – for some reason. I wasn't really sure why.

Since Liam arrived an hour ago, I'd outlined my vision for the house. I tried to paint a picture of a fictional family and how they'd use the house – the back door, where kids could kick off their shoes and bring in shopping bags. Big sliding doors to throw open at a summer BBQ. A cosy front room with a log burner you could curl up next to at Christmas. In the kitchen, I imagined plaster-pink walls, deep-navy-blue kitchen cabinets, and artfully clashing patterns that make you wonder how on earth they work together – a haven of girlishness.

A girly haven that a big stupid man was invading.

'What do you mean?' I twitched.

I'd made a promise to myself not to get frustrated with Liam. Or at least not show my frustrations. Logically, I knew it wasn't his fault – at least not all the time. My ADHD meant emotional regulation was a challenge of mine, and sometimes I could have outbursts of emotions. Sometimes, it was anger or frustration, blissful glee or bubbling excitement. Either way, it was intense and burned bright. And if I suppressed it, it would build and build, like I was in a pressure cooker and then explode.

The funeral was a perfect example.

Nope. Don't go there.

'The plaster is knackered. It's probably as old as the house, eighty years, give or take.'

I waited for him to elaborate until he looked up, and his eyes met mine.

'The kind of work you want to do, especially the new light fittings and switches, I'll need to channel through these walls to put the new wiring in, and the plaster's gonna collapse like a warm Easter egg. It's not gonna hold up a picture frame. And that's just the practical side of it. It's not going to look pretty. The finish on the new paint is going to be shocking.' He shook his head. 'A complete rewire and replaster.'

'Rewire, too?' I squeaked, pound signs flickering across my eyes.

'Yeah,' he said gravely. 'A new buyer will take one look at that fuse board and know it's ancient. It doesn't matter how much you polish the turd, it's still a turd.'

'Charming,' I muttered, and Liam's lips lifted slightly. 'Are you sure it's that bad? Can't we patch it up? I mean, how can you even tell under all this wallpaper?'

Liam reached out and pulled hard on the peeling wallpaper. With it, chunks of grey plaster flew to the ground, throwing up dust everywhere.

I coughed. 'Okay, point proven.'

'I figured you're more of a visual learner.'

Dick. But he was right.

'It's going to be a state. Dust where you didn't think dust could go. Not to mention easier for us lot. With you out of the way, we can work any hours and get this done quickly.'

'It's fine – I'll stay out of the way.'

'It's not just the plaster – we're ripping out your entire bathroom and kitchen. You'll have nowhere to shower.'

'I'll get a gym membership and shower there.'

I was getting desperate now.

'What will you sleep on, a bed of rubble?' Liam raised his eyebrow.

'My air mattress.'

'I'd give that a week until it gets popped by a chunk of flying plaster. Or Jack dropping a hammer on it.'

My eyes narrowed. He wasn't helping.

'Kat,' Liam said gently. Too gently. Like I was a bomb near explosion. 'If we're going to work together, you need to take some of my advice.'

God, I hated he was being sensible.

I raised my hands. 'I can't move out. I've got nowhere else to go. Not from here, remember.'

'Oh, I remember.'

'What's that supposed to mean?' I recoiled.

Liam held his hands up in defence. His eyes danced with humour. 'It's hard to forget with that accent you've got, that's all.'

'Don't do that.' I gestured with my finger.

'What?' Liam's eyes widened in mock innocence.

'Act like I'm going all she-hulk on you. I'm not.'

'You can go she-hulk on me. I can take it,' Liam said cockily. My cheeks warmed, and I wanted to wipe that smug grin off his face.

'Can't you stay at Lydia's?'

I shook my head. 'It's a tiny one-bed. She also complained about the landlord not sorting the mould in the bathroom. I doubt another person showering would help with the black mould.'

'She should have told me,' Liam grumbled. 'Her landlord is useless.'

I ran my hand through my hair, panic rising. 'I can't stay with Lydia, and I can't afford an Airbnb either. Fuck.' Liam watched my hands as I ran them through my hair again. 'This is a disaster.'

'Brian and Sandra have space.'

The prospect of looking at my uncle's face every day and being reminded of my dad made me feel a bit sick. Plus, the funeral fiasco was still hanging over my head. Just thinking about it sent my nervous system wild.

No. I couldn't stay with them. They barely knew me. After two days, they'd get sick of me, and I'd have even less family.

A new idea was growing in my brain, fresh and green.

'How long?' I asked.

'Probably about four weeks, as long as there are no delays.' Liam shrugged.

I nodded. 'I'll figure something out. Don't worry.'

'Are you sure?'

'Yep. Just another obstacle, nothing major.' I smiled.

Liam looked at me for a moment or two, his gaze searching. I did my best to look as neutral as I could.

Finally, his eyes narrowed. 'You're up to something, Red.'

'No, I'm not!' I protested.

Liam hummed and gestured to his eyes and mine with his two fingers.

I rolled my eyes. 'Are you usually this dramatic?'

Liam laughed. 'Me. Dramatic. Funny.'

Then I spotted it. On the remaining plaster. There were some pencil drawings.

'What's that?' I leaned in closer.

'Must have been written on the plaster when that last person decorated,' Liam said as he carefully peeled off the wallpaper to reveal more words.

Written on the walls in messy, juvenile handwriting:

Jim and Brian, aged ten and seven, decorated this room.

The sentence was followed by some funny, albeit disturbing, sketches of three-headed monsters and stickmen with giant hands, as if the boys got bored halfway through helping their parents redecorate.

Grief came hurtling through me as my hands touched the wall, and a memory hit me like a ton of bricks.

We'd driven up to Manchester to visit Uncle Brian, Sandra, and Lydia, just Dad and me. He drove me around Everly Heath, showing me places he'd loved growing up. The Art Deco cinema that showed old movies. His favourite pub where he got served at fourteen because it was the seventies. Some places I can't even remember now. It was so long ago. But he said he saved the best until last, as we drove up this same cul-de-sac. My dad pointed at the house, telling me stories about his childhood. His dad, a mechanic, tinkering on the narrow drive, his mum calling him and his younger brother in from the garden for tea.

A picture of domestic bliss.

'One day, Kit Kat,' he'd said, in his deep Mancunian accent that became more pronounced when he was back home, 'when this house is going to come up for sale, I'll buy it, and we'll do it up together. How does that sound?'

On the long drive back home, like a typical eight-year-old, I'd excitedly detailed all the features I'd add to the house. I wanted a slide from my bedroom window down to the garden. A pink playhouse at the end of the garden. My dad had listened to me, nodding indulgently and chuckling. We agreed over petrol station McDonalds that he would get me a playhouse if it could double up as a pub for him. He held my hand, walking back to the car, promising he'd let me make dens in the garden.

That excited, naive ten-year-old was far away now. But even though I shouldn't, I still craved that promise. The little agreement we'd made together, plotting in the four-hour car ride. Two years later, we'd all fall apart. He would go from a doting father to a ghost. We'd shift to missed milestones and stilted, awkward conversations over the phone that eventually died out.

Where did it all go wrong?

Did he not love me enough to give me those memories, too?

I felt a single tear rolling down my cheek. I hadn't realised I was crying.

'Looks like they had fun here,' Liam said gently, touching the sketches.

I huffed and rubbed the tear away. 'Sorry. I didn't mean to —'

'Don't apologise,' Liam interjected. 'I get it. It's hard to…' He cleared his throat. 'Grief is complicated.'

I laughed, looking up at the ceiling. 'Yeah. Yes, it is very complicated.'

'If you ever want to speak to anyone about it.' He flinched. 'You have Lydia to talk to about it. And Brian and Sandra, too. I'm sure they would be there for you, if you asked.'

I shook my head. 'It's hard to speak to them about it. They had a very different relationship with my dad than I did. You can forgive absent uncles. It's harder to forgive absent dads.'

'I get that.' Liam nodded.

I wiped my eyes. 'Sorry, I shouldn't be trauma-dumping on you. I'm sure you got an eyeful at the funeral as it is.'

I finally met Liam's eyes, and his expression was full of that same pity as at the funeral, and my stomach turned.

'I understand how you feel —' Liam lifted his hand to put… where I wasn't sure.

My whole body screamed to get out of this conversation. I couldn't do this. Not now, not with Liam.

'Anyway!' I said breezily. 'Let's get back to the job at hand —'

'Kat.'

'I'm fine, Liam.' I dusted my hands of plaster. I refused to look in his direction. I was too embarrassed about getting so emotional in front of a stranger.

'Do you want some good news?' Liam asked, his tone brighter. Lighter. I was grateful for that shift.

'Yes, please.'

'I spoke to my dad; you know he and Brian are thick as thieves. Well, he knew your dad as well. They played football together or something like that. Probably back when the ball was made of leather, and everything was in black and white.'

I gave a teary laugh, and Liam's lips twitched. So close to a smile.

'I explained how you wanted to renovate the house, and he wanted to help. So, he said I was forbidden to charge you.'

'Can't charge me?' I squeaked.

'He was pretty insistent.' He looked away. 'Well, you'll have to cover costs for materials, but we won't charge for labour.'

I gawped. 'You can't do that. It's too much.'

Liam shrugged. 'It's not a big deal.'

'That's thousands of pounds, Liam.'

'And if we needed it, we'd charge you. But we don't, and my dad sees you as family. He likes to look after family.' Liam rolled his eyes. 'If he could, I think he'd do everything for free. The man is a softie.'

My eyes were watering again. I couldn't say anything else; my emotions were all over the place, zinging around my body. Before I knew it, I launched myself at Liam, wrapping my arms around his shoulders. He stiffened, but then he relaxed, his palm to my back. I tried to hold back a sob.

'Everyone is so nice here.'

I felt the huff of Liam's laugh. 'Yeah, they are. Bloody nosy, too.'

'It's so weird,' I said, my eyes watering.

'Please don't cry about this,' Liam grunted, 'this isn't anything to cry over.'

'But it's so nice.' I sniffed, pulling out of our awkward embrace. 'Sorry.'

'Don't apologise,' Liam said as he lifted his hand and tucked an errant curl behind my ear.

My face warmed where his fingers brushed, and it took everything not to press my face into his palm. Liam's eyes widened, probably as he realised who he was touching. He dropped his hand like I'd burnt him, glancing away, the tips of his ears pinkening.

'So –' Liam coughed. 'As I said, we'll do all this for free, but you have to promise to at least take some of my advice, okay?'

A trickle of guilt came in.

'Of course,' I replied.

Liam lifted his pinkie. 'Swear on it.'

My lips lifted. 'You're asking me to pinkie swear with you.'

Liam shrugged. 'I'm using your language, Red. Find somewhere to live,' he said, his tone serious, 'and we'll do the rest.'

The guilt continued to trickle, but it didn't stop me from wrapping my finger with his, plastering a smile on my face. Liam's eyes still showed suspicion around the edges.

'Deal.'

Chapter Twelve

Kat's To-Do List

- Tent
- Sleeping bag
- Sleeping pad
- Pillow
- Headlamp
- Camp chair
- Camp table
- Lantern
- Fairy lights

I *did* move out of the house. Technically. The day after Liam's visit, I walked to the little hardware store on the high street. The owner, Ravi, was a sweet, shy man dressed in a leather apron with Heath Hardware embossed on the front. He helped me pick out what I needed – a tent, a sleeping bag, a headlamp, and a lantern. All things suggested when I'd googled 'camping essentials'. For once, I thanked my neurodivergence for allowing me to think outside the box. This was genius. Not only had I resolved the issue, but I'd already planned exactly where to pitch my tent so Liam and the crew wouldn't see my set-up from the house when they arrived tomorrow.

Ravi helped me with my haul to my Uber, the grey sky above us. I wasn't risking walking down the high street and someone recognising me. I'd give it an hour before Liam or Lydia found out. Everyone knew everyone here.

'I hope that's everything you need. If you think of anything else, just let us know. If there is anything we don't stock, I can order it for you,' Ravi said warmly.

'Thank you so much, Ravi. I'm sure I'll be back.'

Almost a week here, I was still shocked to find everyone so welcoming.

Did I love it or hate it?

As I assembled my tent half an hour later, a little guilt crept in about my 'technical manoeuvring' around my agreement with Liam. But I knew it was better this way. I would be comfortable with my own company, even if that comfort were the cold, hard ground.

I rubbed my shoulders as the chilly evening set in, glancing up at the sun that was setting behind a thick blanket of dark grey clouds. I climbed into my tent and shuffled into the sleeping bag, pulling a Kindle out of my bag and did a little wiggle of excitement. This was cosy, a perfect backdrop for the fantasy series with fairies that Willa had recommended. I felt truly immersed into the story as the characters camped across ancient woods. I got to a spicy scene set in a tent, which was very… enlightening when the rain began.

It's fine, I repeated to myself. I'd expected some rain at about seven p.m.

The pitter-patter of the rain was nice anyway – nature's ASMR.

Twenty minutes in, the gentle pitter-patter morphed into an onslaught, and I couldn't concentrate on the words on the screen. The rain pelted the tent, and the sound became deafening. I put my hands over my ears.

The wind picked up.

A gale whipped my tent from side to side.

'Fuck,' I shouted when the water began to seep into the tent, which I had to admit was on the cheaper side.

'Fuck, fuck, fuck,' I muttered as I tried to find where the water was coming in. I blocked it with some of the blankets and towels, which worked well.

I sighed and settled back into my sleeping bag. No excited wiggle this time, but it was fine. Everything had a thin layer of mist, but I wasn't a quitter.

I frowned when I heard what sounded like a branch breaking.

A wet panel of tent hit my face.

It wasn't a branch that snapped.

It was one of the tent poles.

'For fuck's sake!' I shouted as more water began to trickle in. I shoved my boots back on and climbed out, tried to wrestle the tent pole back into shape. I cursed my dad for not teaching me how to camp properly on all those trips to Cornwall or the Cotswolds.

Rain pelted against my face, and my hair and clothes were soaked. Deep down, I knew that even if I managed to get the tent back up, I would never be able to get dry and warm again.

It was hopeless.

I gave a useless, frustrated cry.

Then, the garden lit up, light cutting through the heavy sheets of rain briefly before it was extinguished.

Through the rain and darkness, a figure approached the garden through the side gate, and my heart started to pound quickly. Great, now I was going to be murdered in my own garden.

'Who is that?' I shouted.

'It's me,' a deep voice shouted back, and my heart sank.

Liam's face came into view as he approached the tent, his jaw set. His eyes scanned over me, grazing over my T-shirt that was wet and stuck to my body, and flickered away quickly. His face morphed into a grimace when he took in the pitiful sight of my tent.

Liam crossed his arms, 'So, this was your big plan, huh?'

'Are you going to stand there, or are you going to help me?' I shouted back, trying to hold up the broken tent pole. 'Have you got any duct tape in your van?'

'You can't camp out here, Red.'

'It's fine,' I said while rain ran down the sides of my face. 'It will settle down.'

'This is Manchester, remember? It's kind of known for the rain.'

'That's a myth. There is more rainfall in Cardiff.'

'Semantics.'

'It's true. It will be fine. It's supposed to be heavy for another twenty minutes, then it will be fine.'

'Kat —'

'There isn't even that many centimetres of rainfall due —'

'Get in the van, Kat,' Liam growled. 'We can debate rainfall statistics when we're not getting soaked.'

The rain got heavier and joined forces with a gale-force wind. Liam turned on the heel of his boots, heading back for the van.

Was he going to leave me out here?

I made a frustrated noise. I was out of options and shaking from the cold. So I gave in and ran after Liam, climbing into the safe harbour of his warm van. The smell of wood and pine filled my senses. It was tidy and I wasn't surprised. He had the air of someone who had an anal process for everything and would level anyone with a look if they went against his system. He was the opposite of me. I never did the same task the same way. It was partly why I didn't trust myself to go freelance, even if I could make more money. I know I wouldn't file my taxes on time, and

104

the HMRC would arrest me. I'd be pulled out of my home, handcuffed. And I'd deserve it.

I glanced at Liam through the wet hair stuck to my forehead. We were both panting and pushing the water off our faces. Frustration rolled off us both in waves.

'How did you know I was here?' I demanded.

'Why are you so stubborn?' Liam's voice was like thunder. 'Next time, slip Ravi a tenner to keep quiet. I overheard him talking in the club about a "pretty but clueless" redhead buying a load of camping equipment, and I put two and two together.'

'Ravi said that?' My mouth fell open.

Liam shook his head, 'Ravi looks innocent, but he's the biggest gossip in Everly Heath. He gives Pat a run for her money. I was happy to leave you to your stupid plan.'

'Then why did you come? Why not leave me? I would have been fine.'

Anger flashed in his eyes. 'Because you could have hurt yourself. I sat at home, watching the rain come down heavier and heavier, and I –' He stopped. 'I didn't fancy calling the police about a dead body when I came into work tomorrow. I was going to text Lydia or Brian but you were insistant you didn't want to ask them –' He petered off, running his hand through his wet hair, now jet black. The anger dissipated from his features, replaced with a bone-deep kind of tiredness I was familiar with. Burnout. Liam was burnt out.

Had he even realised yet?

I reached out. I couldn't help it, couldn't stop it. I touched his arm.

'Are you okay?' I asked as Liam's eyes tracked my movement. His eyes came up to mine, frustration burning there now.

'I'm fine,' he said through gritted teeth.

'You seem – like burnt out.'

He laughed humourlessly. 'Of course you'd be the only one to notice.'

'What do you mean?' I frowned, pulling my arm away.

Liam sighed. 'I'm fine. I'm tired.'

Guilt thrummed through me, 'I know I said I'd sort it' – I rubbed my face, searching for the words to explain – 'but I just… I just can't ask them. And I can't afford an Airbnb, even with you not charging me for labour. It's so expensive as it is. I can't believe how naive I was about the costs.'

When Liam sent over a quote for materials for the project, I had to sit down. I hadn't realised how the prices had increased massively since the pandemic, and it sent me into another spiral of self-hatred. I was so incredibly unprepared and naive about this project. Luckily, the money from my dad's estate barely covered it. I was betting I would make some profit on this house.

It both thrilled and scared the shit out of me.

I lowered my hands. Peeking at Liam, I prayed I saw some semblance of understanding on his face. I *literally* couldn't afford to scare him off.

'Okay.' Liam let out a harsh breath. 'I've got somewhere you can stay. You can't camp outside for weeks. We're due rain for the rest of February. And March.'

I swear, the rain bombarding the van was a paid actor.

'You can stay at mine. Don't argue with me until I'm finished. I have an annexe in my garden. I built it for my dad during the pandemic. He had a health scare, and I wanted somewhere for him to stay. But he is as stubborn as you, so he has never used it. It has a little kitchen to make food, and you can have the privacy you want.'

My mouth hung open. This was incredibly generous and would resolve my problem, but the thought of seeing Liam every day made me feel a bit… funny. I had pins and needles running down my back and guilt thrumming under my ribcage. I would be a burden. I would be messy. I would probably accidentally break the shower or smash his collection of vintage Charles and Diana mugs from 1996.

'People will talk,' I said.

'Talk about what?'

'Me and you.'

Liam's eyes were laser-focused on me. 'And what would they say?'

'You know – that you and I…' I gestured between us.

'That you and I what?' he asked, his brows furrowed.

'That you and I are, like, together.'

'Together like sat in this van?' he asked.

I made a frustrated noise. 'No, like having S-E-X.'

'S-E –' His eyes widened, and he gasped. 'Sex!'

The penny dropped. He was mocking me. I rolled my eyes as a wide grin took over his face.

'You're taking the piss.'

Liam's laugh filled the van. 'You make it so easy.'

'I'm serious, Liam.' I couldn't help the smile pulling at my lips. 'You said people are nosy.'

'No one is going to care.' Liam paused and stared ahead, like he was imagining the conversations he would be having at the social club. 'Well, some people might care. A beautiful woman moving into my house isn't particularly normal.'

My eyes widened. Liam turned to look at me, his eyes slightly wide.

'Did you just call me beautiful?' I laughed. 'Does that line usually work?'

'It wasn't a line.'

'Okay.'

'I'm serious. I don't make a habit of hitting on women I'm

107

asking to move in with me.' Liam ran his hand through his hair. 'Nothing like that is going to happen. You'll be safe living in the annexe. I won't… you know. Try it on.'

'Oh.' I tried to pretend I wasn't disappointed. I'd gone from being called beautiful to being completely off-limits. Great. He clearly didn't fancy me, which was fine. It made things a lot simpler, actually.

'Are you sure? I'm not going to be in the way?'

'No more than usual.'

I rolled my eyes, 'If you are sure and only if you are sure. But I want to pay you something.' He protested, but I shut him down. 'Let me pay for utilities.'

'Lydia mentioned you're a graphic designer. That's why you were so offended by these.' Liam leaned forward, pulled a business card out of his back pocket and handed it to me. My nose wrinkled at the boring black card.

'So boring,' I muttered under my breath.

'You're the expert. So you can pay me back by redesigning the logo and get me some new business cards.'

I waved it in front of his face. 'You have to admit, they are boring.'

Liam levelled me a dry look, but his lips lifted slightly.

'We're builders. All of our work is by word of mouth. Handing you that card was the first time I've ever used one of those cards. And that was only because I was worried if I didn't provide you with ID, you'd throw another lamp at me.'

'I didn't have any more lamps to throw. I am lampless.'

'Just as well,' he muttered. 'I think I've still got the bruise from the last one.'

'Baby,' I crooned, and surprise flooded Liam's features at the word, his ears going pink.

Liam coughed, 'Redesign the logo, and we're even.'

'I'll do more than that. I'll design a complete rebrand. Website, socials. The lot. And don't worry, I'll make sure it's sufficiently manly.'

Liam laughed. 'It's your choice. I'll take whatever you give me.' He nodded to the mess of my collapsed tent. 'Have you got everything?'

I groaned. 'My stuff's in the tent. It's probably soaking now.'

'Wait here, I'll go and get it.'

Liam jumped out of the van and returned to the tent with most of my belongings. Liam was clearly an 'acts of service' kind of man. I'd always wondered what it would be like to meet one of those. I'd always dated guys who could say lovely, honeyed words but then would inform the barman that we were paying for our drinks separately. Liam seemed the type to pay for the lot and help you move a sofa into your apartment on a Saturday afternoon. He wouldn't spiral when you asked if he would come to your cousin's wedding.

He was an *all-in* kind of guy.

Climbing back into the van, Liam had rain glistening on his cheeks.

'I couldn't rescue the blankets and towels, but I've got some you can use.'

Liam started the van and pulled off the drive, his words giving me a zip of excitement. I was going to see where Liam lived. He was still a bit of a mystery to me. I imagined the last bachelor pad I'd visited – a loser I'd met on Tinder. I'd taken a chance on him and had been bitterly disappointed when morning rolled around. I left his eerily bare apartment in the same clothes from the night before and a green shoot of regret in my stomach, adding a new branch to my deep-rooted self-hatred.

'Do you have navy sheets?' My thought-to-mouth speed was incredibly fast.

Liam arched an eyebrow. 'You want to know what colour sheets I have?'

'No! Not like that. It's a thing. Men have navy sheets. I saw it as a joke online, and then it was confirmed by pretty much all the guys I've met on Tinder.' My eyes widened. 'Not that I've hooked up with a load of men on Tinder. I don't go home with them until I know they won't murder me in my sleep. I've listened to too many true crime podcasts.' I stopped myself, taking a deep breath. 'Sorry, that was a lot.'

Liam chuckled as we stopped at the red lights. 'No, I don't have any navy sheets. I have white ones.'

'Shocking. I had you pegged for a navy sheet man.'

Liam glanced over at me. 'Disappointed?'

'Not at all; it gives me hope. One guy used empty booze bottles as decor and Fairy Liquid as a body wash.'

Liam shook his head. 'A serial killer.'

'I know, right!'

'I've got proper shower gel.'

'Phew.'

'It's five-in-one.'

I groaned. 'Take me back to the tent. Please!'

He smiled, shaking his head. 'Let's not joke about the tent.'

'Too soon?'

'Too soon.'

Chapter Thirteen

Liam drove us through a modern estate of houses that all had the same kind of look but different configurations – some detached, semi-detached or terrace style. It was clearly an area that had been regenerated recently because it had that new design to the roads that made it feel like a toy town. We pulled up in front of a detached house with large floor-to-ceiling windows and a huge grey front door. It had to be one of the biggest of the designs.

It was gorgeous, even if it wasn't to my personal taste. I also hadn't pegged Liam as modern and sleek. I could see him wearing plaid shirts and chopping trees in a remote cabin in the woods, not wearing a suit, making coffee with an overpriced appliance as this house suggested.

I whistled. 'Very nice.'

Liam shrugged. 'I bought it in a bit of a rush about four years ago. I wouldn't usually go for new builds 'cos they are usually built like shit.' He glanced out. 'And so many of these new estates are pushing people from neighbourhoods they've lived in since they were born. I could justify this, just about. It was a derelict industrial estate.'

'They're pushing people out of their homes? How can they do that?'

'Compulsory purchase. They have no choice.'

'That's not fair.'

'No. Progress is progress, I guess. Gentrification isn't a London thing, you know.' He shot me a wry look.

'Why were you in such a rush to buy?'

Liam glanced away. 'I'd broken up with my ex. I moved into a flat in town for a bit, but it wasn't… practical. I needed somewhere to live and quickly.'

His comments triggered tons of questions, sprouting in my head at speed. But from his tense body language, it was clear that was all the information he would give. So I climbed out of the van, running to the boot in the rain.

Liam's hand covered mine.

'Go stand on the porch.' I wanted to reject his attempt at chivalry, but I was fucking freezing, so I stood undercover as Liam grabbed my bags. Acts of service, indeed. Liam fished for his keys in his pockets and opened the door.

Liam sighed. 'I'll put the heating on. Bloody freezing.'

'Are you sure this is okay?' I blurted out, making Liam stop.

He turned around and came back to stand in front of me. His hair had dried a little bit in the car, making it curl slightly at the nape of his neck. His eyes flickered around my face.

'I told you. The annexe is always empty. It feels silly not to use it.'

I took a deep breath, trying to calm the buzzing in my chest.

'You okay?' Liam said, frowning. 'Are you cold?'

'I'm fine. Just a bit overwhelmed.'

Anxiety.

It was anxiety.

I knew it but couldn't say it out loud.

'That's understandable. You almost got hyperthermia and died tonight.'

'Don't be ridiculous,' I retorted, rolling my eyes. 'You are so dramatic. I didn't get –' Liam's face morphed into a smug smile. He'd goaded me on purpose to get me out of my head.

Liam smirked. 'Can't resist getting a word in. So I know you can't be *that* overwhelmed. Come on.' He gestured down the hallway with his head.

The hallway was modern, with light beechwood floors and spotlights. It was completely bare, with no furniture or pictures hanging on the wall. Two doors led off, presumably to a downstairs loo and a lounge, but I didn't want to nosy around – yet. A beige-carpeted stairway led upstairs. It was like a show home, everything new and shiny, but it showed none of Liam's personality.

I followed Liam and came into an open-plan kitchen and living room. The kitchen was modern and sleek. In my head, my kitchen would be more farmhouse-traditional, something out of a Nancy Meyers film, with clashing patterns and soft colours. Liam's kitchen was the opposite – dark grey slab-fronted units with industrial pendant shades hanging above the island. The kitchen had expensive-looking appliances – an in-built coffee machine, a wine cooler and a double oven. It was obvious that Liam had expensive taste.

I sat at one of the metal barstools. 'Your house is lovely.'

Liam clicked the kettle on. 'I can't take credit. Someone pulled out of the sale after picking all the fittings. I wouldn't have picked it out myself, but it's certainly… out there.'

I frowned. He didn't like the house? Buying a house you didn't like seemed strange. I couldn't imagine it was cheap. It had to be four bedrooms at least, not including the annexe he'd built. He'd built it for his dad, which, I had to admit, was adorable. I was envious that they seemed to be so close.

Even when Liam berated his dad's working habits, he did it from a place of love. Their relationship was clearly strong enough that Liam could be honest. I wondered if he knew how special

113

it was to have frank conversations with his dad without worrying about their relationship breaking down, that it could be the final straw. I'd never had that. I'd never really been honest with my dad about how his absence made me feel. I'd been too hurt.

And I never got the confidence to stand up to my mum when she put me down, either.

'Brew?' He interrupted my thoughts. 'I don't have any alcohol in the house. I don't drink.'

'You don't drink?' I hadn't noticed at the club.

'I quit a few years ago. I – I hadn't loved my relationship with it, I suppose.' He said it lightly, like he didn't want to lower the mood.

'Tea would be lovely. Thank you.'

He poured boiling water into two mugs. I watched his hands grip the handle of the kettle. They were nice hands. I wondered what they felt like, running across skin. A strange shiver ran through me.

Liam's eyebrows furrowed. 'Are you sure you aren't cold?'

I went pink, cringing at where my brain had taken me. I was standing in this man's house, objectifying him. I should be ashamed of myself.

I smiled tightly. 'I'm fine, thank you.'

'I can get some towels –'

'Honestly, I'm fine. You've done enough. I – I really appreciate it,' I said, hoping my face was earnest.

'Did that hurt to say out loud?' Liam asked sardonically.

I rolled my eyes. 'I'm saying I've forgiven you for the car park debacle if that makes you feel better. You don't have to keep trying to repent.'

Liam's eyes widened comically. 'Are you saying I don't have to keep going to midnight mass? Because it was really messing with my sleep.'

114

I held up my hands. 'I mean, I don't know about the rest of your sins.'

Liam nodded solemnly. 'I should probably keep going. Father Nichols would be disappointed.'

'The older ladies need some eye candy. Keeps them from falling asleep.'

'Eye candy.' Liam raised his eyebrows.

Fuck. I could feel heat travelling up my neck.

'Well, you know,' I sputtered, 'their husbands are probably long dead. And they haven't had their eyes tested in a while. So anything will do.'

Was that funny enough to play off my blunder?

'I have been called a last resort before,' Liam said dryly, with an arched eyebrow.

It took me a while to realise he'd quoted what I'd said at the social club.

I winced. 'Not my finest moment.'

'Come on, you can't go back on it now.' Liam laughed. 'You've made up for it with "eye candy". I think I could probably use that to fuel my ego for the next five to seven years.'

I rolled my eyes. 'Typical man.'

Liam laughed as he busied himself in the kitchen, adding milk to the tea. I looked out the bifold doors into a spacious garden, and at the end of the garden was a mini house made of bricks and wooden beams. It looked like something out of a fairy tale, slightly out of place for a residential area, but the garden was big enough that it worked.

'Is that the annexe?' I asked, mouth agape.

Liam joined me at the doors and handed me a mug of tea.

'Yeah.'

'You have to be kidding me.'

'What?'

'Liam. Look at it. It's like, from a film. It's ridiculous.'

'I googled some ideas and picked it. Do you want to have a look? I'll grab your bags.'

He 'googled some ideas'. It looked like a mini version of the cottage from *The Holiday*, for fuck's sake.

I shook my head. 'You are too chill about this.'

Liam leaned to take the mug of tea from my hands. Our fingers brushed, and that familiar shiver trailed up my arm. I glanced up to see Liam looking intently at my hands, his brow furrowed.

'Your hands are cold,' he murmured. He placed our mugs on the sidetable beside the sofa and drew my hands between his.

'I'm always cold,' I explained, my voice going a bit hoarse. It was true. I was always cold, my hands and feet especially.

Liam frowned as if personally offended by the temperature of my hands. He continued to hold them between his much warmer, calloused ones.

'There,' he said, glancing down at me again, and I realised how close we were standing. Our eyes met, and time slowed. Liam's face softened, and I swore that, momentarily, he felt it, too – the electricity. His eyes darted down to my lips, and he leaned forward slightly, like he couldn't help himself.

He blinked, and it was gone.

My cheeks heated. I needed to pull myself together. It was pathetic pining for some man who basically hated me less than twenty-four hours ago.

Liam cleared his throat. 'I need to check the heating is on. It gets cold in there.'

Liam led the way down the stone path to the house. Solar lights were dotted about either side of the path, making it easy to find in the dark. I stood at the door, not knowing what to do next. Liam reached up to the door frame; his shirt lifted, revealing a line of toned skin across his lower back.

'There is a spare key. You can leave it here if you like; it's a pretty safe area.'

He unlocked the door, and we stepped into the annexe, the smell of pine in the air. The cosy room had a small kitchenette on the left, with a dining table and two chairs. Two well-worn armchairs sat in front of an electric fireplace with floor-to-ceiling shelves filled with books on either side. It was homely and sweet but also had that well-worn look, which differed from the modern appliances and furniture in Liam's house.

'It should have everything you need for a few weeks.' Liam dropped my bags onto one of the armchairs and strode to the back of the little cabin, oblivious to my gaping mouth. 'It's a small bedroom, but it has an en suite, too, so you won't need to walk into the main house for the loo.'

'Liam.' He turned around. 'I – I don't know what to say. Thank you. Really, this is amazing. I mean, I can't imagine camping now.'

Liam raised an eyebrow as if to say, *Most people wouldn't be stupid enough to camp outside in February in Manchester*. He turned on the lights, and I peeked around his shoulders into the bedroom. I saw a small double bed with brushed cotton bedding and a sliding barn door leading to the en suite.

'Towels are in the airing cupboard in the bathroom,' Liam said, turning his head towards mine. I stepped back when I realised how close we stood.

'Perfect. Thank you.' I nodded.

'No problem.'

He turned around, and I smiled up at him, wanting to show how much I appreciated this. A friendly smile, nothing more. The corners of his lips turned up. We stood like this for a beat until he stepped closer, and the smile slipped off my face, and I avoided eye contact. Blood rushed to my head, making me lightheaded as his cedar scent filled my senses. I could feel the heat radiating off his body. I didn't dare look up at his face. I couldn't help but stare at his chest, hidden behind a black tee.

'Kat,' Liam rumbled.

'Yes?' I murmured, still refusing to look up. He had a really nice chest.

Liam coughed, which suspiciously sounded like a laugh.

'I need to get past.'

Oh.

I met his gaze and found his eyes twinkling.

'Oh. Sorry.' I turned and shuffled awkwardly into the kitchen.

I wanted to bang my head on the exposed wooden beams until it bled.

'I'll leave you to it,' Liam said. He walked towards the door and put his hand on the door handle, but he turned back towards me. 'We can do some dinners if you like.'

'Oh, you don't have to do that –'

He shrugged. 'I'll be cooking anyway, and I make too much.'

'Oh, okay. That would be nice.' I smiled. 'I usually forget to eat.'

Liam frowned. 'You forget to eat?'

'Yeah, it's a whole – thing.'

'A whole thing?'

'It's my ADHD. I struggle to remember. My friend, Willa, brings me food to my desk and forces me to eat at work. I get so focused on a brief for a client that I forget to eat.'

Liam was still frowning, so I went on.

'It's like I'm…' I searched for an example. 'I'm like a runaway train. I'm impossible to stop. Even if I wanted to, I couldn't. Some people like me get irrationally angry if they are interrupted in their flow. I can get like that sometimes. It depends.'

'You need to eat. I'll make enough for two.'

'Only if you have extra, don't go out of your way…' I petered off, but Liam had already opened the door and walked into the light splattering of rain.

'Lock the door, Red,' he called out.

'Well, good night!' I shouted back louder and went to shower all the rain and mud off myself. In the shower, as much as I tried to stop it, my mind couldn't help but drift to brown eyes and cedar cologne.

Chapter Fourteen

Kat's To-Do List

- ~~FIND OLD TO-DO LISTS!!!~~ Buy a new notebook
- Book design appointments (kitchen/bathroom)
- Thank-you card for Pat (for brownies)
- Redesign social club event flyers (they are gross)
- Call Mum back

'So, just so I can get this right, you've moved in with your builder.' Willa's familiar voice came down the phone. She had texted me about fifteen minutes earlier: *Free for a chat?* I would usually be fast asleep at seven in the morning if it weren't for the fact Liam mentioned he left the house at seven thirty.

Plus, it wasn't like I'd slept.

I'd been too excited to start the renovation, so I was up at five a.m., like a kid at Christmas.

Willa continued, 'The builder you're paying has offered you somewhere to live?'

'Well, yeah, but it's not as bad as you think. He's a mutual friend, I guess. He's close with my uncle and auntie. And he grew up with my cousin, Lydia. *And* he came to my dad's funeral.'

The explanations came tumbling out of me, and I internally

winced at the defensive tone. I did not mention the whole car park debacle but listed off my justifications with no sense of shame.

'Isn't that a bit weird?' Willa asked gently.

'No. Yes. I don't know.' I slapped my hand on my head. 'I think we're friends now. Kind of.'

'Friends?' Willa repeated.

I thought Liam and I were friends. Kind of. We seemed to have settled into a suspension of hostilities since the afternoon tea event at the club. Mostly. He had offered me somewhere to live and made me dinner. Friends did that sort of thing, didn't they? And we'd both agreed that if I lived here, I would rebrand his business in return.

Friends helped each other out.

'Yes, friends.'

I could hear Willa's scepticism from the pause down the phone.

'Be careful, okay, Kat. What do I always say –'

'Don't shit where you eat.'

'Don't shit where you eat,' she repeated with vigour. 'And you're living with the man renovating your bloody house. What if he makes a move on you, and you have no choice but to accept? I know he's a family friend, but – just lock your doors.' She paused. 'But I suppose he has the keys, doesn't he? Given it's his house.' I could hear her frown down the line.

'I'll be fine, Wills. I promise.'

'It's the power balance –'

'I'm rebranding his business in return for staying here. And you know how much I could charge for that if I wanted to.'

Willa hummed, still unsure.

'And I'll keep you updated. It's all on track to finish in two months. Then, I'll be back in London; I can buy my own place and be ready to start work again. All of this chapter about my

dad will be behind me. And you won't have to worry about me.'
I ignored the deflated feeling that gave me.

'I always worry about you,' Willa said dryly.

'Hey!' I complained. 'How are things at work?' I changed the
subject away from my liabilities.

'Fine.' A single-word answer was all I was going to get.

'And John?'

John was Willa's on-again, off-again boyfriend. I fucking hated
John. Willa was the Miranda to my Carrie, always more practical
than me, but it didn't always mean she was invincible. Even if
she'd prefer it that way. John – or as I like to call him, 'fuck-face
John' – was controlling and manipulative. When I'd first met him,
I'd had an instant visceral hatred response. We'd met in the new
buzzy restaurant in Soho, and all night, John had subtly controlled
Willa, monitoring what she ate and drank. I thought maybe I was
going mad because everyone else seemed to like him; even Willa's
dad, who was notoriously hard to impress, seemed to like him.
They went golfing together.

After six months, John persuaded Willa to rent an apartment
with him, but he paid no rent because he had to 'keep up repair
costs' for his piece-of-shit canal boat.

Yes, he lived on a canal boat.

Since then, John had shown his true colours. He'd cheated on
Willa twice, but she took him back. She was hurt and resentful
when I tried to host a mini-intervention to point out how horrible
he was. So, we don't often talk about John.

But since I wasn't in London, if the shit did hit the fan, I wasn't
going to know about it.

However, I promised myself that I'd trust my gut from then
on. I'd trust that part of me that knew something was off, that
raised the hair on my arms. It was like my spidey sense.

'We're not together.' Another minimal word answer.

'Oh.'

When I'd left London, they were back together.

'He's out of the picture. For good now.'

'That's good…' I said, unsure of what I should say.

'Yeah, I thought you might be pleased.'

'Willa –'

'It's fine, Kat. More importantly, when can I come up to visit? I want to assess this new housemate you've got. Check everything's above board.'

'He's not a housemate, Willa.'

'Well, he kind of is, isn't he?'

'He – it's a weird arrangement.'

'If he even thinks about touching you without your consent –'

'Don't worry, mama bear,' I chided. I wish she extended this protectiveness to herself. 'I have family that would knee him in the balls if he thought about it.' After Sandra got up in front of all of Everly Heath to ask for help, I think I could bet on her coming to my defence. And the same with Lydia.

Having a family I could rely on was a strangely nice feeling.

I was about to put off a Willa visit when I glanced over at Liam's house. He was stood in the window looking out at the garden and donned his usual outfit – a black T-shirt, utility trousers and steel-capped boots. A familiar, unreadable expression on his face.

He lifted his cup of tea as if to say, *Want one?*

I gave him a smile and a thumbs-up and internally cringed at the awkward gesture.

'Wills – I gotta go. Can I call you later?'

'Sure. Speak to you later.' And she hung up.

I walked across the pathway to Liam's house to find the bifold doors ajar.

'Morning,' I called out, taking a seat at the island.

'Morning,' Liam replied, pushing over the cup of coffee on the kitchen island. 'I hadn't expected you up this early.'

'What do you mean? I'm coming with you.'

'No, you're not.'

My smile faltered. 'Yes, I am. I want to help.'

'*That* was not a part of the deal. I said it would be quicker with you out of the way. I can't be worrying that you'll fall off a ladder or stub a toe. I have enough to worry about with Jack's weekly trips to A & E.'

Liam moved to the fridge, pulled out something wrapped in greaseproof paper and put it into a backpack.

I trailed after him. 'I need to come with you.'

'Tough.'

'Liam – come on.'

'Don't "come on" me.'

I snorted.

'Childish,' Liam chided.

'I hate to point it out, but it's my house, so I have every right to be there.'

He glanced up, his brows knitted together. He would get some serious lines if he kept frowning this much.

'Wouldn't you rather stay here and relax?' He gestured to the lounge. 'I have Sky.'

I laughed. There was something cute about his innocent suggestion. Like I was itching to catch up on the latest season of *Yellowstone*.

'I'll go mad here. I'm serious. I don't have an "off" mode.'

Liam stopped and stood at the island, pressing his hands on the worktop, levelling me with a serious look. 'There isn't anything you *can* do.'

'I can't knock plaster off some walls?'

'No.'

'Then, can I come to take some videos? I was up all night on Instagram, scrolling through house accounts. I've started one, so I can see how far we've come. Something to remember.'

Liam's lips were a fine line. He looked me over, doing that scanning thing again.

'Fine.'

'Yes!' I beamed. 'Thank you.'

'But no getting in the way.'

'I won't.'

'And don't touch anything.'

'No touching.'

'And don't do anything that can land you in A & E. I'm busy enough.'

I saluted. 'Yes, sir.'

Liam shook his head. 'You'll be the death of me.'

I smiled brighter. 'I won't, I swear.'

'We're leaving in five minutes.'

Liam walked down the hall, and I swear I could hear him mutter something about *wrapped around my finger*, leaving me laughing into my coffee cup.

Chapter Fifteen

I'd weaselled my way onto Liam's little team by the end of the first week. The dream team consisted of me, Liam, Jack, and Freddie, their eighteen-year-old apprentice, who looked at Liam like he hung the moon.

On Monday, I took my little pictures and videos. I cleared the garden of ceramic gnomes. I made five million cups of tea. Meanwhile, the guys took hammers to the walls and had all the fun.

By Tuesday, I was sick of my role as a chief tea maker.

My legs shook, my hands roamed. I itched to do something. So I snuck upstairs and took down the plaster on one of the walls in the bedroom. It was kind of addictive, hitting the plaster and watching it fall to the floor.

'Kat!' Liam's voice called up the stairs. I winced. Heavy steel-toe work boots stomped up the stairs at surprising speed. Liam appeared at the doorway, looming.

'You said you would stay out of the way.'

'I'm a woman, so I should stick to gardening?' I rolled my eyes. 'So backwards, Liam.'

Liam's eyes narrowed. 'No, you don't get to do that –'

'Do what? I'm just saying –'

'I've worked with plenty of tradeswomen. It's not about you being a woman.' He glanced at my canvas trainers and looked like he wanted to pass out. God, he was such a stickler for the rules. 'Shoes,' he barked, shaking his head. 'You're not doing any work until you have some proper bloody boots.'

Ah ha! I felt like saying. If I had the right shoes, he couldn't complain.

On Wednesday morning, bright and early, I stood in Liam's kitchen in a pink utility jumpsuit with matching steel-toe safety boots. I grinned as Liam took in my new garb.

Thank god for next-day delivery.

'What are you wearing?' he said once he picked his jaw up off the floor. His eyes travelled down to my shoes and back up.

'You said I needed to be dressed properly.' I shrugged. 'Now I am.'

His lips were a thin line. 'You said you'd stay out of the way.'

'And you said I needed proper footwear.' I patted his shoulder, feeling bold, even though the touch made my heart pound. 'Compromise, my friend. Compromise.'

'You agreed, Red.'

'Please, Liam. I want to be useful.' I made my eyes go a bit wider. It was the expression I usually reserved for when I'd fucked up – a missed train or forgotten deadline. Puppy-dog eyes were my go-to. 'Besides, the more I help, the quicker it will get done, and you'll be free of me. It's knocking plaster off walls, nothing technical.'

'Don't give me that look.'

'What look?'

He waved a hand at my expression. 'The Disney princess look.'

'I promise I'll stay out of the way when it comes to the dangerous stuff.'

'You better,' he grumbled, and my lips twitched. It seemed Liam wasn't completely immune to my attempt at charm.

As I climbed out of Liam's van, Jack grinned at my outfit. Liam stormed past him into the house, leaving us on my front porch.

'A dog with a bone, you are.' Jack shook his head, smiling.

'How pissed off was he when he saw you dressed like that this morning? No, go slowly. Describe it in detail, please.'

I grinned back, feeling like I'd made a new partner in crime – and the crime was pissing Liam off.

'He wasn't pleased.'

Jack laughed. 'Oh, I think he was something.'

Unsurprisingly, Liam spent the remainder of the week in a foul mood. He seemed to take most of his grumpiness out on Jack. Liam questioned if Jack had ordered the right skip. He questioned him about tiling and barked orders about the skirting boards. At some point, Liam seemed one step away from questioning if Jack was breathing the correct way.

It made me feel bad for Jack and a little resentful towards Liam. Couldn't he give the guy a break?

While Liam was harsh with Jack, he was kind towards Freddie, the very tall, skinny lad who shovelled rubble into the skip better than I could and went bright red when I asked if he'd like another cup of tea. Liam's voice was gentle but instructive when they huddled on the floorboards, chatting through some pipework under the house.

By the end of the week, I'd become accustomed to banging plaster off walls, and Liam hadn't mentioned how therapeutic it was to wield a hammer. It was probably because me, plus a hammer, was his worst nightmare. Knocking off all the plaster from the walls was fun and cathartic. Sometimes, if I got a good section, the entire wall would fall off in one go, and I wanted to squeal. It was even more satisfying than peeling back wallpaper. Or those pimple-popping videos I watched in secret.

However, shuffling heavy plaster in plastic buckets down the stairs was much more challenging. At some point, Liam helped with the heavier buckets. I watched his muscles flex as he grabbed the bucket with only a little strain.

I'd never been the type to go for muscular men. I usually went for the granola hipster type. They usually were decked out in Carhartt, one of those tiny beanies and a signet ring on their pinkie. They would mansplain *The Godfather* trilogy. They would announce that they'd watched the latest Greta Gerwig film as if they had completed feminism. And they were always disappointing in bed.

But I wasn't ever interested in a relationship. I blamed it on my ADHD. *I get bored of them*, I explained if anyone asked why I'd never had a relationship longer than three months, usually either Willa or my mother. I'd never bothered with therapy because it didn't take an expensive appointment to pinpoint my commitment phobia. I was worried about getting hurt. My mum divorced my dad, and he disappeared. Even Willa, one of the strongest women I knew, was messed around by fuck-face John.

Honestly, it seemed more hassle than fun.

But that didn't mean I couldn't appreciate the male form of Liam Hunter.

Objectively, of course.

I cleared the plaster in all three bedrooms on my own. It felt like months of grief and stress had been pounded on the walls, and I felt lighter. Lifting the weight of the hammer had relieved the weight on my chest. Jack was impressed. Liam nodded, and I gave him a smug grin, and he retorted with a roll of his eyes.

I had exactly what I'd wanted – a new purpose.

On Friday, I was finishing hauling the last few bits of plaster when I paused on the stairs. Jack and Liam speaking in hushed tones in the hallway.

'She's living with you? What about Abigail?' Jack asked. His tone was light but loaded with some hidden meaning. Who was Abigail? Was this a girlfriend of Liam's? He'd never mentioned a partner, so I'd assumed he was single.

'Abi is away at the moment. It won't be a problem,' was Liam's terse reply.

Oh my god. Did Liam have a partner? Surely not. I'd lived with Liam for a week, sharing trips back to the house. I would have noticed, even from the annexe, right? Sometimes, I'd sneak a look while Liam cooked, ducking down if he glanced out at the garden. And then I scrambled back to my armchair to play casual when I saw him walk into the garden with a plate covered with tin foil.

Liam brought me food every night. Macaroni cheese with a herby crust. Pan-fried salmon with a bulgar wheat salad. Roasted chicken with greens and sweet potato. I'd never eaten so well. Mum and Graham liked their food bland, saltless and on the table at six thirty on the dot. When I moved out, I ate whatever was in the fridge or stuck to Pot Noodles.

And I didn't think he ever cooked extra for anyone else.

'You know I don't want to overstep.'

'Then don't.'

'I just remember how it was last time you got involved –'

'Jack. I've got it under control.'

The men dispersed, ending the conversation, but it was humming in my mind, a puzzle unsolved. I filed the interaction in my head for now and went to hunt for my phone.

By the end of the day, I was sweaty and bone-tired but happy. I collapsed in a starfish position in the middle of the bedroom. My hair was caked in dust. I could barely see anything through the goggles Liam had insisted I wear. It was even coming from my eyes and nose.

It was horrific, and I loved it.

As I headed downstairs, the house was a skeleton – all wooden floorboards and red-brick walls. Liam was standing in the middle of the back living room, where I wanted the kitchen-diner, with an older man with cropped grey hair.

'Who's that?' I asked Jack, who was standing near me with his arms crossed. Freddie mimicked the stance next to him, making my lips turn up.

'Structural engineer,' Jack said. 'He's overseeing the RSJ.'

'RSJ?'

'Rolled steel joist,' Freddie explained proudly.

'That wall you wanted to remove was load bearing. So, we need to put a steel in to support your house, or it could collapse.'

'I couldn't have done that myself,' I said, less of a question, more of a statement.

'No.' Jack grinned. 'Unless you wanted a big mess on your hands. Liam has done this a million times, though. He knows what he's doing.'

Liam and the engineer were looking over some plans and talking. Eventually, the engineer nodded and left the house.

'Right,' Liam said, 'let's get the props in, and then we can start knocking down the wall.' I brightened at his words. I could help. Liam's eyes met mine and narrowed. 'Kat...' he warned.

'Oh, come on. Look at me.' I gestured to myself. 'I've done a whole upstairs on my own while you slackers were down here. What's the difference with this wall?'

'I think she's earned it, boss.' Jack grinned, and Liam narrowed his eyes.

Liam huffed. 'Fine.'

Once the props were in to hold up the house, I grinned as Jack passed me a hammer. As I hit the wall again and again, earning a 'Jesus, who hurt you?' comment from Jack, I imagined the perfect shaker-style kitchen with a big island. Pristine granite worktops. An Italian coffee machine. I imagined making coffee with that machine, the morning sun streaming through the window. A faceless man coming up behind me and planting a kiss on my shoulder.

Once the wall was demolished, mainly by me, because the guys didn't want to get near me and a swinging hammer, I stepped back.

'Looks good,' Jack said, and Liam grunted in agreement. The space was huge now, maximising the room's light, even through the old milky windowpanes.

Once we were tidied up, Liam turned to me. 'Right – we're done for the day. Do you want to hang around here or come home with me?'

I went a bit pink at his words as Jack and Freddie exchanged a look behind Liam's back.

'Oh,' I started. 'I was going to ask if I could buy you all a drink. To say thank you for starting this so quickly. And for all your hard work this week.'

Liam opened his mouth to reply, but nothing came out. Jack gave Liam a nudge on the shoulder. Usually, I wouldn't dream of looking this messy, but the social club seemed pretty relaxed. I could probably brush out most of the dust and I was too tired to change. I could barely lift my arms; they hurt so much.

'Ah – I can't. But you guys go,' Liam replied.

My face crumpled. 'Come on, Liam. It's Friday. And just one drink. Not alcoholic, obviously.'

Liam stared at me for several moments, pushing his hair out of his face as I did my best to give him that 'Disney princess' look he'd mentioned earlier.

When he glanced away, I knew I'd won. I couldn't hold back the wide grin that took over my face.

'One drink.'

'Perfect.'

Chapter Sixteen

The smell of cedar hit my senses as Liam sat back down next to me, handing me another Guinness and a packet of crisps.

'Thank you.'

Freddie and Jack were across the club, throwing darts. Jack laughed as Freddie hit the cork instead of the dartboard. For the third time.

'No worries,' Liam said, his eyes softening as they met mine.

Sometimes, I could see a glimmer of softness when he was speaking to Sandra or on the phone with one of his elderly clients. And sometimes, he looked at me with his soft brown eyes, his face unguarded. But then, he remembered who I was and assumed his blank, removed expression and I hated how much I missed that soft look.

The doors to the club swung open, and Uncle Brian walked in with his usual mop of unruly ginger hair. The only thing we had in common. Brian scanned the room and looked relieved to see me sitting at the table with Liam. I'd never understand what I'd done to deserve that relieved look.

'Liam,' Brian said with warmth, and they clasped hands, then he turned to me. 'Kat,' he said with a warm, knowing tone and a smile.

'How are you, Uncle Brian?'

'Better now, love.' He smiled sadly and touched my shoulder.

'Have you got a minute? I've got something for you.' He raised the folder in his hands.

'Sure,' I said, following Brian to a quiet part of the club, and sat at a table for two. Brian couldn't look me in the eye as he began.

'I wasn't sure if this would be useful' – Brian put the folder on the table – 'or if it would dig up problems for you. But I thought it was best to share it with you anyway and let you decide. They were left at the last place your dad stayed when he renovated that house in Bath.'

The house in Bath was Dad's last renovation project. He'd sold it before he died. The profits had been used to pay for his funeral and the mortgage on the house in Everly Heath. I had suspected he was about to move back to Everly Heath before he had a sudden heart attack. But that was all it had been – a hunch.

Because I hadn't spoken to my dad in the six months before his death.

Brian cleared his throat. 'When Sandra mentioned you'd moved back to renovate the house, it felt like a sign you were meant to see these. It sounds a bit silly, but it felt like Jim wanted me to give these to you.'

I grimaced. 'You're making me nervous.'

Brian shook his head. 'Nothing to be nervous about. Take a look. It will make sense.'

I opened the folder to find the house's rough architectural sketches. I knew by looking at these plans that Dad had hand-drawn them himself. They were floor plans, but next to them were detailed sketches of the rooms, with a distinctive mid-century style to each. My dad was a seventies kid, so I suppose it was ingrained in him. The sketches had bright colours on the walls – mustard yellow, deep navy, and burnt oranges. Most of these colours were on my Pinterest board, which was a familial coincidence I didn't feel like looking into.

'I think you got your talent from our Jim,' Brian said, pride shining in his voice.

'They are beautiful,' I agreed. 'The colours.' Dad had sketched and used watercolours to add bursts of colour and texture across the plans.

'It brings them to life,' Brian said, and I nodded, dazed.

Dad's plans were a bit more ambitious than mine. He had opted for a side extension to create a walk-in pantry and utility room. A large kitchen-diner. He'd also included a loft conversion to create a large master suite. My eyes stung when I read what he'd named the top floor.

'Kat's room,' I said, glancing up at Brian.

I took in the final page – a landscaped plan for the garden, which included a beautifully sketched Wendy house, but for adults. It had square windows, a little porch, and some sliding doors, which gave it a modern look. Dad had listed it as *Kat's Wendy House*. Tears threatened to overflow. These were the plans we'd made on that trip home years ago. The only thing he hadn't included was the slide from my bedroom to the garden, but I'm pretty sure that wasn't regulation.

But there it was – my Wendy house sat at the rear of the garden. He'd coloured in the green ivy and pink roses.

'But – it doesn't make sense.' I looked at my uncle. 'He never even called. Towards the end, he never called.' My voice sounded strained. I struggled to swallow.

Brian leaned across the table and placed his hand on top of mine. 'I think he wanted to reconnect, and he planned on this house bringing you two together. He never mentioned it to me because I made it clear how I felt about his… lack of contact with you, Kat. I'm sorry. Sorry for you both that he didn't make it right. In time.'

One tear landed on the paper.

Then, it was like a dam opened. My shoulders shook, and I tried to keep my sobs quiet. All the suppressed feelings I'd felt since my dad died came at me in full force – the silent, tense drive to the hospital. Graham's driving, his knuckles white as he tried to get me there on time. His silent prayer that I'd be able to see my dad one last time. My mum was silent in the front seat next to him, processing her own version of grief and stress. The smell of the hospital: bleach and floral disinfectant. The look of pity on the nurse's face when she told us we were too late.

He was gone.

He'd left me again.

Rage and grief had racked me, but I didn't cry.

I'd held it together until the funeral.

And I'd bottled it back up until now.

Chapter Seventeen

Everything was blurry. Blood had rushed to my head.

'I'm so sorry, Kat. I shouldn't have brought them here. I didn't think – I'm sorry.' Brian's arms came around my shoulders, holding me close.

'Red.' A gruff voice came from somewhere behind me. I knew exactly who it was. But for once, I didn't have the bandwidth to acknowledge him. I was concentrating on my breath.

'Shall we step out for some fresh air?' Liam asked, his voice light.

I rose from my seat, suddenly aware of the scene I was causing. Embarrassment rolled through me. I collected the documents, my tears hitting the folder. I suddenly became desperate for any chance to escape any onlookers.

Liam gave me that, like an outstretched hand.

I glanced up at him, and his eyes met mine, his eyebrows pinched. His gaze dropped to the plans.

'I'll take care of these,' he said, and his hand brushed mine. I followed Liam through the side door into a small courtyard with wooden tables and chairs. It was chilly but not raining, thankfully.

Liam shrugged off his coat and handed it to me.

'I'm fine –'

'Don't argue with me.'

I took his coat and put my arms through it. It was warm and smelt like cedar and musk. It was nice. I sat down at one of the tables, feeling numb.

'Wait here a minute,' Liam announced and went back inside.

A few moments later, he came out with a Guinness and what looked like a Coke and popped them on the wooden table in front of us.

'I figured you could do with a pint.'

'Do you mind?' I was suddenly aware I'd never asked if he was okay with being around people drinking.

Liam nodded. 'Oh yeah, don't worry, I'm fine. I – I don't think I'd call myself a recovering alcoholic. I didn't like the person I was when I drank.'

I sensed there was a bit more detail than that.

'Have you ever Split the G?' Liam nodded at the pint.

I shook my head.

'In one sip, you have to drink so that the line hits right there.' He pointed to the G on the Guinness logo. 'Go on, give it a go.'

I took a big sip, put my glass down and waited for the swirling brown liquid to settle. The dark line of the stout was bang-on aligned with the curve of the letter G.

'Beginner's luck.' Liam smiled at me. It was the first proper smile I'd seen on his face, and it felt like an offering. Tentative and sweet. It started a buzzing in my chest, and I couldn't help but look at his mouth. He had straight, white teeth framed by full lips.

'I'll take beginner's luck.' I smiled.

Like a switch, Liam's face turned grave, and I instantly missed the warmth of that smile.

'About what Brian brought you.'

My stomach sank. Liam had distracted me. I'd almost forgotten why we'd come out here.

Liam held his hands up. 'You don't have to tell me if it's private.'

I shifted my glass and ran my fingers over the ridges of the Guinness logo. 'It's okay. They are my dad's plans for the house. He sketched them himself before he passed.' I passed them to Liam, giving him permission to have a look.

Liam opened them, and his eyes widened. 'He drew these? They're incredible.'

My leg shook under the table. 'He was a talented artist when he wanted to be. He didn't get to do it much, though. There wasn't much of an option to be an artist when he was younger. His family didn't have money, so he needed to go into a profession. He became a mechanic.'

Liam frowned.

'Yeah, I know. Artist and mechanic don't add up. He owned a garage in Reading, but it closed when the financial crash hit in '08. I didn't really get the whole story because I was young, and I think my parents were trying to shield me from it.'

'So then he decided to do up houses?'

I swallowed a sip of Guinness. 'I think it was his way of being creative in a practical way. He could put together designs, and he had a great skill set, which meant he didn't need to bring a lot of tradesmen in, apart from some electrical stuff.'

If I was honest, I didn't fully know what my dad did or didn't do on his renovation projects. On the rare occasion we would talk over the phone every few months, he never divulged much information apart from where he was in the country and what he was having for tea. Panic bubbled up inside me when I thought about how clueless I was. My dad had these plans drawn, and I could barely knock the plaster off walls without supervision.

According to Liam, at least.

'Dad had more ambitious plans than me. I can't afford to do this' – I pointed at the plans – 'and turn a profit once I sell.'

'Let me look,' Liam said, reaching for the plans.

I watched his dark eyes scan over the paper; his eyes widened when he read my name. The realisation that Dad had made the plans for me. I should have felt exposed, divulging that information to someone I'd only known a week, but something about Liam's way made me feel comfortable. I knew he wouldn't try to make me feel better with useless words. He would listen and I'd never had anyone *listen*.

'I mean, we could,' Liam said. 'But if you are moving back –' He glanced up at me as if it was a question.

'I'm moving back.'

Liam glanced away, a shadow flitting over his face. Then, he nodded. 'You don't want to overspend.'

'It's fine. We'll continue with the plan we made. I'm happy with it.' I forced a smile, only slightly disappointed. If not for my dad, then for me. Because I had to admit they were bigger and better than my more modest approach.

Liam tilted his head. 'The plan we made is solid. You'll be guaranteed a return.'

'Fine. We keep it as is,' I said, only a tinge of disappointment entering my voice.

I picked up the folder and took the plans out again, running my hand over the sketches. I could feel where my dad's pencil had made grooves, and the watercolours had dried on the paper.

'Kat?' I heard my uncle call out from the side door of the club.

'Out here, Brian,' Liam called into the dark.

'Ay up, you two.' My uncle sat beside Liam, struggling slightly to pull his leg over the bench.

'Alright, old man?' Liam grinned.

'Oi, you. You're not too old for a good hiding, you know.' Brian rubbed Liam's head, messing up his hair. There was a relaxed, natural rapport between them, which made my heart hurt.

'Kat, I'm sorry. I shouldn't have brought the plans here. I —'
He stuttered, looking completely overwhelmed.

'Brian, don't worry.'

'I didn't think you'd get upset.' He cringed, and I wanted to
laugh. In my experience, men of a certain age were oblivious to
feelings. 'If it helps, Sandra's given me an earful in the middle of
the club.'

The image of my auntie giving Brian a bollocking in front of
everyone made me laugh.

'It's okay, honestly. I think being here, well, it's just dug some
things up.'

Brian nodded. Liam was watching me intently. It felt reassuring
to have him here. It was weird that I'd been here about a week
and felt more comfortable around Liam than with my uncle. Even
if I thought Liam was still a bit… skittish around me.

'I'm sorry, love,' Brian said, reaching his hand over to mine. I
knew my uncle was always kind and warm whenever I'd seen
him, but I'd clung to the idea that they 'sided' with my dad
throughout my life. They'd never tried to see me, so they must
be the bad guys. My auntie and uncle were slowly chipping away
at my resolve to keep a distance.

'We don't think we'll be able to follow Dad's plans,' I said,
glancing at Liam.

'That's fine. He wouldn't have wanted them to be a burden.
But keep the plans, Kat. You might buy a house someday and
want some inspiration,' Brian said, a hopeful tone in his voice.

I nodded.

A hand came over mine; this time, it was large and calloused.
Liam's eyes met mine with a silent message.

Do you want to head back?

I gave a little shake of my head. *I'm fine.*

Are you sure?

141

'When you're ready, I can drop you back to the house if you want, Kat.' Brian's gaze flitted between me and Liam. 'I haven't seen it in years. It would be nice to see it again.'

I froze, unsure what to say. Brian didn't know I was staying at Liam's place.

'She's staying at mine, Brian,' Liam said. 'In the annexe,' he clarified quickly.

Brian's gaze shifted between Liam and me. 'Oh, I didn't realise.'

'The house needed gutting completely, so Liam offered me the annexe to stay,' I explained.

Brian frowned. 'You could have stayed with us, Kat. You should have asked. We're here to help if you need it.'

Liam gave me a look as if to say, *See, I told you so*, which made me want to stick my tongue out at him. Despite Brian's offer, I still felt weird about staying with them. I didn't want to look at Brian's familiar body language and expressions daily and be reminded of my dad. Of all that complicated pain and grief.

But then again, I was imposing on Liam. And he didn't owe me anything. So, I should probably take Brian up on the offer, even if it made me feel icky.

'Well, if you're sure –' I began.

'She has her own space at mine,' Liam interrupted. 'Right, Red?'

'Well, yeah,' I said uselessly.

Brian looked at Liam, his head cocked for a moment, then turned to me. 'Well, the offer is always there. You know Sandra is still distraught from Lydia moving out.'

Liam huffed. 'That was six years ago.'

Brian shrugged. 'It might as well be yesterday to Sandra. Speaking of, I better go and grovel. I'll see you two later.'

Brian clapped a hand on Liam's shoulders as he stood up.

Once he was gone, I piped up, 'You didn't have to do that. I can take Brian and Sandra up on their offer if I'm imposing.'

'You didn't see your face.' Liam shook his head. 'No one should be uncomfortable where they live, even for a few weeks. Nothing is worse than having to tiptoe around someone else's place. I get it. The annexe means you have your own space.'

'To leave my socks on the bathroom floor.'

'As long as it's only socks.' Liam's eyes flickered with humour.

'Erm, excuse me. I'm very tidy.'

'Sure, sure. I'll believe it when I see it.'

It struck me then how generous and open Liam was being with someone who was basically a stranger to him.

'Why are you so generous?'

'I'm repenting, remember? Plus, you're entertaining.' He shrugged, but then he held my gaze. His eyes flickered around my face, cheeks, eyes. My stomach swooped. I hated that my body reacted funny when he looked at me like that. I was sure this stupid crush was one-sided, so it was pointless getting all hot and bothered over a single look.

'I like having you around,' Liam said, his voice low, and warmth spread through my chest.

'You like having me around,' I repeated, a bit high from his admission. My face broke into a grin. 'You like me. Oh my god.' I gasped and raised my voice. 'Liam Hunter likes me!'

Liam's lips twitched, and he rolled his eyes. 'Yeah, all right, all right. Don't get big-headed.'

I smiled wider. 'But you like having my big head around.'

'I should never have said that.'

I laughed and sipped my pint, trying to hide my smile.

Chapter Eighteen

My poor attempt to climb into Liam's van exposed how tipsy I was. And that I'd signed up for Lydia's hot yoga class in the morning. And that my filter had completely disappeared.

I'd drank a little more than I usually would, but the day had been a rollercoaster of emotions: excitement, joy, grief, and sadness, all punctuated by the warmth of Liam's watchful gaze.

I'd grown self-conscious about my tipsy status by my fourth pint. It was ten o'clock, probably Liam's bedtime, and he wasn't drinking. Surely there was nothing worse than being around a load of drunk people when he was sober? But Liam seemed happy to sit there, watching everyone else chatter and laugh, sipping a Coke Zero.

Not Diet Coke – Coke Zero.

Sandra whispered that she had ordered it for Liam. 'Don't mention it. He'd only say I was making a fuss.'

I glanced his way to find him looking at both of us, sitting in one of the armchairs next to Jack, Lydia, and Freddie, chatting amongst themselves.

'What are you two whispering about?' he asked, a fake frown on his handsome face. Handsome – when had he got that handsome? His face was so... symmetrical. And masculine. His jaw was sharp and defined like it could cut glass. I wanted to rub my face in his five o'clock shadow. I made a mental note to call

Willa and inform her of Liam's attractiveness. She would want to know.

'Nothing!' I shouted back, grinning.

Sandra called last orders and kicked everyone out. Liam followed me out to the van. The heat of his hands brushed my lower back.

'Do you judge people who do drink?' I asked, shivering slightly. It was now eleven, so it was freezing. I couldn't believe how much colder it was up here.

Liam leaned over and flipped on some switches, making heat blast out of the vents. 'Better?'

'Yeah, thanks,' I murmured.

'I don't judge people who drink.'

'Huh?'

'I don't judge people who drink.'

'Why would you judge people who drink?'

'You asked if I judge people who drink.' His lips twitched.

'Oh.' I hiccupped. 'Well, you probably should.'

'Ah, don't be daft.' Liam was still smiling. His smile transformed his face. His features were usually so neutral and cool. He had a bit of a case of resting bitch face until he smiled, and it was like a switch flipped. His joy flowed across his features so easily when he wanted to. It was beautiful to watch.

'You have a nice smile, you know,' I slurred.

Sober Kat was banging her fists against a locked cage.

'Thanks.' Liam smiled wider. 'You're nice to me after a drink. That's another thing to add to my list.'

'Your list? What list?'

Liam laughed. 'Nothing. You were talking about my smile.'

'Yeah, it's nice.'

'You're a lightweight.'

I pouted. 'I know. It sucks.'

145

'Probably 'cos you're short.'

'I am not short. I'm bang-on average. Average, average, average. Apart from my IQ, which I have been told is below average, which is nice, isn't it?' I hiccupped a laugh.

'Do you want a rod?'

'A what?' I spluttered.

Liam kept his face deadpan. 'A rod. For all that fishing you're doing.'

It took me an embarrassingly long time to figure out what Liam was on about. Then the penny dropped.

'Oh, har, har. Very funny.'

Liam chuckled as he drove us through Everly Heath, the glow of the streetlights setting everything in an orange haze.

'Stop,' I shouted, throwing my hand on the dashboard. Liam came to a screeching halt.

'What's wrong?' His eyes were wide, assessing the danger.

'Can you pull in?' I pointed to the car park.

I unclipped my belt and ran across the grass, searching.

'Kat,' Liam called. 'What are you doing?'

'I haven't seen it yet. I should have seen it by now.'

'Seen what?'

'It's around here somewhere. I just don't know where.' I squinted, trying to see the names on the graves in front of me.

'Wait here.' Liam returned a minute later with a torch and placed it in my hands. 'You use this, and I'll use my phone.'

'You'll help?'

'Are you daft? Of course I'll help. Let's split up, and we'll find him quicker.'

'You shouldn't have said that. That's what you say before you get murdered.'

'What?' Liam frowned.

'In the horror films.'

146

Liam chuckled. 'It's Everly Heath. The biggest crime here is the mystery thief who kept nicking Paul's pears.'

Liam wandered off, shining his torch on each grave as he went.

'Who is Paul? Why did someone steal his pears?' I asked as I took the next row and kept searching.

'The greengrocer. We found out it was the rabbits escaping from the pet shop next door. It was a mystery for weeks.'

I huffed. 'This place is bizarre.'

'Here, Kat,' Liam said, his voice going soft. My heart leapt. I made my way to where Liam stood two rows behind me. I looked down at the epitaph. *James 'Jim' Williams. Devoted son, brother, and father.*

'Devoted.'

Liam gave me a curious look. 'Did you pick it? The words.'

'No, I let Uncle Brian pick it.' I rubbed my forehead. 'Our relationship – if that's what you could call it – well, it wouldn't have fit on the granite.'

'It sounds… complex,' Liam said, his voice uneasy.

Was I making Liam uncomfortable?

'Sorry, I'm drunk. A morose drunk, apparently.'

'It's fine, Kat.' He said my name softly, almost reverent. It was nice to hear my actual name from his lips, not the nickname I'd become familiar with.

'Tell me.' Liam inched his hand around my arm. He placed his hand on my arm tentatively, reassuringly. We both ignored how I leaned into that touch, my head resting on his shoulder. And we both ignored how Liam's arms tightened around me.

'I'm fine.'

'We're a little past "fine", don't you think?' Liam asked, and I turned up to see him looking down at me. He was right. He'd already seen me cry. He knew my family. It wasn't like he was some random stranger asking me. He wasn't just a builder I'd hired.

Liam was… more.

'It's so fucking complicated,' I whispered, as if worried I'd wake the dead. 'People say that grief is love with nowhere to go. But what happens to all the anger and longing and frustration or the crippling disappointment? Where does that all go? What happens when it's not as simple as just "love"?' I glanced down at the grave. 'He left me again. And he didn't even make it right before he left.' My eyes began to burn. I took a deep breath, trying to hold myself together.

I didn't want to fall apart for the second time tonight.

'How do I make it stop?' I sniffed. 'Every time I think I'm over it, it all comes rushing back.'

The streetlamps from across the street illuminated Liam just enough to see the hard lines of his clenched jaw. His pinkie finger moved against my skin, back and forth. I could feel his reassuring warmth standing next to me.

'I don't know, Kat,' Liam answered after a pause, his voice low. 'I think you have to feel it all. It's like a wound. It has to bleed to heal.'

'I don't want to feel it,' I complained. 'I want it gone.'

Liam huffed. 'If it were that simple, everyone would do it. You can drink through it – I've tried that. You can suppress it for a while. But it will come back, and it will come back harder. And grief – grief is the trickiest of them all. It can hit you like a fucking train out of nowhere. A smell or a place sparks a memory, and that's it – you're in the trenches, just trying to climb out.' He was looking ahead, his eyes soft with… sadness.

Pure sadness.

'You lost someone too?'

'I lost my mum when I was twelve. Breast cancer.'

I frowned. 'But Dot mentioned –'.

Liam looked away. 'Dot doesn't remember. She came to the

funeral before she was diagnosed. But she doesn't remember now. And it would be cruel for her to have to hear it again and again.'

'I'm sorry.'

I couldn't imagine losing someone that young. When I was that age, at least I knew my dad was alive, even if he was AWOL. Or did that make it worse? I wasn't sure, but I knew we couldn't have a 'who had it worse' contest.

'It's fine –' Liam's mouth shut quickly, but it was too late.

I raised an eyebrow. 'I thought we were past "fine". And that certainly doesn't sound like feeling it.'

'Have you heard of the phrase "do as I say, not as I do"?'

'Hypocrite.' I tutted.

We stood a little while longer, side by side. I figured the conversation was over and that, in a few seconds, we'd trail back to the van and go home.

Until Liam opened his mouth.

'Losing Mum was the worst day of my life. But sometimes, I wonder if the aftermath was worse. I was the eldest. So naturally, I took everything on. Dad was a wreck because he'd lost the love of his life. My brother was little, and he wanted his mum back. So, I became that for everyone. I started making breakfast. I got Ren ready for school. I helped him with his homework. I did everything to keep the ship afloat.'

My heart hurt for that little kid with too much responsibility.

'I see that in you.' I glanced up at him.

'See what?' He had an earnest expression, eager to hear what I had to say.

I took a deep breath. 'Well, how many favours have you done since the committee meeting?'

'Well, not that many –' Liam kicked a piece of dirt from his boots.

'Come on,' I said. 'Cough it up.'

Liam coughed. 'Seven or eight.'

My eyes bugged. 'Are you joking? For free?'

Liam shrugged. 'Little things, really. Fixing a loo. Sealing a shower. Fitting some cabinets. I'd managed to keep them at bay since I took over from Dad. I had an excuse – new management. We're doing things differently. But when I stood up and volunteered to help you…' He petered off, then glanced up at me. 'Well, it was an open invitation.'

Guilt thrummed through me. I'd caused this.

'I'm sorry. It's my fault.'

'It's not your fault. I could have said no. But I didn't.' Liam shrugged. 'A family trait, apparently.' He glanced up, his eyes soft. 'And I couldn't say no to you.'

My heart jumped, but I kept my voice even.

'You could have.'

'Trust me, I couldn't.'

'Well, you need some boundaries, Mister!' I demanded, my cheeks burned from his words. I needed to change the tone, or we were heading somewhere else. I counted on my fingers. 'You worry about Jack far too much. You spend a huge chunk of your day making sure Freddie gets the proper training.' I cocked an eyebrow. 'You volunteer at the club with the first bat of Sandra's eyelashes. Then, you come home and cook' – I pointed a finger – 'and I know you go to the effort to make extra for me, and then make everyone lunch too.'

Liam's lips twitched. 'Are you telling me off, Red?'

'Yes!' I rolled my eyes. 'You even fold your tea towels in a specific way.'

I'd watched in morbid fascination from the annexe as Liam folded and tucked his tea towels so that they looked like pretty little packages.

'You've been watching very closely.' Liam took a step forward, his eyes flicking all over my face.

I flushed. 'Don't change the subject.'

Liam ran his hands through his hair, which had grown long again, as it had at the funeral. It was floppy, making him look like a nineties heartthrob – a blue-collar Hugh Grant.

'I'm trying not to take on so much. Therapy helped. But it's still hard to say no. That's why I get so angry at my dad sometimes. I'm trying to put some... boundaries up. And he steamrolls over them. He'd have me burn out rather than say no. And half the time, it's not greed or business. It's because he wants to help.'

'I'm sorry for shouting. And I'm sorry if I became another one of those burdens.'

He looked at me then, really looked at me. His usually guarded features were strangely open.

'I didn't mean it like that, Kat. You aren't a burden.'

I shrugged. 'I feel like one.'

'Trust me. You're not. And the shouting was kind of hot.'

A hysterical giggle escaped my lips. 'Hot?'

'Yeah. I'm not going to analyse that.' Liam grinned. 'C'mere,' he said, opening his arms.

I instinctively stepped into them, not caring what this meant. I didn't want to overanalyse this gesture of kindness. Liam's arms wrapped around me, and his chin rested on my head. He was solid and so, so warm.

'I'm sorry about your dad.'

I felt the word rumble through his chest.

'I'm sorry about your mum,' I said into his chest. 'Aren't we a pair?'

Liam pulled back and looked at me. I probably had snot all over me and looked like a blubbering mess, but he smiled. Something had shifted between us – a new understanding. It wasn't a tentative truce based on a silly pinkie promise but something deeper – a friendship, maybe. A green shoot bursting from under the soil; it was delicate and new.

In my bones, I knew Liam was someone I could trust.

A part of me was comforted by that, and the other part of me… the part that had been hurt before.

Well, that part was terrified.

Chapter Nineteen

The drive back was quiet, but not the quiet that made my skin crawl. It was comfortable. Familiar. And thanks to my outburst in the graveyard, my brain was at rest for once. Liam hummed along to a song on the radio and occasionally glanced at me like he was checking I was still breathing. As Liam pulled into the driveway, I realised I didn't want to go to the annexe. I wanted company. Liam's company specifically.

But Liam's words about boundaries rang in my head as we sat in the van, neither of us moving to open the door and walk into the house. It was like we were both content to sit in the car with this new energy humming between us.

Eventually, Liam's security lights extinguished.

'Thanks for −'

'No problem.'

'Night, Liam,' I said, my hand landing on the van's door.

'Do you want to come in for some food? You haven't eaten dinner.' He said it so quickly that I almost didn't hear each word. 'And you drank a lot.' He scratched the back of his head, not looking me in the eye. 'I could make us cheese on toast, if you fancied it.'

'That does sound good,' I admitted.

Liam finally looked me in the eye and nodded, a small smile on his face. 'Come on then.'

As I headed for the front door, my foot hit the wrong angle

on the pavement. Pain shot up my leg. I swore under my breath. Liam was next to me instantly, holding my arm at my elbow.

'What's wrong?' Alarm filled his voice.

'I just rolled my ankle. It happens a lot. Weak ankles. I'm fine.' I put some weight on my ankle, and the pain throbbed there, insistent. But I'd done worse.

Liam frowned, his lips straight. 'It doesn't look okay.'

'I'll be fine. I'll walk it off. Honestly, I always do this. My ankles are like paper thin.'

'You need to watch where you walk,' Liam grunted.

I rolled my eyes. 'Yes, thank you. I'll work on that.'

If he thought this was bad, he would have kittens if he saw all the random bruises that appeared out of nowhere. I could never remember how I'd got them. But then again, I walked through a room like I could move through solid objects. I always bumped my arm on doorknobs or my hip into the corners of tables.

Liam's hands came to my arm, holding me up like I was made of nothing. His shoulders were tense as he unlocked the front door and I realised since that first night, I'd never walked through the front door. I'd always walked around the side of the house so Liam could have his privacy. And now he was basically holding me up, his hands all over me. If it wasn't for my ankle, it felt like we'd come back from a date tipsy and a little handsy.

'Liam, I can go around the side.'

'Stop being daft.' Liam held my elbow tighter, pulling me into him as he pushed the door open. 'I've got some ice.'

'You're fussing.'

'If you don't ice it, it will get worse. Knowing you, you'll end up falling down the stairs.'

'Rude,' I muttered under my breath.

He sat me down at the island and busied himself, getting ice from the freezer.

He flicked his fingers. 'Give me your ankle.'

'I can do it.'

Liam levelled me a look. 'Let me help, will you?'

I rolled my eyes and lifted my legging-clad leg onto the stool in front of me. Liam rolled up my leggings and I did the mental maths on the last time I shaved my legs. God, they had to be prickly as fuck. But Liam didn't seem to care as he placed the tea towel-covered ice pack onto my ankle. He muttered an apology when I jumped a bit when the cold hit my skin. After a few seconds, the shock subsided.

'Better?' Liam asked, his voice low.

I glanced up. Liam was standing closer than I'd realised. His eyes were tracking mine, left to right; his cedar cologne had a citrus undertone. Lemongrass, maybe. Heat rolled off him, making me want to nuzzle closer.

Nope.

I aggressively hit Backspace on that thought.

I swallowed hard. 'Yes. Yeah. Thanks.' I went to take the ice pack from Liam, and our hands touched. 'I can do that −'

Electricity fizzed as Liam's hand was under mine. I looked up. Liam was staring at me like I was something new. His eyes were warm. No. They were hot, like melted chocolate.

'Kat −' His voice was gravelly. Was it me, or was he leaning closer? Blood rushed to my head as he drew closer still, his hand holding my ankle tighter.

Then, I did something I will be replaying until the end of my days.

I leaned forward, pushing up on my good leg and pressed Liam's lips with mine. Liam's body locked up with shock, which had me reeling and pulling back. Fuck. I'd misread the situation. Humiliation was about to burn brightly on my face until I felt Liam's hand draw up my neck and into my hair, holding me there for a moment. His eyes were fixed on my lips.

Then, his lips touched mine again and softened. Tentative and sweet. His hand travelled up into my hair, pushing his palm further into my messy curls. I moaned at the touch.

The noise had Liam pulling back, his eyes wide.

'Kat –' he began, caution in his voice. White-hot humiliation flooded my body. This had to be a nightmare. I would wake up in a few moments in a cold sweat. I squeezed my eyes shut, then opened them. *Nope. Not imagining this.*

I jumped from the stool and could barely hear Liam saying, 'Careful,' as I stepped towards the doors.

'I – I'm sorry. I should go.' I turned to Liam. 'This was a mistake. I don't know what I was thinking. It won't happen again.' I gave a hysterical giggle. 'God, I'm such a fucking idiot.' I slapped my hand to my forehead, picking up the ice pack with my other hand.

'Kat – let me explain.' Liam ran his hand through his hair. 'I didn't want you to think –'

I didn't let him finish his sentence. 'Thank you for the ice pack. I'll leave you to it.'

'Kat –' His voice was quiet and tender, like he was talking to a wounded animal. Pity. The thought of Liam pitying me made me feel sick.

My back hit the cold of the bifold doors. 'We don't have to mention this again. Actually, I'd prefer if we never spoke of it again.'

'I want to talk about it –'

'Well, I don't.' I smiled. 'I'd prefer to die of embarrassment, actually.'

'Kat –'

'Liam, please. Just leave it.'

Liam's eyes were wide, a deer caught in headlights. Eventually, he nodded, glancing down like he couldn't look at me. Like he didn't want to look at me.

Jesus, the hangxiety tomorrow was going to be catastrophic.

'Thank you for – for this evening.'

I tried my best not to limp down the path to the annexe because I knew he'd be watching. Once I'd unlocked the door, I collapsed on the other side, taking deep breaths. I peeked around to look out the window to find Liam pacing across the kitchen, his hands running through his hair.

As I got ready for bed, I played and paused the whole inter-action with Liam from start to finish. I'd misread his body language. Obviously, he wasn't going to kiss me. He was concerned for my ankle, for my wellbeing. He'd been standing close to hold the ice pack to my ankle, and then I'd launched myself at him.

I groaned – my social anxiety at an all-time high.

We'd only been working together for a week, and I'd made things a million times more complicated. We still had two months of work to do. I wanted to throw myself into a wood chipper. I wanted Thanos to snap his fingers, obliterating me into tiny pieces. I'd do anything to be rid of this mortification.

Once I was in bed, the first text came through. I read Liam's name and felt like I'd been struck by lightning. I swiped open my phone with a shaky hand, reading the text through one squinting eye, like my phone might explode at any minute.

Liam: I can hear your brain from here.

Another message came through a few seconds later.

Liam: Can I take you somewhere for lunch tomorrow, and we can talk?

I groaned. I was so mortified I ignored the text. I mean, for all he knew, I was asleep.

Liam: I can see you've read the text, Kat.

Fuck, I forgot about my read receipts. I threw my phone on the bed and collapsed next to it. I lay face down on my pillow, hoping I'd accidentally suffocate myself in the night so I could avoid an incredibly awkward conversation with Liam in the morning.

Chapter Twenty

Kat's To-Do List

- Therapist???

I woke at five in the morning to my heart racing, like I was expected to run from a herd of elk at any moment.

Then I remembered – Liam. The kiss. The fallout. Once my brain caught up with my body, I understood why I was lightly sweating. I sat up, wrapping my arms around my knees, keeping my head down. When anxiety hit like this, it was crippling. I took some deep breaths, trying to calm myself, but it was useless. It was like I was getting ready to jump out of the window at any given moment. I leaned over and checked my phone. Liam hadn't texted again since last night. I couldn't blame him since I hadn't replied.

I texted Willa.

My phone vibrated about three minutes later with her call.

'What are you doing up so early?'

Willa's familiar voice was a temporary balm to my nerves. 'Personal training sessions. I pay Eduardo an extortionate amount of money every month to torture me. It's a good job he's fairly good-looking, or I'd have quit by now.'

Willa rarely noticed when men were attractive, let alone commented on it, so I knew Eduardo was more than 'fairly good-looking'.

'What's up? Your texts were… concerning. Frantic.' She paused before adding, 'Unhinged.'

I began pacing the room. 'I did something stupid.'

'You shagged him.'

I stopped. I didn't expect her to guess so close that quickly.

'His name is Liam. And we didn't *shag*.' Who even says shag?

'Don't change the subject.'

I paused until I reluctantly admitted, 'We kissed.'

'I *knew* this would happen. Some random guy isn't helping you out of the kindness of his heart. He must want to get into your pants.'

'He didn't kiss me. I kissed him. Actually, I kind of launched myself at him. I'd had a drink… or five… and behaved like such a dick, and now I've made everything awkward, and I want to die,' I rushed out, resuming my pacing. 'Not only did I kiss him, but before that, I shouted for him to pull over by the church so I could find Dad's grave.'

'Morbid much?'

'I know.' I panted. 'God, I'm such a fucking freak.'

'Okay, okay. Take some deep breaths.' I could hear Willa locking her door as she left her flat.

'Are you busy? I can call later,' I said, panicking that I was being too much.

'Don't be silly, I've got time—'

'If you need to go to your appointment—'

'Kat.' Willa's tone stopped my spiralling. 'I appreciate you considering me, but I'm fine, and right now, you're not. So take some breaths and tell me exactly what happened.'

I did exactly that, recounting the ice pack, the lean, and the kiss. I explained the graveyard antics and how he told me about his mum. I detailed how Liam kissed me back but then pulled away quickly – then finished off the story by sharing the screen-shots of the texts Liam sent.

'Okay.' Willa took a deep breath, and I could hear the distant sounds of cars beeping and buses going by and I was hit with homesickness. I wished I was in London, as far away from this house, this town, and Liam.

My fight or flight was kicking in, but it was going with flight this time.

Willa continued, 'Look, it sounds like the kiss was mutual, but Liam freaked out. Shit of him, but it could be about anything. You're catastrophising. He asked to talk, so hear him out. He might like you too.'

He might like me too.

I huffed, keeping my voice even. 'I didn't say I liked him. Just because I tried to kiss him doesn't mean I like him. It means he's not bad to look at.'

'Kat.' Willa's tone was bone dry. 'Be honest with me.'

I thought about the past week with Liam. The weird buzzing feeling I got when I watched him walk across the garden with a foil-covered plate. The string in my chest that pulled taut when he was in the room. The high when I got a rise out of him. I was getting addicted to getting a reaction out of that usually stoic, calm expression. I thought about Liam's solid, warm presence beside me in a dark graveyard.

I think you have to feel it all.

'Maybe.'

'Katherine,' Willa chided.

'Okay, yes,' I said quickly, panicking, 'but it's not like he likes me. He was totally repulsed by that kiss, trust me.'

'Oh my god' – exasperation poured down the phone – 'how

old are we, Kat? Speak to him! Be honest! You like him. You never randomly kiss blokes you've known less than a week. Unless you count your spree at uni—'

'Do not slut shame me. I told you I was going through my experimental phase.'

'Exactly, it was a phase, and since then, you haven't exactly put yourself out there, and god help anyone who asks you to be in a serious relationship.'

'I'm not scared of commitment. I haven't found anyone worth committing to.'

'Sure, Jan.'

'Okay, you're right, okay?' I rubbed my temples. I didn't need straight-talking Willa at this time in the morning. 'But it doesn't change anything. It would have to be like all of my other relationships – casual. His life is here, and mine is in London. If it was anything more, it would end in tears. So, there isn't anything to discuss, apart from a stupid, drunk move I made on him.' I groaned again. 'Willa, it was so bad.'

'It's never as bad as you imagine. You let your creativity run wild. Come back down to earth, martian.'

Her words seeped in, a soothing balm to some of my wounds.

'Okay.' I breathed. 'I like him, okay? I like him a lot, and I hate it because I feel so out of control, and I can't stop looking at him and his fucking face and his body. His body, Willa. It's insane, and I haven't even seen underneath his clothes yet. And it's not just physical. He's not what I expected at all. He's really sweet and thoughtful. He danced with his old piano teacher, for god's sake. He cooks because he wants to look after everyone. And he's so—' I took a deep breath in, refuelling. 'I like him, and I'm scared. Terrified. You happy now?'

There was silence on the other end of the phone, apart from the odd gust of wind.

'Willa?'

'I don't think I've ever heard you speak about someone like that.'

'Willa,' I groaned. 'Don't freak me out.'

'I'm not trying to freak you out. It's okay to be scared. It comes with the territory. You have to be vulnerable.'

'I don't want to be vulnerable,' I whined. 'Why can't someone tell me it will be okay?'

'Love wouldn't be worth it without a little risk.'

'No. It's not that. Don't say the L word,' I warned, panic rising in my throat again. God, I needed a therapist.

'You should tell him. Be honest.' Willa added, 'If I can finally finish with fuck-face John, then you can do this too.'

'Maybe.' The thought of confessing my delicate crush to Liam made me feel a bit sick. I wanted to see what he said first. 'I've got to go. I need to face the music.' I glanced over at Liam's house. No lights were on yet, so he had to be sleeping in.

'Text me and let me know how it goes. I'm here if you need me. Wish me luck with Eduardo.'

'I'm wishing Eduardo luck.'

Willa laughed. 'Love ya.'

'Love ya.' I hung up, feeling alone again.

As I showered and got dressed, my mind whirled with wild scenarios – Liam saying he was in love with me, Liam friend-zoning me, Liam kicking me out of the annexe because the kiss was 'inappropriate', Liam quitting the job because I harassed him.

I was making myself a cup of tea in the little kitchen when I spotted a woman and child strolling through the side gate into the garden.

I frowned, putting the kettle down.

The woman had a slim, athletic build and chestnut-brown hair with lowlights running through it, which made it look like glossy chocolate. She glanced around, searching for something with sharp blue eyes that contrasted with her tanned skin. She wore athleisure, but unlike Lydia's citrus brights, hers were warm beige. The woman shouted something to the little girl, who had to be about ten years old, peering through Liam's bifold windows.

Was this woman the Abigail that Jack had mentioned in my eavesdropping?

I was frozen in place, unsure what to do.

Should I go and tell them Liam wasn't up yet?

The choice was taken from me. The little girl's eyes went wide with curiosity, and she pointed towards me. The woman turned and saw me standing in the cottage, her eyes narrowing.

Shit.

She did not look happy, and she didn't strike me as a woman you wanted to cross, but I pulled on my big girl pants and walked outside to introduce myself.

'Hi. I'm Kat. Are you looking for Liam? He's not up yet, he –'

'Is he in there?' The woman nodded towards the annexe behind me.

'No –'

She leaned down and gave the girl a kiss on the head. 'Honey, go knock on the front door again, please.' The girl looked like she wanted to complain, but she nodded and walked away, looking at me with interest.

She lowered her voice. 'Has he been drinking?'

I frowned. 'No, of course not.'

The woman's shoulders sagged. Then, her eyes turned to me, cold and assessing again. 'When I'd told him not to bring women home anymore, he really took it literally.' She huffed, glancing at the annexe. 'He put you in the annexe instead. Well, this hasn't happened in a while. I'd really thought he'd changed but that's what I get when I trust people. At least you're better dressed than

the last one, that bedazzled purple thong put me off my breakfast.'
She glanced down at me, 'You look slightly better dressed.'

'I'm sorry –' I recoiled, then coiled back up like a snake, ready
to snap at retreating heels. 'Who are you?'

'Who am I?' She laughed like I was supposed to know. 'I'm
the mother of his child. Let me guess, Liam didn't mention that
little detail, did he?'

'Mum! Dad's here!' the girl exclaimed.

A record scratch echoed in my head.

Dad.

Liam was a dad.

Chapter Twenty-One

'Yasmin.' Liam's tone was a warning. He was walking hand in hand with the little girl, his hair still wet from the shower. He ran his other hand through his hair, pushing it back. His T-shirt was wonky and damp, like he hadn't dried off properly. The shirt stuck to him like he was in some kind of cologne advert. His eyes were wide, flickering between me and Yasmin and back. The cogs of my brain were moving now. Liam was a dad. He was a dad and hadn't mentioned it.

'What the hell, Liam?' Yasmin hissed. 'We go away for a couple of weeks, and I come back to this again? I swear to god –'

Liam's eyes flickered to me with a pained expression, as if sensing my discomfort.

'Slow down a minute. You're jumping to conclusions,' Liam said, sounding resigned. Tired. 'Abi-chops.' Liam pulled her into his side, kissing her head. 'Did you have a nice time in Formby?'

Abigail babbled, 'Gran and Grandad have a new puppy, Freddie, and he's so cute. I taught him how to sit, and I've got videos of him running on the beach on Mum's phone. Do you wanna see?'

Liam smiled. 'I'll have a look in a bit. Why don't you go in? It's cold, and I need a word with Mum. The Switch is in the cupboard by the TV if you want to go on Zebra Crossing.'

Abigail rolled her eyes, making her look older than her years. 'It's Animal Crossing, Dad.'

'Yeah, yeah.' He ruffled her hair. Abigail moseyed back into the house, leaving three very awkward adults alone.

Animal Crossing sounded really fun right now.

'Liam, you should have let me know you had someone *staying*.' Yasmin widened her eyes at the last word.

'I was waiting for you to get back,' Liam said, tense. 'And I don't owe you an explanation. This is my house—'

'We promised we would communicate about girlfriends,' Yasmin threw back.

'I'm not his girlfriend,' I blurted out. 'We're not — we're not together. He's actually working for me. Or with me. I don't know, the lines are a little blurry on that.' I heaved a breath. 'We're not together. This is strictly business.'

Yasmin and Liam looked at me, dumbfounded at my rambling. Luckily, Liam took over.

'Kat is Brian Williams's niece,' Liam said slowly.

Yasmin's eyes widened as she looked at me, and her face morphed into pity. She knew about Dad, my gut knew it. Liam continued, 'I'm working on her dad's house. She had to move out. Plaster was shot.' Liam lowered his voice. 'This isn't going to work if you don't trust me.'

That sentence was laced with history – tense subtext wrapped in barbed wire. And I didn't feel like getting cut.

'I'll – I'll leave you guys to it.'

Liam gave me a small nod, and I made my way back into the annexe, closing the door and leaning against it, taking some deep breaths.

Liam had a daughter. Liam had a daughter that he hadn't mentioned. No one had mentioned it. Not Uncle Brian or Auntie Sandra. Not Lydia. We'd talked about grief and the house and all the baggage with my dad. I'd drunken kissed him, for god's sake. But he'd never mentioned his own daughter.

I rubbed my chest, feeling the residual anxiety.

How often did he see her?

Oh my god.

What if Yasmin lived here? Had Liam pulled away last night because he was still seeing Yasmin? They hadn't seemed very… happy, but that didn't mean they weren't together. Oh my god, I'd kissed a man in a relationship without knowing. Were they on some kind of Ross and Rachel-style break, and Liam hadn't mentioned it because he was a huge dickhead?

Had I inadvertently become a homewrecker? Because if I were Yasmin, I'd be pissed too.

My head was swimming with possibilities, my hands becoming tingly from panic. I needed to get out. I'd take up Sandra and Brian's offer to stay with them. In a trance, I had begun to pack my clothes into a bag when I heard Liam's voice at the door of the annexe.

'Kat?' He called again, and I heard his footsteps closer. 'Are you decent?' Liam poked his head around the door, his eyes dropping to my bag on the bed. He frowned. 'Where are you going?'

I gave a half-hearted laugh. 'I figured I should get out your hair. I don't want to cause any drama. I've already caused enough fuss as it is. I'll go to Brian and Sandra's.'

'Don't be ridiculous –'

'I'm not being ridiculous. It was my fault. Last night, I mean. I didn't know you were seeing someone or with someone. I mean, you might be engaged for all I know.' I gave a hysterical snort. 'Married even.'

I began shoving more clothes into my bag.

'I should have asked. I'm such an idiot.' Oh boy. My thought-to-mouth speed was becoming supersonic. 'I mean, we did speak about loads of things, about my dad, about your mum. Your job, my job. The house. I mean' – I gestured around – 'I moved in here. But throughout all of that, you never mentioned you had a wife and daughter. A family. I mean, they could live with you, for all I know.' I lifted my hands.

Liam held a hand up. 'Hang on, hang on. You're jumping ahead. Yas is my ex. We haven't been together in – god, it must be seven years now. And yes, Abigail does live with me, some of the time –'

'And that's not something you mention?' I was floating above myself, watching my frustration and anger ripple through my body language, eyes, and hands, but I could not control it. 'I mean, who does that? Who doesn't speak about their daughter to anyone for weeks?'

Liam's jaw clenched. 'It's complicated. I like to keep things private –'

'What kind of dad does that?'

Liam's eyes lit with anger. 'You do not get to sling around accusations.'

'Well, don't you think it's a bit weird?'

'If you let me explain –'

'Yeah, it's fucking weird. Is she some secret daughter? Does anyone even know she exists?'

'Of course people know she exists.'

'I mean, do you know what that feels like? To have someone forget that you exist?'

'Kat. I am not like your dad.' He squeezed his eyes shut. 'I have a relationship with my daughter. Don't project his failings onto me.'

I recoiled, instantly defensive. 'This has nothing to do with my dad.'

Oh fuck.

Was that what I was doing? It took one moment of introspection to realise – yes. That's exactly what I'd done. I'd vented all my frustration and anger at my dad onto Liam. Shame sat heavy in my stomach. It was absolutely none of my business when or where Liam saw his daughter. I had overstepped and freaked out and it was all so fucking irrational.

Freud would have a field day.

The revelation must have shown on my face because Liam's gaze softened an inch.

'You're right, I don't have any right –'

'It's fine.'

I kept shoving clothes into my bag. 'It's not. We don't know each other like that. You're doing me a favour. I don't have any right to comment on your family situation.'

Liam's hands came to mine, stilling me. 'I should have told you. I was going to. I needed to speak to Yas first. What happened with Yas' – he gestured outside – 'well, some of it, I deserve. She shouldn't have jumped down your throat, but I made some mistakes. We'll talk later, yeah? I'll explain everything.'

'Okay.' I bit my lip.

'You'll stay?' Liam stepped closer, holding out his pinkie finger. A ghost of a smile on his face. His attempt to lighten the mood.

Come on, play with me.

I smiled, taking it and shaking it with my own.

'I'll stay.'

'Then I'll see you later.' Liam left the annexe, glancing back at me like I might disappear at any moment.

Once Liam was gone, I collapsed on the bed, my head in my hands. I couldn't believe I just vomited insecure attachment style all over the place. I glanced down at my phone.

Lydia: Pick you up in half an hour?

'For fuck's sake.'

169

Chapter Twenty-Two

'And exhale,' Lydia said serenely as the class of fifteen yogis shifted back into downward dog, with mixed success. I pushed my arse into the air, feeling my hamstrings tighten.

Don't be sick, don't be sick.

But as the blood rushed to my head, it wasn't sick rising up my throat. Heartburn that rose, burning through my chest and up my throat. I collapsed onto the yoga mat, the noise of my body hitting the floor making everyone glance my way.

You okay? Lydia mouthed at me, her face marred with concern.

I gave a strained smile and nodded. 'I'm fine.'

'What's going on with you?' Lydia asked as we queued up in the gym's cafe after class. Lydia's gym was posh and busy on a Tuesday morning.

People were working on laptops while parents rushed their kids to swimming lessons. It had indoor and outdoor tennis courts and pools, several saunas and steam rooms, and even a children's pool with a water slide for all the little Timothys and Jemimas to enjoy. Lydia was nauseatingly popular. We could only take two steps before she was stopped by her clients or regulars, gushing about their personal bests or bemoaning their injuries. Lydia smiled, laughed, and remembered everyone's name. Her brain never lagged and she didn't perform or change into anyone else either.

She was herself – bubbly, approachable, kind.

It made me feel like a pathetic excuse of a human being.

'A bit hungover,' I mumbled.

'Kat,' Lydia said, as we shuffled further down the queue, 'you should have said. I wouldn't have minded if you needed to cancel.'

'I know, I just – I needed something to do today anyway,' I said, picking up a protein bar. It would taste like plastic, but I needed to restore my vitals.

As we got to the front of the queue, a girl with cropped brown hair was taking orders, and her brown eyes lit up when she saw her next customer.

'Hey, Lydia.'

'Hey, Casey.' Lydia smiled.

'The usual?' Casey asked breathlessly.

'Yes, please, and a –'

'A caramel latte, please,' I asked, smiling at the woman who looked like she was going to combust in front of our eyes.

'I'll bring it over.'

'Thanks, Casey,' Lydia said, moving us out of the line and through the cafe to find somewhere to sit near the window. Outside, two ladies in swimming caps were doing laps, more steam rising from the heated pool with each movement of their arms.

'Dad told me you moved in with Liam. I said hire him, Kat.' Lydia snorted a laugh, 'Not shack up with him.'

'I didn't shack up with him!'

'That's how Dad made it sound. How did *that* happen?' She arched a blonde eyebrow. 'You didn't seem all that friendly at the club.'

'Liam said I had to move out. I didn't want to, but I had no choice.' I decided to leave out that I camped in the garden. I could do without that strike to my ego. 'Liam came by the house and offered me a place in his annexe.'

Lydia grinned. 'Bet you loved that.' Lydia's smile dropped. 'You know we're here to help, Kat. Me, Mum, Dad. I mean, half of the club, too. You just need to ask.'

I squirmed. I'd never been good at accepting help.

Apply yourself, Katherine.

I inhaled a shaky breath. 'I'll get better at asking for help.'

'Good egg,' Lydia said, squeezing my hand, 'because Mum is driving me mad. She's chomping at the bit to help. Don't be surprised if you come by one day and she's painting your front room magnolia.'

I knew Lydia was joking, but I internally flinched at the mention of the colour magnolia. Like any millennial, that colour was etched into my brain.

I frowned. 'She never mentioned anything.'

'After Dad brought those plans to the club and upset you, Mum said we were banned from meddling.'

'Caramel latte and black coffee,' Casey said, holding two cups and saucers.

'Perfect, thank you,' Lydia said, moving her phone out of the way. Casey placed the cups down and aimed one more smile at Lydia before leaving.

'Lyd,' I said, lowering my voice.

Her blue eyes lifted to mine, eyebrows raised. 'What?'

'Are we gonna talk about how that woman has the biggest crush on you, maybe ever?' I raised an eyebrow.

Lydia's cup clattered down onto the saucer, her eyes darting across the room to find Casey.

'No. She doesn't.'

I nodded vehemently. 'Yes, she does.'

'She's being nice. I don't even know if she's into girls.'

'She made that guy' – I pointed to the teenager at the till who was going through an unfortunate goatee phase – 'swap with her so she could bring these coffees over here herself.'

'She's just being nice.'

'Look at her face when she looks at you. You're delusional if you don't see it.'

Lydia bit her lip, 'I can tell when guys are interested, but it's so hard to tell with women. I can't tell if they are just being nice.'

'The blight of the bisexual.'

Lydia's eyes widened in mock-horror, 'It's just a phase, Kat. I'll get over it.'

I nodded, pouting. 'You're just greedy.'

Lydia laughed, a dirty deep laugh, 'Oh yeah, greedy and a bit of a slag too.'

I laughed, aware that if anyone took this out of the context, we would definitely be cancelled.

'You should ask her out if you like her,' I said, lifting the mug to my lips. The first sip was the perfect mix of bitter coffee, followed by the sweetness of the caramel syrup. It was what I needed for this hangover. Lydia waved to a table of four smiling older ladies decked out in garishly patterned athleisure. Their workout clothes looked more expensive than a month's rent in London.

'I might do.' Lydia nodded, glancing over at Casey again. 'So…' Lydia's face was uncharacteristically serious.

'What?' I asked, panic rising in my throat.

'On the topic of romance. I should mention a new… development.'

'What?' Panic rose in my voice.

'You and Liam. People have noticed some tension between the two of you.'

I felt my face going red. Had Lydia found out about the stupid kiss? Had Liam told Yasmin, probably laughing it off, and now everyone knew? Or was I that transparent? Was everyone talking about my stupid crush?

'There is no tension.' My breezy voice sounded like I was constipated.

'Well, you bicker a lot.'

'Yeah, we bicker.' I shrugged. 'He sometimes rubs me up the wrong way. That's all.'

I didn't mention I wouldn't have been totally against him rubbing me up the right way…

'I guess people are… reading into it. Everyone seems to have noticed your energy.' Lydia grinned. 'You stare at each other a lot. And Liam signed up to help you, with barely any complaints. He helps out but usually makes people work a bit harder than that. He stood up and volunteered in front of *everyone*. That's as close as Liam would get to a confession of love. He always moans about extra work, even if he does it eventually.'

'Cut to the chase, Lyd.'

'They're taking bets if you'll end up together or not.' Lydia blurted, then squeezed her eyes closed, like a bomb was about to detonate.

'Who are *they*?' I hissed.

'Some people at the club did a whip-round. Then word got around. They were feral when you got upset about your dad's plans – everyone said they'd never seen Liam react like that. Apparently, once he saw you crying, he became possessed.'

My body heated up when I thought about the heat of Liam's palm on my back as he guided me to the terrace garden.

'He was just being nice.'

'Sure, Liam is a softie, deep down. But he's usually a bit more subtle with it. This was something else.'

If word got out about that stupid drunken kiss, it wouldn't just line pockets – it would raise their hopes. I'd end up the town pariah when I returned to London, leaving their golden boy, Liam, in the lurch. Everyone adored him. They'd take his side, and I'd never be welcome back.

And I realised I'd really like to be welcomed back.

'If I tell you something, you promise not to tell anyone?' I asked, meeting Lydia's eyes, the mirror of mine.

She frowned. 'Sure.'

'I kissed Liam,' I announced, cringing. Lydia's jaw dropped. 'It was a silly drunken mistake – my drunken mistake. He was horrified, and I am very, very embarrassed. So I guess I'm saying that Liam and I aren't going to happen. No chance.'

Lydia scratched her arm. 'That doesn't make sense.'

'Trust me, it makes perfect sense. Besides, he still has a thing with his ex,' I said casually.

I was not fishing for information at all.

Lydia snorted. 'Yasmin? No way. They are over, over.' Lydia's eyes widened. 'Did he tell you about Yasmin? 'Cos he never speaks about that. Not to anyone.'

Well, that made me feel marginally better.

'I met her. Thanks for the heads-up, by the way. He never even told me he had a daughter. Yasmin and Abigail came around, looking for Liam, and Yasmin basically slut shamed me, assuming I was one of his one-night stands –'

'Oh my god,' Lydia exclaimed, bordering on laughing, even though I knew she didn't find it funny.

'Yep. She basically implied I was a slag and then asked if Liam had been drinking.'

Lydia cringed. 'Yeah, I could see how she got there. If she didn't know you were staying in the annexe…'

'Who jumps to that conclusion? It all seemed a bit intense.'

Lydia sighed. 'Look. There is some… baggage between Yasmin and Liam. Hangovers from years ago, from when they broke up. I never got the full picture because Liam isn't the biggest talker.'

He always seemed pretty open to talk to me.

I bit my lip. 'What do you mean?'

175

Lydia glanced away. 'Liam should explain, but he went through the wringer a few years ago. He wasn't in a good place after Yasmin broke it off. But then, he got his shit together, quit drinking. Since then, he's been a fucking saint.' Lydia rolled her eyes. 'Borderline boring, if you ask me. Not that he's boring because he doesn't drink, no.' She glanced up to the ceiling, thinking, 'It's like he's shrunk his life. Taking on your project was probably the most rogue thing he's done in years. It's work or Abigail.' Lydia's eyes softened. 'He adores that kid.'

My stomach dropped. I'd accused him of being a bad dad. I'd completely projected all of my daddy issues onto someone who hadn't deserved it. Who was I to judge someone doing their best? Things were clearly a lot more complicated than I'd thought. Nothing was black and white.

'I've got to go,' my coffee clammered down on the table, 'I need –' I wasn't sure what I needed. To apologise? To hide? To make it right? Every option sat in my stomach heavy, like lead.

So I settled with, 'I've got to go,' and make my excuses to leave, pushing past the queue of people waiting for coffee.

Chapter Twenty-Three

My stomach rumbled, caving in on itself.

'Shit,' I muttered.

I opened and closed the kitchen cupboards for the third time that hour. Since Liam had started making all my meals, I didn't need to buy anything for the little kitchenette in the annexe. I checked my phone – eleven p.m. It was too late to order anything; all the restaurants on my phone were closed.

Fuck's sake.

I was pretty sure Liam was asleep, so I shoved my feet into my fluffy slippers and padded outside and down the stone path, mentally berating myself.

All day, I'd done a good job of avoiding Liam. I distracted myself. I reordered the spices in the kitchenette. I attempted to read, shifting in the armchair, but I was too restless sitting in one spot. I bit my lip until it bled and my nails down to the quick. I was in purgatory between a stupid kiss and an awkward conversation. I knew it was cowardly, but I couldn't bring myself to look at Liam. To sweep it under the carpet. To say I hadn't meant it.

A loud screech sounded from the trees, an owl.

'Shut it,' I hissed as I approached the bifold doors.

I tested the handle, and it lowered. Liam had left it open, and I winced as the door creaked. I made a note to lecture him about safety, but how much could I lecture him now? Were we even friends?

I tiptoed into Liam's kitchen, finding a loaf of bread in his bread bin. I thanked some random deity for carbohydrates and placed two slices in the toaster, my stomach roaring to life like a disused engine.

'Kat?' A low grumble came from behind me, and I whipped around, giving a short, sharp scream. Liam stood in the doorway in blue boxers and a dark grey hoodie with white sports socks on his feet. His large muscled thighs were on display, and I held back the thought of running my tongue across those muscles. No. Those were not appropriate thoughts about the man I threw myself at the night before. He ran his hands through his hair, revealing a line of defined muscles above his boxers.

Liam squinted, his hair sticking up at the back. He had no idea he was the perfect combination of cute and sexy right now.

'Are you okay?' he asked, his voice concerned.

He rubbed an eye, coming over to where I stood, frozen, at the toaster. He looked me over, sweeping down my bare legs in my pyjamas – the same floral silky ones I had been wearing when he'd come into my house unannounced. His eyes sat there for a beat longer, making me squirm.

He made a low sound, almost like a groan. The noise shot straight through me and lower. 'Are those the only pyjamas you own, Red?' he asked, voice gravelly. 'Or are you just trying to torment me?'

'Torment?' I arched an eyebrow, 'How exactly would I torment you?'

Liam took a step closer, and the tension was a thick fog around us.

'You have no idea.'

We stared at each other for a moment, until I was the one to blink.

'I'm sorry I woke you up, I'm just making some food. I didn't have anything at the annexe. You've been making so much food for me, so I haven't had to buy anything. I hope you don't mind –' The toaster popped, and I watched Liam's large hand lean from behind me to pick up the toast. His forearms brushed my shoulder. He must have asbestos hands because he didn't even flinch at the heat.

'I'll make you something,' he said, his breath moving my hair. It smelt minty, like he had just brushed his teeth.

Liam's hands came to my shoulders, mercifully covered, but he lingered there like he didn't know what to do next. Gently, he moved me to the side, pulling out a butter dish and pans out from the kitchen cupboards.

I smelt cedar, too. I thought it was his cologne, but maybe it was his body wash.

'Nduja cheese toasty sound good?' Liam asked, his eyes moving back to my legs, lingering there again.

'Yeah, that sounds amazing,' I admitted. 'Thank you.'

Silence fell in the kitchen, heavy.

'Kat –' Liam began, as I blurted out, 'So, have you always liked to cook –'

Liam stared at me for a moment before relenting. 'Yes.'

'Nice. Cool.' I winced. Fucking freak. More silence. I played with the hair bobble on my wrist, looking anywhere but Liam. Eventually, I snuck a peek at him, only to find him looking at me, a smirk on his face, his arms wide across the kitchen work-tops. The pan was slowly melting a knob of butter.

'You hate quiet, don't you?'

'No, I'm fine.'

'Red.'

'Okay, yes. I hate it. Could you please talk about something? Anything.'

'I wanted to be a chef.'

Oh. I hadn't expected that.

'Before the pandemic, I was about to open a restaurant with my brother. Ren and I had signed a lease on a unit around the corner. We'd built the concept and planned the menus. Ren was going to be the general manager and oversee the bar. I would be in the kitchen. The one thing – the only thing I had to do was tell my dad. I was dreading it. I put it off. So when the pandemic happened… well, it felt like a sign. The worst timing in the world to open a hospitality business. It wasn't a good time to take risks. So, I was saved from having to tell Dad.'

I tried not to get distracted by Liam's forearms as he grated cheddar, spread a dark red paste onto the bread and assembled them into sandwiches.

'I can't imagine being that close to something you wanted so badly.'

Liam shrugged, but I could see the sadness in his eyes, even as he glanced away.

'Would you do it again?' I asked. 'If you had the chance?'

Liam placed the sandwiches onto the hot pan, making it sizzle.

'I let him down.'

'Who?'

'My brother. I let him down. It's the reason he up and left the country. He'd quit his job –' Liam hissed as he accidentally burnt himself, turning over the toasty with his hands. I jumped up, striding over to him, instinctively.

'Careful,' I chided as I got a closer look at his hand, which was red and irritated.

'It's fine,' He smiled when I met his gaze. 'I do it all the time.'

We stared at each other a moment, and I wondered if he was

also aware of the last time we stood this close, in this kitchen. Liam was the first to look away, turning to flip over the second toasty, more careful not to burn himself this time.

'You should talk to him,' I said after a few seconds. 'About the restaurant. If it's something you want to do.'

Liam was quiet for a moment and then said, 'Yeah. Maybe.'

'Do you still want to do it?'

'I think about it all the time.' He kept his gaze down, and his cheeks flushed like he was confessing to something embarrassing. 'I think about menus before bed. Wake up the next day wanting to test them out at home.' He shook his head. 'But it's my fault. I chickened out.'

'You should talk to him even if it's an excuse to make things right. I know I wish I had with Dad. Before it was too late.'

Liam turned to me. 'Okay, Red, if it makes you happy. I will.' His tone didn't sound… happy. It was almost resigned. He stared down at the pan; one side of the toasty was a golden brown, the other sizzling away.

'You avoided me today.'

'I —'

'Why?' He turned to face me, his expression frank and earnest. He was so bloody direct. I took a deep breath in.

If he wanted direct, he'd get direct.

'I felt awkward about the kiss situation. And what I said after meeting Yasmin and Abigail. I didn't know what to say. Well, actually, I did know what I wanted to say.' I exhaled, preparing my speech. 'I'm really, really sorry about what I said this morning. I was a total bitch, and I really shouldn't have brought all my baggage into this. And I'm also sorry for the drunken kiss — that was a moment of true insanity that I don't think I will ever live down in my whole life. Like full-body cringing forever.'

'So you hid.'

'What? Did you hear what I just said?'

'I heard you, but I want to understand why you hid rather than saying that to me.'

'I was being a chicken.' I threw my hands up. 'A big fucking chicken.'

He nodded. 'Okay.'

'Okay?'

'If you need to hide for a while, that's fine. But let me know when you need space. I was worried. I didn't like it.' His eyes searched mine in a way that made my throat tighten.

'Okay. I will,' I said, dumbfounded.

Liam nodded and slid the toasty out of the pan and onto my plate, all crunchy yet gooey. I bit into it, tasting the sharpness of the cheddar cheese followed by the smoky, spicy taste of the nduja. It was a perfect midnight snack.

'Do you want some?' I asked around a mouthful.

'No, I'm fine,' He moved closer as I finished my last few bites. 'Did you eat today?' His eyes were roaming mine like he was looking for the answer in my skin or the colour of my eyes. I smelt cedar again, and I wanted to rub my head into his hoodie like a fucking cat.

Ugh, so pathetic.

This was a full-blown crush, and I felt utterly out of control. And I had enough I needed to control – for example, myself.

'Hmm?' Liam asked expectantly. Right. He'd asked a question.

'Ah – no.' I racked my brain. 'I don't think so. I had a coffee with Lydia today.'

Liam tutted. Actually tutted.

Was that hot? Did I want him to tut at me again?

Is that what he would be like in bed? Demanding, coaching, and maybe a little stern. Would he guide my hands to places he wanted them? Would he place my hand in his hair as he –

'Don't look at me like that, Red,' Liam said, his eyes darkened. 'Or I'm – no, we're – going to do something you'll regret in the morning.'

'What – what do you mean?'

'You know what I mean.' Liam stepped forward, taking the plate from my hands, his warm hands lingering on mine. His thighs brushed mine as he leaned forward.

'Oranges,' he murmured near my hair. 'That smell has been driving me insane. At work and then at home, too.'

'Has it?' I asked in a voice that sounded so foreign.

I craned my neck up to look at him. His eyes were tracking mine, gazing into me like he was trying to read me. I glanced down at his lips. They looked so full and soft. Liam's hand reached up to hold my jaw.

'This okay?' he murmured.

'Yes.'

He leaned down and ran his nose along my neck, making me arch into the touch. This – this was incredible. Liam hummed appreciatively and kissed my neck right where it was sensitive. I gasped at the contact. It was such a soft, delicate kiss, but my body did not register it as soft or delicate. It was burning up from the inside, white-hot.

'You make the sounds I imagined, too,' he said so quietly I could have missed it. My hands reached his biceps to pull him towards me. I needed more of him.

Liam's other hand grazed where my shorts met my thighs. 'Driving me mad in these shorts. When I saw you in them the first time at your house.' His hand moved further up, and I shivered. 'I didn't know where to look. I thought it was a good thing you kicked me out. It was a good thing you didn't want to hire me. Because at least I didn't have to see you in these shorts.'

183

I inhaled sharply, lust-addling my thoughts for a moment. Then, I remembered where I was and who said those words to me.

'Liam. What are we doing?'

It was like a pint of water had been thrown on Liam's head. He stepped back, and subtly rearranged his boxers.

'I'm sorry. I didn't mean to –' Liam ran his hands through his hair. 'I swore to myself I wouldn't go there, even when I wanted to. Then, I couldn't deny it anymore. Not when you felt so good in my arms when we danced.' His eyes followed my curves, lighting little fires across my hips and my legs. 'So I told myself I would ask you out properly once I spoke to Yasmin.'

I gasped. 'What – you. You want to ask me out?'

'Yas and I agreed to give each other a heads-up when we started seeing someone seriously so we didn't confuse Abigail. It's not the kind of conversation I wanted to have over the phone. They were due back tomorrow. But then they came over this morning –'

'Wait – Liam. What are you saying?'

Liam took the final step and closed the space between us. My hands couldn't help but wrap themselves into his hoodie. It was softer than I expected, and my squirrel brain idly wondered if he had a thing for cashmere. I could see the flecks of gold in his brown eyes and ridiculously long, dark eyelashes. His eyes searched mine, then got caught on my lips.

'I like you, Kat.'

'You like me.'

'I like you. I think I've liked you since you ran at me with a lamp.' His lips twitched. 'Or maybe since you called me a prick in the church car park. I liked you even more when you were determined to renovate a house all by yourself, with absolutely no experience.' He tucked a strand of my hair behind my ear. 'And I couldn't resist helping you because when your beautiful face drops in disappointment, it's like a punch to my stomach. I can't stand it.' Liam shook his head, like he still couldn't quite believe it himself. 'So yeah. I like you.'

'No, you don't.'

'Yes, I do.'

'I annoy you.'

'You don't annoy me.'

'Liar! I've seen it on your face!'

Liam gave me a small smile. 'I think you're entertaining. Chaotic. Captivating. But you don't annoy me. Usually.'

'"Usually" implies I annoy you sometimes.'

'You're annoying me now.'

'Prove it.'

'Okay.' He stepped back. 'Well, I agreed to renovate your house, and I saved you from a collapsing tent.'

'That was just to gloat.' I crossed my arms.

Liam smiled. 'That was a bonus. I fixed the lock on your house because I couldn't stand the thought of you not being safe. I make you dinner every night because I refuse to let you starve. And 'cos a bag of crisps doesn't count as dinner.' He took a step forward, standing in front of me. 'And there is the fact I can't stop thinking about you all the fucking time. I can't get you out of my head.'

Breath left my lungs at his words, but a bit of me couldn't believe what he was saying.

'But when I kissed you, you looked like you wanted the ground to swallow you up.'

Liam looked at me through dark eyelashes. 'I didn't want the ground to swallow me up. You were tipsy. And you'd had a rough day. You were grieving, and I didn't want to… take advantage. Knowing you might not be in control of all your decisions. That you might regret it.' Liam's face tightened. 'I've woken up and regretted things I've done before. It's not a pleasant feeling.'

185

'I'm sorry,' I said quietly.

'It's fine,' he said, twirling a lock of my hair around his finger.

My eyes were laser-focused on his earnest face as he shared this with me. This was so new, so delicate. We were both walking on a tightrope, both scared to look down. His eyes met mine, then flickered to my mouth. I felt a swoop in my stomach.

He leaned in, whispering in my ear. 'The kiss was everything, Kat. I haven't felt this way about anyone. Ever. So I wanted to be careful. I wanted to do things properly. I've spent so much time fucking things up, and I can't do that again. Not with you.'

His hand touched my elbow and traced it down to my palm tentatively. Exploring. Asking a question. I answered by touching him back. A flicker of relief on his face. It had taken a lot for him to confess.

His chest was heaving, his voice faltering.

Liam was nervous.

So, I made the first move.

I pushed up onto my toes and pressed my mouth against his.

Chapter Twenty-Four

The shock seemed to ripple through his body, briefly freezing him. His hands came up to my face and into my hair. The kiss started slowly and softly as if it was only supposed to be a short kiss, a stolen moment at midnight. My feet were between his, his hand holding a runaway curl at my cheek. His lips were firm and unrelenting against mine but not pushing further.

And I wanted further.

So, I ran my hands into his hair and pulled gently.

Liam listened, answering my demands. He pushed me up onto the kitchen worktop, standing between my legs. My chest flush against his. Then, he deepened the kiss, all tongues and teeth.

'Since I first saw you in this kitchen, I've wanted to press you up against this counter,' Liam said, kissing down my neck. 'Every day since, I wanted to taste you. See if you taste as sweet as you look.'

I made a noise that came out like a half moan, half complaint that he'd moved further from my lips. I was eating up these confessions like my life depended on it. Liam gently bit my neck, and a soft hum came from his throat. I pulled him closer again, drawing his lips to mine, where I wanted them. When his tongue brushed mine, I groaned.

He was good at this. Really good.

He touched, kissed, and pressed in all the right places. His arms roamed but kept me locked in on the counter. I was panting, wanting — no, needing — more from him.

'What do you want, Red?' Liam said, panting lightly. I glanced down and saw that he was impressively hard in his boxers.

'I want that,' I said, leaning over to caress him, but Liam's hand touched my wrist. He brought it up to his lips, kissing the sensitive part of my wrist.

'Not yet.' He grinned. 'It's my turn first,' he said, kissing down my arm. 'I've imagined these hands wrapped around my cock more times than I want to admit.'

I gave a surprised exhale at his words. 'Dirty.'

'You have no idea.' He leaned forward, bringing his lips back to my neck, my collarbone. I guided his hands up to my breasts, and he caressed my nipples, and then he pinched, making me gasp.

'I could get off to that noise,' he said, his eyes meeting mine, molten. I began to unbutton my pyjama top, slowly, watching Liam's face track every movement. His eyes tracked my breasts covered by my lace T-shirt bra. I knew he could see my nipples through the material by the way his eyes melted like chocolate. His hands trailed my waist, coming up and up, grazing over my nipples, making me squirm, needing more. I clasped my legs together, desperate. Liam watched the movement, a small smile on his lips.

'Can I?' he asked, and I nodded.

Liam pulled down my bra and pinched and teased. Then, he lowered his head and took my nipple into his mouth, making me arch.

'Beautiful,' he murmured into my skin, 'so fucking beautiful.'

'Liam —'

One of his hands made its way up my thigh, under my shorts, but lingered there. Waiting. Teasing.

'Please,' I panted, the cold of Liam's kitchen counter burned under my thighs.

'What do you need?' he asked, gently biting, inciting a gasp from me. 'I want to hear it.'

'Touch me. Please.'

Liam hummed in appreciation, as if he liked those words on my lips. He pulled my shorts down in one quick movement. He was just how I imagined. Confident. Maybe a little cocky.

'Kat.' Liam's voice was a warning.

'Yes.'

'Are you aware you aren't wearing anything under these shorts?'

'Yes.'

'And you walked into my kitchen like this?' Liam's head half collapsed onto my chest, giving me a sharp bite under my breast. A punishment. A reward. I wasn't sure which.

'I wasn't expecting this to happen,' I said, my voice low.

'You're a tease,' he murmured as he dropped a kiss on my thigh. He kept kissing his way up to my left hip. Then my right. Kept his hands and his mouth away from where I wanted him so badly.

'Liam,' I murmured, followed by a noise I'd never heard from my mouth before.

Liam chuckled, happy to take his time. He planted a kiss on me right above my clit, and I gasped. My hands went to his hair, pulling. Unconsciously, I opened my legs further and splayed on his counter.

'So responsive,' Liam said, lowering his mouth to plant another closed-mouth kiss on me. I moaned and glanced down to see Liam pressing himself into the counter like he was as desperate as me. Liam brought up his hands and ran his thumb across my clit, circling slowly, painfully.

'Yes,' I murmured. 'More.'

Liam sped up slightly and kissed my thigh again. He kept at the pace until I was panting, my pleasure spiralling up my spine.

'Kat,' Liam asked through the haze, 'can I taste you?'

'Yes.'

Liam slurred something like 'thank god' and lowered his mouth to me, swiping his tongue with precision. He hummed approvingly as he pushed his finger inside me, making me pull harder at his hair. I came, my hips rose off the counter, and I tried to hold back the moan, with little success.

It was white-hot and blissful.

Liam held me through it, murmuring words I couldn't comprehend, then gently kissed my throat, cheeks, and eyelids. Once my heart rate slowed, I sat up. Liam's gaze flickered over my face, taking me in. His chest was rising and falling, and I could see his pulse race in his throat. I reached for him, but he held my arms again.

'You know you've ruined my kitchen. I won't be able to look at this counter without remembering you spread out on it.'

He grinned. He looked so happy. Devastatingly happy. His gaze darted around my face like he was trying to memorise this moment.

Like I meant something to him.

My high dissipated.

I didn't want to lead him on. This had been amazing, but I was leaving. And something told me that Liam was not a 'casual' kind of guy.

I grabbed my shorts, shoving them on.

'Are you okay?' Liam asked, his face full of concern. 'Did I hurt you?'

'No, no.' I reached up and touched the stubble on his handsome face. 'That was amazing. Honestly, amazing. I just –' My smile dropped.

Liam's smile faltered.

I exhaled. 'I like you, too – a lot. But I don't want to lead you on, Liam. My plan is the same. I am moving back home, back to London. I have to. I have people relying on me at work. My mum and Graham…' I trailed off, hoping he got the picture.

'Right,' he said, glancing away.

'But we could keep things casual,' I suggested.

'Casual,' he repeated. 'You want to keep it casual.'

'Well, yes,' I offered meekly. I'd dealt my cards now; I couldn't take them back.

Liam exhaled, running his hand through his hair again.

His eyebrows pinched.

'Hey,' I said, pulling him closer by the arm. 'We don't have to do anything you're uncomfortable with. If it's not what you want –'

'I've done "just sex" before, Kat. It's not my style anymore.'

Disappointment flooded my chest.

'I understand.' I nodded. 'It's not something you're comfortable with. I get it.'

I met Liam's eyes. I could see the deliberation in them. He ran his hand through his hair. His eyes flickered across my face. Then, he gave a frustrated groan, moved and started pacing the kitchen.

'Why can't I say no to you?' he murmured, then walked back to me, pinching my chin between his thumb and forefinger. 'I have some conditions. We can keep things casual, like you want. But we're exclusive. No dating anyone else while you're here.'

'That kind of feels like the opposite –'

'And you let me take you on one date.'

'Liam, both of those things are literally the opposite of casual.'

'One date, Kat.' He smirked. 'I'm not asking you to marry me. Come on.'

I rolled my eyes. 'You are so pushy.'

'Are you going to be able to stop?' Liam asked, caressing my jaw, running a thumb across my lower lip. 'I'm not sure I'm going to be able to stop, even if I wanted to.'

My breathing became uneven. I could practically feel my eyes dilate. I wanted to wipe that smug look off his face with my lips. I wanted to push him away and pull him back at the same time. Liam was right. We'd started something with momentum, something inevitable. How were we going to keep our hands off each other?

People were going to know.

'Okay,' I said. 'I agree to your terms.'

Liam's lips lifted. 'Do we need it notarised?' He went to turn away. 'I can get a solicitor on the phone —'

'Stop it.' I laughed. 'Don't be a dick.'

'I think you like the look of my dick, actually. From the way you were ogling it, about' — he checked his watch — 'five minutes ago.'

My stupid eyes couldn't help but flicker down.

'Make that five seconds.' He laughed, kissing my jaw and neck. It was distracting, so distracting.

'I was thinking…' I sighed and leaned my neck to the side. 'We should keep this… discreet.'

Liam pulled back, frowning. 'Why?'

'Well' — I laughed — 'for one, everyone is taking bets. On us. Becoming a couple.'

Liam stilled. 'Who is everyone?'

'According to Lydia, the whole town. Or at least every member of the club. Apparently, standing up in front of everyone in that meeting was a declaration of love —' I snorted, but Liam didn't crack a smile.

'I'll make them stop.' Liam's lips were straight, and I missed his playful teasing. I took his hand, weaving his fingers through mine and watched as the touch softened his shoulders.

'It's not the bets. They can have their fun. I don't want to leave the town a pariah. People will side with you, their golden boy, not some random woman.'

'I don't care about people.'

'I do –' I said quickly. Too quickly. 'I want to be able to come back to visit. Lydia and my aunt and uncle. I don't want to burn bridges here.' I bit my lip. 'So if you think this will make that impossible—'

Liam pulled me into him, my face pressed into his hard chest. His arms came around me, warm and heavy.

'You're always going to be welcome here, no matter what. It doesn't matter about me. This is your home, too.'

'Thanks,' I murmured into his chest, squished.

Liam let me go and tucked my hair behind my ear.

'But even if it wasn't about that, Liam' – I winced – 'I don't do long-term. So keeping this casual—'

'I get it,' Liam interrupted, his lips pressed together. His eyes burned with intensity.

'Pinkie swear?' I raised my eyes to his.

He raised a dark eyebrow. 'This again.' Liam's pinkie wrapped around mine. 'I'd pinkie swear my life away to you, apparently.'

Chapter Twenty-Five

'Are you my dad's girlfriend?' Abigail asked as she slurped her cereal at Liam's kitchen island, her black Adidas trainers swinging from the barstool.

I sputtered into my coffee, dread settling in my stomach. What the hell was I supposed to say to that? No, Abigail, but your dad and I have a no-strings-attached relationship where he blows my back out and cooks me dinner.

'It's fine if you are,' Abigail said, smiling. 'Mum has a finance.'

'A fiancée?'

'Yeah, that one. Kirsty is really cool. She climbs rocks, and she's a woman. Some people at school think that's weird, but I tell them what Dad told me to say.' She puffed out her chest. 'Fuck off.'

I gave a stuttered laugh. 'Your dad told you to tell other kids to fuck off.'

Abigail nodded, her dark hair the exact colour of Liam's moving around her shoulders. 'Yep. Dad says they are bigamists.'

'Bigots.'

'Exactly.' She nodded solemnly. She shifted in her seat, impatient. 'So, are you his girlfriend? Because if you are, I need to invite you to my next football match. We're playing Heath Prep. They think they are so much better than us.' Abigail rolled her eyes. 'Snobs.'

I swear, this girl was ten going on twenty-five.

'Abs, are you ready to go?' Liam strode into the kitchen, his eyes flickered down my blue jeans and jumper, warming his dark irises. I was relieved to see him, not only because he was wearing a fitted green T-shirt that showed the outline of the chest I had yet to see naked but also so that I could yeet myself out of this conversation about girlfriends.

'Yep. I was just asking Kat if she would come to my football match now she's your girlfriend, and you know Kirsty always comes too –'

Liam winced. 'Abs –'

'I'll come.'

'Are you sure?' Liam asked. His eyes widened as if to say, *You don't have to.*

I turned to Abigail, her face bright and beaming. Who the hell could turn that face down?

'Are you going to win?' I asked, giving Abi a conspiratorial grin.

Abigail grinned back. 'Duh. I'm the *best* goalie. Dad taught me when I was five.'

'Then, I'll be there.'

Liam's face flickered with surprise, shepherding me to the door with a hand at my lower back. Abigail ran to the car, her book bag swinging from her hands.

He leaned in. 'You look beautiful, by the way. Those jeans –' His voice lowered.

'Dad!' Abigail shouted, making us jump. 'Hurry, we're going to be late!'

I laughed as Liam's eyes closed in a wince at Abigail's piercing voice. We all piled into Liam's van and dropped off Abigail at school first. She jumped out of the van, giving a wave.

'See you later, Kat!' she shouted and ran off to her gaggle of friends waiting by the school gate.

195

'She's cute,' I said, turning to Liam.

'She can be.' His lips upturned. Proud. That was a proud dad face.

'You don't have to come, if you don't want to,' Liam said a few moments later. 'To Abi's match. Don't let her twist your arm.'

'I'd like to,' I said. Even if it scared the shit out of me and it felt like we were teetering near 'girlfriend–boyfriend' territory already. The line that I had set in the sand. 'If that's okay with you and Yasmin. I don't want to overstep –'

Liam glanced at me. 'If you want to be there, you're coming.'

'Yes, boss,' I said, adding a flirty edge to my tone.

'Kat,' Liam warned.

'What?' I laughed.

'It's been three days. Don't push me.'

My cheeks burned.

Three days since Liam and I had made our agreement. Three days of missed opportunities. On Monday, Liam had set out earlier than me, flying off in his van to fix some crisis at the Joneses' extension. On Tuesday, Sandra took me for lunch and then to watch Ray, the high-maintenance jazz performer, at the club. Sandra and I silently elbowed each other, our shoulders shaking with laughter, as Ray's toupee flipped up as he stormed off in anger at someone talking too loudly during his set.

Then, last night, Liam helped Abigail with her homework and cooked dinner. I wanted to give them some space together, so I read my book in the annexe. Later in the evening, I got a knock at my door – Liam delivering a hot, lingering kiss and a foil-covered meal.

So we certainly hadn't had time to fully… explore our new agreement. And the tension was painful. It was like I was aware of every breath he took and the moments he was watching me from the corner of his eye, his gaze dragging across my legs or my breasts. I noticed how easily he lifted shopping bags out of the car, his muscles flexing. I smirked when I saw his eyes lingering on my mouth as I finished my breakfast and at his warning glare when I took a bit longer licking the spoon.

Liam's van came to a stop. I heard the creak of the brake handle. The click of our seatbelts.

Our lips met, and I gasped at the contact. Liam's hands were back in my hair. It was hard and fast. Liam's tongue stroking mine. Memories of Liam's head between my legs resurfaced, as they had every moment since.

Then, he was gone.

'Sorry,' Liam said, his forehead against mine. 'I've wanted to do that for three days.'

'You should have texted me.'

Liam winced. 'Abigail —'

'Yeah, it's weird,' I admitted.

'She's back at Yas's tonight.' He winced. 'I don't want it to come across like I want her out —'

'I didn't think that, Liam.'

'She is my priority. Always.' Liam's eyes flicked to me, serious. 'I just want to say that upfront. She will always be my priority.'

My throat thickened. God, that was such a lovely thing to say. I knew the bar was on the floor when it came to fathers. They just picked their kids up, and it had everyone swooning. But it didn't mean it wasn't lovely to hear from Liam's mouth. His expression was serious, like he was ready to jump into action for Abigail, no matter what. I knew from experience how lucky Abigail was to have a dad like that. I'd been without one.

'I know, Liam. I wouldn't expect anything less.'

He nodded. 'Come on.' Liam smirked. 'I need to get through a day without thinking of that mouth.' I snorted, and Liam's eyebrows shot up. 'I'm not joking. I've got a serious case of blue balls.'

'Such a baby.' I shook my head. I leaned across the console, grabbing a fistful of his soft hair. 'If you get through today, maybe I'll come around tonight and –'

'Careful how you finish that sentence,' Liam said, his eyes burning.

I leaned closer and whispered, 'I'll get on my knees and use my mouth.'

Liam closed his eyes and groaned; the noise shot straight to my core.

Liam shook his head, and a grin overtook him. 'You don't know what you just started.'

★

With the first fix on the electrics and plumbing completed, with my cute new antique bronze switches hanging off the walls, Liam enlisted Danny, a plasterer. Danny was in his mid-thirties, with a stocky build, a moustache, and a mullet. His strange blend of New Zealand and Mancunian accents made me want to smile. As Danny set up his radio, Liam got a call to pick up the bathroom materials, leaving me twiddling my thumbs. I paced from room to room, energy humming around my brain and legs.

I bit my lip.

God, I hated having nothing to do.

I poked my head around to see Danny drilling the plasterboard into the walls.

An idea hit: a cartoon lightbulb above my head.

'Danny,' I said, my voice going sing-song.

Danny raised an eyebrow when I asked him. But, like most people being asked about their skills, he enjoyed teaching me and gained enthusiasm with each question I threw at him. He taught me how to fix the plasterboard, mix the plaster mixture with a power stir and then apply a thin coat of plaster over the joints. As we chatted away, I learnt that Danny moved from New Zealand five years ago and had lived all over the UK. He settled in Manchester because he liked the city and had supported Manchester United from afar since he was a kid.

He raised his bushy eyebrows. 'Liam mentioned you were from the Big Smoke. Are you liking it here?'

'Yes,' I said, and I realised I was telling the truth. 'Even if it's a bit mad here.'

'It's barmy.' Danny grinned. 'But I wouldn't live anywhere else.' He arched an eyebrow at me. 'London is mad expensive.'

I nodded. 'It is.'

'And everyone is fucking rude.'

'Liam said the same thing.' I rolled my eyes. 'It's not that bad. People are busy – not rude.'

'Trust me; this town is full of busy people – mainly busybodies. But we still have time to say hello and ask how you are.' Danny shrugged. 'I wouldn't be able to do it.'

'Live in London?' I asked, a bit incredulous.

'I lived in a small town back home. I never liked cities. I get why people do, but even going into Manchester stresses me out. I only go to do my Christmas shopping.'

'On Christmas Eve?'

'Yep.' Danny grinned.

As I began to mix the plaster, I thought about Danny's and Liam's aversion to London. I didn't get it. But then, I hadn't known any different growing up. It was natural to move to London. Could I even imagine myself living somewhere else? I tried to picture myself in this house – living here in this town. I could maybe go freelance, but I was so sure I would fuck it up. But then, a slower pace of life sounded lovely. I could do exactly what I wanted to do. No more shitty meetings with clients I hated. No more packed Tubes. No more roommates and their crusty Super Noodles on the kitchen worktop.

It took an hour to complete one wall in the front room. Danny was laughing at my shoddy attempt when I smelt cedar and rain. Liam. I turned my head enough to see him from my periphery. He was leaning on the doorway, his hands crossed over his chest.

Danny's hands moved to mine, guiding me. 'Just go to the edge.'

I laughed as I tried and failed to push the mixture to the corners of the wall. I couldn't quite angle my wrists in the right way. I stepped back, assessing my efforts. The white mush was patchy and uneven. It looked more like one of those hipster bars in Camden with exposed plaster and Edison bulbs. Fine for a dive bar. Not entirely the vibe for a house someone was going to buy.

'Oh my god, this is terrible.'

'You're a natural,' Danny replied, humour in his voice.

I attempted to make it better, spreading the remainder of the plaster, trying to keep it all even. Once I was done, I turned around to look at Danny.

'What do you think? Any better?'

Danny grinned. 'I've seen worse.'

I snorted. 'Thanks.'

I turned to ask Liam and paused. He was looking at Danny with an intense, watchful expression. His eyes weren't moving from him. A light blush on his cheeks. His gaze shifted to me and darkened with something else. Desire. He was… god. Liam's eyes were dark and stormy.

Jealousy.

Liam was jealous.

I glanced at Danny. His eyes were shifting between Liam and me as fast as lightning, and a new realisation dawned on his face. His smile turned feral.

'Alright, boss?' Danny said, humour at the edge of his voice. 'I was just teaching Kat some tricks of the trade. She's a natural.'

Danny bumped my shoulder.

'I don't remember paying you to flirt, Danny.'

God, it was immature to find it sexy. I needed to grow up. I was a feminist, for fuck's sake. I didn't need some alpha dickhead getting all possessive. But damn. The murderous look on Liam's face sent a thrill up my spine. I'd never had anyone jealous because of me, so sue me. It was a novel experience, the way Liam's eyes tracked Danny's shoulder touching mine.

Danny didn't flinch or cower. He was grinning. He must be so used to dealing with Liam's moods that it made him invincible. Or reckless.

Danny shrugged. 'You know me. I can't resist chatting up a pretty girl.'

'She's a woman, not a girl. And I do know you,' Liam seethed. 'Get back to work.' Liam angled his head. 'Kat, a word?'

Liam turned on his heel and stalked from the room, and I couldn't help but stare at his arse in those utility trousers. I should be angry at him for being petty and territorial, but with an arse like that, I couldn't stay angry forever.

Danny gave me a look. 'I wonder what's got into him today?'

'I'll go check on him,' I said, shuffling from the room, leaving Danny to finish the wall.

'Mhm,' Danny said, returning to fix the wall.

I went into the hallway in search of Liam. A hand pulled me through into the next room, the dining room, and back against a solid chest. The sun came through the window, illuminating the dust and naked floorboards under our feet. Liam's hands were around my waist, holding me to him, my back to his chest. I held back a shiver at his breath at my ear.

'Would you say yes?' Liam's voice rumbled. 'If he asked you out? Because he wants to. I can tell.'

I gave a breathy laugh. 'Why does it matter?'

'Are you trying to make me jealous?' Liam said, voice low.

I smirked. 'That's all it took —'

'I want to spank you so bad right now,' Liam said into my ear, eliciting a shiver through me. I never thought I was into… that. But when Liam said it with a teasing edge to his voice, I was in.

'Would you say yes?' Liam asked. 'Tell me.'

'No.'

'Why?'

'Because of you.'

'Good girl.' Liam whipped me around and pressed me against the door. We moved together, our lips meeting, a clash of tongues and teeth. His weight pressed down on me, pushing me harder into the door. Liam's hands roamed all over me. Then, he pulled back and gave me an earnest look. This was real Liam. No resting bitch face. No schooled emotions.

He was unguarded and genuine.

'You were laughing with him.' Liam tucked a strand of my hair behind my ears. 'Those easy laughs that you make me earn.' He leaned forward, planted a kiss on my neck, and followed it with a nip at my collarbone. He pressed himself against me, and I could feel him, hard, against my thigh.

'Liam.'

'You know what he can't get you to do?'

'What?' I panted.

'He can't make you moan, Red.' Liam's lips captured mine again.

It was like a battle of who could turn on who. He turned me to press me against the wall, and I palmed him, making him grunt. I smiled as he nipped at my neck and whispered my name. Liam's leg went between mine, putting pressure where I desperately wanted it, and I was struck by how ready I was. It would usually take me half an hour of foreplay — at least — to be this turned on, especially when I was so easily distracted, my brain running off on tangents. But Liam had a way of focusing me on my body, how it moved for him, and how it reacted to him.

'We can't here,' I panted, Liam's lips trailing down my neck. 'Danny will hear.'

'You'll have to be quiet, then,' Liam said, pressing his thigh into me, drawing a moan from my lips. I moved against him, desperate. I would be embarrassed later about the noises I was making.

'Yeah, that's it. Ride my leg.' He whispered the last part in my ear, making my head roll back.

I was panting, and the delicious friction of Liam's thigh between my legs scrambled my thoughts. Something about Danny being a wall away, about this being so... public. It wound me up tighter. I was close.

Liam moved his leg, and I moaned. Liam's grin widened.

'Good girl,' Liam said, slipping his hands between my legs. He touched me, and I jolted at the touch. I was so sensitive.

'So wet.'

Liam touched me in circles, and I moaned louder, even as I tried to hold it back. A large, calloused hand came over my mouth, trapping the sound. The movement shoved me over the edge. I saw stars and constellations. The whole fucking cosmos.

Liam murmured, 'Good girl' and 'Fucking yes'.

My heart rate began to slow. Liam held me closer, his hands trailing over my back in soothing patterns.

A clang of a tool hitting the wooden floorboards echoed. Reality hit about where we were and who was in the room next to us. Danny.

Oh my god.

I tilted my head up to Liam. He looked down, unconcerned. Peaceful. I was anything but.

'I can't believe we just did that with him next door,' I hissed. 'Do you think he heard?'

Liam's face split into a grin. 'I hope he did.'

'Liam!' I whacked him on the chest.

Liam's grin widened, and he ran a thumb across my lower lip. 'You started this, Kat. Remember that.' He pulled me back into a hug, his smell surrounding me. I wanted to stay there forever, wrapped up in post-sex bliss. It struck me then that I'd never felt this level of contentment with anyone in my entire life. I was slipping, slowly and all at once, into a life here with Liam. What had I started? And more importantly, how would it end?

Chapter Twenty-Six

Kat's To-Do List

- Prep for design meeting with Liam
- Collect paint samples & fabrics
- Call Mum back
- Do <u>not</u> get attached

'Twenty-two thousand pounds?' I choked, coughing.

My eyes shifted to the designs on the screen of EH Kitchen and Bathrooms. Liam's hand came up and gently patted my back. The shop was brightly lit, the light bouncing off the white quartz countertops they had on display. At the desk, Andrea, the designer, thrummed her pink acrylic nails against her desk as she bit her lip. We had spent the past hour designing the new bathroom and kitchen at Liam's favourite shop, EH Kitchen and Bathrooms.

'It's owned by a local couple, Andrea and Ron,' he explained on the journey while his large hand rested on my thigh. 'They are the only place I go for fittings 'cos I know they'll be the best.'

I'd walked in, excited about the show bathroom on display with a huge roll-top bath. Liam was welcomed like a hero returning from war. Hugs and slaps on the back. I shrunk back a little. It was yet another place where everyone knew everyone. It was like overhearing people speak another language.

'I know, it's dear,' Andrea said, glancing up from the screen, 'the fixtures you picked are top of the range, you see.'

My eyes flicked to Liam. He rubbed his hands across his jaw. The long stubble was turning into a beard, and it annoyingly suited him more. It seemed to bring out his brown eyes. I was worried he wasn't shaving because he seemed to spend every hour at my house these days. We'd had a burst pipe, which caused a leak in the bathroom. Then, the next week, he found rotten floorboards that needed replacing in the kitchen, too. Yet, none of it fazed him.

I'd been the one to panic. But he told me in reassuring tones and soft caresses that it was fine. He repeated that they were minor hiccups and they were still running to the timetable.

Liam frowned at me, quizzical.

What?

I shook my head.

Nothing.

God, the navy T-shirt he was wearing today made him seem so… fuckable. It made his arms look delicious. After our public rendezvous at the house, I had managed to sneak out without seeing Danny's amused face and with my dignity intact – barely. In an act of revenge, I teased Liam on the way home, palming him while I whispered exactly what I would do to him once I got my hands on him. He turned to me, his eyes blazing. 'Wanna put your money where your mouth is?' His eyes flickered down to my lips. I grinned and checked my wrist. 'I believe you are late for the Joneses.'

He swore filthily, sporting a huge erection, and pulled off the drive while I giggled my way into the house for a nap.

Since then, we hadn't spent any time alone. Abigail had the flu, so I volunteered to stay home with her when Liam was forced to firefight problems with the Joneses' extension. Liam had wanted to stay with her, and I could see it was eating him up. He asked if I was sure about fifty times. Once I convinced him, he made Abigail's favourite chicken soup, and I finally shoved him out the door. Abi and I played Animal Crossing all morning. Then, I drafted the rebrand for HBC while Abi slept, her cheeks pink with fever.

When Liam returned, smelling of sweat and rain, Abigail announced she had had a great day and wanted to stay with us for the rest of the week. As much as I wanted some alone time with Liam, I couldn't help but bask in the glory of her words. It was fucking hard to get a pre-teen to like you. They had a discerning taste, but I had passed the test. Plus, it was nice having her around. Liam was playful and light when she was around. It was like Abigail lifted his mood like no one else could – not even me. Abigail got away with murder. Liam let her paint his nails. I finally got to braid his hair, making Abigail snort Coke out of her nose at the sight.

'I could see if we could bring down the price, maybe,' Andrea replied, her eyes scanning the 3D renderings of the designs.

I felt stupid. I proudly showed Andrea my plans, gushing over the dark blue cabinet doors, the herringbone tiles, and the fluted glass cabinets, even though I knew the latter might not be the most practical choice. The finger smudges would be a bitch. My eyes lit up when Andrea mentioned a wine fridge, and I couldn't help but hurl a yes and immediately ask where we could fit it. Liam sat beside me, his lips twitching at my excitement.

For the bathroom, I picked a big roll-top bath with simple white tiles on the floor but accented with a half wall of green tiles on the walls. Liam and I argued over the old mid-century dresser I wanted to source and turn into a double sink with a round mirror and wall lights on either side.

Liam shook his head. 'The vanity unit will be a nightmare.'

'What do you mean?' I recoiled.

'The wood. It's not good in bathrooms. It warps easily and gets watermarks. It's not practical.'

'But it's beautiful. And I can repurpose an old dresser. It will probably be cheaper.'

'Cheaper, apart from all the hours it will take me to fit the sink.'

I leaned in. 'If you can't do it, maybe Danny could help,' I said sweetly.

Liam's eyes jumped to mine, a challenge in them that made my blood hum.

Eventually, I won.

Liam sighed. 'I'll do it, but I warned you. Don't complain when the thing is covered in water stains.'

I grinned. 'Thank you.'

And now, all my hard work convincing him was pointless – there was no way I could afford this design. I'd got so caught up that I'd forgotten to mention the budget. Even Liam was animated, chipping in to recommend particular appliances he'd fitted before and rated. I imagined him behind the huge range oven and flinched.

Throughout all of this, I wasn't picturing an imaginary family at the kitchen island or kicking off their shoes to sit on the sofa. They didn't have blank faces.

I was imagining Liam and me.

I imagined him standing at that oven, which sparkled silver, with that beautiful, determined look when he was cooking something new. I imagined us dancing in the kitchen to Glenn Miller like we had at the club. I was imagining a life with him.

I swallowed hard.

This was not happening. It couldn't happen. There were no strings attached. It was casual.

But as I glanced at Liam, I realised he was watching me, his eyebrows drawn together. His hand came down on my thigh and squeezed.

'You okay?' My heart fluttered. Stupid heart.

'There's no chance I can afford this,' I said, keeping my voice low so Andrea couldn't overhear.

'Andrea.' Liam glanced up, a stubborn angle to his jaw. 'Do you think you could sharpen your pencil on this?'

My head whipped to him. 'What are you doing?' I whispered.

'Trying to get you a better deal,' he whispered back.

'Oh.'

Andrea clicked her teeth. 'I can try, Liam. But it's tricky with customs. You and Kat have picked out some of our more expensive European fittings – the bath and shower.'

'If you can do anything, I'd appreciate it,' Liam said, and Andrea nodded, rising out of her office chair and said she'd call the company and see if any of the prices had come down in the last few months.

'I can't believe you just did that,' I said, flushed.

'What? You never haggled before?'

'No.' I'd never had anything to haggle for.

Liam tutted. God, I wish he'd stop doing that. 'You shouldn't accept the price the first time. There's always some wiggle room somewhere.'

'No.' I shook my head. 'I couldn't do that. It's too embarrassing.'

He chuckled. 'Andrea is used to it. Besides, I bring them a lot of business.'

'Don't you think a lot of yourself?' I teased.

Liam smirked. 'I'm just telling the truth, Red.' He leaned forward, brushing his thumb across my lips. Blood rushed to my cheeks. 'Did I tell you how beautiful you look when you're excited about something? Your eyes light up, a bright blue. For the past hour, I've wanted to take you home and see how I can make you look at me like that.'

'Yeah?'

'Yeah.'

Liam's eyes were like soft brown sugar, flitting from my eyes to my lips.

'If you want the designs, we can make it happen. You just tell me, and I'll fit whatever you want. As long as that look stays on your face, I'll move mountains.'

Air whooshed out of my lungs.

I jumped when Andrea's voice shouted through the shop. 'Fifteen per cent discount, not including sale items.'

She shuffled back to her seat, the noise creaking. 'Brings it down to… about nineteen grand.' She glanced up. 'Or we can redesign something more cost-effective.'

Cheaper. Simple.

I refused to make the house one of those soulless grey temples that landlords charge a million pounds a month to rent. But it didn't mean I couldn't make the fittings cheaper. The designs were more extravagant than they needed to be, that was certain. I'd picked the gold fittings in the bathroom to complement the dark green tiles. Those cost more than standard chrome, I was sure.

I bit my lip.

'Hey,' Liam said, his eyes meeting mine. 'Whatever you want.'

He meant it. Liam would do whatever I asked. He would fit whatever I wanted. And I had a sneaky feeling he would accept whatever I wanted when it came to us, too. He was solid and reliable, like the foundations of a house.

And I was not.

I was flighty and chaotic, and I always changed my mind. I would mess him around and leave a path of destruction in my wake. I knew it. I mean, even Mum didn't believe in me and she was supposed to love me unconditionally. I needed to nip this whole fluttering heart situation in the bud. This was supposed to be a bit of fun.

I faced Andrea. 'Let's go with the cheaper option.'

★

Liam and I walked across the grey car park to his van. Over the past half hour, Andrea clicked 'empty basket' on my entire design, and I felt like I'd drooped like a tulip out of water.

'Kat,' Liam said from the driver's seat, the grey sky flickering past us. Even the weather knew it was a miserable day. 'You're killing me here.'

'Sorry,' I said, sitting up straight and smiling. 'I'm fine.'

'No, you're not.' Liam's lips were in a fine line. 'Come on, let it out.'

I inhaled and, on the exhale, blurted out, 'I just had this vision, and now I realise how stupid and naive it was to get attached. The whole time, this was about profit. Nothing more. But those designs we picked after' – I laughed – 'I hate that I had to choose the cheaper kitchen, not just because it's ugly, but because I know it won't last very long. It will get worn down and look tired in a couple of years. It's not going to last.'

Liam nodded, his hand coming over to my thigh. 'I'm sorry, sweetheart.'

'It's okay, really.' I sighed. 'I think I'm just feeling a bit home-sick, maybe –' I thought about London and my mum and work. And I didn't feel anything, really. Some residual guilt over lying to my mum for so long and dodging her calls. I thought about Willa – 'I think I miss Willa.'

'Your friend?'

'My best friend.'

'How did you meet?'

'We met at uni years ago. Wills turned up to lectures fifteen minutes early with perfectly blow-dried hair and matching stationery. She was sat at the end of a row, so when I turned up late, having slept through my alarm, I sat myself in the closest seat, next to her.' I smiled at the memory of us – eighteen, young and clueless, with so much ahead of us. 'We clicked. It's thanks to Willa that I have a degree. She helped keep me organised and offered to body double with me at the library.'

Liam frowned. 'Body double? Is that like… sexual –'

I laughed. 'No. I can concentrate better when someone is working beside me. I suppose it's like I mimic them.'

'Right. And you miss Willa, being up here?'

'This is the longest we've not seen each other' – I racked my brain – 'probably since uni.'

'Wow.'

'Yup.'

'I haven't seen my mates in six months.'

'Oh my god.' I shake my head. 'You should text them and arrange something! One of you is probably waiting for the other to do it first. Typical men.'

Liam shrugged. 'Never thought about it, I suppose.' We fell silent as we flitted through traffic and headed to the house.

Liam broke the silence. 'Why not just have what you want?' Liam's eyes flickered between mine and the traffic ahead. 'It's your life.'

He made it sound so simple.

'I need to be sensible,' I said. 'I'm not living there. It's just to make sure that I make a bit of profit. Whoever buys it will probably hate the designs anyway.' I shrugged. 'It's better this way.'

Liam frowned. 'They'd have no choice but to love it.'

I gave a small smile. 'Thanks. But it's pointless anyway.'

Liam swerved into a road on the left. My hands hit the dash. I swear I felt the tyres lift off the tarmac.

'Liam! What the hell?' I turned to find a manic grin on his face.

Liam's smile widened. 'I know the perfect thing to cheer you up.'

Chapter Twenty-Seven

Heath Antiques smelt as dank and dark as it looked. In the old converted mill, spindle-back chairs were stacked up to the ceiling next to rows of buffed Chesterfield sofas. Mid-century coffee tables were next to Victorian bureaus. It was dark, but when light did appear, it burst from murky skylights that hadn't been cleaned in years. Everywhere I looked, there was another token from the past – a gaudy neon sign or a dining table with swear words etched into the wood. I was in heaven. Liam was right.

My miserable haze was gone the moment I stepped inside.

'Let's pick out this dresser you keep harping on about,' Liam said, his lips twitching. He raised a finger and bopped it on my nose. 'And you are going to haggle.'

My mouth fell open. 'I can't. And I thought you said it was "impractical",' I said, impersonating Liam's stupid voice.

Liam's eyes twinkled. 'Firstly, I don't sound like that. Secondly, it *is* impractical. But for you, I will add a glass top, so it doesn't get damaged. And thirdly…' He stepped forward, his steel-capped boots meeting mine. His gaze simmered with determination. 'You are going to haggle.'

I crossed my arms. 'You'd do that?'

'Make you haggle? Jesus, Red, the guy who runs this place is a softie. He'll probably give you anything for free once he sees you in those jeans.'

'What — no, I mean fit the glass on top —' I glanced down at my outfit. Not particularly sexy, I didn't think.

'Of course.' Liam pulled me closer.

He was so touchy-feely at the moment, and I kind of loved it. Most guys I'd dated in the past were against physical touch until I was in their bed.

Liam's hands caressed down my arms and grazed along my waist. 'I meant what I said.' His thumb grazed my jaw. 'Anything you want, you can have.'

'Anything, huh?' I grinned, looking up to find him staring down at me. He had a soft look on his usually hard features.

'Anything,' he said, his voice low.

I turned away, my hands on my hips, facing the warehouse. Liam cleared his throat, and I could feel disappointment rolling off him in waves.

Too much. It was too much.

Liam's voice said from behind me, 'Let's test that haggling, huh?'

We spent an hour weaving through the rows and rows of furniture. And while I wanted to take everything home with me, I hadn't found the perfect dresser yet. However, I had found a vintage Ercol dining table with matching chairs, an amazing old dresser that would be perfect for the hallway and glass whisky decanters I wanted to take home. Each time, Liam pulled me gently away, reminding me to stay focused.

I tried my best even as the furniture chanted to me. *Take us home. Take us home.*

'This was a mistake.' Liam shook his head. 'You want everything.'

'I want everything.' I mock-gasped. An antique gold cash till sat on top of a wooden table, the huge leaver you'd pull to open up the till still intact. My hands ran over the metal numbers, pressing them down. They still moved. 'Oh my' — I clutched my chest — '*this* would look so cool in your restaurant.'

Liam arched an eyebrow. 'My restaurant.'

'Yeah.' I waved a hand. 'When you get round to it. And finally speak to your brother.'

'If you have anything to do with it, it's going to look like the jumble sale at Abigail's school.'

It didn't escape me that he skirted around the mention of his brother.

I grinned. 'You have such little faith in me.'

Liam huffed. 'Trust me. When it comes to this stuff, I have complete faith in you.'

'This stuff?'

'I've seen your plans.' He glanced at me. 'They are good. I've worked with interior designers – some good, some bad. I can tell you're talented, even if you need a dose of reality now and then. If I do open my restaurant—'

'Oh—'

Liam held up a finger. 'If. I said if. *If* I open the restaurant. You'll be the first person I'll call.'

'To design it?' I gasped.

'Yep. Only the best.'

The heart flutters were back. He had no idea what those words meant to someone who doubted themselves on a daily basis.

I smiled. 'Thanks. Sometimes I think about—' I paused. 'I think about doing this – as a job,' I said in a rush. 'It's just a stupid idea, and I probably wouldn't make any money. Then I'd end up not being able to pay any bills, and then the bank would repossess my house, and I'd end up destitute. Or worse, back living with my mum and Graham.'

The corner of Liam's lips rose. My face burned.

I turned away. 'Forget it—'

'No, no,' Liam said and shifted my shoulders to face him. 'Why would you think that?' His gaze searched my face. 'Why wouldn't it be a success?'

My mum's voice echoed around me.

Don't take risks. Stop being impulsive. Be sensible, Katherine.

'I wasn't brought up by people who took risks.' I bit my lip. 'And I have a reputation for being… flighty. I've had some failed attempts at businesses before. Stupid stuff, really. A jewellery business. Candle making. Then, I thought I wanted to be a childminder. But all of them failed. Or I failed.'

Liam let out a deep breath.

'Just ignore me. I'm oversharing.'

'Hey,' he said, his arms trailing down mine. 'You aren't oversharing. I asked, remember?' He laced his fingers through mine, walking us down the aisle with old wooden benches. 'Just because someone else doesn't like taking risks doesn't mean you shouldn't. And those other attempts don't mean you'll fail again. And if you do' – he shrugged – 'who cares? If you have about a million careers in your lifetime, who cares, as long as you are happy?'

I snorted. 'Well, the tax man might be a bit concerned.'

'If it means anything, I think you'd be amazing.' He glanced at me. 'You're incredibly creative and driven. Your brain might be hardwired a bit differently, but I've seen the dogged determination when you face your problems.' He smiled, shaking his head ruefully. 'I've been victimised by it, remember?'

I rolled my eyes, my cheeks blushing at his words.

We stopped near some huge wardrobes that looked straight out of a C. S. Lewis novel.

Liam's thumb grazed my jaw, forcing me to look at him.

'I mean it, sweetheart. You clearly don't hear it enough. You are incredible.'

Half of me wanted to make a joke, laugh it off. But the other half wanted to press my face into Liam's chest and pull him close.

I wanted to hear him say things like that again and again. I wanted to bask in those words and ruminate if he really meant them. I wanted to let him prove to me he did mean them.

But I couldn't do that.

I couldn't have him.

So, instead, I showed him. I was much better with my body than words. I pressed my palm against his chest, pushing him against a bookcase in the dark part of the warehouse somewhere that no one would spot us.

'Kat —' he said, and I watched his cocky grin morph into hot desire.

I was determined to make him feel something. I wanted to repay the debt of his sweet, kind words.

My hands roamed across his chest, and I leaned up to kiss him hard and fast. His tongue met mine, and he groaned. His hands came up into my hair, pulling gently.

'What are you playing at?' he murmured into my ear, kissing down my neck.

'Oh,' I said, trying to sound casual, but my voice was pure gravel, 'I'm just getting my own back.'

I sank to the floor, on my knees, and started on the buttons of his jeans.

'Kat —' Liam's voice was a groan and a warning in one. 'You don't — oh, fuck.' I palmed him over his boxers, and his head fell against the bookcase. I grinned, enjoying the power, even on my knees. I touched him a few more times, feeling how big and hard he was. I wasn't sure I could take all of him in my mouth.

'Are you just playing with me?' Liam said, reaching into my hair and holding me there. His eyes were so fucking soft with desire, and I didn't think anyone had ever looked at me like that before.

Liam's thumb reached across my lips, and I opened my mouth instinctively. His thumb dipped into my mouth.

'I've thought about this too many times,' he rasped – molten hot desire. 'You, on your knees. For me.'

I pulled him out of his boxers, rewarding him with a kiss for his confession. He flinched. His palm tightened in my hair. I took him with my mouth, looking up at his face, watching his eyes roll back.

'Fucking hell,' he said hoarsely, that soft accent becoming more pronounced.

I worked him in my mouth, moving my hands in tandem. Liam's hands became gentler, weaving through the curly strands. I glanced up and found him looking down at me with a mix of pure lust and something else – reverence.

Liam brushed my cheek.

'Gorgeous,' Liam said, his dark eyes going hazy. 'You have no idea, fuck, Red. You look so –' He made a frustrated noise. 'Those eyes on me are going to make me come.'

I moved faster until Liam gave a filthy swear.

'Baby,' he said, and I hated how much I liked the words from his filthy mouth, 'if you don't stop, I'm going to come.'

I hummed and kept going. I wanted to do this, to take him to the edge. Make him remember this, remember me, even if this strange arrangement was temporary.

Liam swore as he came, his eyes closing, his head back. I weathered through it, taking him deep and tasting him on my tongue. I grinned as Liam pulled his boxers up and breathed heavily. He looked completely devastated, like his brain had been scrambled. His hair was dishevelled where he'd run his hand through it.

'You're the devil.' Liam picked me up, moving with remarkable speed for someone who had just come undone on their feet.

'My turn.' Liam smirked, hauling me to him, slanting his lips to mine.

'Hello?' A male voice echoed through the warehouse. 'Is someone there?'

'Fuck,' Liam said, his hands moving quickly to button up his trousers. His hand ran through his hair. He turned to me. 'Do I look like I've just had the best blowjob of my life?'

I barked a laugh, dissolving into giggles.

'Oi, you,' Liam whispered, a smile taking over his face, 'I'm serious. You seduced me, and Antony is going to know.'

'Now you know how I felt!' I said, laughing indignantly.

'Hello?' The man's voice was coming closer.

Liam grabbed my hand. 'Come on, let's show ourselves before Ant gets the exorcist over. Again.'

Liam was leading me down the aisle when something caught my eye. My hand fell out of Liam's as I gravitated towards a sideboard in the perfect shade of warm brown – not too dark, not too light.

It was perfect.

I sighed lovingly. 'This is the one.'

I ran my hand over the wood. It was a bit uneven in some places, but the wood's gloss told me it had been sanded back and refinished.

'Yeah?' Liam gave me a small smile.

'Yeah.'

'Antony,' Liam shouted, making me jump.

'Kevin?' Antony called back, sounding confused.

'It's Liam. I'm here with my –' Liam's eyes widened. 'My friend. She's looking at this sideboard.'

'Okay, I'll come over. Are you by Chucky?'

'Chucky –' Liam's hand came to his chest. 'Fucking hell.' I followed his gaze to find a life-size version of Chucky brandishing a huge knife hanging from the rafters above us.

'Was that there the whole time?' I hissed.

A tall light-skinned Black man rounded the corner, an easy smile on his face. His eyes widened when he spotted me next to Liam.

Antony held back a smile and offered me his hand. 'Antony. You can call me Tony. Nice to meet you, Liam's *friend*.'

'Kat.'

'Kat,' he repeated back to me melodically, still shaking my hand.

'Tony. How much for this one?' Liam said, his face still a little red. 'We'll take it today; I've got the van.'

Antony smirked, mock frowning. 'Do you usually escort your customers around reclamation yards, Liam?' He turned to me, holding up his hands. 'This must be a new service.'

Liam sighed. 'How much, old man?'

'Hey' – he smacked him over the head – 'respect your elders.' Antony turned to survey the furniture. 'That's four hundred.'

I coughed. Jesus, that was more than I'd expected. Liam turned to me, his eyebrows high.

'Go on then. Name your price.' Liam smirked.

My eyes widened. I could feel my face turning red as Antony and Liam stared at me expectantly. This felt like too much pressure.

'Er –' I stuttered.

Liam's palm came to my back, touching gently.

Go on, it seemed to say, *you can do it*.

'I could pay you two hundred.'

Antony scoffed. 'Are you trying to swindle me, Kat? You know this is a completely unique sideboard. I sanded it down and refinished it myself. It took me hours. You won't find one in better nick.'

'Oh –' I was about to take back my offer, but Liam's hand came around my waist and squeezed as Antony exhaled noisily.

'Wait,' Liam murmured in my ear.

Antony clapped his palms together. 'I can do three hundred. But no lower.'

I turned to Liam and grinned. He squeezed my waist again and winked down at me. I turned back to Antony, determined.

'Two-fifty,' I said back, trying to be as steely as possible.

'You're robbing me,' Antony said, glancing up at the ceiling like he was praying. 'Two hundred and seventy-five. Final offer.'

I glanced at Liam, who was silently laughing beside me. I turned back to Antony, nodding.

'Deal.' I held my hand to Antony like I'd seen businessmen do on *Dragons' Den*. Antony accepted my hand and shook it.

'I was swindled, but it's a deal. Liam, get your girlfriend out of here before she repossesses my house too.'

'Yes, sir,' Liam said, smiling down at me. Pride shone on his face.

I beamed back. For the first time in my life, I didn't feel like a fuck up. I didn't feel like I was one decision away from ruining my life or someone else's. I felt strong and capable. I felt motivated and driven. And as we lifted the sideboard into Liam's van, under his warm gaze, I felt like I could do anything.

Chapter Twenty-Eight

Liam's To-Do List

- Buy Kat a new to-do list
- Buy Kat some ADHD-friendly snacks
- Plan a date with Kat
- ~~Convince Kat to stay~~
- Get a life

The makers market was hosted every last Saturday of the month. Everly Heath High Street was cordoned off and pedestrianised for the privilege, and I could see why.

It was *rammed*.

I had no idea this many people lived here. The whole street was a sea of bodies shuffling through slowly, pushing through lines of people queuing for coffee and pastries. A huge brass band was performing at the front of the social club, their gold instruments shining in the spring sun. Children were running and playing with their friends, flitting between the legs of passersby. Thirty stalls sold everything from homemade sausage rolls to handmade children's clothes. And despite how busy it was, everyone was so... cheery. Chatty. There were no impatient huffs as people pushed through. No one was trying to speed walk through the crowds on their phone.

People said 'sorry' and 'excuse me' politely as they moved through the crowds languidly.

It was jarring.

Why wasn't this stressful?

I glanced at Liam. He seemed relaxed, his frown lines gone as he rubbed his thumb across my forefinger, leading me through the market. As soon as we arrived, Abigail ran off to see her friends, and Liam slipped his hand into mine, his eyes asking if it was okay. I squeezed back. It should have felt weird. I didn't hold hands with anyone. I'd never got close enough to a relationship to let handholding happen. But I didn't feel that usual suffocating panic. It felt normal, natural to feel Liam's hand in mine.

I stopped to admire a jewellery stand, my hands drifting to a necklace featuring a dainty gold bee on a thin chain. I thought it might be a nice memento to take with me once the house was done. Did I want a necklace to remember this time? I wasn't sure if I'd look back with fondness or grief.

I imagined I would reflect on my time with Liam as a lovely, distant memory, and the thought made me feel sick.

'That's pretty,' Liam said, and I glanced up at him.

'It is,' I admitted. I looked at the price. It was almost two hundred pounds. I put the necklace down.

'Come on, let's go.'

I pulled Liam's hand, dragging him into the crowds, away from my morose thoughts. I wanted to stay in the moment and enjoy myself.

Liam squeezed my hand. 'I've got something I want to show you.'

'Okay.'

We made our way through the crowds. Liam pulled me down a side alley off the main high street. It was quiet.

'This is it. This is where you're going to kill me.'

He laughed. 'You think I would have waited until now?'

He led us to the door of what looked like an abandoned cafe. Liam rooted around in his pockets, producing a key, and opened it.

'Why do I feel like we're breaking the law?' I whispered.

'It's fine. I know the owner.'

'Of course you do. Everyone knows everyone here.'

Liam flipped the lights on. There were abandoned tables and chairs. The lights were flickering slightly. We could still hear children and the band playing.

'Where are we?' I frowned. Liam was walking around slowly, like a bomb could detonate at any point.

This place was important. His shoulders were tense, his brow slightly furrowed.

'Oh.' The penny dropped. 'Was this the place? The restaurant? The one you were supposed to open with Ren.'

Liam nodded quietly.

'Well, it needs some work,' I joked, 'but I'm sure you would have made it amazing. It's got great bones.'

'What would you do?'

'Oh –' I hesitated. 'I've never thought about restaurant design before.' A lie. I totally had. In fact, when he mentioned it at Heath Antiques, I'd already started planning it in my head.

Liam made a 'go on' gesture with his hand.

'Well, some fitted booth seating would work along this wall. Making best use of the space.' I glanced at Liam; he was nodding. 'And also increase covers. I would add some light wood tables and chairs, nothing too heavy because it's on the darker side in here.' I walked towards the beautiful bay windows. 'And definitely get some of those cute half curtains.' I smiled, excited about the prospect of a new project, even if it wasn't mine. 'And I bet you could get some eclectic art prints on the walls, something from a local artist. Maybe someone here at the market, actually. I think I remember walking past an artist with some interesting pieces. We should go —'

Liam was quiet. I'd been planning out a dream that he had forfeited.

I slapped my forehead. 'I'm sorry. I'm getting carried away.'

I walked up to Liam, giving in to the urge to touch him. I touched his hand, and his eyes glanced down at our hands clasped together. But when I glanced up, I didn't see Liam's face full of regret.

He was smiling — a small smile.

'I signed the contract today. It's mine.'

'Are you fucking kidding me?' I squealed, jumping up and down, trying to make Liam join me, but he laughed and pulled me close. His chest rumbled with laughter, contained, muffled by his T-shirt.

'When? How? Your dad —'

'I finally grew some balls and told him. I didn't ask. I told him. I suggested Jack should take over.'

I pulled back, my eyes wide. 'Jack? But you're so hard on Jack.'

Liam frowned. 'I'm not hard on him.'

I cocked an eyebrow. 'You are.'

Liam exhaled. 'Maybe I have been in the last couple of weeks. But that's because I've only started thinking of him as my successor.'

I whistled. 'This ain't succession, babe.'

Liam looked at me sardonically. 'Don't "babe" me. And you know what I mean. Once I started thinking of him taking over, I needed to push him more. I didn't mean it to come off harsh.'

I hummed, unsure.

'I'll apologise to him.'

'You should.'

'I've been in a bad mood the last few weeks.'

I huffed. 'Understatement.'

'It might have something to do with a certain redhead creating chaos in my life.'

I gasped. 'I didn't create any chaos, thank you.'

'Chaos. Good chaos.' He pulled me closer. 'I don't think I would have done this had you not turned up, full of all of your ideas. You inspired me. If you could come here and –'

'Move up to a random northern town, leaving my job and friends, digging up all of my daddy issues, all to renovate some house?'

Liam made a strangled noise like he wasn't sure what to say. 'Yeah, all of that. If you could do all of that, I could do this. I could open Lily's.'

'Lily's,' I mused. 'I like it. Short, snappy.'

'It's my mum's name,' Liam explained, his voice growing hoarse.

'That is lovely, Liam,' I said. 'Really lovely.'

'Ren and I said it would be named after her – the menu is going to be inspired by some of her favourite dishes, after all.'

I nodded. 'And your brother –'

'He won't answer my phone calls right now.' Liam sighed. 'I don't know if it's because he's up a mountain, drinking his way through a city, or just ignoring me.'

'But when he does answer –'

'I'm going to ask him to come back. If he wants to. Come back and help me open this place.'

It was incredible to see the difference in Liam. His voice was clearer, his eyes shone, and he stood taller. Like the restaurant had boosted his confidence. Like he had a renewed sense of who he was.

'And your dad took it well?'

Liam nodded. 'He did. He knew about the plan originally anyway.'

I gasped. 'What?'

'Ren told him everything before he left. He tried to get Dad to push me out of my comfort zone. He wanted Dad to let me go. But Dad said he wanted me to come to it myself. He said I'd never been any good when pushed.'

I nodded. 'Stubborn.'

'Do you want a contest, sweetheart?' He ran his hands up my arms. 'Because I can remind you about a certain incident with a tent and some heavy rain.'

I rolled my eyes. 'And you'll never let me forget it.' I kissed his cheek, a ceasefire. 'So your dad didn't freak out?'

'No.' Liam smiled lightly. 'He'd been preparing for months at home. He knew it was coming. He's already sorted out the next two years of jobs and is getting ready to promote Jack. Plus, he's got some old geezers up for helping out, too.'

'So what you're saying is, you're expendable,' I said, deadpan.

'Cheeky.' He pinched my bum. 'But yes, apparently I am.'

'How liberating.'

'Liberating. Terrifying.' He shrugged and looked around at the abandoned cafe. 'And now I have this.'

'It is so exciting, Liam.'

I pulled away, moving around the room, imagining the restaurant clearly in my head, like I was walking through it.

'I can put together a design plan. I can see it now. Something modern and minimalist, but not boring.' I frown. 'I think we could feature a lot of colour. Reds, greens. The odd blue.' I nodded, biting my lip. 'I need to get home and write these ideas down so I don't forget them.'

'Steady on,' Liam smiled. 'I would love for you to design the concept. There is no one else I would ask but you.' He pulled me closer, his hand on the nape of my neck. 'But we're in no rush.'

I opened my mouth to disagree, but nothing came out. Usually, I would have three different drafts in my head right now. But the lazy, satisfied smile on Liam's face made me want to slow down. I could come up with a design tomorrow.

'Come on, let's go celebrate.' I grinned, pulling him towards the door. 'I can't buy you a drink, but I can buy you some cake or something –'

'Well, speaking of celebrating,' Liam said knowingly.

'What?' I turned around, unease in my stomach.

'A little birdie mentioned *someone's* birthday tomorrow,' Liam said, a song in his voice.

I slapped my forehead, crumpling. 'Fucking Sandra!'

'It wasn't Sandra.'

My eyes narrowed. 'Lydia.'

Liam's eyes twinkled. 'Bingo.'

'Traitor. She knows I hate birthdays.'

Liam pulled me towards him hard. My hands landed on his chest.

He smirked down at me. 'Oh, come on. I can think of very creative ways we can celebrate your birthday.'

My eyes widened, dirty thoughts flickering through my head like a horny flipbook.

'Well, this is cosy.' A familiar, sarcastic, feminine voice pierced through the room.

I turned. Willa was standing at the door with her designer duffel bag and her sunglasses pushed through her blonde hair.

My mouth fell open.

'What –' My gaze moved between Liam and Willa at speed.

Liam squeezed my hand. 'Happy Birthday, Red.'

Chapter Twenty-Nine

'What the fuck!' I squealed as I ran over to Willa, pulling her into a hug.

Willa smelt like her rose perfume. Rich and heady.

'Hey,' Willa said. 'Surprise.'

I pulled back to survey my best friend. Her platinum-blonde hair was straightened to perfection. Light touches of make-up framed her pale skin and bright blue eyes. She had her usual expression on her face – schooled and a little cold.

A bad bitch.

My heart burst – a piece of home, just for me.

'How did you get here? Why are you here? How did you know where I'd be?'

'I came up on the train.' She angled her head to Liam. 'He suggested it would be best to take public transport, despite my aversion.'

I angled my eyebrow. 'Did you book First Class?'

Willa's eyes shifted away. 'Maybe.'

I shook my head. 'Posh bitch.'

'I've got a brand to maintain.'

I shifted back towards Liam. 'Willa, this is Liam. Liam, Willa.'

Willa scanned Liam, assessing. 'We've spoken.'

'I emailed Willa. Asked her to come up for your birthday.'

'Yes,' Willa said, her lips rising at the corners. 'He emailed work, and he was very… insistent. Obviously, I was going to say yes. I was going to point out that I'd invited myself several times. But I didn't get a chance because he had a very compelling speech prepared.'

I turned to Liam. 'A speech?'

Liam shifted on his feet. 'Well, I know how hard it is to get Londoners past the Watford Gap.'

My heart squeezed.

I beamed. 'Thank you, Liam.'

Liam blushed. Actually blushed. 'Don't mention it.'

'I am going to mention it. This is the best gift ever.' I slapped my hands on either side of Willa's face. 'I'm so excited to show you around. I can show you the house!'

'Can you let go?' Willa said, her speech muffled.

I pulled her into another hard hug. She said she hated public displays of affection, but I was one of the rare approved people.

Liam said, 'I thought we could look around the market. I've made you a cheese board for later. I got some wine in. I will be out with Abi, so you two can catch up. I'm taking her to see the latest Marvel film.'

I squeezed Liam's hand. My eyes threatened to well up. He'd thought of everything. He was willing to give me space to hang out with my best friend.

'Thank you,' I murmured, filled with gratitude.

I turned to Willa. She was staring at Liam and me with morbid fascination. I dropped Liam's hand and felt him tense beside me. I glanced up at him, but I found his resting bitch face firmly in place.

Fuck.

I didn't want to hurt him, but I couldn't deny that I was struggling with this. This was not casual. None of this was casual. I'd been lulled into a false sense of security in Everly Heath. But with Willa here, someone from my old life, I felt on display. I wanted to blame it on Liam and send my walls swinging back up, but it was my fault, too. I felt comfortable next to him. I felt loved and seen and looked after.

I was down bad, too.

★

'So, are we going to talk about it, then?' Willa cocked an eyebrow as we sat watching *Clueless* and sipping the Sauvignon Blanc Liam had left us in the fridge.

I'd tried to distract Willa all day to avoid this conversation. I knew it was coming, but I wasn't ready to face it yet – not for the questions that Willa would ask me bluntly. We'd walked through the markets, looking at each stall in detail. We'd gone for a drink at the club, and I'd introduced her to Sandra and Brian, who were having a pint of lager. I'd even introduced her to Peter, who'd grunted in welcome. With Liam gone, we'd got a cab to the house, and I'd shown her the progress on the renovation. I'd watched Willa's face as she'd looked around, nodding, and I nervously repeated that it wasn't finished yet.

I ignored her comment, leaned forward, picked up a piece of Parma ham, and threw it in my mouth. I chewed slowly, trying to focus on the salty taste.

'That man is half in love with you,' Willa said, sipping her wine.

I choked. 'No, he's not.'

'Kat,' she said, her tone flat. 'Don't pretend you don't see it, too. I know you do. You're lying to yourself.'

'I'm not… I know he cares about me. But we've agreed to keep it casual.'

Willa scoffed. 'It's more than that. I watched him today. He pays attention to you, anticipates what you need, but gives you space at the same time. I mean, what man would pay for their best friend to come up from London, First Class, if they weren't in love with them.' Willa threw some pepperoni in her mouth.

'He paid?'

'Yep. He didn't blink an eyelid about the cost. He just said he would send me the ticket. I was sure he would flake —' Willa looked away, and I knew she was thinking about all the times fuck-face John had let her down. Promised her the world on a string, then bailed. 'The tickets came through ten minutes later.'

'I mentioned I missed you.'

'And then he emailed me, begging for me to come up here.'

'I doubt he begged. Liam doesn't beg.'

Willa held out her phone. 'Do you want to see the email?'

'No,' I said too quickly.

Willa shook her head. 'Only you would be like this.'

'Like what?'

'All avoidant.'

'I'm not avoiding.' I stood up, needing to move.

'Yes, you are.'

'Willa,' I moaned. 'I need you to tell me everything is okay. Everything is fine and normal. Nothing has changed.'

Willa nodded. 'I can tell you that. But it won't make it the truth.' Willa patted the sofa next to her. 'Come on, tell me what's got you so stressed.'

I took a deep breath, trying to calm myself.

'I like him. A lot.'

'Yep, that much is obvious.'

'Stop it. I like him. And we… we've been doing some stuff. We kissed. Amongst other things.'

Willa snorted. 'That much is obvious, too.'

I could feel my cheeks burn. 'No, it isn't. No one knows.'

'Babes,' Willa said. 'Liam looks like the cat that got the cream when he looks at you. Like you're edible. It's ridiculous.'

'*You're* being ridiculous,' I said childishly. 'And I do like him, and I know he likes me. But I'm moving back, you know that.' I raised my hands. 'I mean, I've got a month left.'

'Two weeks,' Willa said, inspecting her nails.

'No, four weeks.'

Willa glanced up. 'Two. Think about it.'

Oh. It was my birthday tomorrow.

'Fuck,' I shouted.

How had it gone that quickly?

Liam was almost done installing the boring white tiles in the bathroom, but the kitchen was nowhere near finished. I'd have to move back soon.

'Indeed. So what are you going to do?'

'What do you mean? I have no choice. I've got to come back to work.'

'No, you don't.'

'Yes, I do. I need to come back because you need me.' I glanced at Willa. 'Right?'

'I'd be lying if I didn't need the help at work.' Willa bit her lip. 'But my dad is becoming a bit more involved with the day-to-day of Horizon.'

I got a sinking feeling in my stomach. It was Willa's worst nightmare. Willa had a great relationship with her dad but was overly eager to please him. It would have been a low point to ask for his help. Or worse, he interfered after discovering how bad the situation was.

Willa downed the last of her wine.

'I'm sorry, Wills.'

'It's a good thing. Dad and I will strategise a new approach to keeping existing clients, at the very least.' Willa smiled, but it didn't reach her eyes.

'I can help. I want to help.'

'How?' Willa cocked an eyebrow. 'Are you going to hand out more chewed gum? Maybe this time, you could do used tissues, too.'

I gave her a flat look. 'Cow.'

Willa's lips twitched, and then her face grew serious. 'You are your own person, Kat. You can hand in your notice right now if you want.' Willa's eyes were soft. 'Or if you want, you can come back. But don't pretend I'm the big bad wolf. I will not make this easier for you by ordering you home. It's your choice. And for the record. This is the best I've seen you in years. You look brighter. Happier.'

It was like a foot had been removed from my chest.

'Thanks, Wills.' My eyes began to water.

'No, no. None of that, please.' Willa waved her hand at my face, and I laughed. Willa was allergic to tears. She was repressed as fuck.

'Okay, okay. I won't cry. Stop saying cute shit.' I swiped a finger under my eye.

'So, now that we've cleared that up, what will you do? Stay here?'

'I don't know, Wills. I was so set on coming back. But slowly but surely, this place has got under my skin. Mum always made it out like it was the Dark Ages up here. She said that everyone was backward and nosy. They are definitely nosy, but it's just because they look after their own. It's a real community.'

Willa wrinkled her nose. 'Couldn't think of anything worse.'

I laughed. 'I thought so, too. But it's actually kind of nice. My aunt and uncle have been great, too. Mum made out that they wouldn't care about me, that they took Dad's side in the divorce. But I don't think that's true. Sandra and Brian have been nothing but nice.' I sighed, rubbing my eyes. 'The problem is, Mum doesn't even know I'm here. So if I announce that I'm moving here, it's going to be a big shock. Huge.'

Willa squeaked. 'You didn't tell her?'

'I bottled it. She's called a few times, but I told her I was really busy with work. I don't know how much longer –'

Willa's face had gone pale. 'Kat –'

My face dropped.

'I didn't know you didn't tell her. She called me at work yesterday because she wanted to speak to you, and I mentioned how I was coming up here to visit.' Willa clapped a hand over her mouth. 'I'm so sorry.' Then, Willa whacked me on the arm. 'You should have told me!' She whacked me again, harder.

'I'm sorry, I'm sorry. Stop hitting me.'

Willa relented and said, 'I would have kept it a secret if you'd told me, you twat.'

I gave a sad laugh. 'I know, I'm sorry. Don't worry. It's my fault. I should have told her by now.'

I checked my phone. Nothing from Mum. No missed calls. Not even a text.

Dread sat low in my chest.

'I should have faced it sooner, but you know when I have something big I don't want to face –'

'You hide.'

'Yep.'

'Can't hide from Paula. It's impossible.'

'I know. I just wanted to do something myself.' I picked up my drink and took a sip. 'I think it's helped. Having some space from her. I haven't been doubting myself as much.'

Willa nodded. 'Make sense.'

None of this was a shock to Willa, so I took a deep breath in and delivered the final blow.

I jumped.

'I'm not coming back to work at Horizon, Willa. I think –' I paused, trying to push the words out. 'I want to move here.

Permanently. And not just because I like Liam and want to see where it goes.' The next bit came out fast, the words flowing out of me. 'But because I actually really want to become an interior designer. I'd like to open my own shop, and I think I could do that here. I couldn't afford to take the leap in London. Here, I could. Dad's house is paid off, so I wouldn't need to pay rent or a mortgage. I've been looking at some courses on Open University. I know it's rogue, and impulsive, and probably irresponsible —'

'Hey, hey. Take a breath.'

I took a few deep breaths. I peeked at Willa, trying to gauge her reaction. Her brow was furrowed, but she nodded.

Finally, Willa spoke. 'I think this sounds great.'

'Yeah?'

'Yeah.'

She had a small smile on her face. 'Actually, I think this is the best idea you've had in a long time. You and I both know you've been phoning it in at work. You're lucky that you're such a good designer, or I'd have kicked your arse to the kerb by now.'

A hysterical giggle burst out of me.

Willa nodded. 'I think a new start, a new project, would be good for you.'

'But what if I change my mind? Or what if it fails, Wills? I couldn't face Mum's face if I come crawling back to her, with my tail between my legs.'

Willa's lips went into a flat line. 'No risk, no reward, babes. Them the rules, I'm afraid.'

I bit my lip. I'd been so unhappy at work. For over a year, if I was being honest with myself. Even before Dad died, I'd become restless. It was like I had a persistent shaking leg that wouldn't stop, even if I placed my hand on it and pushed it down.

I thought about all my side hustles, the candle making and the calligraphy. What if all those failed projects were leading here?

'Right,' Willa said with a clap of her hands. 'If we're going to do this. Let's make it happen. Get your laptop out. We're putting together a business plan, bitch.'

I couldn't hold back the answering smile from breaking across my face.

★

It was dark when I felt strong arms come around under my legs and my neck. Someone... someone was carrying me. I was pressed against a hard chest.

'Do you need anything?' a male voice whispered. 'The annexe is open.'

'No, I'm good,' a woman whispered back. 'She seems happy here, Liam.'

'I think she is. I hope she is. She deserves to be,' the man whispered back.

Liam.

My fuzzy brain began to wake. Willa. Liam. After Willa and I had drafted a business plan, I fell asleep before I saw the end of *Clueless*.

'You better take care of her,' Willa said, a warning in her voice.

'I will,' Liam replied. I could hear the soft smile in his voice. 'I'd do anything for her. You should know that.'

'Good.'

I drifted off and woke again as Liam lay me on his bed, giving me a light kiss on my forehead. I tried to wake up. I tried to move. I tried to cuddle into him, but I felt so heavy. So, instead, I snuggled deeper into the sheets, and those strong arms came around me anyway.

Chapter Thirty

~~Kat's To-Do List~~
Everly Heath Pros & Cons

Pros

- Liam
- Brian, Sandra, Lydia – Family
- Pat's brownies – they are fucking insane
- The house is paid off, so maybe I could take an interior design course?
- Liam (again)

Cons

- Willa (I'm pretty sure she's hiding how bad work is)
- I'll miss London, probably???
- CALL MUM, DON'T BE A WIMP

Liam and I stood on Sandra and Brian's porch, holding foil-covered plates and a bottle of white wine, but neither of us had knocked on the door yet. Neither of us had moved our hands towards the large gold knocker on the door. Liam shifted on his feet, and I glanced at him. I wished I could have climbed into his head and read his mind. I had a feeling I would discover he was feeling the same as me – protective of the little bubble we'd had this morning. We lazed around in bed, sipping coffee – black for him, a latte for me. We chatted about inane things, the kind of questions you ask when everything is fresh and new.

I asked Liam about what he was like at school. Predictably, he'd been the sporty type on all the school teams – football, rugby, and even cricket in the summers. I asked how he felt about becoming a dad so young, and he asked me about London – all my favourite places to visit and where I would take him if he ever visited. I saw his face tense for a second when I suggested he visit and swiftly moved on to talk about the restaurants in London – something I knew would distract him.

When we finally got out of bed, I tried not to go bright red when Willa gave me a smug look as I traipsed around Liam's kitchen barefoot and in my short pyjamas. It felt weird having someone else witness our mornings.

Apart from Abigail, they had been ours.

Liam didn't seem bothered at all. He still kissed the top of my head as he went around the kitchen preparing breakfast for Willa and me. Sweet potato hash with smoked salmon and poached eggs. Blueberry pancakes with hand-whipped cream and a strawberry compote. He poured us mimosas and handed Willa her black coffee.

Willa's eyes went wide as Liam plated up. She mouthed, *He cooks too.*

When we dropped Willa back at the station, I tried not to get too tearful as she hugged me tight and whispered, 'Be brave, Kat. He seems like a good guy.' Her eyes flickered to Liam, standing by his van waiting for me. 'And if he hurts you, I'm chopping his balls off.'

I laughed and hugged her tighter, and then she was gone.

In the van, I sniffed. Liam kept glancing over at me.

'Do you still want to go?' he asked. 'I didn't think you might be upset, we can go home –'

I threaded my hand through Liam's.

'I'm okay.' I smiled. 'Thank you for getting her up here. It really was the best birthday present.'

He cocked an eyebrow. 'Better than this morning?'

I blushed. 'Hm. I love Willa, but probably not as much as I love you going down on me.'

Liam punched the air, and I laughed.

★

As we stood in front of my aunt and uncle's terraced house, I regretted not taking Liam up on his offer. The house sounded like a home. The TV was blaring in the front room, and music was playing from the kitchen. I could smell roast chicken and hear my uncle singing to Frank Sinatra in the kitchen.

I felt out of place.

I didn't know the protocol. My family had never done the big, loud Sunday lunches. Mum had always said it was too much food for the three of us.

I glanced at Liam to find him staring down at me, his gaze skirting down me and lingering on my arse, where my dress was particularly tight.

I smirked, momentarily distracted by Liam's stormy eyes.

I knew he liked the tight wool dress I'd picked out this morning. His eyes had widened and trailed over me, up and down, hungrily. He looked ready to throw me over his shoulder and drag me back upstairs. I was sure he would have done it if Willa hadn't been there. The feeling was mutual when Liam wore a hunter-green soft jumper with tapered dark blue trousers and smart white trainers.

His arse looked just as good, but I had the decency to stare when he wasn't looking. Right now, Liam clearly didn't give a flying fuck. His eyes kept trailing over me, heat warming there.

'My eyes are up here, Hunter.'

Liam made a strangled noise. 'I don't think I'm going to be able to get through this meal and hide that I'm clearly obsessed with you.'

I choked. 'Obsessed with me?'

Liam grabbed the bottle of wine from my hand and placed it on the floor. With our hands free, he pulled me closer and kissed my neck.

Liam hummed. 'Just let me get it out of my system. I know you don't want to tell anyone, but sweetheart' – his words made my heart squeeze – 'you look ridiculously hot, and I just want to take you home and do terrible, horrible things to you, and everyone is going to see it on my face.'

His voice grew a bit desperate towards the end. Like he was suffering.

I gasped as Liam nipped at my neck, biting harder than he should. 'Everyone saw us at the market. The cat is out of the bag. We can tell people if you want.'

Liam pulled back, assessing me. 'Are you sure? I don't want to make you uncomfortable –'

'It's just family, right?'

Liam nodded. 'Well –'

He didn't finish his sentence because the door swung open, and Lydia stood in the doorway, her mouth full of food.

Her eyes widened at the food in Liam's hands. 'Is that the chocolate pie?' she murmured through her mouthful.

'It's a torte,' Liam responded in a deadpan tone.

Lydia rolled her eyes. 'Wanker.' She took the plates from him, smelling under the foil. 'Ah, this smells amazing.' She turned around to head back down the hallway. 'Mum! Liam and Kat are here. We can all pretend we didn't see them feeling each other up on the porch for the last ten minutes.'

'Lydia!' Sandra shouted from the front room as my face lit up bright red.

'I made extra,' Liam shouted as Lydia disappeared with the plate. 'It can go in the freezer.'

'Yes, chef!' Lydia shouted back, and I snorted.

'Sandra!' Uncle Brian shouted. 'Where did you put the beers?'

'Are you blind? On the side in the kitchen. In the box,' Sandra shouted back. I could hear Lydia laughing in the kitchen at her dad's expense.

My eyes caught on the pictures hanging in the hallway of shoes and coats. In mismatched frames were photographs of Lydia at school and on holiday and wedding photos of Sandra and Brian from the 1980s, everyone decked out in big, puffy hair and dresses. I spotted my dad with his ginger mop of curly hair.

I couldn't stop the morose thought popping into my head.

He'll never come to my wedding, my brain muttered quietly.

Liam stepped closer, tucking an errant curl behind my ear.

Are you okay? he mouthed.

I nodded, unable to untangle my complicated emotions, even if I wanted to.

He dropped a quick kiss on my cheek. 'We can leave whenever you want. If it's too much.'

I wanted to squeeze him. 'Thank you.'

'Come on, I'll get you a drink.'

We walked into the kitchen, and there was a pop of a confetti cannon.

'Happy birthday!' my aunt, uncle and cousin shouted, along with another grey-haired man who had to be Liam's dad. A

243

crooked birthday banner hung above the patio doors to the garden. A huge table with mismatched chairs was set up for dinner.

Sandra hugged me, and then Brian kissed my cheek, sweat forming on his brow. 'Happy birthday, love.'

Lydia handed me a glass of something fizzy.

Brian dashed back to the oven, staring through the glass as the pale batter puffed up. 'I gotta keep an eye on these Yorkshires.'

'He burnt them last time,' Lydia whispered to me.

'I heard that!' Brian shouted from the kitchen.

Across the room, Liam and his dad were engrossed in conversation. Their eyes came to me, and I flushed. But Liam smiled, and Liam's dad headed for me. My stomach swooped. I'd never met the parents of someone I was... well, whatever we were.

'Dad. This is Kat. Kat, this is Kevin,' Liam said, gesturing to me.

Kevin Hunter had grey hair, a strong, square jaw, and twinkling blue eyes. He was shorter than Liam and had one of those smiles you could feel in the room. I could understand why so many people asked him for help. Kevin struck me as the kind of man you wanted when your car broke down or you had IKEA furniture to assemble. He looked strong, sturdy, and capable.

'Lovely to meet you, Kat. I've heard a lot about you.' Liam's Dad smiled and went to hug me. Everyone was very... tactile. 'I'm Kevin,' he said. 'I heard you've been causing my son grief.'

My eyes widened. 'Oh.'

Liam rolled his eyes. 'He's pulling your leg, Kat. Ignore him.'

Kevin's eyes twinkled. 'He probably needs it.' He looked at his son. 'Someone to shake things up, huh?'

A silent conversation was shared between them.

'So, what do you do, Kat?'

'I'm a graphic designer.'

'And you live in London?'

'For now,' I said, keeping my voice light.

Liam's eyebrows shot up.

'How's it coming along with the house?' Brian asked while opening the oven and checking the chicken.

Liam glanced at me, an expectant look on his face like he wanted to know, too.

'Great,' I said, forcing a smile under the expectation of their gazes on me. 'Thanks to Liam. I don't know what I would have done if he hadn't taken the job.' I turned to Kevin. 'I haven't had a chance to thank you for letting Liam jump on the project quickly and only charging me for the materials. You have no idea how grateful I am.' I glanced at Liam. 'We got off on the wrong foot, Liam and me. So I imagine he wouldn't have accepted without someone to coerce him.' I smiled and shoved Liam with my shoulder.

Kevin's heavy brows knitted together. 'Coerce —'

'Dad —'

Kevin barked a laugh. 'I didn't have to say anything. He jumped at the chance.' Kevin's eyes twinkled as he glanced between Liam and me. 'And now I can see why. I don't think Liam could resist helping the pretty girl he was holding a flame for.'

'Dad,' Liam said, as his cheeks flushed.

Kevin continued. 'Well, obviously, I'd have always helped you, Kat. But it was our Liam who suggested we absorb the labour costs.'

I turned to Liam, and he was scratching his head, looking anywhere but at me. He couldn't have known me for more than a week, and he'd missed out on thousands and thousands of pounds to help me out.

Gratitude surged inside my chest, making my eyes burn.

'Especially strange because he's always on my back for helping people —'

'— Bending over backwards to help people,' Liam inserted.

245

Lydia leaned on the back of Liam's shoulders, messing up his hair. 'Oh, you mean like not charging customers you fancy?'

Liam went a bit red. He was blushing, and all I could do was stare in amazement.

'Liam —' I started, unsure what I was even going to say.

Thank you.

Let me pay you back.

Liam looked at me and said, 'Later.'

'Brian, do you need a hand plating up?'

'No, Sandra. I don't need a hand. Two hours ago, peeling potatoes, however...' Brian replied, walking over with the huge, puffy Yorkshire puddings.

'Touchy, touchy,' Sandra replied in a sing-song voice, making Lydia and Liam chuckle.

Everyone started picking up plates laden with roast potatoes, leeks and roast chicken that Brian had carved. It was all placed in the centre of the table. Liam and Lydia went to the cupboards to pick out wine glasses. Kevin had his hand on the oven door. Uncle Brian whacked him on the back of the head. 'You'll let the heat out, you twat.'

Everyone seemed to have their role, and I was standing next to the table, feeling like a lemon.

'Kat – would you grab the knives and forks?' Brian asked, and relief flooded me – something to do. Once everyone sat down, people began helping themselves to the food piled in the centre of the table.

'Potatoes?' Liam asked, leaning into me. I almost jumped a foot.

'Oh. Yeah. Thanks.'

Liam spooned one huge potato onto my plate and then another.

'Two is fine.'

'Humour me,' he said, spooning on one more.

'Such a feeder,' I muttered under my breath.

'Don't diss my love language, Red,' he said with a smirk.

A love language. Liam managed the table as if he were conducting a symphony. He topped up Sandra's wine glass before she realised it was empty and passed his dad extra greens, commenting on his high blood pressure. He predicted when Lydia would want more potatoes and diligently ladled them onto her plate, making her beam. Then, he laid his arm across the back of my chair. I wasn't sure he was aware that he moved slightly closer each time he moved.

It was all so lovely.

Homely.

My nose stung.

I glanced at Liam, watching the relaxed look on his face. He really was happier sat at a table with his family than he was on a building site. His face was softer. He didn't have that pinched look between his eyebrows.

'What you looking at, Red?'

My lips twitched. 'Just someone who looks entirely satisfied.'

'Not entirely, Red.'

'Can you two get a room?' Lydia made a barfing sound.

'Lydia,' Sandra barked, then turned to us, hearts in her eyes. 'They are so sweet.'

'So come on then,' Lydia said. 'Spill. What's going on? Are you staying, cuz?'

I was expecting Liam to tense, but he didn't. He looked at me expectantly. He was letting me lead the narrative. Usually, I'd want the whole room to swallow me up, but I didn't feel the usual sense of impending doom. Not when Liam had made my birthday perfect and impressed my impossible-to-impress best friend. Not when his arm was on the back of my hair, his eyes stuck on me when I moved around the room. Not when I was so fucking happy in a room with him and my loud, gregarious family, not feeling the slightest bit out of place.

My lips twitched. 'We are —'

The doorbell rang.

Sandra and Brian looked at each other.

'Were you expecting —'

Brian shrugged. 'No.'

Sandra padded down the hallway. The door creaked open, and a high-pitched wail of excitement echoed off the walls.

Ren, Liam's brother, who was supposed to be halfway across the world, strolled into the room, a duffel bag slung over his shoulder.

Chapter Thirty-One

A cacophony of noise erupted as chairs were scraped back. Liam gave a filthy swear, and Brian and Sandra beamed like Ren was a soldier returning from war. Kevin held his son close and kissed him on the head, gruffly asking why Ren hadn't told anyone he was coming home. I stood by, a little awkwardly, as Liam introduced me.

Lydia hadn't moved from her seat. I noticed his eyes flickering to Lydia and losing some of their shine.

I felt Liam's hand at the small of my back. 'This is Kat.'

Ren's brown eyes, so similar to his brother's, met mine. It was almost eerie how similar the brothers were, especially standing side by side. They moved in the same way. They had the same shade of dark brown hair, although Ren's was shorter. They were even the same height. Although if I pointed this out, I was sure there would be a measuring contest, so I grinned at the thought and kept that to myself.

'Hi, Kat.' Ren grinned. 'Suppose I have you to blame for this.' Ren's eyes flickered to Liam's, a joke in them. While Liam exuded a steady calmness, Ren had a fluid cheekiness about him. He had the air of someone who was loved and adored. If I looked up younger sibling in the dictionary, I would find Ren's face grinning at me.

Ren scanned the room, and his gaze snagged on Lydia, who was still sitting at the table, an unreadable expression on her face.

'Hey, Lyds,' he said, his voice hoarse.

'Lawrence,' Lydia replied curtly.

My eyebrows shot up. Liam frowned. I'd never seen Lydia act cold and nonchalant in her life. It wasn't in her DNA. She had a smile and a joke for everyone. She was the life and soul of every room. But when Ren walked in, she'd closed down. She folded her arms in front of her, not looking in his direction.

I'd been led to believe that Ren and Lydia had spent their childhood together, inseparable. Liam said they were two sides of the same coin – best friends.

But these people weren't best friends.

Ren's gaze finally shifted away back to his dad with a cocky smile. But call it ADHD perception or whatever, but I knew the expression Ren wore on his face was longing.

Longing and regret.

My eyes shifted to Lydia.

You okay? I mouthed.

Lydia gave me a quick nod as everyone sat back down and began quizzing Ren. Sandra pulled up a spare chair, and Brian shoved a beer into Ren's hand and busied himself, making a plate of food for the new arrival. It struck me that Brian and Sandra's ties to both Hunter boys were strong.

'How long are you staying, son?' Kevin asked, clapping his son on the shoulder.

'For good,' Ren said, sipping his beer.

Lydia's head shot up. Ren swallowed as he stared at her.

'For good.' Kevin frowned.

'Yep,' Ren said, angling his head towards Liam. 'Liam convinced me. He left me a sappy message about how he'd found his big boy pants 'cos he finally found a woman to inspire.' Ren's eyes landed on me, twinkling. 'I'm guessing that's you, Kat.'

I shrugged, sipping my wine. 'I guess I gave him a good kick up the arse.'

Ren laughed. 'Good.'

'Can you stop talking about me like I'm not here,' Liam grumbled.

'I'm here to help you open Lily's,' Ren told Liam. 'I figured you could do it with the best bartender in the Northwest.'

Lydia snorted, and Ren's eyes flickered to her.

Lydia stood. 'You won't stay. You never do.'

Ren flinched but recovered quickly, replacing it with a smirk. 'I am staying. For good.'

'I'll believe it when I see it.'

'Well, I'll have to prove it to you, won't I? I've done it before. Remember the fifteen hundred metres at school? I won that fair and square.'

Lydia's eyes narrowed. 'And I won it the following year, remember?'

Ren's eyes flickered down Lydia's frame and then back up. 'I remember.'

Lydia's chair scraped back, and she muttered something about fresh air before leaving the room. Ten seconds later, Ren followed, his fists clenched.

'What is that about?' I muttered to Liam.

'I have no idea, but it's probably Ren's fault. He was always the troublemaker. Lydia always tried to smooth over his mistakes when we were kids.'

I knew one thing – Lydia was in for a grilling later.

★

Three hours later, napkins were scrunched on the table, and rings of red wine stained the tablecloth. Ren shared stories about his travels, his eyes wild and captivating. Lydia didn't return to the table but texted me some bullshit excuse about an early start. I was tempted to call her out, but Lydia always had so much patience for everyone, so if she needed time, I would give it to her.

I stood up, running my hand across Liam's back. He had been laughing with his brother and dad for hours. I loved seeing the matching laugh lines around their eyes.

Liam glanced up at me, his hand moving over mine. 'You okay, Red?'

'Yeah, just going out for some fresh air.'

The sound of Fleetwood Mac and the smell of Sunday lunch permeated the room, and I was overstimulated. It wasn't a bad case, but I knew fresh air always set me right.

Liam frowned. 'Are you sure?'

'You worry too much.'

'We can go when you're ready.'

I kissed the top of his head and dipped outside. The fresh air hit my face. Hints of spring had begun setting in Brian and Sandra's garden, and the smell of magnolia and freshly mown grass hung in the air. I closed my eyes and took a few deep breaths.

'Alright, Kat?' Brian popped his head out of the patio doors.

'Yeah.' I smiled. 'All good. Just admiring your magnolia tree.'

Brian stood next to me; the tree had begun budding pink and white flowers.

'That is Sandra's favourite. I planted it here the first summer we moved into this house, almost thirty years ago.' He smiled at the memory. 'It was a right pain. We'd had a cold winter, so the soil was hard as stone. I spent hours making sure the hole was dug deep enough and that it was in the best spot. I bought her a table and chairs so she could sit underneath it. She'd mentioned it was her favourite tree, but we'd been living in a terrace house with no garden. So once we bought this house, I went straight to the garden centre.' Brian laughed. 'She was pregnant with Lydia and burst into tears when she saw it.'

'Never took you for a romantic, Uncle Brian.'

Brian shrugged. 'I'd do anything for her. I'd plant a million more magnolia trees if it made her happy.'

'So, that's the secret to a long, happy marriage, then? Gardening.'

Brian glanced at me, and his expression grew serious. 'It's being willing to make the other person as happy as you feel just to be around them.'

Liam's face popped into my head. Hadn't he done that for me?

He'd refused to charge me for the renovation. He'd wrangled Willa onto a train and paid for her tickets because I'd mentioned it once. He kept cooking for me, and I knew he was keeping a note of my favourite ones on his notes app because I'd snuck a look on his phone.

Deep down, I knew he was trying to give me reasons to stay. He said we were keeping it casual, but his actions spoke louder than his words.

'Do me a favour, Kat.' Brian wrapped an arm around my shoulders. 'If you're considering staying, we couldn't be happier. For both of you.' Brian glanced behind us, where Liam was sitting laughing with his dad. 'But if you're going back. Tell him. Soon. Because we both know he's betting on convincing you to stay.'

My throat closed up.

'I will, Brian,' I croaked. 'I'm just — I don't know what to do. I never imagined any of this happening. I didn't realise you'd all be so lovely —' My voice cracked.

I hadn't realised this could feel like home.

Brian squeezed me tighter. 'I, for one, have been chuffed to get to know my niece better. So whatever you do. If you do want to sell the house and go back down south, do it. But remember you're always welcome back, love. Sandra and I have become a bit attached to you the past couple of weeks, and we don't want it to return to how it was before. Your mum —'

Brian's mouth shut closed. His lips were a thin, flat line. It was the face of someone who was about to say too much.

'What about Mum?'

Brian dropped his hand. 'It's not my place, love.'

'Uncle Brian,' I warned.

Brian sighed. 'Your mum — well, it's been no secret she didn't like it here. Even when she was still married to your dad, she hated coming to visit. She thought everyone was barmy.' Brian shook his head. 'She looked down on us. So it was no surprise your visits stopped too —'

I nodded. 'I know.'

Brian shifted on his feet. 'Well, when your parents divorced and your dad moved back here. She...' Brian winced. 'After they divorced, Paula wouldn't let your dad see you. I told him he needed to get a custody agreement. He needed to fight for you.'

My heart raced, tingles shot down my arms. 'She — she wouldn't do that.'

Brian's face was grave. 'I'm sorry, Kat. If there weren't any reason to bring it up, I wouldn't have. But I think you deserve to know. Your dad — he was really low after the divorce. He took on the blame because of all the money problems he'd caused.'

I frowned. I knew money had something to do with the divorce from all the arguments I'd overheard sitting at the top of the stairs. Dad had invested all the money in his garage, including a loan against the house.

'Your dad trusted the wrong bloke. Someone to do the accounts. But he was funnelling money out of the business. Slowly but surely, taking more and more each year. When the financial crash hit in '08, well, he managed to take it all. He moved abroad with the money.'

I inhaled shakily. 'Does that justify going no contact with your eleven-year-old daughter?'

'It doesn't. But you should know – your dad was in a bad place.' Brian looked ahead like he was remembering that time. 'There were times I wasn't sure he wanted to be here with us. But he came back home and got some help. He was better a year or two later, and I told him to meet you. If Paula hated the idea, I told him to look into custody agreements. Then, one night, he told me. Your mum had asked him to stay away. You were struggling enough at school as it was. You didn't need any more stress. You needed stability. "She's better off without me," he used to say.' Brian shook his head. 'Stupid man. He missed out on so much.'

'I – I don't know what to say.' Emotions swirled around me, a storm cloud brewing. I craved to march back down south and demand my mum tell me it was a lie. Tell me she would never do anything like that. But another part of me knew it wasn't impossible. Mum always wanted things to be as straightforward as possible.

'I understand this is hard to wrap your head around. And for the record, as much as I disagree with Paula's approach, I understand that it was coming from a good place. Routine and stability are so important for kids. But Jim took it to heart. He already blamed himself for the business, almost losing the house. Your mum's parents had to help dig him out of debt. I think he'd lost his confidence to be a dad. A proper dad. I thought you should know that it was complicated. And that if I could, I'd strangle him for not making it right. For leaving you in this limbo.'

It was like someone had added more foreground detail to an oil painting. The details added made sense. Suddenly, memories flooded in of my dad being in bed, unable to get up.

'I wanted you to know that he loved you. I know it wasn't enough. He knew it wasn't enough, but he did love you. He just wasn't strong enough to show it.'

Chapter Thirty-Two

Liam – To Do

- Book Franks
- Call Olivia at Manchester Art Gallery
- Pick up Kat's dress

'White or grey?' Liam asked, holding up the two bags of grout. My brain swirled, and I was thinking about a million things, and none of them were the grout colour for the bathroom. Liam had fixed a half wall of tiles around the whole bathroom, white subway tiles on the walls and up the shower enclosure. The light from the south-facing window reflected off them, sending white light around the room.

It was too bright.

It was clinical.

More importantly, it was boring.

I chewed at my lip. This had been my choice. I could have done something more elaborate, but I didn't. I chose to be practical, and this bathroom was practical. It was inoffensive.

And I fucking hated it.

'Kat.' Liam frowned.

I shook my head. 'Sorry. Yes.'

'Grey or white? Or I can get some other colours if you want.'

As Willa would say, I was fresh out of fucks to give. I was pissed off with the boring white tiles. I was pissed off with my mum. The latter, I had chosen to ignore for the time being. On the drive back on Sunday, I told Liam what Brian had shared. Once we were parked in his driveway, the floodlights illuminating our faces, he'd pulled me into a long hug while a few tears escaped down my cheeks. Since then, three days had passed, and I'd moved through them in a daze. A low level of anxiety hummed. I was unable to concentrate on anything. I was flitting from task to task, each unfinished.

Even when I was at home with Liam, I was somewhere else. Ruminating over what to do about my job, the new career I desperately wanted to explore and the growing feeling that Everly Heath was home. I knew Liam had noticed, but he hadn't mentioned anything. He showed up with gentle touches to my cheeks, bringing me back into my body, into the present. He cooked me food and kept my water topped up. He pulled me into his chest at night, neither of us mentioning that the annexe was outside, unoccupied.

'You choose,' I said, turning back to the bedrooms.

The carpets were going in this week, and I wasn't particularly excited. I was thankful they weren't grey.

'Red,' Liam said, his voice following behind me. I kept my gaze away from him, worried he'd read the misery on my face. His hand came up and cupped my neck, and he planted a kiss on my forehead.

'Talk to me.'

I sighed into the contact, some of my residual anxiety running out of me.

'I fucking hate the white tiles,' I started. 'And I know that is stupid because I picked them, and you took ages tiling, but I hate

257

them. They are too white, and it's too bright in there.' I raised my hands. 'It's boring. Nothing like what I designed. And I hate it.'

Silence.

I finally looked up to find Liam holding back a laugh.

'What?' I asked, exasperated.

'That's all? The tiles?' He lifted my head to look at him. 'I'll take them down right now if you want. I'll go pick up the ones you want.'

I ran a hand across my face. 'No – those tiles are fine. It's not what I imagined, and I knew that would happen. But I didn't prepare myself to see it. To see all of it and be underwhelmed.'

I glanced around the house at the inoffensive white walls and the bare alcoves. I'd wanted to pay a carpenter to install some fitted wardrobes before I realised I'd be spending the money on someone else. My clothes wouldn't be thrown in in a manic hour of tidying before company came over. No, the person who bought this house would probably be all ordered and fold their clothes into perfect squares.

I shook my head. I couldn't believe I was becoming resentful of a fictional person.

'Do you want me to take them down?' Liam asked, and my head whipped up. He wasn't joking. He had his serious face on. He'd spent a whole day tiling that bathroom. 'I've got a hammer. I can start taking them down now. I'll go to the shop now and order the other ones.' I could see the cogs turning in his brain. 'It won't set us back many days. I can move on to the kitchen.'

'No,' I said, my hand linking with his. 'Thank you, but no. I'm being stupid. Childish. This is me banging my feet on the floor. It's a tantrum.'

Liam's lips twitched. 'I'm familiar.'

'Hey! I'm not that bad.'

Liam pulled me into his chest. 'I told you before. Anything you want, Kat. Anything. I'll make it happen. You know that, right?'

I planted my head against his chest, breathing him in. He did make it better. Just breathing in his scent and hearing his steady heartbeat. I supposed that was our dynamic. I was hectic and overemotional, while Liam was steady and rational. We stood there for a few more moments as some of the anxiety dripped away.

Liam kept telling me, through his actions, that he was invested in this relationship, and all I'd done was insist we keep it casual. I'd never had someone so committed to me before, and it was scary. He was so certain of my vision and what I could do. It made me feel invincible and powerful. I wanted to feel like that all the time.

'I was thinking of staying, Liam,' I said in a small voice. I didn't lift my head. I kept my face in his chest. 'In Everly Heath. I'm thinking of staying.'

Liam stilled.

'You —' Liam stuttered. 'You want to stay. Here.'

'I've been thinking about it for a while now. I spoke to Willa about it, and she didn't die of shock. She seemed to think it was a good idea, actually. I'm still worried about Mum. She's going to think I've gone mad. She'll try to convince me out of it; I know she will. She knows I'm here. Willa accidentally told her last week, so I'm waiting for the other shoe to drop.' Liam's hand moved over my back in circles. 'After what Brian told me —' Anger and indignation rose in my chest, burning bright.

Liam's other hand came up to my hair. He kissed the top of my head.

'But I'm scared, Liam. Really scared. I know it doesn't seem like much, but this is big for me. Moving up here after a couple of months. I'm scared I'll turn into my dad and bolt, and I don't want to hurt you.'

Liam's voice was hoarse. 'Okay, okay.'

'What if I fuck all of this up? What if I move up here and then change my mind? What if I throw away a good job, working with my best friend every day for some pipe dream of building something myself?' My voice grew high-pitched.

'Okay.' Liam's voice was calm and solid, his hand still moving against my lower back. His heartbeat had sped up, just a bit. 'You're being brave, Red. I'm proud of you. But all of this is a lot to process. For anyone. So don't make any decisions yet.'

My heart sank. He didn't want me to stay.

Liam lifted my head with his thumb and forefinger.

'Don't work yourself up. Let's take some time for ourselves, just you and me.'

'We can't — we have to finish here.' I gestured around the half-finished room. 'Even if I decide to move up here, we still need to finish this place.'

'Easy.' Liam's hands ran up my arms. 'You're thinking about moving up here, so why don't you let me show you the reasons to stay?'

My brow furrowed, but my mouth quirked. 'What do you mean?'

A bright smile took over his face. I loved it when he smiled like that, like all his defences were down. 'Give me one day, and I'll convince you it's best to stay. Some courage to face your mum. Who sounds terrifying, by the way. Can't wait to meet her.'

I gave a snort and Liam lifted his pinkie finger in front of me. 'Deal?'

'Deal.'

Our pinkie fingers interlocked.

★

Liam's cedar cologne enveloped me. Warmth rolled off him in waves as we stood close. He trailed his hand up my arm, up and down, driving me mad. The train doors opened, and people shuffled to the door. Liam pulled me closer into his chest, out of the way.

My heart still raced to be this close to him. I still woke up craving his rough palms on my skin. The smell of his skin still drove me wild. I glanced up at Liam to find him smirking down at me, like he knew what was on my mind. Smug bastard. He lifted my chin with his thumb and forefinger, placing a soft but insistent kiss on my lips. I tried to kiss him with more fervour, but he pulled back.

'Behave,' he hushed in my ear, making me grunt with annoyance, only making him smile wider.

It was only yesterday Liam promised to give me reasons to stay in Everly Heath, and he moved fast. This morning, he came into our bedroom with flowers and a tray of fruit and pastries. After we finished eating, Liam ate me. He grinned as I came, moaning his name, which will be etched into my mind forever. Once I came down from the high, he swatted away my hand and jumped out of bed in an effort to distract me.

'I got you something,' Liam said as he turned to his wardrobe. The wardrobe that some of my clothes had sneaked their way into. I didn't know who I was trying to kid with this 'keeping it casual' shit. All my stuff had invaded Liam's house. Liam had tried to collect the rest of my stuff from the annexe, but I had insisted it was fine. So my luggage sat in the annexe, like bringing them into Liam's house symbolised something permanent.

Liam opened his wardrobe and pulled out the most beautiful emerald-green dress I'd ever seen. It nipped in at the waist, had balloon sleeves, and a swishy skirt I could imagine would be a lot of fun on a dance floor. I jumped out of bed, running my hand across the silky fabric. It also had an open back, which would look great if I styled my hair up.

'Sandra helped me pick this out,' Liam said, a blush running up his cheeks. 'Since Mum died, well, I guess I haven't had many role models when it comes to women's clothes. Abi won't let me pick anything out for her. If you hate it —'

My nose stung. God, he was so adorable. I couldn't remember a time a man had ever bought anything for me. To be fair, I don't think I let them close enough to allow it.

'I love it, Liam. Thank you.'

His shoulders dropped.

'I thought the colour would look beautiful on you, and you could wear it today,' he said. 'It's supposed to be warm, so you shouldn't be cold.'

'You know' – I smirked – 'you're incredibly thoughtful underneath that resting bitch face.'

Liam grinned. 'You're going to get it now, Red.'

He threw me on the bed, tickling me so much that my chest hurt with laughter.

★

The train pulled into Manchester Piccadilly, and Liam grabbed my hand, speed-walking through the crowds. It was only a Thursday, but the station was packed. Outside, the weather was overcast, the odd ray of sun peeking through the clouds. I followed the natural flow of people, but Liam pulled me back. 'We're not going that way. *That* way is Piccadilly Gardens, and we do not want to go there.' He laughed dryly. 'Not the best impression of Manchester, trust me.'

Liam walked us over a bridge and past some tall buildings, all glass and steel. We followed the tramlines and took the back streets until we stood in front of a Grecian-inspired building with huge stone pillars. The sign read MANCHESTER ART GALLERY, and I was like a bottle of pop, shaken up.

Liam looked over at me, reading my reaction. 'You said you liked London for the art galleries.'

'When –' I frowned, and then I realised it had been when we were standing in the social club kitchen, side by side, preparing sandwiches. It had been such an offhand comment – I hadn't expected Liam to remember.

He bumped my shoulder. 'You'll have to go easy on me. I don't know anything about this.'

I grinned. 'I can show you.'

We pushed through the double doors to find a woman standing in the foyer. She had pink streaks running through her grey hair and wore a red plaid wrap skirt. Her ice-blue eyes were behind oversized red glasses. Suddenly, I felt incredibly uncool.

'Olivia?' Liam asked, extending his hand.

Olivia smiled and shook it. 'Lovely to meet you. As I mentioned over email, you have the place to yourselves for two hours.'

Liam nodded. 'Perfect.'

I turned to Liam, gaping. He scratched his head. 'Well, the thing is… I booked out the gallery.'

'You booked out the entire gallery.'

'Yes.'

'Liam.' My heart began to race.

This was too much.

My feet were beginning to itch.

'Can we have a minute before the tour?' Liam asked.

'Sure,' Olivia said. 'I'll be in Gallery One.'

'Hey' – Liam turned my shoulders to face him once Olivia was out of earshot – 'what's up?'

'This is too much. I – no one has ever done anything like this before.'

Liam shrugged. 'Well, they should have.'

I squeaked. I couldn't look anywhere at him. I couldn't admit that I'd never felt deserving of anything like this. I'd kept the men I'd dated an arm's length because, ultimately, I was scared. I was scared I would get attached and they'd ruin me.

Liam was entirely capable of ruining me, I was realising now.

'You're spiralling.' Liam lifted my chin to meet his stare. 'Tell me what you're thinking.'

I squeezed my eyelids together.

'Can't.'

'Red,' Liam said softly. 'We're better than that. We're honest with each other, aren't we? Whatever you tell me, I'm not going anywhere. I keep telling you I'm here. I'm in this.'

I exhaled. 'No one has ever done anything like this for me. It just feels like a lot. I don't deserve it.'

Liam's breath caught. 'Kat. I want to punch whoever has made you feel like this.'

'You can't – he's dead.' I laughed meekly. 'Daddy issues.'

Liam's lips flattened. 'I want you to listen to me. Really listen, okay? You deserve this and more. You are worthy. You're a bright, shining light to everyone around you. Brian and Sandra adore you. Lydia too. Abi worships the ground you walk on. And I know you don't see it. But I do. So let me do what I can to prove it to you.' His hand clasped the back of my neck and pressed our foreheads together. 'I told you yesterday. Don't think about what is coming. Just be here with me.'

'Okay.'

'Okay.'

'Let's go.' Liam smiled and pulled me into the first gallery.

Chapter Thirty-Three

We stepped out of the art gallery two hours later. The sun decided to stick around, warm on my face. The square in front of the art gallery was basking in the warm sunlight that peeked through the trees.

The tour with Olivia was incredible. We had the whole gallery to ourselves as we walked through each section, Olivia explaining the collection and some of her favourite pieces. The art gallery was beautiful – all parquet floors and glass skylights. They had a huge Lowry and Pre-Raphaelite collection. Liam's face split into a grin as we walked into a gallery full of women with flaming red hair. He snapped a photo of me looking, my curly red hair matching the painting. I watched him smile at his screen and set it as his lock screen.

'That bloke would have loved you, Red,' Liam whispered as Olivia ushered us into the next gallery.

'Hey,' I said, pulling Liam towards me on the steps of the gallery. 'Thank you. I loved it. I can't wait to go back. There was so much I didn't see, even in two hours.'

Olivia had mentioned a huge textile collection, and I was itching for some design inspiration. If I did enrol in that interior design course, I wanted to do my dissertation on those fabrics.

'It was worth it. To see you like that.' Liam smiled. 'You looked so happy.'

I grinned. 'What's next, tour guide?'

Liam grabbed my hand and led me across the square, which had trams running through it.

'Well, you said you liked London for the art galleries,' Liam mimicked, ticking a list. 'Next, food.'

My stomach rumbled at the mention, and Liam threw me a grin. We walked past a huge dome building.

'That's the library, and behind it is the Town Hall. That's where we have the lights turned on at Christmas. It's packed, and we usually get a major A-list celebrity to turn them on.'

I raised an eyebrow. '*Big Brother* contestant from 2005?'

Liam barked a laugh, then gave me a serious look. 'That's their career highlight, Red. It's Abi's favourite day. That and Pride in August. It takes over the whole city. It's a lot of fun.'

'Oh my god. Do you dress up?'

Liam shrugged. 'Abigail might get the glitter out, yeah.'

I laughed, imagining Liam sitting at the kitchen table, Abigail covering Liam's face in glitter.

'I'd love to see that.'

'Maybe you will.'

Our eyes met, and I could see the hope glimmering in his – the hope that I'd be here long enough for milestones written in Sharpie onto a shared calendar.

We passed a grand hotel called The Midland, and Liam nodded. 'That's where Posh and Becks had their first date.'

My mouth fell open. 'Oh my god. Royalty.'

Liam laughed. 'Yep.'

We stopped in front of The Vine & Olive, a restaurant with sash windows and a stripy green canopy. It had a couple of iron tables outside, which I imagined were for when the sun shone briefly and a crisp white wine was on the cards.

'This is lovely,' I said.

'We used to come here a lot as kids. It was Mum's favourite. Best Italian in the city,' Liam said. 'I know the owner, Frank. He tends to be quieter at lunch.'

Liam nodded and opened the door, the bell ringing as we walked through.

'Liam!' a man bellowed.

The man was in his sixties, with dark hair and greys at his temples. He approached us, wearing a white shirt, black trousers, and a red apron emblazoned with the restaurant logo.

He clapped his hand on Liam's shoulder, and I swear I saw Liam wince a little.

'Frank,' Liam said in an indulgent tone.

'Your table is free.' Frank grinned, and his eyes widened when he spotted me.

'Liam, who is this? Ciao. I'm Frank.' He held his hand to me, and I couldn't help but grin. 'Lovely to meet you.' His bizarre blended Italian–Mancunian accent came out.

Liam looked down at me, smiling. 'This is Kat.'

'Liam, you've never brought a girlfriend here.' He raised his eyebrows. 'Must be serious.'

'Frank,' Liam warned.

His eyes widened, feigning innocence. 'What else am I meant to think?'

His arm grazed my shoulder as he angled me towards a table in the window.

'Come on,' Liam murmured into my ear. 'If we don't sit down, he'll keep embarrassing me.'

Frank winked as he brought us some menus, and I could feel myself going a bit red.

'Sorry about him,' Liam said, his eyes twinkling. 'I only come here with Dad and Abigail. It's a bit of a shock for Frank.'

'How long has he had the restaurant?'

'Frank has run this place for… god, it's got to be twenty years now. He's one of the reasons I love to cook so much. He used to give me cooking lessons early on Sundays before they opened. I learnt how to use a knife and make Italian sauces with Frank.'

'So he is to thank for the amazing pasta.'

Liam smiled. 'Yes.'

'He said you've never brought a girl here.' My curiosity piqued. 'Did you not bring Yasmin?'

Liam shook his head, glancing down at the menu. 'It wasn't her vibe. And we were always too busy to come into town. We just stayed local.'

I studied the menu.

Liam cleared his throat. 'The strozzapreti is good. If you are struggling to pick.'

Strozzapreti with broccolini and anchovy butter. My mouth watered. Everything on the menu looked amazing.

I glanced up. 'Do you want to pick us something to share? You probably know all the best dishes.'

Liam hesitated. 'Are you sure? I don't want to be *that* guy.'

'What guy?'

'The guy who says what you'll have. "She'll have the salad." That arsehole in the films.'

My lips twitched. 'Are you going to order me a salad, Liam?'

He wrinkled his nose. 'Fuck, no.'

I laughed. 'I didn't think so. But the Caprese salad does look good, actually. Maybe as a side, though.'

Liam nodded. 'It's really good, to be fair.'

I nodded, acting solemn. 'Okay. I permit you to order that side salad, Liam.'

Liam ordered the strozzapreti broccolini, which was salty and light. To balance the saltiness, he ordered the hearty ragu and finished with a side of garlic bread and Caprese salad. The dishes arrived in traditional Italian bowls, which Liam said Frank sourced from Italy. We shared them in the middle of the table.

'What do you think?' Liam scratched his arm.

'It's amazing. Why do you look so stressed?'

Liam frowned. 'This is one of my favourite restaurants. I didn't realise how nerve-racking it would be to bring someone new here.'

I grinned. 'High stakes, huh?'

I took a bite of the ragu and moaned. 'Fucking hell. What does he put in this?'

'Red,' Liam said, an octave lower. 'Don't make noises like that in public. Or we'll be paying the bill and going home.'

I looked up to find Liam staring at my lips. I blushed and pressed my legs together. He wasn't joking, I could tell. He would pay the bill, whisk us out of here, and take me home. He'd probably undress me slowly. Kissing his way up my body like he had done this morning, and we'd finally—

'Red,' Liam warned. 'Your pupils are like saucers. Pack it in. I want to wine and dine you.'

'Not sixty-nine me?' I grinned.

Liam shook his head until a tall shadow came over our table, and we glanced up to find Liam's brother looking down at us.

'This is cosy.' Ren grinned. 'Really, Liam. I didn't take you for such a romantic. Shall I get some roses, and you can put one in your mouth?'

'Ren —' Liam rubbed a hand over his face.

'Oh!' Ren clasped his chest. 'I'll get Frank to bring out some spaghetti. You can do the bit from *Lady and the Tramp*.'

I laughed as Liam said, 'Remind me why I asked you to come back.'

Ren pulled a chair over, turned it around, and sat, and I could see Liam's blood pressure rising, the veins in his neck pulsing. Ren really pushed his buttons.

'Because I'm the best barman in this fine city? Because you miss me?' He made his eyes go soft and round, and he pouted. 'Because you love your wittle bwother?'

I laughed, a deep belly laugh. This couldn't be more entertaining.

'Eejit.' Liam shook his head, but his lips were twitching. He frowned when he clocked Frank's uniform. 'Are you working here?' Liam's face dropped. 'Ren – you promised you'd work on the restaurant with me. No distractions.'

Ren rolled his eyes. 'I'm not jumping ship. Frank needed some help, so I said I would come and do a few shifts.' Ren picked at his nails. 'I figured it would help if I got back into the swing of things. I have spent a year out of the industry.'

Liam relaxed at his words as Ren bristled. I saw something familiar in Ren – someone sick of being underestimated. I made a mental note to point this out to Liam when we were alone. He needed to ease up on his brother.

Liam gave a nod. 'Good idea.'

Ren leaned forward and stole an olive from Liam's plate.

'So, Kat,' Ren said, chewing. 'We didn't have a chance to catch up the other night when I –' He searched for the word.

'You turned up out of the blue after a year away in the depths of the Amazon?'

Ren pointed at Liam. 'Exactly. What's your deal, then? Dad said you're from London.'

'I'm from Reading. I live in London.'

Ren waved a hand. 'Same, same.'

I raised an eyebrow. 'Would you like it if I said you were Liverpudlian?'

Ren's and Liam's faces morphed into matching grimaces.

'Are you moving up here?' Ren asked. 'Because we'll be busy for the next few months. We're hitting the ground running with the restaurant. I went by the other day, and it looks like shit. We have a lot of work to put in –'

'Ren,' Liam said, his eyebrows pinched. 'She knows. I've told her.'

Ren didn't look convinced. He pointed his finger. 'You might have spoken about it. But have you two thought this through? It's not like you could do long distance, Liam. Even if you didn't have the restaurant, you have Abi.'

Liam opened his mouth, but Ren lifted his palms. 'I just want to know I didn't fly all the way home to finally open this restaurant for you to go saunter off down south.'

'I'm moving up,' I announced.

You could hear a pin drop. Liam's wide eyes met mine. Ren's eyebrows rose.

'And I'm designing the restaurant for you for free. So be nice to me, you little shit.'

Ren gave me a slow smile, then a quick nod.

'Okay. That shut me up.' Ren rose and tucked the chair back.

'Hang on,' I said. 'This doesn't feel fair. You come over here, interrogate me, then walk off. Don't I get to hear any embarrassing stories about Liam?'

Ren's eyes glittered, and he gave a smile. 'What do you want to know, Kat?'

'Ren –'

'Do you want to hear about how he wet the bed till he was seven?'

My mouth fell open as Liam jumped out of his seat. Ren was grinning like the Cheshire cat. 'Or how he couldn't get a girl to go with him to prom, so he took our cousin –'

Liam hauled his brother halfway across the restaurant while Ren laughed manically. 'Wait, wait. Liam – wait. I need to take your drinks orders.' Ren held up his hands in surrender. 'Come on, I'm not going to say anything else.'

'Dickhead,' Liam muttered as he reluctantly let Ren go and returned to his seat.

'Katherine' – he turned to me – 'what is your favourite cocktail, and can I make you one?'

'Oh—'

'I presume you drink?' Ren's eyes shifted to Liam. 'Unlike this one, who couldn't be trusted.'

I scanned my brain for my favourite cocktail. I wasn't sure I had one. I preferred beer, really. I racked my brain to come up with something, anything.

'Has Frank got Guinness on?' Liam asked; he glanced over to the bar.

'Yes.' Ren said.

'She'll have a pint.'

Ren's eyebrows scrunched together. 'Are you sure—'

'Are you sure, Red?' Liam glanced at me.

I grimaced. 'Yeah. I mean, I'm not really a huge fan of cocktails. Willa used to order me her favourite – French 75 – when we went to the bar by our office.'

Ren grinned. 'A Guinness with a side of French 75. Genius.'

Before I could protest, Ren had dipped behind the bar, pulling down the Guinness tap.

'Were you telling the truth' – Liam's voice was thick – 'or were you just trying to get him off our backs?'

My eyes met his and softened. Why was I putting him through this? He was holding so much of himself back, holding half of his heart back. I could see it in his eyes.

'I'm staying, Liam.' My eyes stung.

Liam exhaled hard. 'You're not pulling my leg?'

I laughed. 'No.'

Liam launched out of his seat, grasped my neck and pressed his lips against mine. He poured everything into that kiss – relief, happiness and hope. Vaguely, I could hear Ren, Frank, and the kitchen staff whooping and hollering behind us.

Liam pulled back and pressed his forehead against mine. 'I would have followed you anywhere if I could. But I can't. So this is my chance to ask you properly. Stay. But stay because you love it here. Stay because you want to. But most importantly, stay because I love you.' I took a sharp intake of breath. 'You don't have to say it back. Just tell me you're staying again.'

'I'm staying, Liam.'

Chapter Thirty-Four

We ran across the square, ducking under the canopy of the library. Our dash across had only felt like two seconds, but we were completely soaked. My hair had begun to frizz up already. I laughed at how ridiculous we looked. Rain covered my face and dress. Liam's face was covered too, rain running down his cheeks, his hair flattening on his forehead. He tried to push it back, but it was no use.

The rain hit harder, pelting on the pavements.

'Does it always rain this bad?' I shouted. It was a downpour – April showers.

'You'll have to get used to it.' He grinned and pulled me closer. 'Are you cold?'

I smiled back. His smile was infectious. 'No, I'm fine.'

Liam opened his coat. 'You're cold. You look cold.'

'Okay.' I smiled as Liam pulled me into his chest, his head resting on the top of mine.

I looked up at him, seeing raindrops on his dark eyelashes.

'What's next, boss?'

'Don't call me that,' he rumbled.

'What's wrong with boss?' I asked, grinning. I knew exactly what was wrong with calling him boss.

'I'd stop now, or you'll find out,' he said as he pulled me closer. I could *feel* how much it had affected him. It had affected him big time.

He leaned into my hair. 'You smell so good. It used to drive me mad when we were working on the house. I could smell your perfume in whatever room you'd been meddling in.'

'I didn't meddle!'

'Hmmm. Sure.' He smelt my neck, planting a kiss there. We were basically mounting each other in the middle of a city. I looked around. St Peter's Square was quiet. It looked like everyone else had the same idea – duck under something to keep dry until the worst of the rain was over.

We stood there for a moment, sharing warmth. I leaned up, meeting Liam's dark eyes.

'Can you take me home?' I didn't want to be in a city teeming with people. I wanted to go back to Everly Heath. I wanted Liam's eyes on me and nothing else.

Liam gave me a smirk. 'Sure, Red.'

*

We stumbled through the front door, kissing, and Liam had me up against it in seconds, my legs wrapped around his hips. My green dress had ridden up, leaving my thighs exposed. I could feel the draught from the door as Liam slammed it close with a hard push. He pressed himself against me, and we moaned. Liam trailed kisses everywhere, my neck, my collarbone, my lips, while he ground against me; that coil of pleasure wound tighter with each movement. I pulled on his hair. I wanted to make sure he knew how this was ending.

I wasn't being teased anymore. I didn't care about taking it slowly. I needed him. Now.

'Upstairs,' I panted. 'Now.'

I was going to have him tonight if it killed me. Liam let me go, and I slipped down him. I looked up to see a hungry expression in his eyes.

'Liam. Let's go. I swear to god, if I'm not in your bed in the next five minutes, I'm going to die.'

Liam laughed. 'Yes, boss.'

He pulled me into a fireman's carry, making me squeal in surprise.

'Liam, this isn't what I meant.' I held on tighter as he took us up his stairs. I couldn't believe he could climb a flight of stairs with me in his arms. I was not exactly light.

'You should be more specific, then,' he said as he gave a gentle bite to my neck.

'Just concentrate on where you are going. I swear – if you drop me!'

'I won't drop you,' he said, walking down a long hallway to a bedroom at the end. He kicked open the door and dropped me onto his bed, shifting across me to flip on the lamp beside his bed.

'Can we keep the lights off?' I asked. I rarely had sex in the light. It wasn't my body image or anything like that. It was more it felt strangely… intimate.

'No fucking chance,' Liam said, his voice gravelly. 'I've fantasised about this too many times. I need to commit the real thing to memory.'

'Liam, I've been in this bed a million times,' I said, still baffled.

Liam leaned over me, annoyingly fully clothed.

'Yes, but that was before I knew I was going to get to keep you.'

He cradled my cheeks, then pushed his hands into my hair. Our lips met again, soft at first, then all tongue and teeth, competing for who could make the other moan louder. My hands began to wander first, under his T-shirt, over his abs and his broad back. I pulled at the fabric, and Liam got the message and pulled his T-shirt over his head.

My eyes went wide. I would never get over seeing this guy topless.

Liam chuckled. 'You look like a Disney character again.'

I glanced up. Liam was looking way too smug. He knew he had that lived-in physique, built more like a rugby player than a model. You could tell he worked with his body every day. He had strong arms, a wide chest and a trail of dark hair going down into his jeans.

'You keep looking at me like that, and this isn't going to last very long.' He bit my earlobe. 'And I want to drag this out as long as possible.'

His kisses continued down my cleavage. I felt too hot and claustrophobic to be dressed. I pulled my dress over my head and reached for my bra.

'I'll do it,' Liam said, taking a strap and kissing my shoulder. 'Stop rushing me.'

I wanted to complain, but Liam's expression was... reverent. So, I held back my complaints. He pushed down the bra first, taking a nipple into his mouth, making me arch off the bed. Liam hummed and then moved over to the next. He reached behind me and had my bra off in an instant, even quicker than I'd manage. I didn't know whether to be jealous or thank the previous women he'd slept with at this point.

He kissed down my stomach.

Gently, he bit at the softness of my hips.

'These have driven me mad, your hips. The way you move them. When you squeeze past me at the house. When you get up to get a drink at the bar.' He nipped and then kissed the other. 'I just wanted to grab them. Then I could, but only in private. Now, I'm going to touch you whenever I want.'

'That will scandalise – oh.'

He reached for my underwear, a plain black thong, but he

didn't pull it down like I'd expected. He planted a delicate kiss on me, making me fist his bedcovers.

I lifted my hips. 'Stop teasing.'

'It's only payback, love.' He planted another kiss. 'Payback for driving me mad. For making us wait for this.'

The third kiss he gave me had me moaning, and he took mercy on me, pulling the strip of material off me.

'You. Are perfect,' he said before he lowered his mouth onto me, and everything went taut. With each swirl of his tongue, soft and then harder, I wound tighter and higher. At some point, my hands ended up in his dark hair, pulling at each decadent lick.

'Yes. There.' I moaned as he hit the right spot. He focused there and sped up slightly. Just enough to have my hips rising off the bed. I babbled something about being close and glanced down. Liam's head was down, not looking up at me, focused on me and me alone – a slight smile on his smug face.

One more second of his tongue sent me over the edge, and I moaned his name as I came hard. Liam lessened his pressure and stroked my thighs as I came back down to earth, panting. I was a mess – the good type. All languid and undone.

I could barely put a sentence together, but I gestured for Liam.

'Come here,' I said. 'I need you.'

'We don't have to do anything else, Kat. I just wanted to do that.'

'Stop being so fucking perfect and come here.'

Liam didn't need to be told twice. With a cocky smile I wanted to wipe off his face, he lowered himself over me. He was still dressed.

'Off,' I demanded, trying to undo his belt but failing.

'So pushy,' he said, kissing me and then pulling back to undo his belt. He had his jeans off and then hovered over me in his underwear.

I reached inside and felt him. He was hard, with precum already wetting his cock. I gave him two tugs, making him moan from above me. With two hands, he grabbed mine and put them above my head.

I pouted. 'What? I can't play, but you can?'

'Playing could finish this.' He kissed me hard again. 'Not letting that happen.'

'Fine.'

He kissed me some more, but I was getting impatient. I wanted Liam. I wanted him so fucking much. I wanted him, even when I shouldn't. Even when I'd suppressed it for so so fucking long in a misguided attempt to protect myself. Liam must have sensed my impatience because he pulled down his boxers.

'We can stop at any time. Just tell me,' he murmured in my ears, kissing below them.

His gentle offer, even as he stripped down, was enough to make me melt. It was rare for any man I'd been with to even care enough to make the boundaries of consent as clear as Liam had. I battled the emotions swirling in my chest but focused on the physical. While I was impatient and demanding, Liam seemed focused on savouring this. He kept kissing my cheeks, my lips, and my neck, oblivious to the fire raging inside me.

I'd already come, but Liam hadn't yet.

How was he so calm?

'Condoms?' I panted.

Liam leaned across me to his sidetable, half of his weight landing on me, forcing a strange noise out of me, making me laugh and setting Liam off apologising. Liam rolled on the condom and hovered over me, careful not to put his full weight on me this time.

'Are you sure?' Liam asked, his eyes earnest. Was I sure? My body was screaming yes. There was a bit of my brain, underneath all the lust and urgency, that said we wouldn't be able to come

279

back from this. It said that this wasn't casual. It warned that I would end up being destroyed by Liam, not just physically. But I wasn't going to let that hold me back. I needed this. I needed him. We both needed each other. I could see it in Liam's face as he looked at me now with gentle affection.

'Yes.' I pulled him by the back of his neck to kiss me.

Liam pushed into me, and we both moaned at the delicious sensation. As he pushed in further, I winced a little.

'Are you okay?' Liam asked, pushing his hands into my hair.

'Yes. So good. Keep going.'

Liam pushed to the hilt, then pulled back and slammed back, making me gasp again.

Oh shit. This feels fucking amazing.

Liam picked up the pace, lifted my legs, and he hit a perfect spot. He had his eyes shut, his breath coming quickly.

'Kat.' He moaned in a way I'd never heard before. It sounded amazing coming from his mouth. Liam's hands came to my hips, rocking me harder, and I tightened my legs around his waist, needing him deeper. He slammed into me, and the air whooshed from my chest.

Fuck.

'Too much?' Liam asked, a frown forming.

'Perfect,' I gasped back as he repeated the movement. I continued to pant as Liam changed up the angle and the tempo, slowing down slightly to kiss me, his face close to mine – a look of adoration. I knew at that moment that this was the most intense sexual experience I'd ever had, and it wasn't even over yet.

'God, you feel perfect,' Liam growled between thrusts. His forehead was on mine, and we stared at each other, emotions passing between us. We were so, so close. I couldn't see where I started, and he began. I felt a ball of emotion rise in my chest, threatening to spill over.

'Kat,' Liam murmured. 'I—' I shut him down with a hard kiss, wrapping my legs tighter, digging my heels into him to get him deeper. I knew what he was going to say, but I didn't – no, I couldn't – hear it right now. I couldn't hear it again when I couldn't say it back.

Sensing a shift in my energy, Liam moved and lay on his back, pulling me with him. 'Get on top.'

I didn't need to be told twice. I lowered myself onto him, making us both moan again. Using the headboard for support, I rode him, and it felt so fucking good that I couldn't help but close my eyes and throw my head back. Liam used this angle as an excuse to touch my breasts, then drew them into his mouth, intensifying the feeling up, up, and up.

'I'm close.'

'Come for me. Please.' Liam reached between us and gently rubbed my clit in circles, somehow at the perfect pace. It threw me over the edge, and I moaned as I came in waves. I could feel Liam come with me as he held my hips down, thrusting into me hard, before we both came to a stop, panting. I fell forward onto his chest and felt his heart still racing.

'Christ,' he said.

'Yeah.' I was smiling, boneless. Eventually, I dismounted with a fair amount of grace, all things considered, and Liam took care of the condom before joining me back in bed, pulling me against him. He was so fucking warm, and he smelt so fucking good. He kissed the top of my head.

'I love you,' Liam murmured into my skin.

I wanted to open my mouth, to say the words back, but I couldn't. Time, I just needed some time, and Liam was willing to give it to me. I didn't feel suffocated. Liam's breath was evening out, and his heart rate was slowing.

Then the overthinking kicked in.

It always got worse at night.

I thought of Mum's disappointed face when I told her about another career change. I thought about the stress line between Willa's eyes when she recruited another graphic designer. Or worse, the relief she'd feel that I'd gone of my own accord. Where would I live here? I could move into my dad's house, so Liam and I weren't moving too fast. I could enrol on the interior design course while doing some freelance work for Willa to keep afloat. Mum and Graham would think I was losing my mind.

Liam's breath hitched in his sleep, and he pulled me tighter.

What was I doing? I had Liam. Liam, who loved me. Liam, who wanted me to stay. Liam, who looked after me when I was spiralling. Together, we'd be okay.

I sunk deeper under the covers.

Tonight, I was going to enjoy this.

Tomorrow, I would worry about the rest.

Chapter Thirty-Five

Kat's To-Do List

- Do not spiral
- Do not overthink
- Do not bolt

The sunlight streamed through the blinds, throwing patterns and shades all over the room and the bed. Something hot as a furnace was behind me.

Liam.

I smiled. He was pressed against my back, his head buried into the back of my neck and my hair. I could feel a soreness between my legs, reminding me of last night – his teeth and tongue and the weight of him on top of me. It made me shiver slightly, making Liam move. I tensed, wondering if I'd woken him.

My brain was up, even if my body was still tired. I started to imagine my life in Everly Heath, now I was going to stay. I could see it in technicolour – Liam and I waking up in bed together, in my house or his. He'd make breakfast, and we'd listen to the radio with coffee cups in our hands, kissing now and then between songs. Then, I realised the family I'd always imagined buying my dad's house no longer had blank faces.

They were Liam and me.

I bit my lip, thinking about those damn white tiles. I wanted to beat myself for not seeing this coming and picking whatever fucking design I wanted for the house. Of course I was going to stay. The more I thought about it, the clearer it was. Everly Heath was always going to charm me to stay. Liam had warned me. And he was right.

'What are you thinking about?' I jolted at the deep, amused voice behind me. 'You're just lying there with your eyes wide open.'

I shifted, turning in the bed to face him. I tried to keep as far away as possible in case of morning breath.

'I was just thinking how stupid I am.'

Liam's face dropped. 'You aren't stupid.'

'I am. I should have seen this coming. I should have realised I was falling for you too.'

Liam's face softened.

'It's okay, Red.' He pulled me into his chest. 'You had to come to it in your own time. You're that stubborn.'

'I am not stubborn,' I mumbled. 'But now I have boring white tiles.' I moaned miserably into Liam's chest.

His shoulders shook with laughter.

'They are just tiles, Red. You do know I'm a builder, right? I can get them replaced tomorrow.'

'Not just the tiles – everything. I would have done it differently if I'd known I would stay.'

Liam hummed and traced his hand over my back in little circles. It calmed me after a few seconds.

'Let's take it day by day,' Liam said finally. 'We'll figure out what we want to do with the house. Mine too. If we wanted to sell both and buy a bigger one, we could do that.'

I tensed.

'I don't want to sell Dad's house.'

'Okay,' Liam said. 'Then we could sell mine. Whatever you wanted.'

'It can't be what I want all the time.'

Liam kissed my head. 'I'm happy when you're happy. This house hasn't meant anything to me since I bought it. I could leave it behind, and I wouldn't give it another thought.'

'But what about Abi —'

'You can design a room for her at yours, maybe?' There was uncertainty in his voice, like he wasn't sure if he was taking it a step too far by mentioning his daughter. But it had the opposite effect. I shot up in bed.

'Oh my god, do you think she'd let me design it?' I squealed. 'I wouldn't just paint it all pink if she thinks she's over pink. I know she wears a lot of blue.' I shifted. 'Oh my god, I could get her one of those trundle beds so when she has friends over, she can have them to stay. I used to love sleepovers when I was a kid.' Even if it was always at my friends' houses, not mine. It was Mum's idea of hell having more children in her house. I was more than enough. But I didn't mention that to Liam because his face broke into a beautiful wide smile.

'What?'

He shook his head. 'You are something else, you know that?'

'What do you mean?'

Liam didn't explain; he launched himself at me, and I made an unladylike squeal as his weight came on top of me. He kissed me, hard and fast.

'As much as I love this,' I said, giving his bum a swat, 'you've given me a new hyperfixation. I need to google stuff for Abi's room.'

Liam laughed. 'Day by day, Red. Let's take it day by day.'

'Okay.'

He kissed me and pulled me under the covers.

★

'Coffee?' Liam asked, barefoot in the kitchen after we'd finally got dressed. I insisted that we dress in separate rooms to keep our hands off each other after several failed attempts. Liam certainly had stamina, which was impressive for someone who hadn't had any action in a long time.

'Yes, please,' I said, smiling, no, not smiling. Fucking beaming.

It was ridiculous.

I came around the island, not able to spend time not touching him. He pulled my arms around his waist, my cheek pressed against his back. A few weeks with this man, and I'd turned into some needy barnacle, clinging to him while he made my coffee.

Pathetic.

I loved it.

He leaned to the cupboard above, taking me with him, and pulled out some caramel syrup.

'I got this for you,' he said, half turning around with a wry smile.

'You noticed,' I said. We'd got drive-through coffee once. Only once. And I'd ordered a caramel latte because the option was there.

I felt Liam shrug. 'It's been hard not to notice you, Red. Even when I tried my best not to.'

My heart burst, and I planted a kiss on his shoulder as he poured some syrup into my coffee, stirred it, and then turned around, handing me the mug. I reluctantly let him go and replaced him with coffee.

A fair trade, just about.

I took a sip and hummed. 'It's really good.'

Liam smiled. 'Good.'

We looked at each other, and I could tell we thought the same thing. How normal and natural this felt. Waking up in the same house and making coffee.

I loved him. I realised it then. I loved him and this mad town. I was really going to do it. Not run and hide like I usually did. Or doubt myself. I was going to do it.

The doorbell sounded.

Our heads whipped around at the sound.

'Abigail?'

Liam shook his head. 'She's at this music weekend with school.'

My phone buzzed – a text from Lydia.

Lydia: Your mum came by the house. I'm sorry, I tried to keep her away, but she was insistent.

I leaned and looked through the peephole to see all five foot three of my mum. Her lips were a flat line, her nose flared.

Oh, she was pissed off.

Fuck.

Chapter Thirty-Six

'Mum. What are you doing here?' I said, attempting an airy tone.

Mum's eyes narrowed with her typical headteacher look. Her eyes flicked up and down. 'I'm here to see my daughter, my daughter who moved counties and kept it from me.'

I stared at the floor.

'Willa let it slip last week. I'm sure she mentioned it. I wanted to come up sooner, but I was at work. This is inconvenient, Katherine.' She said it like I'd asked her to come up here. 'You wouldn't pick up the bloody phone.' She huffed like the words took something out of her. She never swore. 'But once Willa let the cat out of the bag, I understood why.' Mum sighed. 'Really, Katherine. What on earth were you thinking? How much debt are you in renovating that shell of a house?' She glanced up at Liam's house. 'And renting while you do it? What a waste. I brought you up better than this.'

'I'm not renting –'

'Well, are you going to invite me in?' She put her hands on her hips.

I glanced at Liam, standing behind the door, trying to communicate with his eyes. His face went calm with a decision. He swung the door wider, revealing him next to me.

'Mrs Williams. I'm Liam Hunter.' He extended a hand. 'It's lovely to meet you.'

I could hear a tightness in Liam's voice. He used it when he spoke to the Joneses. It was his voice reserved for snobby arses.

We were lucky we'd got dressed and changed. But something about Liam's still-wet hair and bare feet felt... intimate. Like he was used to being casual and half-dressed around me. And I knew Mum had got the gist by how she surveyed us from our toes to the top of our heads, her eyes assessing. Mum wore the same expression when I was sixteen, and my boyfriend was picking me up to see *The Hunger Games* at the cinema.

'It's Ms Evans,' she replied. 'And who exactly are you?'

'Liam – Liam is the builder working on the house.'

Her eyebrows shot up into her hairline.

'The builder,' she said with disdain. 'The builder you're living with.'

I ignored the last comment. 'Liam has been great, Mum. He jumped on the job quickly, and it's almost done now.' I glanced at Liam, needing backup. 'Right?'

'It's almost finished now, Ms Evans.' He shifted on his legs. 'A few more weeks, then it'll be finished.'

'Weeks?' Mum said, alarmed. She shifted her gaze to me. 'That's what they always say, Katherine. Double it. It will take twice the amount of time they say it will.' Her eyes moved to Liam. 'And double the cost, probably. How much is this costing, Katherine?'

Anger began to simmer in my chest at my mum's poor form. I'd never seen this snobby side of her before. The way she looked down her nose at Liam. The scathing referral to 'they' like Liam's profession was inferior. I'd always thought Mum pushed me because of my disability. I'd thought she pushed me to overcome and persevere. But had it come from elitism? A disdain for professions that weren't acceptable to her? She had certainly looked down on artists, but I'd figured that was because it was such an unstable career.

How hadn't I seen this?

I stood ramrod straight. 'Liam is a professional, Mum. He's done this for years. I think he would know how long it will take to finish, especially when we are at the tail end of the renovation now. And I used the money left to me by Dad. I don't see why you would need to know how much I spent. It's my money to spend.'

My gaze turned cold, and Mum's cheeks flushed red hot.

She sputtered. 'Well. If the house is almost finished, why are you still living here?' she asked pointedly. 'Surely you could live out of a room while it's finished.'

I baulked. I could have moved back this week, probably. But I hadn't wanted to.

'Liam offered his annexe.' I gestured outside. 'I've been staying there.'

I could feel Liam's eyes shift to me, and guilt burned in my chest. I should have come out and admitted that we were together. I had planned to, eventually. But I hadn't expected to be ambushed. I needed to prepare my script perfectly and try to predict Mum's retorts.

Mum's eyes shifted over our clothes again.

'I just— I came around this morning to discuss more details about the house. Invoices, etcetera.'

Liam's shoulders tensed at my words. Mum ignored my defence anyway. I deflated. I'd shown my cowardice for nothing.

Mum crossed her arms. 'I had to find out from Brian and Sandra. They looked at me like I was a terrible mother for not knowing where you were. Why didn't you tell me, Katherine? I told you this was a mistake. It's a money pit. Your father had some grand plans about renovating the place, but it was a misplaced rose-tinted view of his childhood.' She shook her head. 'And, of course, he had to drag you into it. Even from beyond the grave.'

'This wasn't for him. It's for me. So I can get some closure.'

Mum scoffed. 'This wasn't going to give you any closure. Selling it and being rid of it would have given you closure. Trust me. There was no need to come up here and dig everything back up.' She sneered at 'up here'. 'You need to put the house on the market and come back home. I've heard from Willa that she's struggling at work, and you've taken off and left her in the lurch. They might be selling – closing for good. What will you do for work then?' Mum pressed. 'You need to think about your future, and trust me, it won't be up here. Really, Katherine. Use your brain.'

Liam stepped forward, the warmth of his body behind me. He leaned his arms above me on the door frame. 'Do not speak to her like that. Not in my house, not ever. If you'd let her get one word in edgeways, maybe she'd explain why she is here. And exactly *why* she felt she needed to keep it from you. Amongst other *revelations*.' Liam levelled my mum with a knowing look, and alarm filled her expression.

'Liam,' I said, warning him, and I could see regret flood his features. His chest was heaving. I could tell he was ready to throw more words at my mother.

This was my battle, not his.

Mum turned to me. 'What is he talking about, Katherine?' She asked Liam, 'Would you give us some space, please?'

'Mum,' I warned. 'This is his house.'

'I'll go,' he said, his touch lingering on my shoulder. 'I'll make us some breakfast.'

'Well, he's a delight,' Mum announced after Liam was out of earshot. 'You know how to pick them, Kat. I mean, a builder, really? And one that is quick to anger, at that.'

I closed my eyes. 'Why do you have to do that?'

'What? Question your romantic choices. I'm your mother.'

I clasped the door. Out of anger or for support, I wasn't sure. 'You put me down, Mum. It makes me question myself. I'm an adult. I'm twenty-seven years old, for god's sake. Don't you think I can make my own decisions?'

My mother's cheeks coloured, flustered. She wasn't used to me using my voice. She wasn't used to me pushing back. I'd heard so many sharp remarks and put-downs from her mouth. Had Graham not played the peacekeeper, I think I would have pushed back a lot sooner. There were only so many sharp words and looks that someone could take.

And Graham wasn't here now.

Mum scoffed. 'I don't put you down. I want to make sure you make the right choices. When you were little, you were so lost –'

'Yes, I know I was. But I'm not little anymore. You can't use my disability to defend how you treat me, Mum.' I got straight to the point. 'Did you ask Dad not to see me anymore? When I was younger?'

Mum's eyes widened. Her mouth was a perfect 'O'.

And that's all I needed. I knew then it was true. I closed my eyes again, a deep-rooted disappointment anchored in my chest. It hurt.

Mum jumped into defensive mode. 'Is all of this about your father? Really, Katherine. He was unstable. Flighty. Unpredictable. He'd never come to your parents' evenings or ballet recitals, even when I reminded him. He took off, and you needed a dad who could be there. Not let you down.'

My nose and eyes burned. She was right. But she was also wrong to have pushed him away. And I was stuck in the middle, living the realities of their failures. My dad hadn't owned up to his. He hadn't had time. But my mum could.

I sighed. 'Dad was unpredictable, yes. But you pushed him away, Mum. You made it worse. Can't you see that? How and when I wanted to have a relationship with Dad – that was my choice to make.'

'It's not that simple when you're a mother, Katherine —'

'My name is Kat,' I barked. 'Everyone calls me Kat. I've been Kat since I was a kid, and I know you know that.' My breath was heaving now. I'd never raised my voice like that. I squeezed my eyes shut. 'I know I struggled at school and all that uncertainty when you were already a single mum juggling a lot. I don't know what I would have done in your shoes. But the choice has been taken from me twice now. Because he's gone.'

The last word choked out of me.

I thought about my dad at his lowest. He was not able to reach out for help, even from his brother. I thought of Brian's strained, worried face when he told me how low he'd been, and my heartbroken dad wasn't able to pull himself out of it. But I was heartbroken for myself because I was the one who lost out. I lost Dad and was left picking up the shards of our relationship. The broken memories and promises cut my hands and made me bleed.

And now it was all coming out, flowing strong.

Mum's face flickered with pain; then she schooled it. She took a step forward. 'I know you've taken his death hard. I understand, I do. But I don't regret my choices, Kat. You don't understand what it was like. How overwhelmed you become —'

I smiled sadly. 'I get overwhelmed, Mum. Sometimes life is a bit much. But that doesn't mean I shouldn't live it. It doesn't mean I'm not capable.' I thought about Liam's words. 'I can't be mollycoddled anymore. I have to push myself. And if I get over-whelmed, fine. I'll get over it. If you wanted, you could support me through that. Help me instead of making me hide from everything.' I lifted my eyes to hers. 'You've made me risk-averse. You let me believe he didn't love me.' My voice broke.

Mum's face softened. But then, her mask was back on.

'Does this look risk-averse to you?' Mum gestured around Liam's hallway. 'Living in some random man's house, you've only known a few weeks? Does leaving your job and a stable income behind sound risk-averse? If that was my plan, I did a poor job of it.'

I closed my eyes, taking a deep breath. I wanted a new job, a new life. I wanted to stay with Liam. I was in love with Liam.

'I want to stay.'

Blood rushed to my head. That was it. I'd said it. And once it was out, I couldn't stop.

'Liam and I are together. I know I've only been here a little while, but I found a home here. I like it here. And it likes me back. I'm moving up here, and you can't convince me otherwise.'

'I don't know what to say. This is so incredibly selfish, Katherine. What about Graham and me? We're not getting any younger, and you want to move two hundred miles away. What if something happens and we need help?'

'You said you were going travelling next year. So what difference would it make?'

Mum scoffed. 'Travelling. Who on earth told you that?'

'You did. You and Graham have all those travel books. You said after retirement –'

'That's a dream, Katherine. It would be nice to travel the world, but we have a life to consider. Responsibilities. Normal people don't just drop everything. And at our age...' She laughed. 'We could never do anything like that.'

I thought about all the times Mum limited herself. All the examples flickered through my head. She loved to bitch about her boss but never went for a promotion when he resigned. She always complained about the house but never put any work into repairing the creaky floorboards or touching up paint. She could travel and see the Pyramids and the mountains in Peru, but she wouldn't leap.

She liked her life to be small and manageable.

Nothing I ever dreamt about was small and manageable.

She was never going to understand me or Liam or Everly Heath. She'd never understand why I wanted to move here and how it wasn't daunting to me in the slightest. I wanted to share all of this with her, but I imagined her repeating it back to me, all the words sounding ridiculous out of her mouth.

The whole idea sounded silly – a pipe dream.

Mum shook her head. 'I knew this would happen. This is why I'm so hard on you, Katherine. This is just like your dad – unreliable. I mean, if you don't think of Graham and me, then think of Willa. She's been left in the lurch. She put faith in you when she hired you after all those dead-end jobs after university. She trusted you, and now, when she needs you most, you abandon her to renovate some hovel.'

Tears burned under my eyes, but I didn't open them.

Mum placed her hand on my shoulder. 'There's no need to cry, darling. I'll send the estate agent details, and we'll get it sorted.'

I took in a shaking breath and gave a sharp nod. I felt like I was twelve again.

'Good. I've got an open return on the train, so I'll head back.' Judgement laced her voice. 'I doubt I'm welcome here. I'll book you on a train for this week, and we can sort everything remotely, okay?' Mum patted my shoulder again. 'We'll sort it all out, darling. Get you back to normal.'

Mum left in a blur. I remember shutting the door behind me. I slid down the back of the door and burst into tears. I smelt Liam's cedar scent first, and then I felt his strong arms come around me and hold me.

Chapter Thirty-Seven

Mum sent me the train ticket on the Monday after her visit. She emailed it to me with no message. I'd opened my phone to look at it several times.

Liam had given me space after Mum's visit.

After she left, he led me to his sofa, pulled a blanket over me, and brought me bowls of food and cups of tea with reruns of *Gilmore Girls* on in the background. Liam's eyes searched mine like he was looking for signs of life. I fell asleep on his sofa, but he pulled the blanket higher and kissed my forehead.

On the second day, I went back to the annexe. I didn't want to burden Liam with my pathetic wallowing. I needed to pull myself together and get over it. Either stand up to my mum or go back to London. I screamed at myself to make a decision, but I couldn't.

So I just lay in bed, paralysed by indecision.

Mum had chipped away at any confidence Liam or Everly Heath had instilled into me. Any faith in myself or my abilities was gone.

On the third day, I was asleep when I felt the covers move, the weight on the mattress and the smell of cedar. It was a moment before he spoke.

'Red,' Liam said, his voice hoarse. 'Talk to me.'

'I can't.'

'Why?'

I shifted, facing him. His brows were wrinkled, but his eyes were open and loving. Like he wanted to make it better. He lifted his hand and rubbed his thumb across my cheek.

'Ren gets like this. I know the signs. He can't move for a few days. I used to bring him meals to see some sign of life. It's probably why I love cooking so much.' Liam leaned forward and kissed my forehead. 'Take as long as you need, Red. But come back to me, will you? When the fog is gone.'

My throat made a choking noise. I squeezed my eyes to keep the tears from overflowing.

'You deserve better than this, Liam. Abi, too,' I whispered, my voice raw. 'Someone reliable. Not some headcase who can't even stand up to her own mum.'

'Hey, hey.' He pulled me into his chest. 'Why don't I be the steady one for you, huh? You keep things interesting for us. Drag me into your chaos. I can take it, Kat. Talk to me. I'm going mad here. I feel like I had you for a moment, and one visit from your mum and you're gone.'

'She was so mean.' My voice broke. 'And I know it's ridiculous. Willa would tell me to forget it. Ignore her. But Mum has ingrained so much of her opinions into me. I don't know what is my idea or hers. I doubt myself. It's like I'm paralysed.' I stifled a sob. 'I'm such a fuck up, Liam. I'm sorry.'

'You are not a fuck up,' Liam said, pulling me tighter into his chest. 'You've never been a fuck up, Kat. She doesn't understand you. It sounds like she's never tried to.'

My tears stained his dark blue T-shirt. 'I don't know what to do. I want to stay, I do. But it's like I've had the wind knocked out of my sails.'

Liam's fingers drew back and forth on my back, soothing me again. Always soothing.

'Let's take some time then,' Liam said, and I pulled back.

My heart raced. 'Are you ending it?' I wasn't sure what I would do if it ended like this. Under the covers at midnight. Like the whole relationship was something I'd dreamt up.

'No, you muppet.' Liam gave me a sad smile. 'Let's take a beat for a bit. I'm opening the restaurant. You need to prove to yourself that this move is something you want. We've got a lot on our plates.'

'You – you want me to go?'

Liam took my head in his hands. 'I don't want you to go, ever. But if letting you go now will let me keep you forever, then I'll do it, Red. Two months to tie up any loose ends, then you come back. I'll have opened the restaurant, so I'll have some of my life sorted, too.'

'You already have your life sorted.'

'It might look like that, Red, but it's not true. I'm terrified that it could fail. Terrified of losing you.'

'I don't want to go.'

'Then are you going to stay? Even when you aren't speaking to your mum. Even when you think Willa needs you? You aren't that kind of person, Kat. You might be chaotic sometimes, but I know you like your relationships neat and tidy. Go and come back. Make me work for it. Ruin my life, Red,' Liam teased.

I huffed a laugh at his joke. Even when it felt like my world was caving in, Liam could still make me laugh.

In Liam's arms, I thought about Willa. Mum made it sound like things were a lot worse than Willa had made out – which was so Willa. She would undersell how bad it was if it meant I could be spared from the stress. I could work for her while she found a replacement. I'd have to move in with Mum and Graham, which made me mentally recoil, but at least I could convince them that this wasn't a fluke. I was serious about this move. I was serious about becoming an interior designer. And I was serious about Liam.

I could use the time to enrol on the design course. I could pack my scattered belongings between Willa's flat and Mum and Graham's house.

'I hate that you know me so well.'

'You love that I know you so well.'

I muttered 'piss off' under my breath, making Liam laugh. He drew me closer, against his chest, and I listened to his heartbeat, steady. Always steady. I didn't have to say it, but I knew we both knew the decision was made. We sat in each other's arms for a few moments.

'Two months. We come back together in two months,' Liam said. 'But no contact.'

My heart lurched.

'Liam—' I started, but he interrupted.

'Kat, I won't be able to stay away if we're speaking every day. It will make it so much more painful knowing you're only three hours away. Ren was right. I'd drive down south to see you for twenty minutes. He needs me here. I owe him that, like you feel like you owe Willa. Two months, no contact, and we'll come back together. What do you say, Red?'

'I hate it.'

'Me too.' He kissed my temple. 'But I've looked at this a million different ways, and this is the only thing I can think of.'

I hummed.

'In two months... if you still aren't sure about us. If you change your mind—' Liam's shoulder tensed, like the idea made him recoil. 'Don't come back, Kat. Don't get my hopes up. If I see you standing in front of me, just to see you leave again. I don't think I'd recover from that.'

'I'm coming back, Liam.'

He kissed me again, this time, my cheeks, my eyelids, and my forehead. Tender, soft kisses that took away the sting of my tears.

'I've said my bit.'

'I'm going to miss you,' I whispered.

I pressed myself into Liam's chest, inhaling him, squeezing him tight.

'I'm going to miss you too, Red.'

His hands were in my hair, his lips on my forehead.

'Come back to me.'

I left the next morning, creeping out of the annexe so I wouldn't wake Liam, who was sound asleep, lightly snoring with his hand over his eyes. On his kitchen island, I left a note and a USB that I knew contained a ridiculous number of files.

As promised, for HBC & Lily's. Don't invite nosy designers into your home if you don't want them to redesign every aspect of your life – Red x

Chapter Thirty-Eight

Six Weeks, Four Days and Nine Hours Later

Kat's To-Do List

- Quotes for moving companies
- Clean out room at Mum & Graham's
- Draft job description for Willa
- Pay the last instalments for Dad's house
- Gifts from London for Abi??
- Reply to Sandra
- **<u>Do not text Liam</u>**

'Kat.' I heard a voice, but it was miles away. My attention was fixed on the logo of Organism, a computer software company. Something about the logo was off, and I couldn't put my finger on it.

The all-male company was often referred to as 'orgasm', so the logo needed to be formal and masculine. Nothing that hinted at sex toys. No bright colours. Essentially, boring as fuck, like the snooze-worthy onboarding call Willa and I sat through with their team. Clients like Organism would have had me itching my skin a few months ago, and Willa would have put them with Clara or

Kieran. But things had deteriorated over the last few months. Willa's dad had got involved in the business in an attempt to save it. Clara and Kieran had been made redundant. I took a voluntary pay cut that Willa reluctantly agreed to — a clear sign things were much worse than she'd let on when she visited Everly Heath.

On the outside, Willa seemed fine. Her dresses and pencil skirts were immaculate. Her tone with demanding clients was formal and professional. But I knew her better. She'd started going to Elias's most nights. I'd go with her when I could, and she'd drink a bottle of wine, stumbling out to call a cab to her apartment in Soho. The next morning, there were no signs of her hangover, apart from the condensation of her Diet Coke on her desk.

I'd tried to speak to her about it, but she shut me down, and Willa didn't like to be pushed.

We were both relieved when Organism signed the contract for twenty grand for a complete rebrand. And for her, I would do the work. Smile at clients. Get it finished on time. And I promised to celebrate with her at Elias's, even though the thought of crowded bars and sticky floors made me feel ill. It made me think of my auntie's smiling face, ugly patterned carpets and Liam's gaze on me.

But for Willa, I would go and smile and sip champagne.

Besides.

It was my last week at Horizon.

One week, and I'd go back home.

'Kat.' The feminine voice was louder now, so I pulled off my headphones. Willa was standing next to me, a look of concern on her symmetrical face. Her eyebrows pinched. She tucked a strand of blonde hair behind her ear.

I looked up at her. 'What's up?'

Willa pointed a pink nail to my screen. 'You've been looking at the screen for five hours straight.'

302

'And?'

'You haven't looked up, tried to make a cup of coffee and failed three times. Nothing.'

I shrugged. 'I want to get this done for you.'

'Who are you, and what have you done with Kat Williams?' Willa said it dryly, but I knew she was hiding her concern under the joke.

I smiled. 'Still here, Wills.'

Her eyes narrowed. 'I don't want you working yourself to the bone for me, you know. You need to tell me if you're working all hours. I don't care if it's your last week.'

'I know, I know. God, you're such a mother hen sometimes.'

Willa rolled her eyes. 'Someone has to be.'

Sometimes, I wished someone would swoop in and look after Willa for once. I kept that thought to myself because god knows she wouldn't let me do that.

Willa wiggled her Best Boss mug I'd bought her for Christmas last year in my face. 'I'm making a coffee. Do you want anything?'

I nodded. 'A brew would be nice, ta.'

Willa raised an eyebrow. 'A brew.'

'Tea. Tea would be nice.'

I checked my phone. The timer read seven days, three hours, and forty-five minutes left. I thought of deep brown eyes, wide shoulders, and insufferable smirks. I thought of the smell of tree sap and petrichor. I thought of Lydia's dirty laugh and the smile lines by Brian's eyes.

One week, and I could get back to Liam.

★

The following week, Willa and I took a short walk across our office to Elias's. It was as buzzy as usual for a Thursday night. Apparently, nothing had changed in London but me. The cold air conditioning of the bar made me shiver, and the sound of the blonde woman's laughter behind me was piercing. Even Elias's had lost its shine.

Willa pushed us through the crowd towards two barstools with signs hooked on the metal bars. One said *Evil Witch*, and the other, *Old Hag*. Elias had bought them as a joke one Halloween. 'Something to keep your seats reserved, ladies,' he'd said with a too-white smile.

Usually, Willa and I argued over who got the old hag seat, but today, I slipped into it.

A strangled noise had me looking up to find Elias staring at me wide-eyed. Elias had olive skin and cropped dark hair. His shirts were unbuttoned far too low, showing off a muscular, hairless chest.

'What the fuck —' he said, a slight accent lingering from his upbringing in Greece til he was fifteen — 'happened to you?'

I frowned, my eyes flickering between Willa and Elias, who shared knowing looks.

I raised my hands. 'I'm fine! I don't know what your problem is. Either of you.'

'You look terrible.' Elias grimaced. 'Your skin is so pale. You have bags under your eyes. You look —' He clicked his tongue. 'Dead.'

'Dead,' I repeated hysterically.

'Elias,' Willa chided. 'She doesn't look dead.'

I raised a hand. 'Thank you.'

'She looks dug up.' Willa took a sip of the champagne Elias placed in front of us. My mouth fell open as I turned to my so-called best friend.

I made a noise in my throat. 'Pot, kettle, bitch.'

Willa pointedly looked away, and Elias gave an amused whistle as he turned, opened a bottle of prosecco, and artfully handled six flutes in one hand.

'Elias's right,' Willa said after a moment. 'We're going through it.'

'I think you'll find he said I look like shit, not you.'

'Trust me, under this make-up, I look like shit.'

I touched her knee. 'Wills, let's talk about it. It might make you feel better.'

Willa gave an acute shake of her head. 'No. I can't right now.' I deflated, and Willa turned to me. 'I will when I'm ready, Kat. I promise.'

I squeezed her knee. 'Good.'

Willa and I turned to watch Elias shake up a margarita. His biceps flexed, and Willa threw an olive in her mouth as she openly ogled him.

'Willa.' I smiled for the first time in weeks. 'You are incorrigible.'

'He knows what he looks like. And I know he isn't exactly batting for my team.'

I hummed and glanced behind us. Aidan sat in a booth on his own. His hair was floppier than usual, as if freshly shampooed. Our eyes met, and he looked down and pushed up his thick-framed glasses to inspect the menu.

'Aidan is sat over there.'

Willa stiffened but made a nonchalant hum. 'He comes here every Thursday.'

'To see you?' I teased.

Willa huffed. 'I seriously doubt it. We are not friends.'

'I don't think he wants to be friends, Willa,' I said in a sing-song voice.

'Ridiculous,' Willa said, sipping her drink. 'We've been rivals since we were kids. It's always a battle of how he can win. By now, he's probably heard from his dad about –' Willa couldn't even say her own business name out loud. That was how ashamed she was of how things had gone. 'He's probably here to rub it in.'

I glanced back over and found that Aidan was gone.

'He's gone.'

'Who cares about Aidan? We're here to celebrate our client win, baby!' Willa said, knocking the rest of her champagne back. 'Elias, another, please!' she shouted across the bar.

Willa turned to me. 'I'm going to miss you so much.'

I bit my lip and told her the thought that had haunted me for two months. 'What if he's moved on, Willa? It's been weeks, and we haven't spoken. We only knew each other a few weeks, for god's sake. I miss him so much, but it also feels like a dream now I'm back here. I've wanted to call him a million times, but he asked me not to. So what if I go back and see him and it's not the same? Or he laughs and says he didn't mean it. Or he is seeing someone new? I wouldn't blame him.'

I would blame myself.

Willa whistled, shook her head, and thanked Elias as he placed two full champagne flutes in front of us. Mine was still half-full. 'The man is in love with you. You made a dramatic, romantic pact. And apart from the whole no-contact thing, he is sickeningly good at communication. You think he's going to forget about you in two months?'

'I don't know.' I held my hands. 'No one has ever been in love with me. I don't know how quickly someone can move on.'

Willa swivelled the barstool and clasped my head in her hands. 'I don't do soppy. So I will say this once, and I want you to hear it. I love you,' Willa said. 'And it would take me longer than two months to get over you, I promise.'

My chest warmed. 'It is so freaky when you're soppy.'

Willa grinned and let my head go. 'I know. You need to go back, Kat. Don't chicken out.' After a while, I turned. Her cool blue eyes were watching me. 'You're miserable. I can see it. Anyone can.'

'I miss him so much.' I groaned. 'But I don't even know what the plan is supposed to be. Do I rock up on the day and say hello? We never planned how this is supposed to happen, and now I'm spiralling.'

'Kat. Listen to yourself.' Willa sighed. 'You're in a position most people would kill for. You have a man waiting for you. A man who adores you so much that he let you go so you could sort your baggage. Well, my baggage, I guess. I can't even dream up a man that well-adjusted.' She gulped her drink. 'Trust me, before I swore off all male kind, I tried.'

I bit my lip. Willa was right.

'However, we need to talk about what you're going to do about your mum.'

I groaned. 'I don't know, Wills. We're barely talking. At first, I tried to talk to her, to convince her. But now, I've accepted I need to move without her approval.'

Willa nodded. 'Good. Let her sweat a bit. The only way she'll start to respect your word is when you start living by it. If you keep flaking on your plans because she puts you down – it's a self-fulfilling prophecy.'

I nodded. I thought about all the plans that had deflated with a word from Mum. 'Yeah, you're right.'

'I'm always right. Go home, tell your mum you're moving to Everly Heath and don't let your mum convince you out of it. Did you just get déjà vu?' Willa pointed to her glossy lips. 'Oh yeah, that's 'cos I've told you this shit before.'

Chapter Thirty-Nine

The Tube was stuffy, and my throat felt tight as a bloke played the accordion, and I stood next to the armpit of a man with some serious body odour issues. Everything was too loud and hot and smelly. Overstimulated, I changed onto the Elizabeth line to Reading, which smelt moderately better. At the other end, I jumped into a cab, preparing for a lecture from Mum about wasting money.

But this time, I had a response.

I wasn't a fuck up.

I was a grown-ass woman. I was capable and creative.

I was more than her low expectations of me. I was capable and creative. I repeated the words like they were my morning affirmations. I might even paint it on my mirror in red lipstick.

I tipped the cab driver, pushed open the creaking gate and walked up the weeded path to Mum and Graham's Victorian terrace. Next door, our neighbours, Will and Patrick, were watching reruns of *Gogglebox*. I'd spoken to them twice in my entire life and not given it a second thought. After two months in Everly Heath, that was bizarre to me.

I tiptoed into the house, placed my keys in the bowl and tried to kick off my shoes without making any noise. Mum and Graham would be in bed by nine, and it was ten thirty. I'd been at the bar later than I'd planned with Willa, and while I wasn't drunk,

I was definitely tipsy. Willa and I had planned what I would say to Mum tomorrow. I was leaving in two weeks.

Willa kept repeating the same point – they were welcome to visit, but I wouldn't accept any negativity at all. By the end of the first bottle of champagne, Willa role-played Mum. She aced the flat look Mum gave me when she was disappointed. As Willa wagged her finger, and we both burst into laughter, Elias watched on and shook his head as he wiped down the bar. Elias usually let us stay later when leftover handbags and empty pint glasses littered the tables.

'In here, Katherine,' Mum said, and I froze like a teenager caught climbing through the window after dark.

I corrected myself, repeating my affirmations. I held my head high as I walked past the front room, which had become colder and dustier since I left. I strode into the little galley kitchen at the back of the house, trying to emulate how Willa walked around the office in her pencil skirt.

'Hello,' I said, opening my mouth to apologise for my late arrival, but I snapped my mouth shut.

Graham and Mum sat at the wooden kitchen table we used for breakfasts and lunches. The orangey wooden kitchen cabinets were cosy, making the room feel smaller. Graham was a full head taller than Mum, even seated. Their hands were cupped around steaming mugs of tea on the faded polka-dot tablecloth.

We'd had it since I was twelve.

Before I'd left, I thought Mum and Graham's house was charming and eclectic. Now, everything was thrown into a new light. It was a mausoleum. I wanted to throw open the windows and let some breeze in. I wanted to donate all the crap they held onto. Stupid trinkets Mum was curating, all items holding her back from doing what she wanted to do – travelling the world.

'Sit down, Kat,' Graham said, and panic rose in my throat.

'What's happened?' My brain searched for some kind of cata-strophic event. Dad was already dead. Oh god, was it cancer?

'Nothing bad,' Graham said with one of his soft, reassuring smiles. I never understood how Graham and Mum worked together. She was so prickly and unrelenting, and he was so soft and pliant. Maybe that's why they worked.

I pulled back the chair, suddenly conscious of my alcohol breath and how the room was slightly spinning.

'We want to talk to you about Everly Heath,' Graham said, and surprisingly, Mum didn't bristle like she usually did at the mention of the town.

I sat up straight. 'You aren't persuading me to stay here. I told you from the beginning that I was going back. I needed this time to make sure everything was sorted with Willa.'

And with you, I wanted to say.

I wanted to shout that Liam and I agreed that I hadn't returned here with my tail between my legs. I wasn't going to have my mind changed.

I hadn't stopped thinking about Liam for weeks. Each morning was a brutal reminder when I rolled over, searching for him. The dreams were the worst – they taunted me with moments of Liam in the kitchen, kissing me. A blend of memories. I missed waking up next to him, his scent around me, the weight of his arm across me. I missed the tree-lined walk to the club and, most worryingly, Ray, the jazz singer and his polyester waistcoat. I missed laughing with Lydia and Sandra at the club. I even missed the light sheen of rain on my face on the walk home.

'We know, Kat,' Graham said, glancing at Mum. 'And we've had some… discussions about your move. Mum and I didn't agree at first.' Graham reached over to pat Mum's hand, and Mum's head nodded an inch. 'I think it would be good for you to have a fresh start somewhere new. And this chap of yours –' Graham paused.

'Liam.'

'Yes, Liam. Well, you mention him so often, so I suppose you are rather attached to the chap.'

My lips twitched. 'I am.'

I'd been trying to recreate some of Liam's recipes at home for Mum and Graham. I never got them right, but each one got better, and I loved mentioning his name at the dinner table. I revelled in the way Mum's eye twitched. I didn't give a fuck what she thought anymore. Just mentioning Liam's cooking and Lily's made me feel like I hadn't dreamt him up. He was real. And I'd be back soon.

It made my heart ache but in that lovely, painful way.

'I'm not going to ask for your permission,' I said, and Mum's eyes flickered to mine. 'I'm a grown adult.'

'No, we know,' Graham said, ever the diplomat.

'You hurt me, Mum.' The champagne had loosened my tongue. 'You lied to me. You pushed Dad away. You let me believe he didn't love me.' My voice broke, and I saw regret etched on Mum's face for the first time. 'I've grown up terrified of letting you down, like I did at school. So I've done everything you said just to get a glimmer of approval from you. You picked my university. You suggested I work for Willa. I stopped seeing anyone you didn't approve of. I wrote relationships off completely because I knew there was no point. I couldn't make you happy.'

Mum opened her mouth, but I held up a hand.

'Let me finish. You owe me that.'

She gave a small nod.

'I've been stagnant. I was bored out of my head. And okay, maybe that is a bit to do with my ADHD, but so what? It took Willa pushing me to do anything about it. I've found where I want to be. I know it's a risk. But I can't live like life isn't about taking a little risk. It isn't living, Mum.' My eyes flickered to

Graham, his bespectacled face uncharacteristically intense. 'You should both live yours.'

'Kat,' Mum said, and I tried not to react at the use of my nickname. 'I realise I've made a lot of mistakes. If you can believe me, whatever I did was out of love. It was because I thought it was best —'

I opened my mouth, but Mum stopped me. 'I was wrong. I'm realising that now.' She glanced at Graham. 'Graham made me see how blind I've been. I'm sorry.' She inhaled. 'I can't say I'm happy about you moving to Everly Heath. I don't understand it. But I don't have to. I need to accept it's what you want.'

My mind reeled. Not in any universe did I expect Paula Evans to admit she was wrong.

'Well —' I paused, unsure what to say. 'Thank you.'

'So, we figured you'd want to see this.' Graham slid over a white envelope. 'We haven't opened it.'

I spotted the familiar sprawl, and my hands darted across the table to snatch it. It was Liam's handwriting. I was used to seeing it on my walls where he'd made measurements or on notes he left on the island when he left early for work and left me in bed. I ripped open the envelope and let out a little noise. Something between a whine and a sigh.

'What is it?' Graham asked, frowning.

'Nothing,' I said, my eyes burning as I scanned the invite, my brain lagging behind. Next weekend. Friends and family. Then, a little handwritten note in the corner. *You pinkie promised.*

My heart pounded, adrenaline pumped. I stood up, my chair scraping back. Then, I stopped myself.

What did I think I would do — run two hundred miles?

Mum's hand went to the invite. 'Did you design this?'

'How did you know?'

'I always know your designs,' she said, lowering her eyes. 'I can tell by the colours. You always favour reds and oranges. Sometimes teal.' Mum took a deep breath and met my eyes. 'I know I don't always say it. But I'm proud of you. I've always been proud of you. I promise to work harder to make sure you know that.'

My nose burned, and all I could do was nod.

I glanced down at the invite. I'd used swirly cursive letters to spell out Lily's – strong, bold colours for their branding, an ode to Liam's strong, no-nonsense attitude. The deep blues and burnt oranges captured his steady, thrumming presence. I'd be happy if that were my last graphic design job, ever. For Lily's. For Liam.

I said goodnight to Mum and Graham and headed to pack up my life.

Chapter Forty

It was balmy walking up Everly Heath High Street. My heels sounded on the pavement as I passed the social club, which was suspiciously quiet. The day had been blistering sunshine, and the smell of barbecue and freshly cut lawns hung in the air, reminding me of my last visit in June – for Dad's funeral. A year on, and I could still feel some of that lingering grief like fingerprints smudged on glass.

It wouldn't leave. I didn't want it to. That familiar tug was painfully reassuring, like a rope against the skin. It meant I had loved someone. I loved Dad despite all his mistakes and distance. Some days, when clouds circled, I felt he didn't deserve my love. But other days, like today, I could sit in that reality. I loved my dad, and returning to the place he loved filled me with bittersweet comfort, whether I wanted it to or not.

It was a momentary comfort as my thoughts shifted to Liam, spiking my cortisol. I tried to focus on the sound of my heels clopping. My steps slowed as I approached the side street Liam and I had walked down a few months ago.

Low, orange light poured from the window as I stood and looked in. My heart burst when I saw the turnout. Everyone I'd ever seen in Everly Heath was packed into the tiny restaurant. Lydia and Sandra sipped flutes of champagne. Pat and Ravi gossiped by the bar, their heads leaning in together conspiratorially. Dot sitting on one of the booths, her legs dangling above the floor. Even miserable Peter had the grace to look impressed with a nod and a downturn of his lips.

Yasmin laughed as Abigail wrinkled her nose at the smoked salmon blinis passed around by Ren, who ruffled Abi's hair; she wrinkled her nose again.

My heart jumped when Liam strode out of the kitchen and into the bar. He had the air of someone who was comfortable, familiar in their surroundings, and I figured he'd probably lived in this restaurant for two months. I watched him carefully lay more champagne flutes on the copper bar. As he turned, I saw he was wearing a hunter-green apron with my logo – no, his logo – in the centre. His hair had grown longer, long enough to be pulled back into a ponytail. His beard had grown, too.

As he turned, I saw a wild look in his eyes and a determined edge to his jaw, even under his beard. Fulfilment, I realised. Purpose.

Liam's face broke into a grin as he spotted Frank, pulling him into a hug – a warm welcome for the man who had inspired him. Liam looked up from Frank, glancing at the door with… anticipation. He was looking for someone, waiting.

His eyes met mine and widened.

My heart gave a painful lurch. I wasn't sure why, but suddenly I turned on my heel, walking back down the alley. This was too public, too much.

'Kat!' Liam's voice was nearing. 'Kat.' My damn heels weren't letting me move any faster.

A hand landed on my arm, and I had no choice but to stop. I turned around, and Liam was smiling – a wide smile, a hundred-kilowatt bulb.

I blinked, wondering what I'd done to deserve that smile and what I would do to keep it, keep him, in my life.

'You're here,' he said, smiling. 'Why did you run off?'

'I –' I squeezed my eyes shut. 'I'm not sure. I panicked. Half the town is in there.'

I rubbed my temple. I was fucking this up. Liam touched my hand, gently pulling it away from my face.

'Hey, it's okay.' Liam ran a hand up my arm. 'I'm just happy you're here. I hadn't planned on so many people. But you invite Pat, you're inviting everyone.'

We just looked at each other then. I took in the small smile on his face, the smile creases around his chestnut-brown eyes. His face softened.

'I missed you,' he murmured, and then I was in his arms. I launched myself at him so hard that he took a step back at the force and gave a husky laugh.

'I missed you, too,' I whispered into his neck.

'How have you been?' he said. 'I want to know everything.'

We shifted, and my feet hit the ground, but we didn't separate. We just stood in each other's arms.

'Miserable. London was hot. And usually it's hot in June but this time it was worse. Like suffocating. And moving in with Mum and Graham was tedious. I only did it so I could prove a point. I kept talking about you and Everly Heath, partly to piss off my mum, which was a stupid teenager move, but I couldn't help it.' I inhaled for the next words. 'Willa is miserable too, but she won't let me help her. I tried my best to sort what I could, but I get the feeling something bigger is happening that she won't share with me. And I missed you every day. I wanted to strangle you for saying I couldn't call or text. I was going to FaceTime you for sex one night, to see if you'd cave –'

Liam gave a shuttered laugh. 'I probably would have.'

'Damn it. I knew I should have given it a go.' I sighed. 'But annoyingly, I'm glad I went back. I helped Willa land some clients and recruit someone else. And Mum seems to have come around to the idea of me moving here. She was actually quite nice when I left. She and Graham helped me pack up my stuff.'

I was suddenly aware I was waffling. I closed my mouth, and the silence held for a moment. I pulled back to see Liam's lip turned up, but he was staring at me with that resting bitch face.

'Say something!' I said, my hands flapped uselessly.

'Just checking you were done,' Liam said, hiding his smile. 'Sometimes you get a second wind.'

'Ugh, what do you want me to say? I should never have gone back. Because I will –'

My words died as Liam stepped forward and pressed his lips against mine. His chest pressed against my own. The world roared with white noise, but my head was quiet. Peaceful. Until Liam's teeth grazed my lower lip, teasing me, and blood roared in my ears.

He pulled back, and I swallowed my disappointed noise.

Liam cradled my neck. 'I've been miserable. More of an arsehole than usual. Sandra banned me from the club.'

'She banned you?' I gasped.

'She held a public vote. Everyone voted yes.'

I gave a strangled laugh.

'Don't laugh.' But his eyes twinkled. 'I was a mess because I missed you. God, it's been so quiet.'

My eyes narrowed. 'Excuse me –'

'Too quiet,' Liam murmured, his hands gripping my hair.

Our lips met. Relief and the smell of Liam's cologne flooded my senses. Liam's hands fell to my neck, pulling me closer and deepening the kiss. He kissed my cheeks and forehead like I was something precious.

Liam's eyes were soft, flickering between my lips and my eyes.

'I've got something to show you,' Liam said as he grasped my hand and led me away from the restaurant, which was teeming with people.

'What about the party?' I said, frowning. 'Liam, we can't leave.'

'It can wait.'

'Liam. You've worked so hard on this. We can't just walk off –'

Liam turned, clasping my head in his hands, planting a quick kiss on my lips. He grinned down at me, a glint in his eyes. 'I've been waiting two months for my life to restart again. Trust me, the party can wait. This can't.'

Chapter Forty-One

Liam stopped the van outside my house, a small smile on his handsome face. He'd run his hand through his hair on the drive over, his gaze shifting to me and back to the road, like I was going to disappear at any time.

'What's going on?' I said, walking over to him, taking his arm from his hair and threading his fingers through mine. It was a relief to be able to do it. To touch him again.

'I –' Liam began. 'I'm not good with all the words.'

My lips turned up into a smile. 'All the words?'

'You know what I mean. I didn't go to uni. I can't write you poetry.'

'Liam, if anyone wrote me poetry, I'd die of embarrassment.'

Liam pulled me closer, pulling me into a quick kiss, his hands still wrapped in my hair when he said, 'This is my way of saying I love you.'

My heart pounded at his words as he pulled me towards the house, and then I noticed it. The front garden had been neatened, and the moss and overgrown plants had been trimmed back. A new porch light had been fitted. The door had a fresh paint of colour – a pale pink.

Then – I glanced through the front door windows and pulled back.

I turned to him. 'Liam. What did you do?'

Hope and happiness blazed through Liam's dark eyes.

'I've been waiting to show you for weeks. I've kept all the photos I wanted to send.' He threaded his fingers through mine to pull me towards the door.

As it glided open, my jaw fell open.

Parquet flooring was shining up at me. A cream carpet runner led up the stairs, with new spindles painted black. It smelt of fresh paint. A huge round mirror hung above the console table.

Three framed pictures hung, empty.

Liam clocked my gaze. 'I figured you would want to pick out the pictures. I didn't want to assume who you'd want in them – this isn't for me. This is for you. I've still got my place, so we can live separately, if you'd prefer.'

'Liam.' I squeezed his hand, grinning up at him. I'd never seen him so flustered. 'Take a breath.'

His eyes took me in, moving across my face. 'I want you to enjoy this.'

Liam put his hands on my shoulders and ushered me into the first room, the lounge. The deep blue walls made the space feel cosy and homely. A log-burning fire sat at the hearth, and on either side were fitted arched bookcases, which looked familiar...

Then it hit me.

I turned to Liam. 'My Pinterest.'

He'd gone on my Pinterest and recreated it.

Liam shrugged. 'It was public, and you made it easy. You catalogued each room so I could replicate what you'd designed. I was impressed. I've worked with a few interior designers, but none were as thorough as you. And before you say anything, I chose to do this. I'll take the hit.'

He'd paid for all of this. He must have spent a small fortune.

'You –' I stuttered. 'You've done each room.'

My eyes almost bugged out of my face. I hadn't held back. I'd gone all out. Bold Farrow and Ball paint, floral Sanderson wall-paper, and expensive furniture from West Elm and Soho Home. I'd gone down a rabbit hole until three in the morning and made notes and lists. It was my dream house, an ideal scenario. But I never actually planned to decorate it like this. I'd planned to find some cheaper alternatives.

'How – how did you have the time? What about the other fittings?'

When I'd left, this house had been half finished.

'I had some help.' Liam smiled. 'Pretty much everyone chipped in. Every labourer at the club. I couldn't keep Brian and Sandra away. They kept coming to do odd bits after work. And Lydia helped with some of the heavy lifting.' Liam hooked his arms around my shoulders, pulling me into his back. He planted a kiss on my neck. 'Unsurprisingly, you are very popular. Once Pat caught wind, I had a whole list of volunteers. Carpenters, painters. Someone who tried to sell me solar panels. I held off on that, but if you need them installed, I know a bloke.'

I made a choking sound.

Liam murmured, 'But even if they hadn't helped, I would have done it. It might have taken me longer.'

I stood there, Liam's arms wrapped around me, in the same room we'd crossed paths in all those months ago. I'd got him so wrong. I'd presumed he was an arsehole, grumpy, uncharitable. But he was the opposite.

'I – I'm lost for words.'

'First for everything, Red.' I could hear the grin in his words. 'Come on, there is more.'

I let Liam tour me around the house. It was surreal seeing a house I'd designed on a social media app in real life. Liam had replicated my perfect kitchen and somehow improved it. Originally, I'd planned for a small kitchen and island, but Liam had shifted the design to make room for more units. It made it more practical, with a perfect triangle between the oven, sink, and bin. He'd installed the brass handles and a huge Belfast sink I'd dreamt of.

He'd created the dining nook I'd added to my board one day without a second thought. I'd loved it, but I'd figured it was a pipe dream. Now, it was in front of me. I wanted to sob. It was so beautiful. Liam told me that Sandra had spent hours painting it in Farrow and Ball's Railings, the dark blue complementing the soft, almost pink kitchen cabinets.

'She wanted it to be perfect,' Liam said.

The bathroom we designed months ago was installed upstairs. The first design, not the pared-back one. A vintage dresser held the sink, making the rustic tiles and the soft blue wood panelling on the walls pop.

'What – what did you do with all the other fittings?'

'I donated them,' Liam said with a grimace. 'A bloody field day at the club. People bartering over a bloody bathroom tap.'

A laugh burst out of me, and Liam's lips twitched. He ran his hand over the bathroom dresser.

'As promised.'

'As pinkie promised.'

My eyes met Liam's, and I tried to show him what this meant to me, how much I appreciated it. He raised a thumb to my cheek.

'I wanted to see this, what you created.'

My eyes burned with tears. 'Thank you. Thank you so much. It's beautiful.'

'There is one more thing.'

'Liam. I can't take anymore.' I shoved my head into his chest. 'I might combust.'

Liam's chest shook with laughter. 'One more, that's it. You aren't getting anything else for the year.'

I pulled back, pouting. 'Not even a Christmas present?'

'Maybe your present will be me.' Liam kissed my lips, his tongue stroking mine.

My hands began to roam until he pulled them off him, and I groaned. He grinned.

'Come on, I can't wait.'

'Neither can I,' I muttered as Liam led me downstairs.

In the kitchen, Liam opened the French doors onto the garden. The most extravagant Wendy house I'd ever seen sat at the end of a new stone path. Liam had painted it a soft pale green, and it had a little porch with two rocking chairs. The windows and doors were real and solid, not just made of timber and plastic.

Tears formed now and ran down my cheeks silently.

'I took a look at your dad's plans. I couldn't do everything in them – he had a lot of ideas. But if we wanted, we could extend into the loft next year with Jack's help.'

Liam opened the doors and turned on the lights, and I suppressed a sob.

A huge rustic wooden desk sat in the middle of the room on a large rug. On the wall hung a huge pinboard, and pinned to it were samples I'd ordered for the house months ago. Samples that now made up the cushions and wallpaper of the house behind me.

Next to them, my dad's draft plans for the house were on display, too.

A craft table and an easel with paint supplies were on the other side.

'This is for your interior design projects, but I found out you liked to paint watercolours when you were younger,' Liam said, his deep voice filling the room, 'so I ordered you some paints.'

'How –'

'I asked Graham. I got his number from Brian, and he seemed more pleased to hear from me than your mum had been. He promised not to say anything to her. He sounded like he was living out his spy fantasies.'

'Why – why did you do this?'

'Call Graham?'

'No, all of this, the house. This office.'

'I like to think of it as a studio.' Liam scratched his head as he took a deep breath. 'When I asked you to come back. I realised I didn't have anything to offer you.'

My face softened. 'Liam –'

'I know – you'll deny it. But you're giving up this big life in London for me. So when you left and I was alone. Well, I couldn't just sit on my arse. I needed something to do.'

'Other than opening a restaurant.'

Liam shrugged. 'Ren was great with it, actually. He took on a lot more than I'd been expecting him to. He hasn't dropped the ball once. So I spent a lot of time here when I wasn't with Abi or at the restaurant. I wanted to be able to give you something.'

I took a step forward, itching to touch him. Liam seemed to read my mind and stepped forward to pull me into him. My chin on his chest, I looked up at him.

Liam kissed my nose. 'I think this is the first time I've seen you speechless.'

I cocked an eyebrow. 'You met me at a funeral where I was literally speechless.'

Liam wrinkled his nose. 'I don't count that.'

'Yeah, because you were a dickhead.'

'I think you called me a prick, actually.' He smiled, and I laughed. 'I think I probably fell in love with you then. You leaned out your window and called me a prick. That was it.'

I rolled my eyes but wanted to burst. Combust. So many emotions running through my body, I had no idea how to siphon through them.

Liam tugged at my hand. 'Come on, there's a lot more to see.'

'Don't you have a soft opening to get to?'

He looked sheepish. 'I may have given you the wrong timings on your invite.'

I raised an eyebrow. 'You're conniving when you want to be.'

His eyes burned into me. 'I knew what I wanted, and I needed to make it happen. I'll beg, borrow, and steal if I have to. Now, come on.' He tugged at my hand. 'I've been waiting to show you this for weeks.'

'But I want to stay with the bookcases,' I complained, staring at them like I was Gollum. 'So pretty.'

Liam laughed. 'I think you'll like the kitchen more.'

'Am I dreaming?' I went to pinch myself. 'I must be dreaming.'

I thought about my life at home since I moved back. The sadness I felt when I dropped my bags in the hall of Mum and Graham's house – the feeling of defeat. I'd lost again. I'd failed. Another unsuccessful hobby I'd taken up and then dropped. Mum was right.

Then, I thought about living in Everly Heath. I'd never felt lighter or more at home. I'd been supported, even with the heaviness of my relationship with my dad, that flipping between grief and resentment. They'd rallied together and built me a fucking home. A proper home. Just like the one I'd imagined. And I think it was something like my dad had imagined when he'd drawn up those plans.

So, it made my decision easy. For once, I knew my impulse was so right that it wasn't an impulse.

'So, would we live here?' I mused, playful.

Liam's eyes flickered, but he was still reserved like he was holding back.

'Yes. I'll sell the house. I don't care about it anyway.'

'So, you'd make me breakfast every morning.' I pointed to the main house. 'In that kitchen?'

'Kat —' Liam warned, the deep timbre of his voice making me shiver. 'Don't play with me.'

I turned to him, smiling up at his handsome face, which was flickering between disbelief and hope. I decided to put him out of his misery.

'I'm staying.'

His head shot up.

'What?'

'I want to stay. Here, with you.'

'You're moving here? We're doing this?' Liam's eyes were wide, still disbelieving. I stepped closer, wrapping my arms around his neck and leaning closer.

'Well, you did make this house the most perfect house I've ever seen —'

'You did that —'

'And built me an art studio. Then you told me you love me. I'm afraid you won't be able to get rid of me now.'

'I don't want to,' he said, pushing me up onto my new desk, his mouth on mine, insistent and urgent. His hands were every-where: on my neck, my cheeks, like he was trying to kiss every bit of me at the same time. Like he couldn't decide where to start.

He pulled away. 'You're staying.' We were both out of breath.

'I'm staying.' He kissed me again, somehow even more urgent and fervent than before.

'How long have we got?' I gasped between kisses.

'Long enough.'

One Year Later

To-Do List

- Pick up Abi from school (Liam)
- ~~Food shop (Kat)~~ Already done it, Red
- ~~Prep food for tonight (Kat)~~ In what world?
- ~~Collect Mum and Graham from the station (Kat)~~ Sandra and Brian are on it
- ~~Make sure we have enough napkins.~~ I brought some over from Lily's
- Just get ready, beautiful. I love you – L

'Abi! Kat!' Liam bellowed up the stairs. 'We're going to be late!'

'Shit,' I muttered furiously, flicking through my make-up bag, and Abigail laughed beside me.

We had been applying eyeliner for the past twenty minutes, sitting at my dressing table in our loft room. We sat on matching stools, the mirror lights illuminating our irises – mine blue, Abigail's a deep brown, like Liam's. I bought Abi her own after she liked to linger by my dressing table, asking me what products I used.

'Oh yeah. I've seen someone use that before,' she said after I showed her my Lancôme mascara. 'Some millennial on YouTube, I think.'

She pretended to play it cool until I bought her a tube, with Yasmin's approval, and she jumped up and down, squealing. I will never forget the force of her hug around my waist, her small arms wrapped around my middle, and Liam's satisfied smile watching us together.

Since then, we've always done our make-up together.

I checked my watch. 'Shit. Seven twenty. We are late.'

Abigail hummed, concentrating on applying her eyeliner. We promised Liam to leave at quarter past by the very latest. I glanced over at Abigail. Her dark hair had grown so quickly this year. Her mouth was open in a perfect 'O' as she applied her mascara. Her eyeliner was impeccable.

I frowned. 'How the hell are you doing that better than me?'

I swear she was practising this shit without me.

The girl was almost twelve and could apply make-up better than me – the cheek of it.

She shrugged. 'I skive PE so I can practise.'

My eyes narrowed. 'I'm going to pretend I didn't hear that.'

Either Abigail was comfortable with me or testing how outrageous a statement could be before I was forced to tell her dad. Abigail had forgotten that I had a step-parent. I was well-versed in manipulation strategies. But as Abigail's teenage years set in, all grey moods and apathy, I was selfishly grateful to be seen as the 'cool' one. Abigail saved her fights for Liam and Yasmin.

I had to take *some* wins, right?

'Katherine! Abigail!' Liam shouted.

'Dad!' Abigail shouted back. 'Per-fec-tion' – she sounded out each syllable – 'takes time. Didn't anyone tell you that?'

We giggled as Liam loudly grumbled something, and when we were ready, Abigail and I walked down the two flights of stairs. The little 1930s semi was no longer a project or a deadline. It was a home now – scuffs on the skirting boards and recycling piled up by the bins. Abi had her own room at the back of the house, and we'd had a lot of fun designing it together. She'd gone for a powder-blue wallpaper with birds and florals. A very sophisticated choice that I thought would take her into her teen years at least.

I walked down the hallway with a wall full of bright and eclectic art prints we'd collected at art fairs and markets around the Northwest. Amidst the prints were a scattering of photos taken over the past year. Liam and me next to the Christmas tree, his arms wrapped around my waist, his kiss on my temple. Liam and Abi playing football on the beach when we visited Yasmin's parents in Formby in February. Lydia and I with our medals after we completed a 10K in April. Mum, Graham, and me climbing a mountain in the Peak District on their visit a couple of months ago.

A snippet of our life up here, all on the walls of this house that wasn't supposed to be mine. But now it was ours. Liam sold his house within a few months and moved in. I told him he could keep it or rent it out, but he insisted on selling it.

'I don't give a shit about that house, Kat,' he'd said one morning while trailing his hands across my bare hips as we stood in the kitchen, looking out at the garden on a bright morning. 'It was just a house. This is home.'

Liam used the money from his place to do a huge loft conversion, making us a master bedroom, walk-in wardrobe and en suite with a walk-in shower. I got to design all over again, staying on Pinterest until the early morning hours. Liam grinned and shook his head when I showed him the expensive marble I picked for the shower.

Then, the next day, he ordered it.

The loft conversion gave Abigail the first floor to herself and her friends during sleepovers. We had plenty of space when Willa or Mum and Graham visited. Mum was slowly coming around

329

to Everly Heath. She and Graham visited every three months at least. They were starting to get on with a lot of the locals in their own way. On their first visit to the club, they sat in a quiet corner with their lager shandy, but I didn't mind. Mum was making an effort, like I'd asked her. I could accept she had her own way of doing things. Then on the next visit, Graham had one too many and started chatting to Peter. I was convinced it was game over. The men couldn't be any different. But then, Peter's face lit up and they talked for three hours, bonding over their shared love of Egyptology.

Last week, I'd been tidying and I'd found a list of walks they wanted to do in the Peak District, and it made me well up.

'Finally,' Liam grumbled as Abi and I descended the stairs. His eyes softened as he took us in. Abigail was in a racerback mid-length dress with platform trainers, her hair styled in braids down the back of her head. She looked cool – like her mum. Meanwhile, I tried to ignore the way Liam's gaze travelled up my body. I was wearing a new floral green dress, summery and feminine – a homage to the dress he'd bought for me last year on our first date. Liam scanned over my curves and I had a feeling he was thinking how much better the dress would look on the dark hardwood floors of our bedroom later.

'Ew, Dad,' Abigail said, ever insightful. 'Stop perving.'

I laughed, and Liam's eyes flicked away. 'I was not.'

'You so were.' Abigail scrunched up her nose.

Liam kissed Abigail's forehead. 'Go get in the car, trouble.'

'Happily.' She held out her hand for the keys, and Liam dropped them in her palm.

'You can start it but do not move it. Not again. We'll piss off Pat if we run over Noodle.'

'I barely ran him over,' Abigail argued as she walked out of the porch. 'He was in the way!'

I chuckled, shaking my head. 'It's only going to get worse.'

Liam smiled and shrugged. 'I've got help.'

I arched an eyebrow. 'I'm busy being the favourite, thank you. I'm not raising my head above the parapet.'

'Coward,' he said and pulled me into a searing kiss, his palms travelling down my hips and down to my bum. 'You look fucking incredible.'

I smiled into his kiss and thought about how this was the same man I'd called a prick in a car park. Both of those people felt so far away like we were completely different people.

Liam pushed me against the wall, his thigh coming to rest between my legs, and I melted. A year on and he could still set me on fire with one kiss.

'Do we have to go now?' I complained, my heart racing.

Liam chuckled. 'It's your party, Red. I think people would notice if you were missing.'

I groaned, pushing Liam's chest away so I didn't press him closer to me. Liam's smug smirk told me he knew exactly how distracted I was.

'Come on, you're going to be late.' Liam laced his hand through mine and ushered us towards the pink front door.

I raised an eyebrow. 'Can I be late to my own party?'

Liam laughed. 'It's a good job I told you the wrong time. Now, we're bang on time.'

I swivelled towards him. 'Not again.'

Liam shrugged, a wide grin on his handsome face. 'And yet, you fall for it every time.'

★

I bit my lip as the last of the evening sun lit up the KAT WILLIAMS DESIGNS sign, giving it a warm orange glow. It felt obnoxiously big. Too big. It dwarfed the little shop I had picked because of the adorable bay window. The outside was painted a soft white, and I was sure it would get dirty in the winter. I could paint a new colour to reflect a new season – burnt orange for autumn, dark blue for winter, and duck egg blue for spring. I shifted on my feet, my gaze drifting back to the sign. Liam stood beside me as Abigail had already run into the shop to find her mum.

A year ago, Liam's restaurant was full to the brim with people, all buzzy and warm and full of laughter.

Now, it was my shop opening, three doors down from Liam's restaurant, which, after a rave review from a well-known national restaurant critic, was booked up weeks in advance. Now, I had people asking me for favours in the club – bookings at Liam's restaurant for their daughter's birthday or a big anniversary they'd forgotten about. Liam always kept a table back and called it the Everly Heath Tax. He usually took care of the bill if he liked them well enough.

I gnawed at my lip. 'Is the sign too big?'

'No, love.'

'I think it looks stupid.'

Liam rubbed his hand across my arm. 'It's perfect.'

'Are you sure? Maybe I should call the signage people and ask them to mock up something else –'

'Kat.' Liam turned my shoulders so I faced him. He tilted my head up to meet his eyes. 'You've worked fucking hard for this. All those nights studying and the money you saved to open this place.' Liam offered the money to help, but I said no. I wanted to do this on my own and know I did it myself. He reluctantly agreed because he knew how much that mattered to me.

Liam continued, 'The hard bit is over. No more working from the Wendy house, Red.' He stood behind me, hugging me from behind. Kissing my neck. 'Now you have your own shop, so everyone knows where they can hire the best fucking interior designer in the Northwest.'

My lips twitched. 'Maybe in the country.'

Liam smiled. 'There she is.'

I exhaled a groan. 'Okay. Let's do this.'

Liam pushed open the door, and the little bell I installed last week gave a delightfully camp ring. Two of Liam's floor staff, Mia and Adam, welcomed us holding trays of champagne. Liam had closed the restaurant for the night and insisted on catering the launch event.

'Thanks, guys,' I said, accepting a glass of champagne. Nerves bubbled up in my stomach.

Everyone I loved was squeezed into my tiny shop. Lydia and her girlfriend, Casey, stood by the wall-to-ceiling display of fabric samples. They had been going out for almost a year once Casey finally got the courage to ask Lydia on a date. Casey smiled and waved at me, her naturally warm disposition lighting up the room. Lydia turned and met me with a big smile.

I laughed as she pointed at the champagne and mouthed, *Nice*.

Ren was standing on the other side, standing alone. His charcoal trousers and white tee stood out against the burnt orange of my wall of prints. It was always a surprise to see him off-shift. He never seemed to take a break from Lily's. I wasn't sure he wanted to. He stood away from Lydia. He was subtle, but I noticed him stealing glances at her. Things were still off between them since he'd appeared at my birthday dinner. They were supposed to be childhood friends, but they were cordial. Distant. Everyone in Everly Heath seemed to notice it, whispering behind their hands when Lydia and Ren were in the same room. But whenever I brought it up to Lydia, she changed the subject.

'There you are, darling.' Graham and Mum came out from behind some curtains, like some sort of magician's act. 'Lovely display in the windows. We had to take a look.'

Mum and Graham looked tanned. Freckles across Graham's cheeks showed they'd been somewhere warm.

'How were your travels?'

'It was a holiday.' Mum's lips pursed. I'd been teasing her about it being a trip of a lifetime. 'A three-week cruise doesn't constitute itself as travelling.'

I grinned and shrugged. 'Sounds like it to me.'

Graham's eyes lit up. 'It was amazing, Kat. They had performers every night and a casino! I'd never bet before, but I was quite a blackjack fan by the end. And the sand in the Bahamas was white, and the water was like a bath.'

Mum smiled. 'It was nice to have a break.'

My eyebrows rose. That was a rave review when it came to my mum. Five stars.

Mum touched my forearm and nodded. 'Everything looks lovely, Kat.'

I couldn't keep the pride from my smile. 'Thank you.'

Liam slung his arm around my shoulder. 'She's outdone herself. Again.'

'She has.' Mum's face turned up to Liam's, respect shining there. 'I hope you both have a lovely evening.'

'Oh, Kat. I wanted to ask if Peter is coming along. Just I found out about this dig —'

Mum pulled at Graham's checked shirt. 'Come on, darling. Let's leave the lovebirds.'

'Next time, then!' Graham laughed, raising his flute.

I laughed, turning to Liam. 'They seem happy.'

'I was thinking the same,' Liam said. 'And I think your mum likes me now. That's a relief. Not sure I could face that stare again.'

I nodded. 'The scary teacher stare. It's famous.'

'I can see why.' Liam shuddered.

I laughed. 'Who's the coward now?'

'Self-preservation, Red. It's self-preservation.' Liam grabbed another champagne flute from one of the trays and took my empty one. 'Now, go on. Work the room.' Liam nodded at the crowd behind me. Several people were watching, most of them friends, but I had some clients in mind I wanted to speak to today. I knew Pat wanted some rooms redesigned in her house, and Liam's ex-clients, the Joneses, were also here, and they had thick wallets.

I took a deep breath and stepped forward into the crowd.

★

'Such a good party, Kat,' Pat slurred as she teetered towards the door with Auntie Sandra on her arm. 'Such a fun night.'

'It was marvellous,' Sandra agreed. 'Even Peter seemed in good spirits.'

'I'm so glad you had a good time,' I said, trying to suppress my laugh, as the two friends walked in a zigzag.

'Oh!' Pat gasped, turning. 'Did we tell you, Kat? Peter said he'd let Noodle come to the club!'

I laughed. 'Yes, you did.' They'd told me three times already.

'It's 'cos he was buzzed on champagne. But I'm holding him to it.' Pat hiccupped.

I opened the door, the bell dinging, and the two friends laughed their way up the street, where I knew my uncle was waiting in his car to drive them home. I turned around to assess the damage but found the room was immaculate.

I frowned. There had been tons of napkins and empty flutes, but they were all gone. Then, Liam appeared from the kitchenette at the back of the shop, rubbing his hands with a tea towel. He grinned when he took me in, throwing the tea towel over his shoulder and leaning against the wall.

'One hell of a party, Red.' He smiled.

I exhaled. 'I'm kind of relieved it's over. Even if the real work starts tomorrow.'

'You're the boss. Give yourself the day off.' He strode over to where I stood next to the huge custom drawers I'd had installed in the centre of the shop, holding all my samples.

'Hey,' Liam said, cradling my head. 'I'm so proud of you, you know.'

'Thank you.' I blushed. Even now, I was shit at accepting praise. 'My feet are killing me.'

'Take a load off,' Liam said as he lifted me up on top of the drawers in one movement, making me squeal.

'Give a girl some warning, Christ.'

'Should I give you a warning about this?' Liam said as he sank to the floor, on his knee, and my stomach swooped, my heart racing. My hand flew to my mouth as Liam reached into his pocket, pulling out a little velvet box. 'I know you said we should wait until you opened the shop. But technically, the shop is open, Red.'

Liam opened the box, showing off a marquee solitaire diamond ring. The light from the wall lights bounced off the stone, reflecting off it.

'Katherine Williams, will you do the honour of my life and make me your husband?' Liam's smile was gone now. He was in serious Liam mode, as if he had run through this scenario in his mind countless times before and wanted to take it seriously.

'Yes,' I laughed. 'Yes, I will.'

Liam was off the floor instantly, his arms around me and his hands in my hair. He tilted my neck back and kissed me, his tongue brushing mine, his teeth grazing my lower lip. Eventually, we stopped but didn't pull away from each other, his hands around my neck. Pure joy gleamed in Liam's expression as he slid the ring onto my finger.

'Yours forever,' he murmured onto my lips. 'Promise?'

'I pinkie promise.' I gave a watery laugh and wrapped his finger around mine.

Acknowledgements

Firstly, I'd like to thank my incredible parents, who, in addition to introducing me to the merits of Bridget Jones and Monty Python, have always supported my numerous creative endeavours – despite the questionable singing and terrible dancing. I promise I'll always do my best.

P.S. You should not be reading this.

To my siblings, Laura and Jack – your infinite chaos, squabbling, and neurospiciness make you hilarious. You keep my mind brimming with jokes (see: insults).

P.S. I know you two aren't reading this.

Aurora, this book exists because of you – your steadfast encouragement, knowledge, and pure joy for stories have shaped it from the start. Olivia, thank you for giving me the time, space, and structure to make it happen. Growing beside you both has made me a better writer and without your support, I wouldn't have made it past that first draft. I count my lucky stars that we met on the steps of the central library that chilly November day.

P.S. You two have over-read this. Go touch grass.

A huge, ginormous thanks to my agent, Saskia, for your unwavering support and belief in this book. You totally got it from day one, and I'm over the moon to have you in my corner. To Rebecca and the team at Bedford Square – thank you for taking a chance on me and the Everly Heath world. To my gorgeous, lovely friends – thank you for pushing me up that hill, taking free headshots of me, and nodding and smiling while I forced yet another romance recommendation or Taylor Swift theory upon you. You know who you are, and I love you.

To my oldest friend, Manchester – the place I made my home. You're weathered and cantankerous, and I suspect you'd hate the attention, but consider this a little love letter to you.

To my first readers and champions of this book – the ones who left thoughtful reviews, posted on their socials, and took the time to message me about how much this story, and its representation of neurodiversity, meant to them. You are the reason I started writing, and you are the reason I'll keep going. Thank you.

And finally, to my husband, Charlie. Thank you for the small cups of coffee I don't drink and the large glasses of wine I do. For your steadfast encouragement when doubt and imposter syndrome creeps in. For reading my favourite books just to understand my passions. I'll never have the words to express how much I love you, but I promise to spend my whole life trying.

About the Author

Maggie Grant is a neurodivergent writer who crafts romance with heart, wit, and a dash of spice. When not writing, she's likely sipping wine and devouring romance novels. She lives in Stockport with her husband and their dog, Paddy.

📷 @maggiegrantauthor

Bedford Square Publishers

Bedford Square Publishers is an independent publisher of fiction and non-fiction, founded in 2022 in the historic streets of Bedford Square London and the sea mist shrouded green of Bedford Square Brighton.

Our goal is to discover irresistible stories and voices that illuminate our world.

We are passionate about connecting our authors to readers across the globe and our independence allows us to do this in original and nimble ways.

The team at Bedford Square Publishers has years of experience and we aim to use that knowledge and creative insight, alongside evolving technology, to reach the right readers for our books. From the ones who read a lot, to the ones who don't consider themselves readers, we aim to find those who will love our books and talk about them as much as we do.

We are hunting for vital new voices from all backgrounds – with books that take the reader to new places and transform perceptions of the world we live in.

Follow us on social media for the latest Bedford Square Publishers news.

🐦@bedsqpublishers
ⓕfacebook.com/bedfordsq.publishers/
ⓞ@bedfordsq.publishers

https://bedfordsquarepublishers.co.uk/